Honorbound

John K. Potter

Bloomington, IN Milton Keynes, UK

authorHOUSE®

AuthorHouse™
1663 Liberty Drive, Suite 200
Bloomington, IN 47403
www.authorhouse.com
Phone: 1-800-839-8640

AuthorHouse™ UK Ltd.
500 Avebury Boulevard
Central Milton Keynes, MK9 2BE
www.authorhouse.co.uk
Phone: 08001974150

First published by AuthorHouse 11/7/2006

ISBN: 1-4259-7857-6 (e)
ISBN: 1-4259-7099-0 (sc)
ISBN: 1-4259-7100-8 (dj)

Library of Congress Control Number: 2006909168

Printed in the United States of America
Bloomington, Indiana

This book is printed on acid-free paper.

This book is dedicated to all my friends and buddies in the 6922nd at P Y DO, and those at Yale who patiently taught me the intricacies of the Chinese customs and language.

And, of course to my best friend, my guide, my life, my wife Lynn, and to my children (sorry I know you're grown up) John and his wife, Kim, and my daughter, Meredith and her son, (my grandson) Logan.

PROLOGUE

Somewhere near Palung, China, August 1960

Peasants planting rice stalks in the stifling heat of the day stopped their work to stare at the odd procession slowly moving up the old road to their village. In the front, an old cart with two wooden wheels, pulled by an ox waddled up the old road. Atop the cart, in a crude bamboo cage, a naked man, his hands handcuffed to the top of the cage, dangled and swung freely as the cart bounced around in the deep, timeworn ruts of the road. The ox cart driver, a small, older Chinese man, dressed in a faded blue padded coat, matching blue pants and a straw hat that had seen much better days, shuffled barefoot alongside the cart and occasionally flicked the ox with a long bamboo pole to keep it moving. He paid no attention to the man in the cage.

Beside the cart, on each side, three Chinese soldiers, their rifles slung over their shoulders, plodded listlessly along. Their boots stirred up small whiffs of dust. Their sergeant trailed behind the cart. His burp gun was slung over his shoulder, and he squinted over the top of his wire rimmed glasses. Behind him, an olive-drab 1940 American-made Packard sedan with a red star painted on each of the doors trailed the procession and bounced along in and out of the ruts.

In the back seat of the car a stocky, rather bloated looking Chinese Colonel squirmed each time the car jolted back and forth as if he could never get comfortable. His aide, a grey-haired Captain, sat beside him and stoically peered at the vast countryside of the rolling hills around them. The car's driver fought to keep control of the car as it veered from side to side.

The man in the cage was a thin, wiry Caucasian, whose hair was matted with blood. His haggard face was covered with dirt and rivulets of sweat ran down to his chin. He struggled to remain standing. When he saw ruts coming ahead in the road, he tried to brace for them, but he was simply too weak. Because his hands were cuffed to the roof of the cage, he could neither sit nor kneel. As long as he stood upright, the handcuffs attached to the roof of the cage didn't cut into his wrists, but if he slipped or began to pass out, the rough edges of the cuffs ground against his wrist bones and sent tremendous pain cascading down his arms and into his already beaten and bruised body. His lips were parched, and he was in great pain, not only from the sores on his wrists, but from the many bruises and lacerations on his sun burnt body. He winced with pain every time the cart ricocheted off a deep rut. His mind understood why he had to be alert and try to stay on his feet, but the exhaustion combined with the pain wouldn't let his body do as his brain said. He tried to think about something, anything, but his agony was too severe.

Whenever the cart crossed over a particularly rough spot in the dirt road, he would lose his balance, or slip on his own sweat or blood and would hang by his hands until he managed to get his feet back under him and stand again. But, from time to time, he simply could not get to his feet, and the more he struggled, the more the pain grew until he passed out.

Each time he passed out, the sergeant yelled at the ox driver to stop. He ordered one of the soldiers to prod the man and determine whether or not he was faking. If he determined the man was not faking, the sergeant made two soldiers in the squad run to the back of the car and draw a bucket of water from the water barrel tied to the trunk. The soldiers doused the man in the cage. The shock of the water usually would arouse him. If it didn't, they would pour more water on him until he was conscious. Then the procession would continue.

This procession slogged its way for nine days through the sparsely populated back country of Sheni Province. The soldiers longed to come to a village where they could rest. On this day, as the cart topped a ridge, the soldiers smiled. In the distance was a village at the top of a ridge. They began talking and chattering as their spirits rose. They wanted the cart to go faster and urged the driver to whip the ox. The old man tried, and the cart sped up only to fall into a very rough section of the road. The prisoner screamed with pain as time after time he slipped and lost his footing. The soldiers laughed at him and prodded the ox driver to go even faster. The soldiers' high spirits climbed higher only to be dashed when the man passed out again.

The procession stopped. The reawakening routine began again, but after three buckets of water were poured on the man, he was still unconscious.

The officers in the car watched as the soldiers poured more and more water on the man hanging limply by his wrists. When the man failed to respond, the Captain got out of the car, walked to the cage and looked at the man. He reached in, grabbed the prisoner's leg, shook it violently and screamed at the man to stand up. The prisoner's body jerked involuntarily. The Captain repeated the procedure twice more. The captive stirred and opened his eyes. The Captain didn't say another word but just stared at the man.

Slowly, in extreme pain, the prisoner managed to stand again. He looked down at the Captain. He wanted to kill him and everyone in sight.

The Captain looked the man over carefully, assessed his condition, turned and walked back to the car. Before he got in, he commanded the procession to continue.

The Colonel moved over to allow room for his aide to get in. "And? Doctor?"

"He can survive one more stop," the Captain said.

Two hours later, the cart stopped in the square in the center of the village. The two hundred and sixteen curious people of the village immediately surrounded the cart and peered in at the man hanging by his wrists. He tried to stand, but slipped a few times before he regained his footing. The villagers began shouting and taunting the man in the cage. They spat on him, threw rocks at him, poked him with sticks and called him vile names. He wanted to yell back at them, but he had no energy.

The Colonel and the doctor got out of the car after about twenty minutes of observing this behavior. The soldiers immediately made a path for the officers to the front of the cart. The villagers scampered out of the way. When the Colonel, a squat man, in his mid-forties, held up his hands, the crowd immediately fell silent. He took off his high-peaked hat, wiped the sweatband with his handkerchief, and put it back on. The Colonel waited until he had the complete attention of every person in the village square. His small black eyes scanned the faces of the villagers to make sure they all were watching him. When the villagers made eye contact with the Colonel, shivers of fear trickled down their backs.

"Comrades," the Colonel began in a high-pitched, singsong voice, "this foreign devil sneaked into our country to destroy our way of life. He is our enemy, as are all foreigners who come to China." He spoke slowly, in a crisp Mandarin dialect, and weighed the villagers' reactions as he parroted the party line. "We brought him to your village so you could see one of our enemies for yourselves. We also wanted you to see what happens to our enemies when they are caught. And I assure you, all enemies of the state are eventually caught."

The man in the cage pretended to be unconscious, but he actually listened very carefully. Through a haze of pain and exhaustion, he interpreted every word into English.

"We will not execute this man because as Chairman Mao says, most men are good inside. If they stray, it is up to the people to set them back on the right path. We believe this man can be reeducated and possibly become useful to the state. If not, of course, he will die. We will rest in your village. Make places for my men among you. Return to your homes."

The crowd quickly dispersed. Many of the villagers looked back at the man in the cage, shook their fists in anger, and kept on going.

The Captain ordered the soldiers to get the man out of the cage, wash him, and put him on a stretcher.

When he heard the Captain's orders, the prisoner whispered a quiet, "Thank you, God," and passed out.

CHAPTER ONE

Peking, China, February 1959

Beads of cooling sweat broke out on Roger Walters' temples as he walked down the musty, narrow, concrete-walled hallway of the bunker three stories beneath the Forbidden City. Roger, although anxious, tried to remain calm for this meeting. He had a plan and needed all his wits that morning. His freshly laundered olive drab People's Republic of China army uniform was crisp, starched and pressed, but there was a hint of dampness under each arm.

As he approached the door, clearly marked in Chinese characters *Authorized Personnel Only*, he took a deep breath, stopped and knocked once.

"Ching lai," called a high-pitched voice from behind the door. Roger took off his cap, rubbed his hand over his shaved head flicking away the beads of sweat, opened the door and stepped in.

"Ah, Captain Walters," a large trim Chinese Major said as he motioned for Roger to come into the dimly lit conference room.

Roger gave a short bow to the Major, Major Yu, and looked around the room at all the familiar faces. He recognized Captain Liu, a thin bespeckled man who specialized in codes, and Major Gauting, a round-faced man with a Mandarin mustache and narrow black eyes, who was the head of intelligence for the United States sector. He nodded to Captain Shi Shin, a light-skinned tall man with an ever-present enigmatic smile, who was a propaganda specialist, and, of course, his commanding officer, Colonel Chin Su Yang.

Colonel Chin, the chief of intelligence and security for the Republic of China, was a large man with a big belly that strained the buttons on his uniform coat. His round face was outlined by slicked down shiny black hair, black pencil-thin eyebrows and a thin mustache.

The long, polished walnut conference table took up most of the room. In the center of the table sat two porcelain pots of tea. At each place cups, note pads and pencils were carefully arranged. On the wall to Roger's left hung the ever-present portrait of Chairman Mao. A well-lit map of the world faced the door. It was dotted with brightly colored pins.

Even after six years, Roger still felt uneasy among the Chinese High Command. He believed he'd won their confidence, but he'd also seen them turn on their fellow officers for the smallest infraction. Roger never doubted his loyalty to them, but sometimes he felt because he had been a turncoat after the Korean War, they might still regard him as a possible risk. He was especially aware of this as he prepared for this particular meeting.

His thoughts were interrupted by a knock on the door, and Colonel Chin called out, *"Ching lai."*

The door opened and a muscular Chinese officer with his head shaved and his eyebrows plucked to a fine line entered the room. He carried a gunmetal grey briefcase. His eyes were cold as steel, and his jaw set as if he were clamping down on a bullet with his teeth. He silently studied each person in the room. There was a momentary, involuntary hush.

Colonel Chin stepped forward, "Ah, Wu Ting, come in."

Wu Ting nodded, went to the head of the table and sat down. He placed the briefcase on the table in front of him, but he did not open it. The others took their places and made themselves comfortable. Walters' chair was at the far end of the table. This was, in its own way, a rebuff to the Occidental.

The weekly staff meeting covered several items. Roger sat patiently as long, verbose reports were made on everything from non-working locks on office doors to undercover activities in the United States.

Two hours later, Colonel Chin announced, "Now we will turn to our most important matter, our internal security. Comrade Wu Ting, you have a report?"

Wu Ting opened his briefcase, took out a several papers and rose from his chair. He towered over all the others in the room, except Roger. Wu Ting held the file high and said, "Colonel, there is a traitor in our intelligence unit. The cryptographer, Comrade Sz An."

Obviously shaken, Colonel Chin said, "Why do you say this? Comrade Sz is one of our best operatives. His last operation was carried out with extreme efficiency. His reports seemed to be very thorough."

Roger watched both men. He stifled the urge to smile.

Wu Ting, knowing that Colonel Chin held his position of authority, not for his intelligence, but for his vigorous, yet careful, administrative abilities, chose to be tolerant of the Colonel. He breathed a deep sigh of exasperation and in a slow and deliberate fashion outlined the case against Comrade Sz. "It is true Comrade Sz prepares excellent reports," Wu Ting began, "however, I must point out that he has been the chief coordinator for three important operations during the past year. Each failed. And failure gives our enemies new insights into our operations."

Roger could see the concern on Colonel Chin's face.

"Sz's last operation is conclusive," Wu Ting continued. "As you know, the idea of hollowing out African art statues and filling them with heroin came from Comrade Sz himself. He was assigned the operation as a way of rewarding his intelligence. Comrade Sz went to Africa to supervise the operation. On his instructions, we sent dummy shipments of these African art works to New York for over a year so the customs officials would become complacent. All during that time, not one case of the statues was ever opened by the customs officials. But, the very first shipment in which we packed raw heroin into the statues was not only searched, but all the heroin was discovered. The entire shipment was confiscated."

Roger sat back and watched Colonel Chin squirm in his seat. This is going well, he thought.

3

"I need add only one other point. The American officials were rather clumsy in their handling of the case. Why? Because they picked out only the statues containing the heroin." He paused and waited for this to sink in. The room fell silent. Wu Ting walked to the map. "Only one person knew all of the details. Sz An. Each of our other agents knew only one facet of the operation. The packers did not know where the shipment was to be sent, and the shippers did not know one another, and so on." Wu Ting put his briefcase on the table. He opened it, took out a file marked "Top Secret," held it up, and handed it to the Colonel.

"This is a report from one of our undercover agents in Africa who was assigned to follow Comrade Sz," Wu Ting watched the Colonel scan the file. "As you know, it is standard operating procedure to have all our agents under surveillance whenever they are out of the country. Comrade Sz did not know our surveillance agent in Africa. That agent reports that Comrade Sz met for over an hour with an American CIA agent in a hotel room. The Americans, if you will pardon me Comrade Walters, for the most part, are not very clever in hiding their identity when they are assigned in foreign countries."

Roger nodded in agreement.

Colonel Chin sagged back in his chair, threw the file on the table, and heaved a great sigh of disgust. Everyone watched him carefully. After a few moments, he spoke. "Comrade Wu, I commend you on your diligence and thoroughness in this matter. It is sad to learn that one of our own men would betray us so."

Wu stood erect, obviously pleased that he had convinced the Colonel of his case against Sz and proud that he had been given recognition.

"We shall arrest him immediately and send him to our work camps."

"Yes," said Wu.

Roger Walters leaned forward in his chair, paused a moment then said, "Perhaps there is another option." All of the officers turned toward him, surprised and mystified by this remark. Roger slowly got up from his chair and walked to the other end of the long conference table. "I think it would be to our advantage to make use of a traitor in our midst."

Wu looked at the Colonel. The Colonel motioned for him to sit. Wu frowned, but sat as he was instructed. They all studied Walters very carefully.

"This, Comrades, is a classic problem in espionage - a double agent exposed without his knowledge. If we arrest Comrade Sz," Roger paused again until he was sure every man in the room was hooked, "we have one spy, one traitor. But who, we must ask ourselves, does he report to? How many others are involved with him? Do you know the answers to these questions Comrade Wu Ting?"

Wu moved around uncomfortably in his chair. He was very much aware of Walters piercing eyes. There was a long silence.

"Comrade Wu?"

"We only know of the CIA agents in Africa. We have not yet been able to find out whether he has enemy contacts in China, but I am sure under intensive interrogation... "

"Possibly, but doubtful," Roger interrupted. "Agents of foreign powers are usually fanatics who are difficult, if possible, to break. They would rather die. No, I don't think we would get much information from interrogation."

"I agree," interrupted Colonel Chin, "Go on Comrade Walters, you seem to be driving toward a point."

"Thank you, Colonel. I propose we use him to benefit the state. We use him to expose his own network of spies. Now, I admit, that I have had time to think this over because I first learned of Comrade Sz's traitorous actions yesterday." He looked over to see the surprised look on Wu Ting's face and nearly chuckled out loud. "Since that time, I've been thinking about the best way to use this traitor, and I believe I have a plan which will answer all our questions. For example, who is he working for?"

"I say the American CIA," offered Wu.

"Possibly, but we do not know for certain. Furthermore, we do not know who his contacts are here in the People's Republic or outside our borders. We must, for the sake of the people, find out and eliminate all of them as well."

"By all means," said the Colonel.

"I propose we give Comrade Sz some vital, top-secret information which would be so important that he would have to act on it."

"He would take the information to his contacts, and we would follow him and arrest them all," Wu interrupted.

"That is a little crude Comrade, at best we might get three or four low level couriers. No, we must be much more subtle. We must make our plan so precise that we arrest not only the couriers, but their leaders as well. If my plan works out the way I think it will, we will have a fat imperialist agent from the United States as well."

Roger returned to his place at the far end of the table and picked up a manila folder. "The details are in this plan for each of you to read, but I will give you the basic idea. Since the United States Intelligence community knows that I have been working for your intelligence department for the last five years, I am certain they would like very much to have me in their hands. So, I shall hand myself over to them."

"You will defect?" said the astonished Colonel Chin. "That would be madness."

"You're right. It would be. No, I shall not defect, I shall merely make them think I want to defect so they will come after me," he said with a wily smile. He could see the others beginning to smile as well.

"I shall become friends with Comrade Sz, secretly, of course. When I feel the time is right, I will tell him that I want to defect back to the United States. If he is a smart agent, and I believe he is, he will think this is a trap and report me to you, Colonel Chin. You will then reward him with a higher position... your aide."

"Go on," Colonel Chin said. A slight hint of a smile crossed his face.

"You will tell him that you shall keep careful watch on me. You, Wu Ting, will call Comrade Sz in and ask him about my movements. I am sure he will say nothing against me. You will inform him that you have had several bad reports about me and that you are thinking of sending me away to a security camp to be reeducated. This should make Sz act quickly. I will tell him that I want to escape but I do not trust any Chinese. I will say I want an American to get me out."

"An American? Why?"

"To find the head of the snake."

Everyone in the room nodded.

"How long do you think this will take Comrade?" asked Wu.

"I would say, if all goes well about three to six months."

"That is a very long time."

"Please, Wu Ting, that is just to set up the operation. I believe it will take nearly a year to complete the entire plan, depending, of course, on whether or not the Americans take the bait. But remember, as the Chairman teaches, 'The patient fisherman catches the biggest fish'."

Roger sat down satisfied he had won the day. He answered several questions thrown at him by Colonel Chin and the other officers about the details of the operation. After an hour of both important and petty questions, silence filled the room. After a minute or so, Colonel Chin addressed the group. "Do you have any further questions Comrades? Wu Ting?"

"No," said Wu, "No, I have no more questions. I believe Comrade Walters has thought this matter through very carefully."

"Thank you, Comrade." Walters smiled.

"Anyone else? No? I have no further questions at this time, but I reserve the right to review this operation at a later date," Colonel Chin said as he pushed back his chair and stood.

"Then it is agreed that we implement my plan?" asked Roger.

"It is agreed," nodded the Colonel. "How soon do you plan to put the plan into operation?"

"Immediately."

CHAPTER TWO

Muncie, Indiana - August 1959

Alex banked his BeechCraft Bonanza left and began the downwind leg of his approach to the Muncie, Indiana, airport. It was a hot, lazy day. The wind sock at the north end of the airport hung still.

Alex felt both drained and exuberant. He looked at the clock on the instrument panel - three ten. He yawned and reflected on the day. Rising before dawn, Alex had had his first meeting in Springfield, Illinois, at seven in the morning, and his last meeting in Indianapolis broke up two hours ago. He felt good because in his briefcase were two lot purchases, one lease agreement and one contract for two station sites in Peoria. His best day in a long time. Time to celebrate.

Alex pulled back on the throttle back to slow his air speed, and the plane seemed to hang in the air as it drifted down to 2,000 feet. He scanned the sky. He didn't see any other planes, no clouds, just a blue, hazy sky on this hot, Saturday in August. Heat waves radiated off the steel roof of the one hanger, and the peeling paint of the word "Muncie" wiggled with the waves. The combination control tower, office and coffee shop, located beside the aircraft tie-down apron, was the only other building. The airport was surrounded by green corn fields laid out in perfect squares.

As he turned into his base left, he looked down and saw a long, black sedan turn into the parking lot near the control tower. A

Lincoln he thought. Strange. He hadn't seen that car before. Two men got out. Alex frowned. Who the hell were they he wondered.

He checked the altimeter. He was still at 2,000 feet. He throttled back, and the plane descended slowly. He focused on his instruments as he turned into his final approach. He couldn't help but see the two men standing beside the black car. They both wore sunglasses and were dressed in seemingly identical black silk suits. It was too hot to wear a black suit, he thought.

He again focused on the instruments in front of him and mentally ran through his checklist for landing. "Gears down," he said out loud. He pulled the lever and heard the landing gears begin to descend. "Flaps to three quarters," he reminded himself. Alex throttled back to make sure his descent was smooth, lined up on the runway, and guided the plane to a perfect three-point landing. When he felt and heard the familiar screeching sound of the wheels as they touched the runway, he relaxed. He complimented himself on the good landing. He stopped at the end of the runway, turned left to make sure another plane wasn't behind him, then taxied to the tie-down apron in front of the control tower.

Benny Johnson, an 18-year-old, freckle-faced boy who worked at the airport as a general "do anything, anytime" guy came out of the coffee shop and guided Alex's plane to its usual parking spot.

Alex cut the engine and turned off the master switch. He reached behind his seat, grabbed his briefcase and his small suitcase, opened the door and handed them down to Benny.

"Have a good, trip, Alex?" Benny asked as he took the cases and set them down behind the wing.

Alex got out and walked to the trailing edge of the wing and jumped down. "A great one, Benny. Found four spots."

"Where?"

"Two in Peoria, one in Springfield and one just outside Indianapolis."

"You're gonna be rich," Benny said admiringly.

"From your mouth… "

"To God's ear."

"Right." Alex gave Benny the "thumbs up," picked up his two cases and started toward the control tower. "Gas her up, and check the oil, Benny. After that, just roll her into the hanger. Bill's going to do a 50-hour check up for me."

"Wilco," Benny said raising his right thumb.

Alex looked over at the two men by the car. They hadn't moved since he first saw them from the air. They were watching him. Strange. He pushed open the screen door and went into the control tower. It was hot, and the old osculating fan simply moved one bit of hot air to another place. Alex wiped his brow and called out, "Hey. Joe," as he put his briefcase on the counter.

From a door behind the counter Joe Parsons, the owner of the airport, came out yawning and scratching himself. He was a heavy set man in a white shirt and black tie -his everyday uniform. The sweat marks under his arm pits were clear and dark. He was wiping his brow as he came up to the counter, reached under it and pulled out a pilot's log. He passed it over to Alex.

"Did you get your 400th hour?"

"Yep, and two more," Alex replied as he took the book, found the right page and logged in his flight. "Anyone call?"

"No, but you got a couple of visitors, Alex. Damned unfriendly, too," Joe said as he tipped his head toward the parking lot. "You want me to go with you?" he asked warily.

"They say what this is about?"

"Nope. Just said to let you know they were here. Can't tell what kind of guys they are with those damned dark sunglasses. Frankly, Alex, I don't like their looks."

Alex grinned. "Real bad guys?"

"Could be."

"Well, there's no time like the present. Guess I'd better see what they want."

Alex kicked his suitcase over toward the counter. "Look after this, Joe," he said as he patted his the briefcase on the counter.

"You sure you don't want me... "

"Might keep an eye open," Alex said. He walked out the screen door leading to the parking lot. The asphalt pavement was hot. Alex wiped the sweat from his right eyebrow with his index finger and nodded to the two men. They didn't move or acknowledge his nod. The first thing Alex noticed as he approached them was that they didn't seem to be sweating. He couldn't see a bead anywhere.

Leaning against the driver's door, the tall, thin, hawkish looking man just kept staring at Alex. The other man, heavier, but not fat, and a lot shorter, stood rock still with his hands behind his back in a sort of military parade rest attitude. Alex instinctively knew they were either F.B.I. or possibly C.I.A. Nobody else, he thought, could stand out in the sun in this heat and not sweat. Neither man made a move to greet him. They just waited until he walked up to them.

Alex stopped a few feet away and assessed the men. He decided that the one leaning against the driver's door was the head man. He smiled inwardly. He'd seen these kinds of guys many times before. He was almost one of them. But he was smarter. Alex walked up to the tall man and said, "You wanted to see me?"

"Yes, Mr. Hunter. We would like a few moments of your time," the man said in a passionless, monotone.

Alex estimated the taller man to be six foot six, about a half a foot taller than himself. He was thin and his nose twitched slightly as he stood there. He pushed off the car, reached into his inside coat pocket and produced and small I.D. wallet. He flipped it open and revealed his identity. "Herman, J. R., Central Intelligence Agency." Then nodding to his partner, "And this is Agent Robert Lessing."

"I see."

"You look a bit warm, Mr. Hunter. Why don't we get comfortable in the back seat? The car is air conditioned."

It was only then that Alex noticed that the motor of the car was idling. He nodded, "Okay."

Lessing opened the back door. Agent Herman seemed to coil up like a snake and slither into the back seat. Alex followed. Lessing closed the door but remained outside.

"There, isn't this better?" Herman said, indicating the cool air flowing out from the vents.

"Feels, great," Alex said.

11

Agent Herman paused and took off his sunglasses. His eyes were big and brown, and his eyebrows were dark and heavy. He arched them as he spoke in a low and even cadence. "I'll get right to the point, Hunter. We want your help. Your government needs it. We think you're the right guy."

"Oh? Why me?"

"Roger Walters."

Alex's brow pulled in tight. He looked at the agent over the tops of his eyes. He wasn't sure he'd heard the agent right. "Roger Walters?" Alex said dully. It was half a question and half a confirmation.

"Roger Walters," Agent Herman confirmed.

Alex sat back. His mind was racing. Roger, that son-of-a-bitch, he thought. Roger, my best friend-turned traitor! He could see Roger grinning at him and then walking away and boarding a Chinese truck at Panmunjom on that cold afternoon in Korea. Roger was a turncoat, and Alex hated him for that.

"Mr. Hunter," Agent Herman said softly.

When he heard his name called, Alex shook his head as if to wipe out those memories. "Sorry. I wasn't expecting that."

Agent Herman nodded.

"Besides, I thought Roger was dead or something."

"Quite the opposite, I'm afraid. He's one of their best intelligence people."

"North Korea?"

"China."

"Well, all that language training must have paid off for him."

"You were a better Chinese linguist, Mr. Hunter. But, that's not what this is about. We hear he wants to come out, and we need someone to go in and get him. You know him pretty well."

"I thought I did. That was six years ago. I think we both must have changed a lot."

"He knows you. We think he wants you to come and get him."

"He wants me?"

"Not specifically."

"Specifically what?"

"He has made some demands. One is that whoever gets him out must be an American."

"So why don't you go?"

"Bad joke, Mr. Hunter. We need you. You know the man, you know the language, and you took a brief visit to China, unauthorized I'll admit. You've got all the qualifications."

Alex chuckled, "Boy, have you got the wrong guy. Even if I did want to help your guys out, which I don't, it's been a long time since I played those games. And, most importantly, Agent Herman, I don't like the guy, and I don't have any intention of playing his game. Sorry, conversation over. It's been interesting meeting you." Alex threw open the door and started to get out when Agent Herman grabbed his arm.

"This is no game, Hunter."

"Whatever. I don't want any part in it." Alex tugged loose from Herman's grasp and got out.

Agent Lessing stepped in front of Alex to block his way. Instinctively his fists clenched and his eyes narrowed. "You're not going to stop me. Are you?"

Agent Lessing looked at Agent Herman who also got out of the car. Herman shook his head and Lessing moved aside. Alex looked back at Agent Herman then walked back into the control tower.

"That went well," Agent Lessing said. "He didn't even recognize you."

Agent Herman sighed, "It's only round one, Bob."

"Did you use the murder on him?"

"No, I promised I wouldn't. Perhaps that comes later. I'm just following orders."

The two men got back in their car and drove away.

Alex and Joe watched the car disappear down the road. "You must've made a good impression, Alex," Joe noted. "Although they did seem a little miffed."

"I hope so."

"Maybe they won't come back."

"Could be, but something tells me they will."

"Yeah, I know," Joe said as he patted Alex on the shoulder.

CHAPTER THREE

Alex threw his briefcase and bag in the back seat of his pride and joy, a perfect 1952 light green Buick Super Convertible. "I'm home, baby," he said as he slid into the driver's seat. He put the top down on the car and settled down in the hot seats. "Home," he said and sped off toward downtown Muncie.

Alex liked Muncie. It was a basketball town, and he loved playing even though he failed to make the cut his sophomore year at Muncie Central. It was located in the heart of the corn belt about 60 miles northeast of Indianapolis. His father and mother grew up there. He knew many of the people in town. He prided himself in getting to know new people. He was like the town, warm, friendly and outgoing. That was his persona.

Inside, Alex was a mess. He couldn't get over his wife committing suicide in Japan while he was in Korea. He was always trying to repress the memory of seeing her falling toward him from the fifth story balcony of their apartment in Tokyo. It was six years later, but he still had nightmares of that day. His mind was constantly searching for the answer to why she did it. He felt they were happy, he didn't sense any hostility or fear during the year and three months they'd been man and wife. He was always going over those last moments.

He'd faced the three stages of grief, sorrow, anger, and self-blame, and yet, he had never found a plausible answer. As a result, Alex never remarried. He couldn't, he told himself. What if I was the reason she killed herself, he kept asking himself. Slowly over the past years, he built a solid wall around himself to shield his dark side from the rest of the world, but it couldn't hold out the memories.

Alex drove to his office, an old Victorian house built about 1910 on Jackson Street near the city square. He'd bought it with his first commission. He remodeled the charming two story house and made the first floor his offices. The second floor was his space. There, he could be alone with his past. While his living room, kitchen and master bedroom were considered "tasteful macho" with leather chairs, a four-poster bed, etc., his second bedroom remained locked to the outside.

It was his "house of memories" as he called it. Not a shrine or dark haven, but a bright room where those things he loved as a boy were arranged carefully in a logical order: To his right was a dresser. On top were various pictures of his grandparents on his mother's side on their farm, next to them his grandparents on his father's side, his grandfather in his World War I uniform taken the day he was killed and his grandmother who died in a accident working in a war plant. Then his parents. His mother, Ruth, holding him on her lap, and his father, Frank in his Air Corps Navigator flying suit, and of course, their wedding picture. And, last but not least, a picture of the three of them taken just before his mother's tragic heart attack when he was a senior in high school. On the wall above the dresser were his high school achievements: pictures of him playing football, on the basketball team, his senior picture with the autograph pages of his year book pasted all around it, a picture of him standing beside the old Packard he drove in high school, and various pictures of him with dates at proms and other outings.

On the wall over his bed were his most prized pictures: getting his Eagle Scout Award as he stood beside his parents, the wedding pictures of he and his beloved Crissy smiling and cutting the cake. A picture of him in his Air Force uniform and the last picture he and Crissy had taken of themselves in Tokyo in January 1953.

Hanging next to the window on the other wall were two pennants, his high school, and the Cincinnati Reds baseball team.

And on the coat rack in the corner near the door was his high school letter jacket for football.

Alex visited this room less and less frequently, but today was different. The meeting with the CIA guys had dredged up memories. Memories of Crissy, Roger, Japan, and Korea.

Alex stared at the portrait of Crissy. He still had a hard time believing she committed suicide because of him yet he couldn't imagine any other reason for her to take her own life. The thought of this always took his breath away. Then their was the picture of Crissy, Roger and him taken at the wedding. Roger looked as happy as he had ever been that day. But, then came that awful day a month after Crissy died when Alex was called into his commander's office and told by two CIA men that Roger had defected when he was in Panmunjom. Roger became the secret twenty-second turncoat. They told Alex that that information was still classified, but he should know what happened to his best friend. Alex remembered walking out of the office with the distinct feeling that they weren't telling him everything. Now he knew what it was - Roger defected to join the Chinese intelligence service. Why? He asked himself for the millionth time. Alex sat on the bed and closed his eyes. He needed to think before he made this major decision.

On Monday morning, Alex pulled in the driveway alongside the office/house and parked in back near the separate two car garages. He went in through the back door which led into a small kitchenette where he noted with pleasure a pot of coffee brewing. He went down the long hall and walked into his offices at the front of the house. The reception area had been the parlor. It was large, bright and airy with floor length windows along the front of the house. There was a sitting area by the windows with a leather sofa and two wing chairs, and in the middle of the room was his secretary's big Queen Anne cherry desk. Matching cherry files occupied the wall opposite the door.

"Hey, anybody here?" he shouted.

The door to his office opened and Ginny, his long time secretary and best friend, poked her head out. Her oval face was highlighted by her shiny black hair in a page-boy cut. Her eyes, big and brown, seemed to be smiling all the time, and her cute nose sometimes wiggled when she laughed. Ginny had a figure any beauty contestant would die for. "Hey yourself," she said. "I didn't expect you back until tomorrow. Why didn't you call?" Ginny asked. She felt hurt that he hadn't seen her over the weekend.

"Finished early and I had a lot on my mind. How're things?"

"Just fine. And how did the pride of Hunter Real Estate make out? Successful trip?"

"You got it. Bought two lots, got that lease agreement in Springfield signed and leased a site in Peoria. So, all in all, not bad."

"Not bad?" Ginny said. She gave a long whistle and an admiring arching of an eyebrow. "I'd say very well." She flipped her hair back and looked up to him. "In fact, I'd say very well."

"Yeah," he said. "Very good. Could've done better, but... "

"You are something else, Alex," Ginny chided him. "You never give yourself credit for anything."

Alex ignored the barb and put his briefcase on her desk. "Any calls while I was gone?" he asked as he slumped down in the large overstuffed leather sofa.

Ginny went to her desk and picked up a stack of notes. "Well, Mr. Brown at the bank called to say that the mortgage Harry Wilson applied for went through and you can close on the house whenever you and he want. I called Mr. Wilson and told him and said I was sure you'd call him as soon as you got back. The cleaners called to say that they can't find that pair of pants you said you left there." Ginny glanced at the message pad on her desk. "Oh. A Mrs. Johnson called several times about the house at 210 Walnut. Larry Brinkman called you for a golf date last Saturday and, of course, you were gone again. I think he's getting fed up with you. You'd better call and make up."

Alex gave a big sigh of resignation and slowly got up from the couch. "Okay, love. First, call Wilson and the bank and set up a closing on the house for tomorrow afternoon if possible, about three

17

or four, then, call those damn cleaners and tell them I'm sure I left my brown pants there, and I want them back today!"

Alex crossed over to the desk and reached down and tore off the message from the pad. "I'll call this Mrs. Johnson later, and I'll take care of Larry, too." He started to go into his office, stopped, turned around to see Ginny looking at him strangely. He cocked his head and raised his eyebrows.

"You look funny," she said.

"Funny, ha ha?"

"No. Kinda, I don't know, preoccupied maybe."

Alex nodded. "Preoccupied maybe." He went into his office.

Ginny frowned. She knew something wasn't right. She sighed and went to her desk, tucked her skirt under her shapely legs and sat. Her lips were pursed. She was worried.

Alex closed the office door, took off his sport jacket, hung it on the old coat rack in the corner and sat down behind his large mahogany desk in his squeaky high-backed swivel chair. He leaned back and cradled his hands behind his head and closed his eyes. His mind kept calling up the memories. The last time he and Crissy were together, they'd gone up into the mountains at the southern end of Japan to a place he'd heard about called Bepu. It was a small village situated near the top of a mountain. It's claim for fame were the many flowered gardens that dotted the hillside and around the small homes. Bepu wasn't a tourist trap but a genuine hideaway, which gave everyone who visited a taste of the genuine Japanese culture. They'd laughed and had a wonderful time. Not once did Crissy even hint that she was unhappy or troubled in any way. In fact, they'd made plans for the future and both agreed on two tow-headed kids. He searched his mind for any clue that she was planning suicide then, but once again, the search was fruitless. Next came the nightmare. He was standing on the side walk in front of Crissy's apartment in Tokyo when he heard a scream and looked up to see Crissy falling toward him. He sat up and opened his eyes. Beads of sweat were rolling off his forehead.

Outside, in front of the office, the dark sedan pulled up to the curb. Agent Lessing turned off the engine and turned to his partner, "I tell ya, Frank, it would get him on board instantly."

"You're probably right, but the brass said no dice. Nothing is to be said about his wife and Roger Walters. Nothing. No hints, clues or winks. All they said was 'try again'."

"I still don't get it. If he knew Walters killed her, he'd jump at the chance to go in and get him."

"I think that's what scares them the most. They think, and I gotta admit so do I, that his first instinct would be to kill Walters rather than bring him back to us. That's not the mission. The mission is to go in, get the guy out, and let us see what we can get out of him. After the interrogation is over, then they'll tell Hunter. Not before."

"But what if he refuses to go?"

"We don't let him refuse. We find a motivation that touches him and makes him want to go. Today we try, duty, honor and apple pie."

"And tomorrow?"

"How about begging?"

They both laughed and got out of the car. "Remember, not even a hint about the murder. Nothing."

"Got it."

Ginny was putting away the last of the papers in the file when Alex yanked open the door.

Her immediate reaction was to be wary. Something in his eyes told her to beware. "You all right?" she asked.

"Yeah. I'm fine," he said, "Get me a drink.'"

"It's a little early isn't it?"

The look Ginny got from Alex was hot steel. She immediately turned on her heels and went out to a file cabinet in the corner, opened the bottom drawer and took out a bottle of bourbon and a coffee cup. She set them down on her desk in front of Alex. He quickly poured himself a drink and downed it.

"Whoa! Was it something I said?" Ginny asked.

"Nope," Alex said. He poured himself another drink and downed it.

"I know I'm gonna regret this, but what is it?"

"My past. My rotten past just caught up with me again. I can't lose it."

"Wanna talk about it?"

"Nope."

"Might help."

"Nope."

"Was it about those two guys in the black suits at the airport?"

"How did you know?" Alex frowned.

"Joe Parsons called to say you were on your way. He said you acted funny when you left. Thought I should know."

"Joe's too good a friend."

"He cares," Ginny said. "So do I." There was a sadness in her big, brown eyes.

Alex sagged. "I know. I appreciate it. It's just that what happened out there at the airport is off limits."

"Joe thinks they were Government men."

"Joe thinks too much."

"Okay. I'll butt out. Just trying to help."

Alex nodded and walked around the desk, stood in front of her, and put his hands on her shoulders. She felt a tingle down her spine. "Ginny. I swear to God if I could say anything I would. This is just something I have to deal with by myself."

"Sounds pretty serious."

"Yeah. It is. I need to think. Would you close the door on your way out? And take the rest of the day off."

"You sure?"

"I'm sure. Oh, and take this bottle and put it back where it belongs," he said holding up the bourbon. "See you tomorrow."

"Alex, if you need…," Ginny said as she took the bottle.

"You'll be the first one I'll call," Alex interrupted. He held up three fingers on his right hand, "Scout's honor."

Ginny was replacing the bottle when there was a loud knock on the front door. She stopped and turned.

"I'll get it," Alex said as he approached the front door. Alex looked through the fine curtains that shaded the glass inset. He saw the outlines of two men standing in front of the tinted glass front door. He did not like what he saw.

Alex spun around and barked, "Ginny, "Go home. Now." Ginny started to protest, but the stern look on Alex's face told her not to. She looked at the front door. He shook his head. Ginny shrugged, picked up her purse, walked down the hall and out the back door. She was really worried. She'd never seen him like this.

When Ginny closed the door, Alex reached for the door knob.

CHAPTER FOUR

Alex slept fitfully all night. He wanted to dismiss the meeting in his office with the two agents, and the whole Roger Walters' thing and get on with his life, yet he couldn't get his mind off of what Agent Herman kept saying about Roger's value to the CIA. Why didn't they just go in and get him? Why this thing about Roger wanting someone he knew to come and get him? And why me? It didn't make sense. Finally about five in the morning he fell asleep.

An hour later, a passenger disembarked from an American Airlines Electra that had just landed at the Indianapolis airport. He was a tall man, six foot two, with a long, angular face and long arms. He was very trim and the dark suit fit him perfectly. His blond hair was combed back severely with a part right down the center of his head.

As he came down the steps, he stopped and put on dark sun glasses. He surveyed the arrival area. He saw a black Lincoln sedan parked almost under the wing of the plan on the tarmac. He walked briskly toward the car. Agent Lessing quickly got out and opened the back door. The man slid in, and the car immediately sped off.

"I really don't have time for this," the man said to Agent Herman who was sitting beside him. He pulled down his black tie and loosened his collar. "Bring me up to speed."

"Hunter didn't believe us. He seemed to think... "

"Seemed to think, agent?" The man interrupted. "I want facts."

"Sorry, Major Brady," Herman said and he turned to look directly at the man. "First, you were right. He reacted to Walter's name. It was a strange reaction, sort of fear and pain. Anyway, he got over that. I explained that he was the last man and all that and told him that Walters was valuable and that we needed to get him out."

And the "Duty, Honor and Glory" meeting?

"Unsuccessful."

"Bottom line?" Major Brady asked.

"He thinks the whole idea is, in his words, 'screwy'."

"Can he be convinced?"

"I'm not sure."

Major Brady nodded. Herman turned around and nodded. The car sped up and turned onto Highway 67 toward Muncie.

At ten that morning, Alex walked out of the bank with a big smile. His commission was one of the biggest since he started his real estate business three years ago. He kissed the envelope, and put it inside his coat pocket. The closing had gone without a hitch, both the buyer and the seller were happy, he was happy, and all was right with the world. He walked the four blocks to his office, but when he turned the corner there was the black Lincoln. "Aw, shit," he muttered.

When he walked into the outer office, Ginny was typing. She glanced up and nodded toward the three men in black suits who were seated in the reception area. The three men stood when Alex entered.

"Hi. How'd the closing go?" Ginny asked.

"Great," Alex said, not taking his eyes off the men.

"Yea! I get paid," she said in her best perky voice.

She noticed no one laughed. "Alex, these gentlemen would like to see you about buying some property," Ginny said as she stood up.

"Ah, yes. Property. Well, what did you gentlemen have in mind?" Alex asked.

"Perhaps we should talk in your office," Lessing said.

"Alone." Herman added.

Alex did not like the looks of the third man who was big, trim, and starred daggers at him. "Ginny. I feel like a doughnut to celebrate. Do we have any in the kitchen?"

"Nope."

"Be a good girl and go get us some at the market. You gentlemen want some?"

Lessing nodded, but the other two didn't move.

Brady reached in his pocket and pulled out his billfold. "Yes. I think that is a very good idea. We'll treat because we know you're going to help us Mr. Hunter." He handed Ginny a ten-dollar bill. "Take your time, miss. We have a lot to talk about."

Ginny glanced at Alex out of the tops of her eyes. "You sure you want doughnuts?"

Alex nodded toward the door. "Yes. Doughnuts. Now."

Ginny got the message. "Doughnuts it is," she said pulling her purse out of the bottom drawer of her desk. "It'll take a few minutes."

"Fine," Alex said and indicated the door. Ginny nodded and practically ran out the front door.

"This had better be good," Alex said as he walked toward his office. The three men followed him to the doorway. Brady held up his hand to the other two, "I think Mr. Hunter and I should discuss this alone."

Lessing and Herman nodded and returned to their seats on the sofa.

Brady closed the door behind him and faced Alex who was standing behind his desk. "I'm sorry to be so blunt. I hope your secretary doesn't go call the police or anything."

"Ginny's a pro. She'll get the doughnuts."

"I think we got off on the wrong foot, Mr. Hunter," Brady said holding out his right hand. "This business is very serious. May we begin again?"

Alex warily shook Brady's hand and gestured for him to sit.

Brady sat down and took off his sunglasses. His cold black eyes trained on Alex's eyes and never varied from them. "I understand that at one time Roger Walters was your friend. Close friend. And I can understand your reluctance to get involved with him again. But, I know that he used you at Panmunjom to defect. And that his actions got you into some trouble with CID, but the matter was quickly cleared up. That said, Mr. Hunter, Roger Walters has risen to one of the most important intelligence positions in the Chinese security service. He has become the most valuable asset we could ever hope to get a hold of. Because he's so valuable, we feel it is best we follow his rules when it comes to his calling the shots as to how he wants to come back to the States. Are we clear so far?"

Alex, in spite of himself, liked the man sitting across from him. This was a no bullshit guy. "Clear."

"Good. The way we read his request, you are a key to getting him back. Believe me, we searched for other people to do the job, but, frankly, you are our best bet."

Alex didn't take his eyes off Brady.

"As a professional, I'd really rather have a trained agent doing this, but we don't have one who fits the bill. We need you, Mr. Hunter.

"Mr... "

"Brady, Hiram."

"Mr. Brady. I understand all that. I think I understand Roger's value to you guys, but I'm not the right person for this job. First of all, it's been five years since I spoke Chinese to anyone except Mr. Lum at the Mandarin Inn restaurant. I couldn't ask for a newspaper let alone make my way inside China. My body is not my temple anymore. It's more like a pup tent. I don't think I could run twenty yards without puking my guts out. As to covert training, I haven't had any training since that little trip I went on in '53, and everything was set up for me. I was there for less than 20 hours. And, as I recall, I was younger, stronger, and more gung ho."

"Details, Mr. Hunter."

"They may be details to you, but they're reality to me."

25

Brady got up and paced for a minute then put his hands on Alex's desk, leaned in, and stared directly into his eyes. "You don't understand anything. Walter's 'value' as you described it, is priceless. Walter's knowledge of the inner workings of the Chinese intelligence operation could help prevent everything from skirmishes to all out war. He knows how many agents are working in the U.S. right now, and he probably has met several of them. He knows what they are planning. Hell, that son-of-a-bitch knows things we haven't even thought of. Getting him possibly could save hundreds maybe thousands of American lives. And you, mister, are in a position to help save those lives."

The attack on Alex had the desired effect. Alex was taken aback at the forcefulness of Brady's position. He wasn't like the other two, he was straightforward and from the look in his eyes, he was telling the truth. Alex was rocked, but he wasn't prepared for the next thing.

"It's your fucking duty, Hunter," Brady went on. "You are, at least were, and we think you can be now, a damned fine soldier, linguist, and agent for your country. We think you can do this job or we wouldn't be here now. We're willing to bet all our marbles on you. We'll risk everything to see to it you have the best training, support and protection possible. Your country needs you, damnit."

Alex let everything soak into his brain. He hadn't been talked to like that since he got his instructions as to how to debrief the U.S. POWs when they returned at Panmujom. A thousand quick flashes of those days passed before his eyes in the matter of a few seconds. It made cold chills run down his spine. He looked down to see his hands clenched tightly together. He was torn. Part of him wanted to say no. To say it wasn't his fight anymore. He did his bit. Another part felt the responsibility and duty associated with it, and another part was insecure. He was scared of what might happen, and scared he might not have the ability to accomplish the mission. He got up. Brady followed his movements with those piercing black eyes. Alex ambled to the window and looked out at the beautiful summer day. His stomach was churning, and he felt weak in the knees. It was almost too much to comprehend at one time. He didn't know what to say or, frankly, to do. He just stood there looking out and hoping that time would give him an answer.

Brady watched him without saying a word.

Finally, Alex turned. "What about my business?"

"We'll take care of it."

"How?"

"It's just another detail, Damnit."

"And Ginny?"

"She'll be here when you get back. Enough about details."

Alex looked at Brady. Brady peered into Alex's eyes without saying anything for a long time. Then, he broke eye contact. His voice changed to a more sympathetic tone, "Alex, I know this is a lot, and it's coming faster than you can handle right now. I wish we had time to discuss each and every detail, but we don't. We're not sure how long Walters is going to wait for us. We don't know how long we have before Colonel Chin, Walter's section head, finds out about the defection, and we don't know long we can hold the current bunch of our Chinese agents together. We need you now."

CHAPTER FIVE

Peking, China, December 1959

Sz An shifted uncomfortably in his chair in the back of the restaurant. He was worried. It was not like Roger Walters to be late. Also, he still had not heard from his contact about getting Walters out. He was beginning to wonder if there was something wrong at that end.

Sz An took a long drag on his cigarette and decided to give Roger two more minutes. If he didn't come by then, he would leave and try to set up another meeting. It was also possible, he surmised, that Colonel Chin was getting suspicious or had arrested Walters. Enough, he said to himself, negative thinking clouds the mind. He sat back and closed his eyes for a moment. When he opened them again, Roger was standing over him.

"Sorry, I'm late," Roger said sitting down with his back toward the door. He gave no other explanation.

"I, too, am sorry, Meng Shenshang. I still have no further word."

Roger hated his Chinese name, Meng. It meant dream, and he was often kidded about it. Sz An's brief report of "no progress" surprised him. It had been nearly four months since he convinced Sz An to try and get him out of China. He thought that for sure some news of the "rescue plans" would have been forthcoming. This isn't good, he thought. In addition, he was finding it more and more difficult to deal with Sz An because he didn't trust himself. This cat and mouse game was beginning to wear on his nerves.

"Is there a problem with my request?" Roger asked.

"I don't know. My contact has not talked with me in two weeks. I'm not sure whether there is a problem or whether he simply hasn't gotten any new information other than that which he passed on."

"You mean about Washington working on it?"

"Yes."

"How long should you wait before contacting him?"

"That is up to him. He makes the decision as to where and when we meet."

"I see."

Sz An pushed back his chair. "I will contact you as soon as I have any information." With that, he turned and walked out the front door.

Roger watched Sz An leave. He wasn't sure if he was being led along for some reason or whether Sz An was a double agent. Also, he was frustrated. Neither he nor any other of the agents watching Sz An could figure out how he got information out of the country to the Americans. Sz An had managed to elude his tail only twice, but the next day, Sz An always walked out of his apartment precisely at six A.M.

Roger was certain his plan was going to work, but this annoyance about Sz An was putting him to the test. He took a deep drag on his cigarette and let the smoke out slowly. He reminded himself that the Chairman always said 'patience was his friend.' He would play this out no matter how long it took.

CHAPTER SIX

100 Miles Due West of Waco, Texas, March 1960

The bedroom was pitch black. The man in the bed breathed slowly, evenly. It was quiet. Very quiet. Slowly, without a sound, the doorknob turned. Silently, the door opened a slit. A pair of almond-shaped eyes pierced the darkness. The door slowly, quietly opened just enough for two men, dressed in black, to slither in and close the door behind them. The room was once again pitch black. The only sound was that of the man in bed who was breathing even more slowly and evenly.

The two men remained perfectly still and waited until their eyes became accustomed to the darkness. They waited and fought to control their breathing. Sixty seconds later, they could make out the outline of the man sleeping peacefully. They inched their way toward the bed. They separated and silently approached - one on each side. The man on the left side of the bed pulled a long hunting knife out of its sheath. Holding it with both hands, he raised it above his head, held it for an instant over the body on the bed, and plunged it downward.

The plunging knife was met with a flurry of bedclothes flying upward. At the same time, the wrist of the man holding the knife was met with a sharp blow causing him to cry out as he dropped the knife. The knife fell harmlessly onto the center of the bed and was instantly wrapped in a mixture of sheets and blankets. The other man, who was approaching from the right, felt a sharp pain as he was kicked in the rib cage just as he was about to leap onto the bed. He let out a huge gust of air as he reeled backward over a chair. His arm swept the lamp off of the night table.

The man with the knife was so stunned when the knife spun out of his hand that he hesitated. The sleeper grabbed his right arm and pulled him face downward onto the bed, and with his right hand and dealt him a sharp karate blow to the kidneys that evoked a muffled scream of pain from the man.

Alex was up in a flash. The other attacker was struggling to get up from behind the chair, gasping for air. Alex shoved a chair brutally against him, pinning him against the wall, then he landed a sharp uppercut, and the unconscious man slid down the wall in a heap.

Alex whirled around and leaped onto the bed. Both of his knees landed on top of the man spread face down across the bed. Alex pushed his face into the bed clothes and grabbed at his throat from behind with both hands and squeezed.

Suddenly, the lights went on in the room. The brightness momentarily blinded Alex.

"Alex! Don't kill him!" barked a strong voice.

Because Alex was operating on sheer instinct, it took a moment or so for this command to sink in. When it did, he released the man and rolled off the limp body.

Two uniformed men were standing in the doorway. One was Brady in his Air Force uniform with the gold oak clusters on his shoulders. The other man was an Air Force Master Sergeant named Jack Kelly. Kelly was 35, and the hash marks on his sleeve indicated he had been in the service fifteen years. He was a big man about six feet five, well-built, without an ounce of fat. He had a flat top haircut that was perfectly level and deep-set eyes that flashed about the room surveying the damage but constantly flitting back to Hunter.

"You bastard," Alex said getting up and starting toward Brady.

Kelly stepped between the two men, "Easy fella... it's just part of the training."

"Training!" Alex screamed at Brady, "You son-of- a-bitch, that guy almost killed me!"

"Oh, I think he would have stopped short of that," Brady said nonchalantly.

"You think?" Alex was incredulous, "You mean to stand there and calmly tell me you <u>think</u> he would have stopped?"

"We had to know how soundly you slept."

Kelly took Alex by the arm and tried to lead him away from Brady, but Alex stood his ground. "Look Brady, for the past three months now I've been 'trained'. First it was the intensive refresher course in Chinese, then the karate, geography, morse code, code names, escape routes, not to mention the fifty or so agents' faces, names and descriptions I've had to memorize. We go at it for twenty hours a day, seven days a week and now you wake me up in the middle of the night with this cockamamie stunt!"

"Frankly, Alex, I wish we had another six months, although I must say I was surprised and pleased by your reaction to the intruders. You are a quick learner," Brady said.

The man on the bed groaned and rolled over holding his kidneys. He was an oriental about five foot five. His almond eyes were glazed. He shook his head to clear his mind.

Kelly walked over to him and helped him to his feet. They both looked at the still unconscious figure pinned against the wall with the chair. The Sergeant ambled over to that man and pulled the chair out. The man, also an oriental, slumped over and fell to the floor. Sergeant Kelly reached down and slapped the man's face. His head snapped back. He didn't react. He was still out cold. Kelly tried to revive him again with another slap but still no effect. He reached down and lifted the small man up. Using a fireman's carry, Kelly took him out of the room.

Alex walked over to his bed and began picking up the covers which had fallen on the floor. Brady stopped him. "Before you go back to sleep, let's go over a few things."

The other assailant began shuffling out the door. Brady called to him, "Chu Li, what did he hit you with?"

Chu Li stopped at the door, rubbed his wrist, and winced. "The one I taught him this afternoon."

Brady smiled and nodded. Chu Li went to the door. "Get some sleep," Brady called out.

Chu Li nodded and closed the door behind him.

"How come they get to sleep and I don't?" Alex asked as he wearily sat down on the bed.

Brady went over to the overturned chair, picked it up and picked up the lamp and put it on the night table. He sat on the foot of the bed, folded his arms and looked straight at Alex, "Now, let's get started. Who's Yu Ling?"

Alex sighed and fell back on the bed and stared up at the ceiling as he began ticking off facts to each of Brady's questions in a low monotone voice, "Yu Ling, old fisherman in Tsingtao Harbor. His junk is moored at Shin Yi dock, slip number 12. Recognition code Yang Fang, countersign Bai Fang if the coast is clear, Yu Fang is the signal to get out of there fast... "

Three hours later, sunlight streamed through the bedroom window and slowly moved into Alex's eyes. He squinted at the light and covered his eyes to shade them. He and Brady had been at it constantly since the "attack," and he was dead tired. He ached from head to toe. He slowly got up and staggered into the bathroom. He splashed cold water on his face as he continued to talk with the same monotone, "Red brick building at 113 Lyou Shan Lu. The signal is to ring the bell twice, knock twice, and ring the bell three times."

"Bell twice, knock twice, bell four times!" Brady interrupted loudly.

"Four times?" Alex repeated. "Damnit Brady, I can't think any longer, I've got to get some sleep."

Brady got up from the chair and went to the door of the bathroom where Alex was hanging over the wash basin, "Alex, you know as well as I do that all this information must be second nature to you. Your life depends on it."

Alex turned his head toward Brady. His bloodshot eyes pleaded for sleep. "I know," he said quietly.

Brady looked at him sadly. He knew he was pushing Alex almost beyond his endurance. He also knew that he had to go on pushing Alex until he reached the breaking point. All his experience told him that Alex could take more, and he had to find out just how much more.

"Come on Hunter, think! What is the signal?"

Alex's face grew grim as he realized that Brady wasn't going to give in. "Ring the bell twice, knock twice, ring the bell four times!" he shouted, and an echo came out of the wash basin.

"That's better. Now wash up and meet me in the screening room in fifteen minutes. Don't be late." Brady commanded, and stomped out the door.

Once outside the door, Brady stopped and leaned up against the wall. He was tired, very tired. His only consolation was that Alex was progressing very fast. In fact, much faster than he had anticipated when Alex first arrived. He could still see Alex getting out of his small plane on that abandoned air strip a hundred miles north of San Antonio. Alex wore a smirk on his face and walked with a slight swagger. He's too cocky to take it, Brady thought. He's fat around the middle and probably terribly out of shape. This'll take at least six months if at all. An aging pretty boy, what'll they think of next?

Brady knew he had greatly underestimated Alex. He pushed himself off the wall and slowly walked down the corridor to the stairway and started down to the screening room in the basement. On his way down, he stopped in the kitchen on the main floor of the old three story house in the residential section of Dallas and got a cup of coffee from the urn that was always kept full. The coffee was hot, and it lifted his spirits a bit. He drew a second cup and went down the back stairs to the screening room.

CHAPTER SEVEN

Upstairs Alex washed his face with cold water to wake himself up, then ran the hot water and washed with soap, lathered his face and shaved in a drunken-like stupor. When he finished, he rubbed his clean-shaven face and peered into the mirror. Whatever happened to the happy-go-lucky smile buddy? he thought. You sure got yourself into a real mess this time. Why couldn't you just have said no and settled back to the nice, dull routine at home? He noticed the lines on his face were deeper than he ever remembered, but he knew he was in better physical shape than he'd been since the time he went into China back in '53. You were young then, he mused, eager and full of get up and go, now look at you, he thought, you've only been up for about forty hours and already you're dead tired. Why back then you could go for 70, 80 hours without feeling this tired. He shook his head, took off his pajamas and turned on the shower. "One thing's for sure, you got your old build back, handsome," he said out loud. He slapped his stomach and stepped into the shower.

Alex was two minutes early getting to the screening room. The huge basement of the old house had been partitioned off and each room soundproofed. The screening room was about twelve feet long and about ten feet wide and the walls and ceiling were covered with white acoustical tile. At one end of the room was a table with a 16mm projector and a slide projector. There were four chairs near the projectors. On the opposite wall was a large screen. The room was lit with florescent lights and very bright. Brady was loading the slide projector when Alex came into the room.

"There's a cup of coffee over there for you," Brady pointed to the cup on the floor beside one of the chairs.

Alex bent over, picked up the cup, and took a sip. "It's cold. How the hell long has it been here?"

"If you want to heat it up, go up to the kitchen and get a fresh cup." Brady motioned to the door. Alex took his cup and exited nearly bumping into Kelly.

"He looks pretty good." Kelly commented as Alex disappeared out of earshot.

"He's holding up better than I thought," Brady answered, "But we'll see. He's got the basics down pretty good, now. We start pushing him. I don't want to let up on him for a minute."

"Whatever you say, Major."

"How's his code work coming?"

"Well, his sending and receiving are quite good, he's up to about 65 characters a minute on both, but his deciphering is still pretty slow."

"How slow?"

"About four words a minute."

"I want him up to ten by the end of the week. It doesn't do any good to get the codes if he can't read them quickly."

"Major," Kelly sat down and looked over at Brady still loading the projector, "there's still one thing I don't understand. Why are we teaching him an out of date code and transmitting techniques? Why not give him our newest methods? They are much simpler."

"Kelly, we have on our hands an agent who is being thrown in for one mission. He's relatively inexperienced. If he should make a mistake and get captured, I'm not sure he could withstand the new interrogating techniques. I'm not gonna risk our new stuff on this mission. He has enough to survive. That's all he needs. He doesn't need to know our new stuff. Am I clear?"

"Yes, sir."

Brady finished loading the projector, sat down next to Kelly and lit a cigarette.

"Boy, he sure took old Chin and Chu Li apart last night," Kelly said with a chuckle.

Brady smiled, "He sure did. That's a good sign."

"What's a good sign?" Alex asked as he entered the room.

"Nothing Alex. Shut the door will you and get the lights?"

When the lights were turned off the room fell into darkness, Brady, using the hand switch, turned on the slide projector and flipped to the first slide. Alex took his seat beside Brady and looked at the image on the screen. "That's Sz An, my contact. He works for Walters and knows him well. He will help me set up the escape," Alex said as he looked at a slide of Sz An in his uniform with the red star on his hat. "He will have any last minute information I will need to get Walters out."

And so another day began. Before the day was through, Alex had spent another nineteen hours working on all phases of the plan and the alternate escape plans. He memorized everything carefully and could repeat the slightest detail back. His knowledge of the street layouts of Peking, Tsingtao, and Tientsin were faultless. He knew how to read all the street signs, military signs and shop signs he would have to know. He knew all the agents by sight, mannerisms and voice patterns.

During the next week, he was instructed to speak only in Mandarin Chinese. The words came back to him quickly, and soon he could talk to his teachers about any subject in nearly twenty dialects of Mandarin. His proficiency in code work surpassed even the best expectations Brady had outlined to Kelly. His physical prowess was that of a twenty-year-old - reflexes, speed in running, karate, ability to stand long hours without sleep all increased dramatically. He was feeling pretty chipper at the end of eleven and a half weeks.

Then one night, just as he was finishing deciphering a message, Brady came up to him, "Alex, let's call it a night."

Alex looked at his watch, it was only five thirty in the evening, he gave Brady a wary look.

"So early?"

"Well, Kelly here tells me you've come a long way and I think it's time you had a little rest."

Alex was immediately suspicious, "Okay, Brady, something's up. What is it?"

"All right, I'll level with you. You've progressed to the point where a brief rest is in order before we start on the final phase of the training. You've done a good job so far, but you've got a long way to go, so we figured you were due for some, entertainment."

Alex cocked his head, "Entertainment?"

"What kind of girls do you like Alex?" Brady said with a straight face.

Alex was surprised by the question, and somehow offended. The suggestion by Brady sounded like a cheap offer. He sat there and stared at Brady, anger boiling up inside him.

"Brady, just what do you have up your dirty little sleeve?"

"Nothing spectacular, I just thought... "

"Don't." Alex interrupted, "Don't think for me. Right now I don't want a girl. I came here to do a job, and I don't need that kind of... encouragement. You know Brady, I never would have believed you would stoop to being a pimp to get your job done."

"Now hold on, Hunter," Brady protested, "My job is to get the best out of you. Some men need that kind of relaxation to perform at their peak. Maybe you don't, but I had to ask... it's my job."

"Some job."

"Yeah, some job. It's what I do because I know the technique works, and if you don't want that, fine. Espionage is a dirty game and sometimes I play the dirty side, but I'm not a pimp and I resent your taking that attitude. Now go get washed up and dress up for dinner. We're having company. The subject is closed. Get out!" Brady yelled.

Hunter got up and started out the door, but stopped and looked back at Brady who was getting red in the face. Alex smiled, I got to him for once, he thought, and he smiled as he went out the door.

CHAPTER EIGHT

The dining room of the old house was furnished with mahogany chairs and a table. The highly polished oval table was set for four places. Already seated at the table was Brady at one end and to his left was Sergeant Kelly. On his right, dressed in a very low cut, powder blue silk gown, was a very beautiful blond. She was about five foot three inches tall, 38-24-36, with electric blue eyes. Her hair was golden, with every hair in place. The up-sweep hairdo, the perfect make-up and posture, and the smile that exuded charm and breeding made her the vision of a Greek goddess.

When Alex came in the door and saw her, his face dropped a full three inches. He just stood there for a moment taking her in then looked in Brady's direction. Anger began to fill his eyes. "Brady, I thought I told you I... "

"Relax, Alex," Brady interrupted, "I'd like you to meet Lieutenant Clark of Air Force Security Service."

Alex looked back at her in surprise and doubt, "Oh really. You're in the Air Force, huh?"

"What's the matter, Mr. Hunter, don't you approve of women in the service?" she said with a smile.

"Let's put it this way Miss... "

"Lieutenant Clark."

"Well, let's put it this way, Lieutenant, I didn't know they had women in the service like you."

"That, Mr. Hunter, can be taken two ways," she said looking him over carefully. Then a sly smile began to appear at the corners of her mouth. "I'll take it as a compliment."

"Don't be too sure it was intended as one," Alex looked away, his mind racing. Brady is too much, he goes out and gets a hooker and is now trying to pass her off as a Lieutenant in the Air Force, Alex said to himself. I would have thought he was smarter than that. He must think I'm an idiot.

His thoughts were broken by Brady. "Sit down, Alex."

"No thanks Brady, I don't think I'm hungry." Alex turned and started to go back out the door.

"Hold it, Hunter," Brady commanded as he quickly stood.

"Major, perhaps I'd better leave. Mr. Hunter doesn't seem to care for my company," the Lieutenant said as she pushed back from the table.

"Stay right there, Nancy," Brady snapped and gave her a look that could stop a charging bear. "Hunter, I don't know what's running through that brain of yours, but I think you had better come back in here and apologize now."

"For what?" Alex demanded. "You bring a hooker here for me, masquerading as an officer, and I need to apologize? Nice try." Alex turned away again, but by the time he could reach out for the knob again Kelly was out of his chair and rushing toward him.

"Hold it, Kelly," Brady said. Kelly stopped, but he didn't take his eyes off Alex. "Hunter, Lieutenant Clark isn't what you think. She's my administrative aide. I demand you come back in here and apologize right now!" Brady shouted.

Alex paused and looked first at Kelly to see that he wasn't about to spring, then to Brady. He swore he could see fire shooting out of his eyes. And, finally, to the Lieutenant whose eyes were looking at the floor, her chair still pushed back from the table. He saw her hands shaking. He felt like a fool. He exhaled, bit his lip and slowly approached the table. Kelly backed off and went to his chair and stood behind it. Brady watched Alex carefully. The girl didn't move.

Alex didn't know what to say, partly because he felt embarrassed, and partly because he had a feeling in the back of his mind that he was still right, she was a hooker. Discretion is the better part of valor, he thought, and he stopped beside the girl and looked down at her trembling hands. A single tear fell from her cheek and left a dark blue spot on her dress just beside her white gloved hands.

"Lieutenant Clark, I... I'm sorry." Alex managed to get out in a halting manner. "It's just that this afternoon the Major offered."

She looked up at him, a tear running down her cheek and simply said, "I know. I suggested it."

"You suggested it!?" Alex blurted out.

"Yes, I thought a little relaxation might be in order," she said, still looking at him. She couldn't help herself. She began to laugh. His face was like a little boy with his hand caught in a cookie jar.

After the initial shock wore off Alex, too, began to laugh, and so did Kelly. But Brady just sat back, put his napkin on his lap and eyed the elegantly set table.

"Lieutenant, I'll bet you're the best administrative aide in the Air Force. I can see you think of everything," Alex said as he pushed her chair back into the table. "I must say, I would never have thought that. I really do apologize."

"Forget it," she said. "I can understand your... concern... but I'm a little disappointed in myself. I thought I dressed rather tastefully, and here I just look like a tramp."

"No, no you don't Lieutenant," Alex said quickly.

"Just call me Nancy," she replied.

"Nancy," Alex said remorsefully. "You don't look like one at all, I mean, you look... beautiful. It was the circumstances, not the company that... "

"I understand. Let's drop it shall we? Major, may I have another drink? And I think Mr. Hunter could use one too."

Brady came out of his stupor and glared at Alex. "Hunter, if you jump to wild conclusions like that on your little trip you're gonna end up a dead man!"

Alex pondered that remark for a moment, then shrugged it off. He took his seat at the other end of the table opposite Brady. A

41

waiter came in and filled his water glass and asked if he would like a cocktail. "Scotch and soda," he replied. Then he turned back and faced the assembly. They were, for the most part, just staring at him. "Well, what do you want? I said I apologize, didn't I?"

When his drink arrived, Lt. Clark raised her glass, "May I toast to your good luck on this mission Mr. Hunter? And may you return safe and sound."

The others grunted an affirmation of the toast and drank silently.

Alex just sat there. He didn't know what to think of the girl. At first he was sure she was a hooker, but now he wasn't so sure. Alex then raised his glass in toast. "To my most beautiful mistake," he said nodding toward Nancy.

Brady looked at him and heaved a big sigh. The sergeant laughed.

The lieutenant laughed too, but there was an air of nervousness in her laugh.

"I hate to break this little game up, but I think you ought to know that the lieutenant here is not only my aide, but she is an expert on China. She has been very helpful in setting up the logistics for this mission."

Alex wasn't surprised she was intelligent, but he was surprised that she knew anything about China. "How did you come to be an 'expert' on China, Lieutenant?"

"I lived there," she replied simply.

"You lived there? When, twenty years ago? Why you must have been only about six or seven when you left."

"Sorry, Mr. Hunter, but I left there only two years ago. You see, my father was the Swedish Ambassador to China. I lived in China for twelve years." She was very serious.

"What are you doing in the American Air Force then? I thought all Swedes were neutral."

"Technically speaking they are, but I'm an American citizen." Shrugging, she said, "It's a long, complicated story. You probably would find it very boring."

"I've got all night," Alex quipped, then he looked up at Brady, "Haven't I?"

Brady moved his drink to one side as the waiter served the soup. "Thank you," he said to the waiter. "All night? Not quite. A few hours at the most. You should get some rest, I but let's just see how things go."

"Okay. Let's see." Alex downed his drink, looked at his soup, looked at Brady, then to the girl, then to the Sergeant, then picked up his spoon and started eating.

It was nearly an hour before they finished the last course and were having coffee. The talk at dinner had been light, polite, and, to Alex, dull. Kelly, Brady, and the girl were laughing about an incident involving a person Alex didn't know. He slid his chair back from the table and started to get up. The other three looked up.

"Going some place, Alex?" Brady asked.

"I think I'll hit the sack, you all obviously have things to talk about, and I'm a little tired."

"I'm sorry," Nancy protested. "We sometimes go off on tangents like that about things around here. We didn't mean to exclude you from the conversation. Please sit down." She motioned to his chair.

Alex hesitated, he didn't want to stay. He was bored.

Kelly rose from his chair, "Good night all, I have an early appointment tomorrow." And, just as quickly as that, he left.

Alex frowned a bit, but when Brady also asked to be excused, Alex was downright suspicious. "Hold it, Brady. What's going on?"

"Nothing. I have a long day tomorrow, too. Right now, I have some paper work to take care of. Stay and have another cup of coffee with the lieutenant. You might learn something new about modern-day China." He started out of the room, but Alex stepped in his path.

"Just a minute Brady. At the risk of stating the obvious, I think you and the lieutenant have cooked up something fishy."

Brady looked Alex right in the eye and in a dull flat monotone said, "Alex, nothing 'fishy' is going on around here. We just felt it

43

might be good for you to talk to someone besides us for a while to relax some of the strain you've been under. No tricks, no fancy maneuvers, just plain, old hospitality. You'd do well to just relax and enjoy this night, not long from now you'll wish you were back here. Goodnight Nancy."

"Good night, Major."

"Good night, Alex."

"Something tells me... good night, Brady." Alex watched Brady go out the door and close it softly behind him. Alex looked at the door for a second, then turned around to face the Lieutenant. She was still sitting primly at the table with the cup of coffee in her hand. Her cool, blue eyes peered at him over her coffee cup.

Alex walked over and stood across the table from her. He looked into her eyes, but for the life of him, he didn't know what he was looking for. "Well... "

"Well, what?" Nancy said, putting her coffee cup down.

"Well, what is going on? What're all the funny looks and innuendos for? Was I a bad boy or is there something about to happen?"

She leaned forward propping her chin up by her hands, elbows on the table and looked up at the handsome man in front of her. She gave him a slow look up and down and then spoke softly. "I really couldn't say. They don't tell me everything either."

"Come on now, do you expect me to believe that? I saw that little look he gave you just before he left, and I saw you acknowledge it. What's going on?"

"Oh, that," she said, getting up from the table and going over to the large drape-covered window at the opposite end of the room. She parted the curtains and looked out into the night.

"Yes, 'that'," Alex said impatiently.

"Well frankly," she said turning around and facing him, "The Major was reminding me not to upset you tonight. He thinks you are getting close to the breaking point."

"The breaking point! Why that son-of-a-bitch! I can take all he can dish out and more!"

44

"Easy, Mr. Hunter, relax. There's no need to get mad about it. The Major's been doing this kind of training for a long time. He must see something in your behavior to lead him to believe you're on the edge, so-to-speak. But maybe he's wrong. At any rate let's just relax a bit... unless, of course, you want to get to bed," she said as she coyly glanced back at Alex. She ambled to a set of double doors at the far end of the dining room and opened them. There was a large comfortable room, with overstuffed chairs around a heavy oak coffee table and lamps in each corner of the room turned to the low setting. At the far end of the room was a huge fireplace ablaze with the logs crackling. Directly in front of the fireplace was a large circular heavy-pile white rug and on both sides of the rug were identical high wing-backed chairs with foot stools facing one another. Directly opposite the fire was a large sofa. Nancy walked the entire length of the room until she was near the back of the sofa then she turned, sat on the back edge, and faced him.

Her pose, the lighting, the fire, everything was perfect, just like a page out of one of those high fashion magazines. Alex stood there and took in the full effect.

"This is some room," he said slowly walking toward her while glancing at the various paintings and small objects of art carefully placed around the room. "It looks like what I'd imagine a millionaire's living room would look like."

"It was once owned by an oil millionaire. He donated it to the government just before he was sent to prison for tax evasion. As I understand it, Major Brady knew the man some years back, and when he found out about the government seizing it for back taxes, he convinced someone in Washington to let him have it for his special projects. Actually the house is ideal. It is large enough to house all the different training areas necessary including the firing range in the basement and, of course, the screening room. Brady decided to keep this room just as it was, and the dining room, of course, so the staff could enjoy themselves in a relaxing atmosphere."

"The teacher's lounge as it were."

"Yes, would you like some brandy?"

"If you're going to have some."

She moved over to a servant's bell hanging by the door and pulled the chord twice. Almost immediately the waiter appeared at the door leading to the dining room. "Yes, Lieutenant?" the waiter called.

Alex was startled and turned around to see the waiter.

"Any special kind of brandy, Mr. Hunter?"

"Frankly, I rather have Grand Marnier."

"Lieutenant?"

"Cognac."

The waiter turned and vanished into the now darkened dining room. Alex went over to the tall floor to ceiling windows and looked out at the manicured court yard. "I didn't know any of this existed. From what I've seen up to now this was just a compact little school. Are there any more rooms I haven't seen?"

"A few, mostly offices for the staff. Rather military I'm afraid." The waiter returned with a tray on which were two bottles, one cognac, the other Grand Marnier, and two snifters. He put the tray on the bar and went back out into the dining room closing the doors quietly behind him.

Alex watched him, then turned toward her. He chuckled to himself, "Something tells me I'm in a dream world, and I must say I'm not sure whether I like it or not."

Nancy crossed over to the bar and poured out generous drinks for each of them. She handed Alex his and sat down on the sofa and curled her long tanned legs up under her. Alex crossed over to the sofa and looked down at her. His pulse was racing, and he was perspiring a bit. He started to sit down on the sofa but changed his mind and went over and looked at the fire for a moment. She sat perfectly still. He turned around from looking at the fire and saw her looking at him, sizing him up. Suddenly, he burst out laughing. A small frown crossed over her face.

"I was just thinking," Alex mused, "This is just like a scene out of a bad B-movie. The beautiful woman and the spy, both uncertain of the other's next move."

She laughed, "Ah, but she's always the spy."

"Touche," he said as he sat down in one of the chairs across from the sofa.

"You never did tell me about how you ended up in the Air Force."

"Oh, it's a long story."

"You said that once before. I'd kinda like to hear it."

"Okay," she said, as she got more comfortable and relaxed. She leaned her head back on the sofa. "As I said, my father was the Swedish Ambassador to China for twelve years. He had lived in China for most of his life. In 1930, after university, he was appointed an attache. He was only an aide, but he liked it there, and by pulling strings, managed to stay there almost uninterrupted for twenty-eight years. He returned to Sweden at least once a year for briefing and traveled all over on his vacations."

"So you were born and raised in China," Alex asked.

"No, I was born and raised right here in the U.S. The product, you might say, of my father's indiscretion. My father met my mother while he was visiting here before the war. He didn't know about me for nearly seven years. Then, my mother took sick, and I guess swallowed her pride. She wrote him about me. By the time he found me, my mother was on her death bed. She died hearing his promise to take care of me. His wife, who lived in Sweden, couldn't stand to 'live among those dirty oriental people', never knew. She was shocked, of course, to learn about me, but she came from a very proud family and wouldn't divorce him. She made him put me in school in Switzerland so there wouldn't be any scandal. Am I boring you?"

"No, no, go on."

"Well anyway, when I was twelve, my father's wife died. He decided I should get out and see the world, so he took me with him to China as a Swedish citizen."

"And the Chinese didn't know that you were really an American?"

"Not for a long time. But one day two years ago, they came to the Embassy and ordered my father out. Somehow they found out the whole story. I'm afraid the story shocked many of the people in

Sweden, because we left there six months later for the United States. My father is now working for your government in some capacity or another as I do. So, now you know why I know a great deal about China."

The waiter poked his head in the room and asked if they would like anything else, he was about to retire for the night. They said no, and he shut the doors behind him.

Nancy moved and sat in a very provocative pose. She flipped her hair back and took a long, sultry look at Alex. He watched her move. He had to turn away and look at the fire.

"Alex, come and sit over here beside me and relax," Nancy said beckoning him with her eyes.

Alex got up, faced her and approached the couch, but instead of sitting down on the couch, he sat on the arm of the couch. "Would you mind pulling your dress down a bit...uh... it's a little distracting. Actually, a lot distracting."

Nancy smiled, tugged at her dress and got it down almost over her knees. "Better?" she asked looking seductively into his eyes.

Alex took a deep breath, "Yeah, better." Then, suddenly, he got up again and walked to the window and looked out.

"Alex, what are you thinking about?" she said getting up and walking toward him.

He heaved a big sigh and turned around. "I'm not thinking about anything right now," he said staring out the window. "You know, there's only one word to describe that garden in the moonlight, 'beautiful'. And then I turn around and see you and I think the same thing -'beautiful'." He smiled a boyish smile and walked over to her. She braced herself for his next move. It caught her completely off guard. He reached right around her and picked up his glass and held it up. "Another drink?"

She broke out in laughter, and shaking her head negatively, she went back to the couch and flopped down again. "I give up, you're something else, Mr. Hunter."

A knowing smile crept over Alex which she did not see, and by the time he had fixed his drink and walked over to the couch, he quashed the smile. "Just what do you do, Lieutenant?"

"Well, I keep records of all the trainees, their progress, their idiosyncrasies, their skills, and I keep the Major informed of all the reports sent in by the various instructors. I keep busy."

"I see."

"As a matter of fact, you've been doing remarkably well in your training. Better than most I've seen."

"Thank you."

"Mr. Hunter, " she began.

"Alex, please," he said.

"Alex, I've read all the reports on you. I hope I'm not being too invasive, but I do want to say how sorry I am that your wife... "

"Committed suicide." Alex shrugged and walked over and stood in front of the fireplace with his back to Nancy. "I thought that might come up."

"I'm sorry."

"It's all right. Well, actually, it's not, but I guess I try to forget it, but it's not easy."

"Must you forget?"

"Those kinds of things you never forget, but you learn, sooner or later, to accept the reality. For me it was later. I accept it, but I hate it. You know why? Cause I don't understand why. I think if I knew why she did it, even if I thought it was wrong, I could accept it better. But I don't know, and I never will."

Nancy watched him sag a bit.

A tear ran down Alex's cheek as he peered into the roaring flames. He could see Crissy falling toward him. He wanted to catch her, but it wasn't to be. Then after a few moments, Alex stiffened. He rubbed away the tear and set his jaw. He turned and faced Nancy. "Well, looks like time for bed."

Nancy said, "I feel like such a fool. I should never have... "

"Sure you should have. Brady needs to know how I am on that, and a woman gets a much better reaction. It's all right. I understand why you brought it up. Well, is that the end of the third degree?" Alex asked as he put his glass down and started for the door.

"It wasn't meant to be a third degree, Hunter. I was just curious," Nancy said with an edge of anger. "Brady didn't put me up to it either."

"Really?" Alex stopped. He looked back at her trying to probe with his eyes to get beneath her words and find out what was the real meaning behind this 'innocent' meeting so carefully arranged.

Nancy got up from the couch and walked up to Alex. "Go if you want. I have no hold on you. I'm just curious about a man who is about to go on a dangerous mission. I want to know why. Why are you doing this? It is just a man thing, or is it deeper?"

"Good question - which I've asked myself a number of times lately."

"And... "

"Hard to say. Duty, honor, to help my country, those are some reasons."

"All the reasons?"

"No. I guess you could say I'm curious, too. I want to see the look on Roger Walters' face when we meet for the first time in a long time. I want to know why he defected to the enemy. Yep, I'd say curiosity is a big part of the rationale."

"Walters was a friend, wasn't he?"

"I thought so until that afternoon at Panmunjom. It all happened so suddenly. I gotta find out what made him go out, and why."

Nancy looked at him over the tops of her eyes. Brady was right. One of the triggers was Roger Walters, she mused. Now, let's just hope Walters doesn't spill the beans about Crissy's murder until they get him back in the States, because if he tells Alex, one of the two of them won't make it back. She wondered what would happen the day those two met. "You don't know why he defected?"

"No. He left me in deep trouble when he went. They thought I knew about it in advance."

"And, you didn't?"

"Not a clue. I was probably more surprised than anyone."

Nancy smiled. So much for that phase of the interrogation, she thought. She thought very carefully before making her next move.

She kissed him on the cheek, and said, "Good night." She walked briskly toward the doors to the dining room.

Alex reacted quickly and cut her off before she could reach the doors. He grabbed her arm and spun her around to face him. He now held both her arms in his powerful grip and looking into her eyes he slowly and deliberately spoke, "Cool it, Lieutenant, the game is over. We both know why you're here in this all too perfect set up."

"Do we?" Nancy asked acidly.

"We do. You were sent here tonight to relax me and to see if my attitude toward the mission had changed. Well, it was a nice ploy but Brady didn't need to go the whole route. For the record, what I just said is how I feel. This is a mission I want to do because my country wants me to do it. Same attitude, same reason as before. As for catching me in an unguarded moment by getting me to relax, forget it. If there is one thing I am, it's single-minded. The only time I want to relax is after the mission. Now you can go back and tell all that to Brady."

Nancy nodded and lowered her head a bit still looking right at Alex but now with a rather soulful expression. "Alex."

"Yes?"

"May I have a drink?"

"I think we can both use one." Alex crossed to the bar and fixed the two drinks in silence while Nancy watched his every move. He brought the drinks over and sat down on the couch beside her and handed her the drink. "Okay, so I am a little uptight."

"Me, too," she said. "I'm sorry, too. Maybe I did come on a bit like Mata Hari. Can we shake and be friends?"

Alex turned and saw the slight smile on her face and he, too, began to smile. "Shake," he said extending his hand.

Alex stifled a yawn and sat up a bit. "Well, I must say the hours around here aren't too good."

"I know, I type up the schedule for training."

Alex perked up immediately and turned to her, a question burning in his mind.

51

Nancy caught the look immediately and held up her hand in protest, "Huh uh… no dice. I won't tell you what's on the schedule for tomorrow."

Alex, now with a sly grin on his face, moved toward her, "Come on Lieutenant, be a good girl."

"Sorry, but orders are orders."

Alex reached for her but she was a bit too quick this time. She got up and went around in back of the sofa. Alex hopped up and gave chase, first around the sofa and then as he reached across it, he fell over onto it. He rolled off and came up on his feet and chased her around a chair and caught her around the waist. He pulled her over to one of the chairs and turned her over his knees. Both of them laughed hysterically.

"Now come on," he said raising his hand as if to spank her, "be a nice girl and just tell me what little goodies Brady and his band of villains have cooked up for me tomorrow."

Nancy was weak with laughter, "Sorry, you know the rules, it's classified."

Alex raised his hand higher.

"Don't you dare, Alex Hunter!"

He gave her a sharp, but not too hard, crack on the butt, and she felt the sting.

"Alex, ow! Ow! I won't talk."

He gave her another crack a little harder this time. "Torture will get you no where."

""Oh? Why not?"

"Because… "

He gave her another crack.

"Because I don't know. You can't get information from an informant who doesn't know the answers."

Another crack, just a little harder, but enough to bring tears to her eyes. She stopped laughing. "Really, I don't know. I don't know."

"Come on, you type up the schedule. You know the routine."

"Not tomorrow!" she said covering up her backside with her hands, "I was off today."

"You can come up with a better one than that lady," Alex said giving her another spank but this one less hard.

"Ow, it's the truth, damnit! Stop!" Nancy began fighting for real, and she pushed herself off his lap and fell on the floor. She got up and started to hit him with her fist. He grabbed her hand and started to pull her back on his knee, "Ah, temper, temper... "

"Alex, stop!"

Alex looked at her and he could see she was getting mad and the game ceased to be fun. He let her go. She pulled away and straightened her hair and clothes, "Boy, for a tired man you sure move fast !"

"Training my love, training." Alex got up and straightened his tie and went for his drink he had left on the table by the couch. He picked up hers too and handed it to her. "To training... and the chase."

"To training and catching," she said coyly.

Alex stretched his arms and rubbed the back of his neck.

"You are tired. I can read the signs. Time for my special services."

"Oh? And just what might they be?" Alex asked with a bit of devilment in his eyes.

"You, Mr. Hunter, are looking at one of the world's most accomplished masseuses. Of course, my talent comes naturally since I am Scandinavian by blood. Why, I once rubbed the back of the Chinese Ambassador to Sweden."

"Hummmm, pretty exciting!"

"Not really," she said as she led him over to the couch. "Frankly, he was ninety-one and not what you would call the sexiest man in the world." She motioned for him to lie down on the couch. He tried, but he was too big for the couch.

"Somehow I just don't think these couches were meant for comfort, forget it, nice try," Alex said as he struggled back on his feet.

She began pulling off his coat, "For goodness sake, improvise man. Don't they teach you things like that here? Kick off your shoes, let me help you with your coat, now down on the floor, there in front of the fireplace."

"I sure hope you know what you're doing lady," Alex said as he kicked off his last shoe, opened his collar and laid down on the soft white rug in front of the fire. The embers were just glowing now and the room was made even darker when Nancy turned off one of the lights by the couch. Nancy kicked off her shoes and hiked up her skirt and sat down astride Alex's back. He tucked his arms under his chin, and she reached down and began to gently rub his neck.

"Ohhh, does that feel good," he said, already relaxing.

Slowly her fingers worked their way into his aching muscles, first squeezing them, then rubbing them, then seemingly cutting deep into them. His head began to swirl with a combination of pain and euphoria. She started on his neck and then down his spinal column vertebra by vertebra - probing, massaging, sometimes with tenderness, sometimes with sharp forceful strokes. He had never had a back rub so invigorating and yet relaxing. His fingers and arms and legs began to tingle as the blood rushed to them. He began to feel as helpless as a newborn baby under the expert treatment. A drowsiness came over him for the first time in years, a drowsiness that made him forget everything. He felt a nice warm blackness come over his mind, and he was at her mercy. She rubbed his back, his legs and arms. He shut his eyes and let go of reality. Then she got up and rolled him over and knelt beside him rubbing his forehead and his temples, then his chest. Now, as her educated fingers reached his thighs, he felt a new awakening, a more basic one and instead of tightening up, he felt released. He reached up and touched her long soft blond hair and ran his hand behind her neck and massaged it for a moment then slowly and deliberately he pulled her face to his and kissed her gently but lovingly.

The zipper on her dress broke the silence. She zipped it up, and silently went to the side of the couch and picked up her shoes. She looked down at Alex lying there in front of the fireplace sleeping peacefully. She put his shirt over his bare chest . She walked to the door, opened it and was startled by coming face to face with Major

Brady standing in the hall. She put her finger to her mouth, tiptoed out the door and closed it carefully behind her. They walked a short distance down the hallway and then stopped.

"Well?" Brady inquired.

"He needed sleep more than me I'm afraid, but I can assure you he doesn't talk in his sleep. I'm going to bed. I'll be in about three. Good morning." Nancy gave her report curtly and with a twinge of disappointment. She walked briskly to the elevator and pushed the buzzer.

Brady chuckled at the report. He returned to the room and quietly opened the door and crept in. He walked over to where Alex was lying and gently put his hand on Alex's shoulder. "Al… " was all he got out when he felt a sharp pain in his stomach and all the breath was suddenly knocked out of him by an accurately placed fist. He reeled back and found himself flat on the floor doubled up with Alex standing over him ready to continue the attack.

"Oh, it's you Brady. I thought it was another of those midnight raids," Alex said as he looked down to see Brady writhing in pain. Alex got down on one knee. "Are you all right?"

"Fine," Brady managed to answer between gulps for air. "Just let me lay here for a minute and catch my breath." It took nearly three minutes until Brady was able to slowly get to his knees.

"I'm all right now, just help me up will you?" Brady held out his arms. Alex grabbed hold of them and helped him to his feet. Brady was still woozy.

Alex hitched up his pants, "What's on the agenda today?"

"Something a bit more fun I'd say."

The orange and white parachute popped open at about five hundred feet above where Major Brady and Sergeant Kelly stood in a remote field several miles from the compound.

Alex looked down at the two figures coming up at him, and he tried to steer the chute down right on top of them but the wind was too big a factor. He drifted over them and landed about a hundred yards from them. He landed well and rolled over once and came up on his feet. He tugged at the shroud lines and the chute collapsed.

He unsnapped the chute and walked away leaving the chute to drift away with the breeze. When Brady and Kelly saw the chute being carried away, Brady motioned for Kelly to go after it.

Alex walked up to Brady, and they both watched the comical chase of man against wind. After Kelly caught it, Alex turned to the Major.

"You've sure got a hell've a way of having fun."

"Well, one man's fun is another man's folly I guess. In fact, you did so well I think you're ready to move on to bigger and better things."

"What bigger and better things are you talking about? Or is that a secret too?"

"No secrets between us. Pack up and be ready to leave in an hour."

CHAPTER NINE

March Air Force Base, California, April 21, 1960

Alex and Nancy were crammed into the observer's section of the giant B-52 bomber as it leveled off at 35,000 feet high above the Pacific. Alex was sweating in his cumbersome flying gear, but Nancy Clark seemed cool and comfortable. They'd spent the last three hours with Major Brady going over the latest intelligence reports on Sz An, Alex's contact on the Chinese mainland. At the airfield, after they climbed on board, Brady said goodbye and headed off in another direction.

"We've got about five more hours to go until we reach our destination do you have any more questions, Alex?" Nancy asked, talking loud to be heard above the whine of the engines.

"Just a couple. How long will it be until they decide to drop me in?"

"Frankly, I don't know. Since you are a quick learner, I'm sure you've fouled up their time table. The last words I heard from the Colonel co-ordinating this thing in Tokyo, were, 'Oh, shit.' Major Brady flew on ahead to oversee the rest of the elements of the operation. I know they want you to get in, get Walters, and get you both out as soon as possible. The longer he stays in China, the greater the possibility he will be discovered."

"I know. I want the same. You know we've talked a lot about the mission, but I haven't kept up with the politics of China since

I was discharged in '54. What's happening there? What are the people like now? I know that when I was inside in '53 they were so frightened and distrusting of each other I wasn't sure who to trust. Turns out things went okay, but I was on pins and needles the whole time. Was it still that way when you left?"

"Well, it's changed a lot. I remember how it was in 1949 when Mao took over. There were a lot of victory parties, a lot of happiness and relief when they threw out Chiang Kai Shek. But there was also a lot of fear of the communists, too. It was the Hundred Flowers era, but within I'd say six months, the Communists began a concerted effort to control the lives of each and every person. They used spies to spy on spies. They took from the rich and gave to the poor, but the government actually owned everything. As you know, before the Communists took over, there were over 250 dialects of Chinese. People in the north of China could not understand the people of the south. Mao changed that. Every person was required to learn the Mandarin dialect, and it helped to unify the country."

"Warlords were killed or surrendered their land to the government. Echelons of control were established with those in the party in control. Everyone reported to another person in the community. By 1951, only the high Party officials were allowed to express an opinion, and their opinions were always consistent with Chairman Mao's. You're right, fear was the basic tool of the government. The Korean War also helped to unite the country because they were fighting a common enemy. The propaganda against America was very intense. You couldn't turn on a radio or walk down a street without seeing the banners. It definitely helped the people to band together for the common good."

"After the war ended, the struggle for their minds still went on. All the people were required to meet daily for 'education'. To miss one of these sessions was not allowed. The punishments were cruel and frequent. There were many people killed by the communists."

"Then, in 1958, the Chairman announced the 'Great Leap Forward' a plan to help the ailing economy. He also decided that rather than kill the dissenters, he would 'reeducate' them. He sent farmers to the city and city workers to the farms. He made skilled workers do menial tasks and put people with no education in charge of universities and schools. It was a strange time, but I can only image how strange it was for the average person. By the time I left, things had quieted down. I'm not sure whether fear or the mass reeducation phase caused it, but the common people seemed to adapt to Communism by the Summer of 1958. Since that time, they seem happier. I saw many smiles on the streets of Tsingtao when we boarded our boat. Oh, they still aren't free to say everything that comes to mind, but for the most part I think they believe the government is good for and to them."

"So they are satisfied with their lot?"

"That is hard to say, but they seem to have stopped all resistence to Chairman Mao and the Communist Party. I think they are content to let things be for a while."

"So it's live and let live."

"Mostly. The only trouble I see is that the government has broken up into two factions - the pro-Mao and the pro-Lin Pao people. This could damage the central government, but last I heard, Mao seems to be doing something about it. He is backing the young people. He created this uprising of the youth, all educated under communism and Mao's leadership, of course, as a springboard for a purge of the followers of Lin Pao. He calls it a 'cultural revolution', but what he means is that anyone not thinking like him is... well, is not working for the people. He is encouraging the youth to attack the intelligentsia, the teachers, and the professional people both physically and psychologically."

"Attack?"

"For instance, I got a letter the other day from an old friend who recently escaped from China. Her husband was an administrator in a university in Canton. One of the youth groups made up of students in the university, burst into his office and dragged him out into the street and put him on a platform. They tied signs on him, threw garbage at him and criticized him for never having worked in the fields alongside the people. They made him confess that he was working more for himself and his own self glorification than for the people, and they hounded him down the streets tearing his clothes and spitting on him. She said that that night when he finally got home, he realized he would soon be forced to work in the fields and would probably never be allowed to return to the university. They managed to sneak out of Canton to Hong Kong. The irony is that in spite of this, both her and her husband still see Chairman Mao as the savior of the people. At the end of the letter she closes with a quote from Mao, 'It is well known that when you do anything, unless you understand its actual circumstances, its nature and its relations to other things, you will not know the laws governing it, or know how to do it, or be able to do it well.' So you see, they are now true believers of Mao. He has become a god to them and his philosophy has become like law. As I grew up watching this strange phenomenon grow, I, too, began to see and at least understand that the reason these people were so susceptible to this way of life was that they never had any one person to look up to."

"What about Chiang Kai Shek?"

"Chiang seemed to be fighting only his own people and if anything, by the time the war with Japan was over, he was hated more by the Chinese people than almost any warlord or emperor."

Alex nodded. He had heard that many times from his teachers in school and from several of the Chinese officers in Korea he interrogated. "Anything else?"

"I get the picture," Alex said. "Think I'll get some shut-eye."

The B-52 landed at Tachikawa Airbase in Tokyo, Japan, at four A.M. There was a soft rain falling. Several Marines surrounded the plane when it came to a stop. Alex and Nancy were quickly taken from the plane to another small, unmarked plane. It's engines were already warmed up. They got on board and the plane took off into the darkness.

Less than an hour later, their plane landed at a small air field in northern Japan. The only lights on the runway were coming from the headlights of two jeeps. Alex had a very eerie feeling about things. Time was getting short and he knew it.

They were met by Major Brady, Kelly, and two other Air Force officers, one dressed in flying clothes.

"Welcome to Japan, Hunter," Brady said rather formally, "How was your trip? Pleasant?"

"If you call being cooped up in a B-52 for thirteen hours pleasant. Although, I must say the company was great."

Nancy smiled, "Why, thank you, sir."

"I'd like you to meet two more of the team." Brady first pointed to a tall, blond-haired Air Force Officer in his early forties, a little on the hefty side, but looking sharp in his tailored uniform, "This is Colonel Al Mason. He's in charge of communications for the project. He'll be the one you'll contact in case of an emergency."

Alex shook hands and noticed right away that his grip was strong and sure. "Colonel Mason."

"And this is Major Buck Warner." The major stepped into the light from the headlights. He was still dressed in his flying suit and wore an overseas cap cocked to the right. Major Warner was a small man only about five foot six. He was in his early thirties and the most prominent feature about this man was he was bald as a cue-ball. He, too, had a firm grip when they shook hands and he looked right into Alex's eyes. "He'll get you in and out," Brady said.

They all turned their backs as the small plane taxied away from them so the prop-wash would not get sand in their eyes. As soon as the plane taxied far enough away, Brady motioned for them to get into the jeeps, and they drove off into the night. It was beginning to rain when they pulled up in front of an old Quonset hut set back in a wooded area at the far end of the runway. All the lights were out except for a bare bulb hanging over the door. Brady unlocked the padlock on the door then reached in his back pocket and took out a card; the others did the same. Brady opened the door, and they all filed into the darkened room. Suddenly, it was bright as day as all the lights in the room went on, and Alex nearly jumped out of his skin when he heard a booming voice. "Halt. Stand and be recognized."

When his eyes became accustomed to the light, he saw two towering U.S. Marines standing in front of him, with bayonets drawn, pointing their rifles at the five of them. The three identified themselves by holding up their I.D. cards. The guards immediately took down their arms, stood at attention, and saluted.

Brady returned their salute and told them to take their posts outside the building. They moved quickly, each one giving both Alex and Nancy the once over.

"Over here Alex," Brady pointed as he walked to a large relief map built on a table in the middle of the room. The hills, and valleys were carved out in minute detail. "The length of this table represents one hundred statute miles. It is an exact replica of the terrain, the drop zone, and down here, he said pointing to the far end of the table, is your pick up zone. We want you to become familiar with every road, hill, valley for the entire route."

"That's quite a layout," Alex remarked.

"That's just part of it," Brady said. He picked up a remote control. "Here's the other part." He pressed a button on the remote, and at the far end of the room, a wall-sized projection screen began to mechanically unwind. When it was all the way down, Brady pushed another button and a slide came up on the screen.

"Colonel Dzai Feng Chin," Alex said. "Head of Chinese International Intelligence, fifty-four years old, graduate of Oxford, magna cum laude, served first with Chiang Kai Shek as an aide. He participated in the 'Long March' after he became disenchanted with Chiang. He is a long time friend and advisor to Chou En Lai. Walters reports directly to him."

"Very good, Alex," Colonel Mason said. "Very impressive."

Another slide came up on the screen.

"Tien An Mien Square, Peking."

"Your meeting place."

"The northeast corner near the palace."

"He will be there on May first."

"May day."

Brady turned off the slide projector. "Now, let me explain how we're gonna get you into China without the Reds knowing it." He nodded toward Buck. "The major had an idea, and he has been secretly practicing for this mission for the past four weeks. He'll be your pilot. The point of departure is here." Brady walked over to the wall and drew the drapes apart revealing a large wall map of Japan, Korea, and China. He pointed to Kyushu, the southern most island in the Japanese islands, "at our base at Fukouka. Just south of the city it just so happens that the terrain there is somewhat similar to your drop zone. Major Warner will take a direct northwest course from here, over the Yellow Sea," he said tracing the route as he spoke, "avoiding any land mass, to the point of entry." He pointed to an area on the northwest coast of the Gulf of Chihli. "From there he will turn 30 degrees north and pass over the coast. The drop zone is here, 20 miles south of Tangshan. Why don't you take it from here, Buck."

Major Warner motioned for the group to assemble around the large relief map on the table. With a pointer he showed Alex and the others, the exact point of entry and traced the terrain as he spoke. He talked in a low gravelly voice, slowly and carefully. "First, I'd better explain that near Seoul we'll make a maneuver that will seem to the Chinese radar as if we are going to land there. What we will actually do is drop down to an altitude of two hundred feet and head out back out over the ocean. As far as we know, the Chinese have not yet installed the low scanning radar at any coastal station in the region. If we're right, they can't pick up planes flying at less than three hundred feet, so they shouldn't be able to see us. We'll fly low over the water from Seoul to about fifty miles from the mainland, about here. We'll run with no navigation lights, no markings. We'll cross over the shore about here, twenty-five miles South of Tangshan and climb to about two hundred and fifty feet. We'll continue from there at a heading of 70 degrees for another hundred and six miles." He stopped the pointer. "You'll eject here, Point Able, about seventy-five miles east of Tangshan and about a hundred miles north-north-west of Taku."

"Eject?" Alex was wide eyed, "at two hundred and fifty feet?" He quickly glanced over at Brady and the others in disbelief. "I'll be killed dropping out at that level."

"We don't think you will," Buck said calmly.

"You don't think!?"

"Nope. We've done several tests. The equipment hasn't failed once. The two tests with live people proved that if the chute opens at 100 feet, you'll be okay if you know how to land going that fast. The increased power of the ejection charge will blow you up and out of the aircraft to a height of a hundred to a hundred and fifty feet above the aircraft, and that is our only danger."

"Only danger?"

"Yes, we estimate you will reach a peak altitude of about four hundred feet. It is possible that you will be picked up by their radar. It would only be a small blip on the radar - wouldn't be up there for more than one rotation of the scanner. And, chances are the guys on duty will either be asleep or not paying much attention."

Alex was still shaking his head incredulously, "Let's get back to this 'ejected' thing."

"Look Mr. Hunter, we did our homework. We're damned sure you'll be all right." Buck said with confidence.

"But, if it will make you feel better," Brady interrupted. He walked over, pushed another button and a movie projector lit up. As the film played on the screen where the map had been, Alex and the others saw four different tests of the ejection system and the two 'live people' tests. Afterwards, Alex still shook his head.

"Satisfied?" Brady asked.

"What can I say? It looks okay, but I don't know."

"Trust us Alex," Major Warner said. "We wouldn't hurt you for the world."

Alex couldn't help but smile. "What else can I do? Okay, I'll try it."

"It's the best way to get you where we want you. Besides, we don't want Chairman Mao to know you're in town, do we?"

"No, we don't."

They all laughed at his sarcastic tone.

The briefing went on for about three more hours until Alex knew nearly every step in the operation backward and forward. "Okay, Alex, that's enough for today. I want you to go with Colonel Mason now and get a physical and a shot which will make you sleep for about eight hours. When you get up, Colonel Mason will go over the emergency communications procedures with you. After that, we'll all meet in the mess hall at 1700 for dinner, then we'll come back here for a final briefing. Take off time is 2200."

The news that the mission would begin in less than twenty-four hours rocked Alex. He had been expecting a few more days of briefing and a chance to at least try out the communications equipment, the codes and the ejection maybe, but all of a sudden all his waiting was over. He walked quietly out of the hut following Colonel Mason.

After he had gone, Major Warner, Lt. Clark and Major Brady gathered around the table once again. The mood was somber. "What do you think, Buck?" Brady asked.

"You know him better than I. I was surprised he didn't put up more of a fight about the ejection."

"Me, too," Nancy said.

"Yeah, that worries me, too. Anything else?"

"Hell, Brady, the question of the day is, 'Can he do it? Can he get the job done?" Buck said putting his hands on his hips. It was more like a challenge than a question.

Brady rubbed his face and sat down on the edge of the table. He licked his lips and said, "Yes. Yes, he can do it. Frankly, I'm much more worried about the other end of this thing. Sz An is a good agent, but is he that good? My sources seem to have a lot of confidence in him, and I respect their opinions, but who knows? The other thing is, is Walters on the up and up? All we have to go on are the reports from Sz An. What if he's been compromised and is being used? It sure as hell is possible. There a thousand things that can go wrong as we all know. But to get back to your question, Buck. I'm sure Hunter will do his best."

Nancy nodded in agreement. "But."

"But?" Brady said, frowning.

"But has he the heart to kill Walters if he has to?"

"That I don't know. No one does. Especially Hunter."

"Are you going to tell him?" Nancy asked.

"Tell him what?" Buck asked.

"No. It might cloud his judgment," Brady interjected. "Remember this is a mission to get someone out, not killed. After it's all over, we'll tell him."

"Tell him what?" Buck asked again.

"I can't tell you, Buck," Brady said. "Let's get some breakfast and some shut-eye."

After he woke up, Alex spent nearly four hours (not nearly enough in his opinion) working with the Colonel on the codes and re-familiarizing himself with the radio that Sz An was supposed to have to use in an emergency. They went over once again the Chinese radio procedures he had been taught while still in the U.S. For the next four hours, he and Buck went over the entire drop step by step so that Alex was clear. He practiced his landing curl, but there was no way to practice the ejection. They also went over the pick up procedures, and when and how it was to be accomplished. Alex liked the pick up idea better than the ejection one. He joined the others for a quiet dinner. Not much was said - everyone was in his own world.

It was 1900 hours when the four of them finished their dinner. Alex changed into his flying suit. They assembled once again in the Quonset hut. They went over every aspect of the operation, stressing the last minute changes necessary because of moving his entry date up from the original schedule. They went over the contacts, the entry plan, the exit plan, alternate escape plans, places, names, dates, timing, everything. Finally, Alex was asked to go over the entire mission step by step.

He heaved a big sigh and began. As he went through each phase correctly, the strained faces of everyone else in the room seemed to relax more and more. "And finally, you will pick us up here," he pointed to a flat area on the model south of Peking with the pointer, "and we go winging out in the beauty of the early dawn."

"Good Alex," Brady exclaimed patting him on the back, "you've got it down to a tee." Brady ground out his cigarette in the overflowing ashtray and looked at his watch. "Time to go." He walked to the door and held it for Alex and the rest.

Alex stopped at the door, turned and looked around. "Sure hope it goes as easy as this briefing." He pulled up the zipper on his flying suit close to his neck and walked quickly and calmly to the waiting jeep.

When the jeep pulled up at the apron of the runway, Buck Warner, who had left the briefing early to pre-flight the modified F-80 Shooting Star, greeted Alex yelling to make himself heard. "Welcome, meet the Low Ball Express," he said, pointing to the carefully camouflaged plane. "We're here to help ya Chief." He shook Alex's hand again as if he had just met him and motioned him toward the plane. Alex started to go but Nancy grabbed his arm and kissed him. "That's for luck," she yelled above the noise. Alex smiled and said, "Thank You." Colonel Mason shook his hand firmly.

Then Brady took him aside and cupping his hand next to Alex's ear gave him one last instruction. "Remember Alex, we want him out alive, unless you can't do it. If you can't... make sure he doesn't help them either." Alex looked at Brady and his mood again went from feeling rather happy about the mission to the somber realization that he was going off to a war, a war where the odds were against him but the strategy and timing worked in his favor. He shook Brady's hand and nodded his understanding of the last instruction and walked to the plane.

The crew chief, a trim old Master Sergeant, helped him into his seat and fastened, him in securely. This man, whose sole responsibility for the past weeks had been to make sure this plane was in perfect condition for the mission, eyed Alex just once in a fleeting moment, otherwise he was all business. He hopped off the wing and went to the front of the plane and gave Buck the thumbs up.

Major Warner closed the canopy and returned the thumbs up signal to his crew chief.

Colonel Mason, Brady, Lt. Clark and the crew chief stood silently in the darkness. Each with a different prayer for Alex and Buck. The sleek jet taxied down the ramp and onto the runway. Buck pushed the throttles forward revving up the engine. The shrill whine got louder and louder as the Major kept the brakes on while he checked every gauge and dial one last time. Then he released the brakes. The F-80 Shooting Star shot down the runway, its small red and green navigation lights flashing into the black infinity. The jet lifted smoothly off the runway and disappeared in seconds.

"It's a couple of hours until we get to the Seoul checkpoint, so if you want to take a nap, I'll wake you," Buck's voice came over the intercom. "It should be smooth enough to sleep like a baby. I've got a flight plan for under ten thousand feet so you won't need the oxygen mask."

"Thanks," Alex replied waving at the figure in front of him then realizing Buck could not see his wave. "I'll try it."

Alex loosened his harness some and tried to get comfortable but couldn't in the small cockpit. He leaned his head back and closed his eyes. For some reason the first thing that entered his mind was an old World War One song, "It's a Long Way to Tipperary". He smiled to himself and closed his eyes. For a while he saw colors melting with no images behind his closed eyes, then he began going over the mission one more time in his mind.

"Alex, we're making our fake approach to Seoul now." Buck's raspy voice in the intercom snapped Alex back to reality. "When we level off at 200, we'll turn north. From here on out I'd like you to help by keeping an eye out for anything but the stars. My radar will probably spot ships, but if you see any little boats let me know."

"Roger."

The jet made a long swooping lazy turn. The closer they got to the ground, the darker it seemed to get. He could see the lights of the city below, and to the south the runway lights of Kimpo Air Base. A thought flashed through his mind. It had been nearly seven years since he had been over this very same air field, when he was leaving Korea, after interrogating the returning GI's from the Korean prison camps. He could see, in his mind, many of the faces of these men, some who had been prisoners of war for nearly three years. Their faces were blank, their minds dull and slow. A cold shiver went down his spine.

The F-80 approached the runway just as if it was going to land. Alex could hear the radio crackling with landing instructions, wind direction velocity, runway number, and altimeter setting. The plane was soon about fifty feet over the runway, but it didn't descend any further. It just kept flying at that altitude. Buck banked to the left after passing over the end of the runway and headed due west. The compass on Alex's instrument panel read 270 degrees. Minutes later Buck banked right to a heading of 330 degrees. They were on their way toward China.

"There's a small packet for you in the map pouch to your left Alex. Open it and read it, then leave it in the pouch. From here on out we must maintain radio silence. The signal to jump is on your right. It's the green one to your right. See it?"

The small green light lit up, it was slightly to his right and at knee level.

"I see it,"

"Good. I'll turn it off. The next time, I'll flash it three times for you to get ready and when it lights up for five seconds, eject. Good Luck." There was a small click in the intercom. Alex knew that was the last time he would talk to anyone until he was on the ground in China.

He reached in the map pouch and took out a large white envelope and opened it. There was a small note. He switched on the map light and read, "Alex, we don't really know what you will be up against over there, but I hope we have trained you for every contingency. You are on your own now. If you feel you want to change anything at any time do it. The only thing we ask is that you do everything in your power to accomplish your mission. Bring Walters out, or if necessary, kill him. No matter what happens, we all want you back safely. God's speed."

Alex placed the note back in the envelope and put it back in the pouch. His mouth felt dry and he was sweating underneath his flight suit. It's all been a game so far, he thought, but now it's the real thing. He closed his eyes and said a short prayer, "God, help me to do my best. To do my duty. I think it's important for a lot of people. Thanks for being there for me all the time. I hope I can be there for you, too. Amen." He swallowed hard, took a deep breath and then he began to go over his mental check list. He checked his suit and parachute buckles to see that they were securely fastened. He felt for and found the lever that would trigger the ejection charge below him. "It'll hit you in the ass like a ton of TNT," Alex remembered Buck Warner say. He felt for the canvas curtain he was to pull down over his head just before he ejected so his head would not be snapped off by the impact. He reached inside his suit and pulled out his shoulder holster 45 automatic. He checked the magazine, made sure the safety was on and returned it to its holster. He went over the ejection steps mentally three times. Buck would flash the green light three times ten seconds before he was to go. Buck would then open the special sliding canopy over Alex's seat. Then, when they were over the drop zone, Buck would turn on the green light. Alex would then pull the curtain over his head and pull the lever. From there on, it was up to God and the mechanics who had rigged the outfit. With any luck, 22 seconds from the time he pulled the lever, he would be safely on the ground.

The next hour Alex spent going over and over the instructions in his mind. He couldn't concentrate on anything else. Suddenly, he heard a tapping noise and looked up front. Buck was signaling with his hand to look down. Alex did, and in the darkness he could make out the sea just a few feet below . Then, in a flash, the sea was gone. It was land below the plane. They had passed over the China coast.

What seemed to be an eternity lapsed again. He waited. Every minute seemed like a hour. Then the flashing green light flashed three times. Alex fastened his helmet on tightly, re-checked his gear and reached for the curtain. His heart was beating faster and faster. He took deep breaths to calm himself down just as he had been trained. Every nerve ending in his whole body was throbbing. Suddenly, the canopy slowly slid back over his head. The roar of the wind was deafening. He tried to concentrate. Think, damnit, he told himself over and over. Then there it was - - the green light.

CHAPTER TEN

150 Miles South of Peking, China, April 28, 1960

Buck Warner was right. The ejection seat hit Alex in the ass like a ton of TNT. He shot out of the F-80 Shooting Star just like the name implied. He was catapulted more than a hundred and fifty feet straight up. The night air was cold and the shock kept him from panicking. When he reached the apex, the seat separated from the man, and Alex began free-falling. He tumbled head over heels. His arms were flaying in all directions, and his legs were almost running in mid-air. Alex was completely disoriented. The spastic spinning combined with the instantaneous acceleration put a tremendous stress on him. He felt like he was going to black out. Got to control my fall, he said to himself, and then he remembered Buck's instructions,

" Tuck your feet and pull your arms across your body. The chute will open.!" All he could think of was when? When's the chute going to open? He struggled to bring his feet together and cross his arms over his chest.

It seemed like an eternity until the parachute began to deploy pulling him back skyward. The actual time was five seconds. It took another three seconds until the parachute was fully open. Alex was jolted by the impact of the chute popping open above him. He felt as if he was stopped in midair. Suddenly, he was aware of the silence. No more rush of wind, sounds of shroud lines pulling, the ejection seat falling. Nothing. Perfectly still. He opened his eyes and realized that he had closed them when he pulled the ejection curtain over his head and had never opened them since. He was swinging in a wide arc. Alex instinctively reached for the shroud lines, pulled hard on the right line to cut down on the swaying motion. He knew that if he continued to swing back and forth, he might very well land in a bad position and break a leg... or worse. The swaying motion slowed and then stopped. He looked down, and it was a good thing he did. The ground below was coming up at him very fast. He was only about fifty feet from the ground! He put his legs together and bent his knees slightly to take the impact.

Alex hit the ground with a thud! The sting on the bottom of his feet sent a quick message to his brain - tuck and roll! He rolled over just once and with amazing agility and a lot of luck, he came back up on his feet. He remembered to pull hard on only one of the control lines to collapse the black chute.

It worked! The damned thing worked. The whole thing worked! He smiled to himself as he pulled and the chute gathered near his feet. He quickly unsnapped his harness and looked around. Nothing but silence. Alex gathered up the chute in a ball and put his foot on it, pulled off his helmet, checked the equipment in the various pockets of his suit, and was relieved that his .45 automatic was still snug in his shoulder holster. Still no sounds. Not even a breath of wind. He checked his surroundings. The moon was at half, and because it was a clear night, he could see fairly well. Alex took his map from the zippered pocket on the right leg of his flying suit. He was in a plowed field just as the briefing said it would be - to his right was the wooded area, and in front of him was the old, deeply rutted road.

He didn't want to stay out in the open for fear someone had seen his descent. He picked up the chute, his helmet and carried them inside the tree line of the wooded area, got out of his flying suit. Under his flying suit he was dressed in the uniform of the Chinese people, blue sailcloth pants and a blue, quilt-padded coat. Alex pulled a cap out of the suit along with another map, and his knife. He took off the coat, put his shoulder holster on and put the coat right back on. It was cold. The ground was hard, almost frozen.

There was very little breeze and it was very quiet. He listened again. Satisfied no one was near, Alex quickly gathered up his flying suit and helmet and wrapped them in the chute, rolled up the whole thing into a tight ball and tied everything with the shroud lines and put the ball beside a tree. He'd take it with him once he got his bearings.

He stepped out of the edge of the woods and tried to find where he was on the map of the drop zone. If he was right on target, there should be a small hill just to the north and small creek to the west. Using his compass, he walked along the tree line in an easterly direction. He stopped and listened. Sure enough there was the sound of running water in front of him. The creek was to his left. He was to follow the creek northward. As he looked up, he saw the small hill right in front of him. So far, so good, he thought as he retrieved his ball of stuff and returned to the creek. The creek bed was partially frozen over. He found a place and began to cross when he slipped and one of his shoes got wet.

After about a half an hour, he started feeling the cold. The ground was hard, and the frost penetrated his shoes. His foot was wet, and he was shivering. How did the Chinese manage to stay warm in these clothes he asked no one in particular as he trudged over the hill. On the other side, he stopped again to look around. He couldn't make out any details of his location because the moon slipped behind some clouds. It was too dark to read his map and he didn't want to turn on his flashlight for fear someone might see the light.

He looked up and waited for the clouds to part again. He tapped his feet, partly to get them warm, but also partly out of impatience. Finally, the clouds separated, and the light from the half-moon lit up the area for a brief moment. Alex quickly scanned the map and the area. Out of the corner of his right eye he thought he saw his rendezvous point - a hill with a sharp point and one lonely tree. His heart started beating faster. At last. He started walking toward the hill when the moon again hid behind heavy clouds. It was so quiet that the only noise he heard was the sound of his own footsteps. He walked on until he thought he could see the tree only a few hundred feet away. Alex stopped and crouched down. He listened, straining to hear something or someone. Nothing. He waited. Still nothing. He started to get up again when he heard a noise. It sounded like the breaking of a twig. He stopped and slowly, carefully put down the ball of stuff, and slid his hand inside his coat and reached for his .45 pistol. He pulled it out, and without moving his feet, he looked around in all directions. He could see nothing in the darkness. He waited for three minutes, but there was no other sound.

As a precaution, Alex kept the gun in his hand, picked up the chute and his flying clothes, and stood up. He began moving forward. He took each step carefully, setting his feet down as softly and noiselessly as possible. Even so each step sounded like a cannon shot.

Finally he reached the tree. He looked around. No one was there. Had they not been told? Were they captured? Had the plan been changed again and Brady not been able to get to him in time? Where the hell was his contact? Now the perspiration of walking changed to the cold sweat of fear. He put the chute and flying clothes down beside the base of the tree and inched his way around the tree. This is ridiculous, he thought to himself. If anybody could see him, they would laugh. A man walking around a lonely tree in the middle of nowhere. He looked at his watch - 3:20A.M. Peking time. The contact was nearly thirty minutes late.

He waited. There was no sound except the rustling of a slight wind that had come up in the last few minutes and the sound of his breathing. Alex could see his breath becoming denser as the temperature dropped even more. He looked at the illuminated dial on his watch again - 3:47. His heart was going faster now as he realized that dawn would break in a little more than an hour and he would be trapped out in the open. He didn't dare light up a cigarette. His hands were getting very cold, and he put them in his arm pits to keep them warm. His eyes searched the horizon for any sign of movement.

"Nide fangdz dzai nar ma?" a high pitched, singsong voice pierced the stillness. It seemed right on top of Alex. He spun around in the direction from which it came and dropped to the ground. He took

the safety off of his .45. His heart was pounding. His eyes strained to see where the voice came from. He could see nothing. Suddenly, he slapped his forehead. That was the recognition sign. He looked around the tree once again, took a deep breath, and slowly called out in Mandarin in a loud whisper, "*Wode fangdz jer.*" He waited. No reply. He cocked the pistol and the sound of the mechanism seemed deafening. Then he remembered. The counter sign. He'd used the wrong one. Again, he called out in Chinese, "*Nide fangdz dzai nar?*"

The voice replied, "*Wode fangdz shr lo shan.*"

It was the right counter sign and Alex gave a huge sigh of relief. "*Haugile!*" he called. Then, not ten feet from where Alex lay, a figure rose up from the ground with a Russian-made burp gun at the ready. It looked to Alex as if the person was wearing the Army uniform of the People's Liberation Army. Alex could not see his face. He was in silhouette. The man lowered the gun from the ready position and using the sling, put it over his back. He began walking toward Alex.

"Welcome to China, Satan," the man said in excellent English.

Alex had almost forgotten. His code name in English was 'Satan', in Chinese, 'foreign devil'. It was funny to be called by his code name, he thought.

Alex slowly got up from his prone position and stood near the tree with the trunk of the tree at his back. He watched the man approach. In the bright moonlight Alex saw that his contact was not young. He was stout and walked with a slight limp. His face was round and his almond-shaped eyes were narrow and decidedly slanted. He wore a blue quilted coat, dark pants and rubber-soled shoes. His hat was at a jaunty angle and cheerful smile greeted Alex.

"Sz An?" Alex said, extending his hand.

"Yes," the man said. ""We must be going immediately, the sun will rise soon." Sz An picked up the chute and flying clothes. "Is this all you brought with you?"

"Yes, everything is packed up. But I couldn't find the ejection chair."

"I found it. We must not leave anything here that others might find. Come with me."

Alex and Sz An started off down the northern slope of the hill. They walked through a plowed field and up another smaller hill. After about ten minutes, they came to a road. Leading the way, Sz An led Alex across the road to a clump of trees. Hidden among the trees was an American Dodge army truck, vintage about 1944. Alex climbed into the front seat alongside Sz An. They drove off.

"You surprised me," Alex said in Chinese.

"Can we use English? I'm so out of practice," Sz An said with a smile.

"Sure," Alex said. "I guess my Mandarin is pretty bad."

"Sounds good to me. No accent. Natural."

"Good."

"I didn't mean to surprise you by sneaking up on you, but I wasn't sure whether or not you had been picked up by the radar and were taken prisoner."

"Well, that surprised me, the English I mean," Alex said. "I didn't expect to hear any until I met with Walters."

"Oh, you see, everyone in Special Unit Four, Comrade Walter's unit, must speak English. Any one of us might be sent to the United States on a mission so we must be trained and ready."

"Where did you learn English?"

"My parents taught me. They had worked for a Christian missionary for many years. The missionary was from Wales. During the World War II was put into the intelligence command for General Chiang Kai Shek. In 1944, a Mister Smith of your OSS secretly recruited me to do some spying for the Americans."

"So, I had worked for both Mister Smith and General Chiang for three years. And because the information I provided to him proved to be valuable, Mister Smith paid me handsomely. Then early in 1948, Mister Smith asked me to desert General Chiang and join The Long March led by Mao Tse Tung. He seemed convinced that Mao's army would eventually take over China. He said he wanted someone on the inside. I agreed, and, so, I have been working for America - the OSS, now you call it the CIA -for a long time."

"What is this Special Unit Four you referred to?"

"It is our special intelligence unit devoted to infiltration and espionage in the United States. Walters is the head of the planning division of the unit."

"I see. And how long have you been in Special Unit Four?"

"About three years."

"And you've known Walters all that time?"

"No, I just began working in the planning division only about a year ago. Until that time I didn't know him, I had only heard about him. I was put into his unit because I had submitted to the Chief of Intelligence several ideas he liked. Six months ago I was promoted to his staff, and I am now one of his three project coordinators."

"Then you see Walters frequently?"

"Yes, nearly every day."

"Do you think you know him well?"

"As well as most I think."

"What's he like now?"

"To me, he is a brilliant man, a good strategist, careful planner, and a total perfectionist. He demands, and gets full cooperation from all who work for him, and he expects everyone to do their jobs to the best of their ability. He is reasonably even tempered, in fact, I do not know of any time when he has lost his temper. But, the thing that impresses me most about him is how cunning he is. He is very tricky."

"Tricky? How so?" Alex's ears perked up. Most of what Sz An had said he knew from his past experience with Roger, but this was a new wrinkle.

"He is a master of taking plans submitted by his coordinators and adding a new twist or changing a few elements and thus creating a very successful operation. He has been so successful that I am sure he has given your people many troubles."

"I see. He adds twists?" Sz An nodded. Alex leaned back and began to think. "It doesn't sound like Roger. He used to be very matter of fact and always a straight-line thinker. Roger wasn't the type to be a masterful thinker. Either he's changed, or... what am

I thinking, of course, is he's changed." Alex shook off the thoughts and turned to Sz An. "Is there anything else I should know?"

"No... except there is one thing about him that I have seen only recently. Up until a few months ago, he expressed much hatred toward the Americans around the other staff, but lately, with the three coordinators, he seems... well, he seems more tolerant."

"Tolerant? How so?"

"I really don't know how to explain it, but he seems to have some sympathy for the Americans. And the kinds of missions he is developing are subtly different - less hate-filled. It is as if he is no longer as dedicated to the overthrow of the American government as he once was."

"Do you think the others have noticed this?"

"I'm not sure. The other coordinators don't talk much about their work so I can't tell whether or not they see this change."

"I see." A change in attitude, he thought. Less interested or at least less competent in his work. Why? "When did you first notice this?" Alex asked.

"Just a few months ago."

"Was this before or after he contacted you about leaving China?"

"Oh, much before," Sz An assured Alex.

"Sz An. Why you? Why do you think he let you know his feelings about leaving China?"

"I don't know. Just what he told me. He felt I was an understanding man. I think he felt that way because... well, because I listened and did not criticize. We talked for a long time and became comrades gradually. I think he felt I earned his trust. Many times I thought he was testing me. I even thought for a while that he might suspect or know that I worked for American Intelligence, but there has been no evidence of that. I am accepted in all the inner circles. Perhaps it is a combination of these things that persuaded him I could be a 'friend'."

"Do you trust him?"

"I must say it took me a long time to feel I was getting the truth from him. As an agent, I have been very cautious; he could have been leading me into a trap. But at every turn, he convinced me by his actions that he was sincere. And, just before I contacted your people, an incident occurred that finally led me to believe in him. We were planning a training program for a group of dissident American youths in Cuba. The program was to train these people to set up organizations on college campuses that would spread dissent about the way the government of the United States was handling the civil rights movement. In the program there was a section on how to handle questions from progovernment people to sway them from their positions by ridicule and fake logic. The original program called for the answers to be provided by using the teachings of Mao. The answers were to be memorized. However, Walters modified this plan by instructions which said not to use any direct quotes of Mao for fear it might expose the leaders we had trained, and he had us paraphrase the sayings in more colloquial language. This might have worked had he not changed the meaning of many of the paraphrases slightly to make them illogical and thus not nearly as effective. He also made it easy for any CIA or other government spy in the group of youths to identify others of the group by requiring the assignments of the smaller groups or cells to be posted. He said this was necessary because some people might be exposed, and if they were, they could not go on to another college and work with their fellow comrades. The effect of this was to broadcast who was where and when. Information any spy could use to great advantage."

"So you think he sabotaged the entire program?"

"Yes, and very cleverly. I saw him do it in front of the other coordinators and sell the idea to Colonel Chin."

"Well, it seems he may have changed his mind and regretted his past actions."

"Satan, there is one thing more I should tell you."

"Yes?"

"Last month he asked me if I had heard anything about his being replaced. I had not. But he seemed to feel that he was being phased out. Then the next day, I noticed that he received a directive from the office of the Director of Intelligence that he would no longer be required to submit reports to the Assistant Director. That is strange because it means his reports go directly to the Director which is very much out of character for the administration. And, right after that, he was not invited to a very important staff meeting."

"So you think his theory might be correct?"

"I thought so at the time, but now I'm not sure."

"What do you mean?"

"Not long after the incident about the staff meeting, he seemed to get back in the good graces of the high command. It was not quite like it seemed before, I sensed some strain in the relationships between Walters and Colonel Chin, but things seem to be improving."

"One last question, Sz An, how did he go about asking you to help him?"

"He didn't directly. One night, after we became friends for many months, while we were drinking, he became very melancholy. He began talking about his childhood and his 'old house' and 'his friends back home' and things. Then he asked me if I thought it would be possible for him to return to America. He asked if I thought the People's Republic would allow it."

"And what did you say?"

"I said I didn't think they could let him go back because he was too high up in the intelligence department."

"That makes sense. In fact, rather obvious."

"Yes, but you must know that they let many of the turncoats from the Korean War return to America without much trouble."

"I know, but I understand that none of them were in sensitive places in the government."

"Did you ever find out why he chose to put his trust in you?"

"All I know is what he told me. He said he had made it his business to know a lot about people and he followed his instincts."

"Sounds like a pretty thin story," Alex mused.

"I know, I felt that way too. I even felt he was setting up a trap for me by getting me to say something against the government, so I waited for nearly two months before getting my information to one of our agents. During that time there was no indication that I was being entrapped or anything. Of course it would have been difficult for them to detect anything since I knew they were possibly watching me."

"You think they were following you?"

"I had to assume it. So, I resorted to *jwodza hwa* - 'table talk' to get my messages out."

"Table talk?" Alex was puzzled. "What is that?"

"Oh, I suppose it is no longer taught. It is a system to prevent enemies from capturing a whole line of agents. Only two are vulnerable. The rest don't even know each other."

"But, how?"

"Simplicity is the genius of this system we developed when the Japanese occupied our country. A message is written, in code of course, and the first man puts it in a envelope, a matchbox, something small enough to hold in the palm of your hand. The first agent takes it to a restaurant and places it under the table somehow. Some restaurants had special places for messages. That agent leaves and another sits at the table and picks up the message and goes to another restaurant and places the message under that table, and so on until it reaches its destination. That is why we called it 'table talk'. Only the next agent in the line knows the agent delivering the message so if they are captured, they can only reveal the identity of two people and the line of agents is safe. I chose to meet Comrade Walters in such a restaurant and just for fun left my messages there while we were meeting. I enjoy a bit of danger. It keeps me young."

"Right under Roger's nose."

Sz An smiled and nodded.

"Well," Alex said with a chuckle in his voice, "It looks like you handled everything well. Where do we go from here?"

"It's not too far. I'll wake you when we get there."

Alex nodded. He was very tired. He slid down in the seat and closed his eyes. Sleep came on him like a soft blanket. The truck sped on down the road.

An hour later, Sz An roused Alex and turned the truck off the road onto a dusty side road. On the horizon the sun was coming up, first a bright star, then instant light. It was going to be a clear cool day. Alex could see the outline of a small house nestled in a clump of trees. Sz An drove into the small barn at the back of the house. They walked to the house. The air was cool and crisp, and Alex found himself being wakened from his foggy sleep mode. By the time they reached the door of the house, he was alert. The house was small and built of crude bricks. One of the windows was knocked out, and it looked like no one had been near here in many months. Inside, the one-room house was cold. There were scattered pieces of broken furniture, a wooden bench that had seen better days and a wood-burning stove in the center of the room. Sz An walked over to the stove and opened the lid. He reached down inside the stove and turned a hidden handle. Immediately, the floor near the bench started to move and separate, exposing a hidden stairway. Sz An motioned for Alex to follow him, and they descended down the dark stairs to another door. Sz An pushed a button and opened the door with a key. He explained that the button must be pushed three times before the key is inserted and twice after before turning the lock or the entire area would be detonated by one hundred pounds of TNT. Alex whistled.

Sz An reached around the corner to the left of the door and turned on a single high intensity light that lit up a large table in the middle of the room. The table was covered with maps and some blueprints.

"This used to be a command post for the Japanese during World War II, Satan. Very few people ever knew about it. It was abandoned in 1942. Your intelligence people learned about it near the end of the war and gave me its location a couple of years ago. I did not use it until I had word of your impending arrival, and I had a hard time getting the mechanisms to work. The electricity is generated by that old gasoline engine over in the corner. It generates enough electricity to last about three weeks when the lights are not used, and about twelve hours when they are used. I finally figured out the system. It works very well. I charged the batteries just before I met you tonight so we have a lot of time. While I am gone, you will have to keep the engine running at night to recharge the batteries. "

Sz An walked over to the table and spread out a large map of the streets of Peking.

"Before we go into Peking, you will have to wait two days. During that time, you must memorize this area around T'ien-an-men Square. You must also memorize this route to a pick up point here, in case something should go wrong."

Sz An pointed out the routes clearly three times. Then he began to go through his plan to get Walters out of Peking.

"Two days from today is the celebration of May Day in T'ien-an-men Square. There will be thousands of people in the square to participate in the celebration. Over here in front of the Great Hall of the People will be a large reviewing stand for the dignitaries of the Party and several visitors from other friendly countries. Walters will be a part of the official Party dignitaries and will go to this stand. He will arrive at exactly 7:20 AM. By that time, the square will be filled with people. The first official ceremony, the military parade, will begin precisely at 7:30. He will leave the stand at five minutes to one to attend the banquet lunch held in the Great Hall. After the lunch, at two, he will no longer be required to be with the dignitaries. I will meet him here and lead him to the rendezvous point here in the staging area for the People's Southern Army. We will have a truck waiting."

"We?"

"Oh yes. It is necessary that we use one more man to insure success. He is a man whom I trust implicitly. His name is Wu Ting. During the past few months he has managed to work himself into the Peoples Southern Army as a driver and will be our driver."

"Tell me a little about Wu Ting"

"Wu Ting has been training with our unit for the past two years. Walters and I both like him. A couple of months ago Walters caught him stealing some of our plans and forced him to admit to him that he was stealing the documents to sell. He was planning to escape to Hong Kong. He thought he could sell the documents and get enough money to go to Taiwan. Walters didn't turn him in, instead he brought him to one of our meetings and promised him that if he helped us, when Walters got back to the U.S., he would help Wu Ting get out of China safely. Walters had him transferred to the Army and managed to get him the job as a driver with the

Southern Army Unit that was to be given the privilege of attending the ceremonies in Peking. He knows nothing of our plan except that he is to meet us at the staging area at the allotted time."

"Do you trust this man?"

"Yes. He is very scared and could be punished severely if Walters were to turn him in, and I believe he is sincere in his wish to go to Taiwan."

Alex looked at Sz An and walked away from the table for a moment then turned around and returned. "O.K., if you both think we need him and you both trust him."

"We need him and trust him."

"Okay." Alex nodded.

"Now Wu Ting will be waiting here," Sz An pointed to a spot on the map, "and during the lunch period, I will get you from the truck I have been driving and take you to Wu Ting's truck. You will wait inside the truck and I will bring Walters to you. Then we will wait until the truck convoy pulls out to return to Canton, and we will go with them."

Sz An went over the plan several more times, and, after giving Alex instructions on how to get along inside the cellar for two days, he left.

As he went out, Sz An closed the trap door and very carefully covered up all the tracks in the dusty room with a small feather duster and then covered the tracks to the barn. He backed the truck out and drove down the long driveway to the road which led to the highway. He stopped, backtracked on foot and carefully covered the tire tracks to the barn. Then he sped off down the highway toward Peking.

CHAPTER ELEVEN

Peking, China, April 30, 1960

Roger pulled the large steel door open and entered the Great Hall of the People on the north side of T'ien-an-men Square. It was late, nearly eleven o'clock at night and the long, main hallway was dark and empty except for the few guards stationed at regular intervals along one side. The guard at the door snapped to attention when he saw Roger. Roger paid no attention to him and quickly made his way down two flights of stairs to the familiar hallway which led to Colonel Chin's office. The light coming from beneath the Colonel Chin's door cast eerie shadows on the floor. It was the only light in the hallway. Roger knocked in code. The lock on the door clicked, and the door opened slowly. Wu Ting nodded to Walters and stepped out of the way. Colonel Chin was seated behind his well-worn wooden desk piled high with papers. A metal lamp on the desk provided the only light in the room. Roger walked to the desk and stood at attention.

"Close the door and lock it, Wu Ting." the Colonel commanded. He did and stood alongside Walters. Colonel Chin looked up and smiled.

"It is nice to see you again Captain Wu. How does it go in the South?" Colonel Chin asked with a wry smile.

"It goes as well, however, I must admit I will be glad to return to my rank. The life of the common soldier is a difficult one."

"It does you good to return to work alongside the People, Captain Wu," the Colonel said with a smirk in his voice. "Please, Sit." Wu sat in one of the two chairs facing the Colonel's desk..

Colonel Chin turned his attention to Roger. "Comrade Walters, tell us how you are progressing with our traitor Sz An," the Colonel directed.

"It goes better than I could have hoped, Colonel. I just returned from seeing Sz An. He has made contact with the American spy and has brought him to the city."

"Where is he hiding him?" Wu asked.

"He wouldn't tell me, but we shall have plenty of time to find that out later. The big question is how the American slipped into China undetected. We must have a weak point somewhere."

"What is the next step?"

"To let them believe I am going with them. Sz An outlined a plan. It is not a particularly good one. Everything is as we expected."

"Good"," said the Colonel, very self-satisfied.

"I will be met by Sz An after the luncheon and taken to your truck, Captain," he said nodding at Captain Wu Ting. "The American should have already been brought to your truck. We will ride with you in the convoy out of the city. From there we will proceed to our next contact in the South. Do you know where Sz An intends to go, Wu?"

"No, he has not told me the exact destination."

"Frankly, I was hoping he would tell you. It would have made the next steps easier; however, we have planned for this eventuality," Walters said.

"You are referring to the tracking device Comrade?" asked the Colonel.

"Yes. Perhaps now would be a good time to go over this part of the plan. Could you call in Major Dzu and have him bring his diagrams?"

The Colonel nodded and rang a buzzer under his desk. A small door in the far corner of the room opened and a very slender Chinese officer with steel-rimmed glasses entered smartly. He was carrying a large leather briefcase. Roger took the briefcase from the major and removed series of technical diagrams and a small metal pin from of the briefcase. He spread the papers out on the colonel's desk and began explaining, "These are the schematic drawings explaining just how the mobile tracking unit works. Here you see... if."

"Never mind explaining how the device works," Colonel Chin interrupted impatiently. "Just explain how you plan to use it."

Roger stifled a sigh of disgust. "As you know Colonel, we could capture the American agent at any time, but we feel it is important to see just how he plans to escape, and what contacts he makes on his way out. In that way we will get the most information possible."

The Colonel nodded dully.

"Now this pin," Walters picked up the small metal device on the table, "is actually a small radio transmitter. It is preset to a specific frequency. We have sewn one just like it into the seams of my underwear in case they should want me to change clothes. The transmitter will give off a signal that can be picked up for over thirty miles on a specially equipped radar truck. The truck will follow us wherever we go. Whenever Sz An and the American stop, if they meet or talk with anyone, the local police will pick up those people they meet with after they leave the area. In that way we will cut down the spy network as we follow them."

"Just how reliable is this device?"

"If I may, Comrade," the major interrupted, "We have been testing this device for nearly a year. We have made every conceivable test including dropping a five hundred pound weight on it. We have tested it in a deep mine shaft and..."

"Yes, yes, enough, I believe you have been thorough," interrupted the Colonel. "Go on with your plan Comrade Walters."

Roger spent an hour with the Colonel and Wu Ting and the major. Each step of their plan was carefully worked out, including special signals in case he should be in trouble and need the assistance of the special police force in the radio truck. The meeting broke up about midnight, and each went their separate ways.

It was a balmy night in T'ien-an-men Square. There was a gentle breeze, and he could almost hear it wafting over the cobblestones. He stopped and looked around. It was quiet, very quiet. In front of the Great Hall of the People, newly erected, was the reviewing stand for the annual May Day celebration. The stand was nearly two hundred yards long, the size of two football fields, and he knew that tomorrow over a thousand dignitaries and world officials would stand for nearly five hours as the ceremonies of the May Day celebration took place.

In a few hours he, too, would be standing there alongside many dignitaries. He would be relegated to the back row, but he hoped that when his job ahead was successful and he had exposed the American agents and the network of spies in China, he would finally be accepted as a true "comrade" and move down a few rows. What an honor that would be!

He remembered the first time he stood on that platform in 1954 along with all 21 of his fellow turncoats. What a sight it had been. To see the vast Army parade before them, and the various groups of peoples from each of the provinces of China numbering nearly a million in all. They were all awestruck at the enthusiasm and discipline of the people. He had not understood them at that time. He had not understood that they were celebrating not a victory over foreign enemies, but victory over the oppression of thousands of years of warlords, starvation, poverty, and disease. Now, after six years of "education" and observation he understood. The communists had given the people a new lease on life. They had done it with violence, fear and intimidation, but still he felt Communism was good for the people. He knew that most were better off than ever before. It took five years of loyal service before he was asked to once again stand on that platform. His only regret, he thought, standing in the almost mile-square courtyard, was that he was not Chinese. He understood, even now, that most of the common people still looked down on him and regarded him as an "outsider" a "Yang Gweidz", a "Foreign Devil". He was doing his job, and doing it very well, but he was not part of "the people."

Roger walked down the dimly lit street toward his apartment. He was pleased with the meeting and especially his plan. It was foolproof.

As he walked along, he thought to himself how much Peking had changed over the years he had been here. The crowded dirty streets, filled with milling people looking for food and a place to sleep, had long since been cleaned up, and now there wasn't a single piece of trash lying about anywhere. Gone were the starving people, the beggars, and the ever-present soldiers. A sort of serene peace pervaded the air and streets. He was as amazed as anyone that the government had been so successful in "educating" the people in such a short time. He knew that very few people nowadays locked their doors in Peking. He felt very safe walking even this late at night. It was a good feeling, and he was in high spirits.

He approached his apartment in the newly-built People's Community Housing Center only about a half mile from the square. The concrete block apartment complex housed nearly 20,000 workers and military officials. His room was on the third floor, number 322F. He went quietly to his room and opened the door. Like all the other doors in the Center, there was no lock on his. He didn't feel he needed one. Nothing had ever been taken from his room in the three years he had lived here. His room was small, about twelve foot square, with a small bathroom to the left as he entered the room. He didn't have much in the way of furniture, a bed, slightly oversize and built especially for his six foot one frame, a desk with a lamp, two small chairs and a large overstuffed chair and ottoman with a floor lamp next to it. There was a small bookcase next to the desk. The closet was on the wall next to the bathroom. He took off his blue quilted coat and hung it carefully on the wooden hanger. It was chilly in the room. He looked at his watch, it was one o'clock, the heat had been turned off now for about two hours and the chill of the night air was beginning to creep in under the metal window sills. The heat would not be turned on again until six o'clock. He went into the bathroom and rinsed off his face, then he went to the overstuffed chair and slumped down in it, and turned on the floor lamp. He picked up three American newspapers, The New York Times, The Washington Post and the Los Angeles Times which were lying by his chair and began reading. They were only four days old. He wanted to make sure that he was current on American politics so he could converse with the American Spy. The part of the trap he did not explain to the Colonel, was how he was going to get the American agent to trust him. He would just have to play that by ear, tomorrow.

CHAPTER TWELVE

150 Miles South of Peking, China, April 30, 1960

Alex was just putting the finishing touches on his make-up when he heard the outside door open. He quickly turned off the light and trained his burp gun on the door. He heard footsteps on the stairway, then slowly the door opened. "Satan?" Sz An called out.

Alex lowered the barrel of his gun and turned on the lights. "Damnit, Sz An, we need some sort of signal. You scared the wits out of me."

"Sorry, I should have called out at the door." Sz An stopped and gazed at Alex. "You have done an excellent job. You look Chinese. I was afraid you might have looked very theatrical. It is very natural."

"Thank you, you look very Chinese too. It's walnut oil. I just hope I can get it off." They both laughed. Alex looked at his watch. "You're early."

"Yes, there has been a slight change of plans, the truck convoy that we are to join is making better time than we thought so we must leave right away."

"How did you find that out?"

"Walters is helping to coordinate the arrival of the various delegations to the ceremonies, he warned me. We must go."

As Alex finished putting on his People's Liberation Army uniform, Sz An inspected the various crates stored around the room. "Did you have time to check the special equipment Satan?"

"Yep, and as nearly as I can see, everything is there."

"How long do you think it will take to put it together?"

"Well, with the three of us..."

"Four." Sz An corrected.

"Four?" asked Alex, "But there will just be you, Walters and and me."

"And Wu Ting."

"Wu Ting? Why is he coming along?" Alex questioned as they left the house and got into the truck.

"Walters told me that Wu Ting feels he is suspected of dealing in the black market foods, and is very frightened. Walters asked if we could take him along, and I said I did not know. Walters insisted, and I agreed so as not to upset him. Besides, Wu Ting has been of great help during the preparations."

"I see," Alex rubbed his chin.

Outside, the twilight air was crisp and cool. They got into the Army truck and drove off down the long lane dragging the specially prepared tree branches to cover up the tire tracks. When they got to the highway, Sz An took the drag off and pulled it behind a few scrub trees and got back in the truck. They drove to near the crest of a hill and stopped. Sz An and Alex got out and walked to the top of the hill. Alex could see the highway not too far away. An Army convoy was crossing the intersection at that time. The Red Stars painted on the sides of the truck had a small white dot on the left point. Sz An pointed out the dot and explained that this was to show that the trucks were from the Western Peoples Army who were coming from the Jhansi Provence. They could not join this convoy because the white dot on their truck was on the lower right hand point indicating they were from the Army of Nanking.

The convoy passed and all was quiet. They waited at that same spot until after dark. Sz An told Alex to stay with the truck and that he was going down nearer the highway to see the markings of the next convoy that was due soon.

It was only a few minutes later when the headlights of another convoy appeared. Sz An came running back and said the markings of that convoy were the same as the ones on Sz An's truck. They started their truck but did not turn on the headlights. Again they waited until the last truck passed through the intersection, then Sz An drove down the hill, turned onto the highway and then turned on his headlights. Sz An sped up and blended in with the convoy.

CHAPTER THIRTEEN

Peking, China - May 1, 1960

It was four o'clock in the morning when the convoy pulled into the staging area about a mile from T'ien-an-men Square. Alex had climbed into the back of the truck because only one person was supposed to be driving. Sz An opened the window to the back of the truck and motioned for Alex to wait. Alex settled down behind the row of fake boxes in the truck and tried to put things together. So far, so good. The only wrinkle in the plan so far was Walter's insistence that this guy Wu Ting go along. Something funny about that, he thought.

Two hours later, the back flap of the truck opened. Alex didn't move from his place behind several boxes. He heard men talking in Chinese. They were knocking against the boxes that covered his hiding place. He heard one of them say that the boxes contained the wrong equipment for the parade, and he seemed to be chastising the other for bringing the wrong stuff. The other was trying to get a word in, but the first man was talking too fast. Finally the other shouted at the top of his voice that this was not his truck, that his truck was over across the way. The other apologized profusely and their voices trailed off. The flap swung closed. Alex released his grip on the burp gun he held in readiness and wiped the beads of perspiration from his forehead. He no sooner had relaxed when the flap opened again only this time the voice he heard was familiar.

"Satan, Satan, it is me Sz An. Come to the back of the truck."

Alex pulled the cover back and crawled out between the boxes to the rear of the truck. He peeked out and saw a huge crowd of soldiers standing and milling around in the square. They were getting their uniforms ready for the parade. There were nearly one hundred trucks in the large area near T'ien-an-men Square.

"Climb down quickly so as not to draw attention to yourself," Sz An commanded.

Alex hopped off the truck and Sz An motioned for him to follow. They walked across the parking area. From time to time they mingled with other soldiers. Alex kept his knees bent to make sure his height didn't call attention to him. Alex's eyes darted back and forth looking for any sign of danger. No one seemed to pay any attention to him and soon Alex felt less nervous. They went around a corner and came into a narrow street. Sz An and Alex walked quickly down the street four blocks. They stopped in front of a small house. Sz An wiped his feet and Alex followed suit. They went in the double doors, through the clean courtyard, to a small ornate door. Alex followed. They went down a narrow hallway directly to a small room. Sz An knocked twice, waited a moment then opened the door. They went in. Alex closed the door behind him and turned to see Sz An shaking hands with Wu Ting. The sight of it nearly knocked Alex off his feet. Alex's mind was racing at top speed, Where had he seen Wu Ting before? What had he done? Alex went through the motions of an introduction and some light conversation without thinking about it, all he could think of was that Wu Ting was someone he should know. Who? Who, Damnit!?

Then he heard it, the slurred 'is' sound, combined with a soft 'ir' at the end of action words. It was a memory key, as Brady used to call it, to remember certain agents accents. Now he remembered. Wu Ting was known to Alex as Wan Yu Tan, a highly trained member of the Chinese secret police and the first Chinese citizen ever taken into the KBG. Wan had since denounced the KBG as a Russian "revisionist" group and had exposed many of the Russian agents acting inside China. There was no doubt that Wu Ting was working for the Party, a real fly in the ointment. Did Sz An know? Did Walters? Who the hell is on his side?

"You seem to be distracted Satan," Wu Ting said in a loud voice.

Alex came out of his thoughts and looked again at Wu Ting, then smiled, "I was just thinking about how well things are going I'm sorry, you were saying."

"We were talking about the plan for getting Walters into the truck without being seen." Sz An said.

"Oh, yes, I guess my mind wandered. Would you mind going over the plan again?"

"Yes, the plan is to have Wu Ting meet Walters at the entrance to the Great Hall and ask that he come to headquarters, pretending a special message has come in. No one will suspect this. He will then escort Walters directly to the truck. You and Walters will climb in the back of the truck, and Wu Ting and I will drive out with the convoy," Sz An explained.

"Right, the only tricky part will be climbing into the truck without drawing attention to ourselves," Wu Ting cautioned. He looked directly at Alex and a cold chill went down Alex's back. "We must act naturally as if loading something."

"Good," Alex said as his mind raced to decide what to do next.

Wu Ting had brought some food and the three of them ate quickly. They went over the plan two more times to insure the timing then they checked their watches and agreed that by seven that night it would be dark enough to get into the truck.

Alex asked Wu Ting about the arm band on his sleeve.

"I am an acting leader for a youth group from Peking. The arm band identifies me as a member of the corps and, as you can see, the word leader is imprinted so," he pointed to the character inscribed in yellow on the armband.

"But I thought the special youth groups were students organized to ferret out dissenters of the policies of Mao."

"That is true, but there are certain leaders chosen from the ranks of special Party groups for this celebration. I was elected an honorary leader for the day," Wu Ting said, just a little too proudly. "I'll will lead the ceremonies this morning." He looked at his watch. "It is time for me to go to the staging area. Are you coming Sz An?"

"Yes, I must go to the reviewing stand. The ceremonies start precisely at 7:30 this morning." Sz An gathered up his coat and hat and started for the door. "You will be safe here, Satan. The man who lives here is gone for reeducation."

Alex, thinking quickly, casually remarked to Sz An, "Oh, by the way, don't you want to take some of these cakes to eat on the stand if you are to stand there for so long a time, Sz An. Maybe Walters would like some."

"Oh, that is a good thought," Sz An said. He stopped at the door and came back to the table and gathered up some cakes in a handkerchief. Alex knocked one off the table and bent over just as Sz An did to pick it up. In a whisper he said, "Wu Ting is a traitor. Come back here as soon as you can."

Sz An did not even look at Alex, he simply continued the motion of picking up the cake. Then turned and faced Alex. "Thank you for the suggestion," he said in a normal voice, then left with Wu Ting.

Alex peered out the door and watched the two men going down the hall talking and laughing. He shut the door and sat down. He was depressed and worried. Was Sz An in on the plan with Wu Ting alias Wan Yu Tan? If so, why hadn't he been arrested by now? What the hell is going on? What if Wu Ting really did want to defect just like Walters? What if Walters was in on the deceit with Wu Ting? Don't panic, he thought, if Sz An is in on a plan to have him captured, there is nothing he could do. But, if Sz An came back without soldiers, then perhaps he is on the up and up.

His thoughts were interrupted by the sound of the door outside opening. He reached inside his coat and took out the .45 he had hidden there and trained it on the door. There was a knock. Not a signal knock nor a commanding knock, just a knock. Alex hesitated for a moment then he heard the knock again. If it was either Wu Ting or Sz An, they would know he was in there. Just then he heard a voice, a woman's voice calling outside the door.

"Chan Wu Yi? Chan Wu Yi, are you there?" The voice called out twice more but Alex stayed still. Then he heard the footsteps go away and the door close. Alex looked at his watch, it was two minutes until six. No time for Sz An to get back before the beginning of the ceremonies.

He sat in the room for nearly an hour, slowly growing more and more anxious. He ran through the options he had. He paced the floor, watching, waiting, hoping that he could come up with a plan to get to Walters without the help of Sz An or Wu Ting. But everything he thought of required him to go to the reviewing stand. He didn't know where Walters lived, he didn't know Walter's itinerary after the luncheon and what's more, he wasn't even sure he would recognize Roger after all these years.

Finally, in desperation, he decided he would chance it and go out into the square and look for Walters. If he could see him on the reviewing stand, possibly standing beside Sz An, he would try to find a way to contact him. Alex put on his coat, stuffed the .45 into his belt and started toward the door. Again he heard the door outside open and footsteps coming toward his door. He slipped back into a corner and waited. This time there was no knock. The door just opened and there stood Sz An.

"I'm very sorry Satan, I could not get back before now. I just managed to slip away for a moment. What you told me just before I left, is it true? Is Wu Ting a traitor?"

"Sz An, I'm really not sure, but I think he is. I've been sitting here trying to put two and two together and what I come out with is five.".

"I don't understand."

"Well, first of all Wu Ting is a notorious member of the secret police. I recognized him from the pictures we have on file in Washington. His real name is Wan Yu Tan. He has been a member of the elite secret corps for several years. Secondly, as I understand it, Walters introduced you to Wu Ting."

"Yes, that is so," Sz An injected.

"And finally, you tell me that Wu Ting wants to escape with us. It could be that Wu Ting or Wan Yu Tan really does want to defect. If that is so, there could be no problem, but frankly I smell a rat. I think he is working for the secret police in which case, he may be leading all three of us into a trap. Something tells me that the trap idea is more likely. If I'm right, the other question is, is Walters in on the trap or not?"

"Why would he be in on the trap?"

"I don't know. That's the part that puzzles me, Sz An. Why a trap and why such an elaborate one?" Alex looked at his watch, - 7:00.

"Sz An, how can we get Walters without Wu Ting,?"

"I don't know. The plan is to have Wu Ting meet him after the luncheon and bring him back here. If someone else meets him, and he is in on the plan, he will become suspicious."

"I know, the problem is how to get rid of Wu Ting." Alex paced around the room thinking. Sz An followed suit. Finally Alex stopped. "Sz An, does Wu Ting know which truck we are taking?"

"Yes, I'm afraid he does, and he knows which convoy we are joining."

"Well, that kills that idea. Wait a minute. What if... " Alex cut himself off. "No, that won't work. Sz An, we must find a way to get Walters out and get Wu Ting out of the way."

"I have an idea," Sz An said quickly. "What if we overpowered him and left him here?"

"That would work, I guess, if nobody else knows our meeting place, but we will be in the midst of a convoy of soldiers. We must get rid of Wu Ting some other way. And we must make it look like Wu Ting ran out on the operation or something so that if Walters is in on the trap he will not be suspicious. What is Wu Ting doing now?"

"He is leading his special youth group unit in exercises in the square."

"What if he were to be exposed in some way as anti-Mao? What would happen?"

"The youth groups would capture him and possibly even kill him."

"Good, now how do we do that?" Alex asked both Sz An and himself.

"The only way he could be exposed is if he were to say something against The Chairman, which he surely would not do."

"Right, but what if he were to do something… something that could be interpreted as anti-Mao?" Alex's brain was working hard. He instinctively knew he was working in the right direction, but he couldn't come up with an idea. He strained for an answer, an answer to his own question. The blood was rushing to his brain, his temples were throbbing. What? What? The lines in his face deepened and he paced nervously. Suddenly, Alex grabbed his hat and headed for the door.

"Where are you going?"

"To the square."

"You are taking a great chance, Satan. There are nearly a million people out there. Your make-up is good, but anyone might see that you are not Chinese and suspect you."

"That's a chance I'll have to take. I've got to have a look at the area. We've got to try something, we can't just stand around here and wring our hands. Time is running out." Alex snatched the door open and started out. Sz An followed closely behind buttoning his tunic and running to keep pace. When they stepped outside, the side street was empty. Sz An led the way to the square. As they rounded the corner, Alex saw the T'ien-an-men Square for the first time, he stopped dead in his tracks. He could not believe his eyes. The entire square was a sea of humanity. There had to be at least a million people there. All were dressed in costumes of their native provinces. Many were in tightly organized groups consisting of from three hundred to four hundred in some groups, to maybe five thousand in others, Alex guessed. Each group was carrying placards with pictures of Mao and anti-American posters. Many of the posters read, "Death to the Foreign Devils." The groups moved in marching precision from one spot to another gradually moving to get in the choice position in front of the reviewing stand to execute their precision drills or exercises. Alex was dumbfounded.

The military parade was just ending. A long row of Russian-made tanks were exiting onto the road leading north away from the square. These were followed by rocket launchers passing by the reviewing stand. Finally, a large missile mounted on a huge truck passed the reviewing stand just as a squadron of MIG 23's passed over the square. The noise of the jet engines was deafening. The military units dressed in the brown woolen uniforms, carrying Russian-made rifles marched out of the square near where he was standing.

As the last soldiers left the square, without a signal, the leaders of each group of civilians from children to old men gave commands in quiet voices and each individual group moved as one person. There were large blocks of young people smiling and all dressed the same in the blue cotton trousers and white shirts with various colored arm bands. They sang as they marched from one position to another. There were Tibetan Monks with prayer wheels spinning and colorful costumes. There was a unit of teachers of all ages all dressed the same in the blue coats and pants and the black loafer-like shoes all standing in neat rows but talking to one another. Near the reviewing stand was a group of teenagers and next to them very young school children all dressed alike in white shirts and blue pants and dancing around a huge maypole-like device. And there were other blocks of people all orderly, all dressed uniformly, most in the blue pants and blue coats of the working people. One group stood out, about five thousand people all dressed in white pant suits with flared trouser legs and with red bandannas. They were doing complicated exercises with perfect precision.

Sz An pointed to a group of young people almost halfway across the square. "There is Wu Ting's group - the *Shaunyandwei.* They are wearing yellow arm bands. They are the older teenagers who are great supporters of the Revolution." They were far across the square. Alex saw Wu Ting wearing his yellow arm band and ordering his group around.

"I must get back to the reviewing stand," Sz An said. "Perhaps you can think of something, but be careful. And don't start a riot. You could easily be killed."

Alex watched Sz An walk away across the square toward the huge reviewing stand with the Red flags of the People's Republic of China sticking high in the air. He walked around the square and studied the buildings, a harmonious blend of the old and the new. To the north, stood the Great Hall of the people; built of grey stone, with huge wings sticking out at each end of the building and the center area studded with four story high pillars. To the west, was a large pagoda-type building, probably built in the ninth or tenth century, with the red and green enameled paint shining in the morning sun. On the northwest corner was a complex of buildings circa the late 1900's, frame in structure with gables and a built-in clock. To the east was a canal, built probably eight or nine hundred years ago, with the stone sides and a road stretching along the far side. Along the road government buildings, each topped by a huge red star, stood in neat uniform rows. In the south was a large park, where thousands of people gathered to picnic on the well-manicured lawns. There were small groups of people dancing some of the traditional dances. Children were running and playing just as they do anywhere in the world except for one thing – they were not throwing things or climbing on the statues that dotted the park. On the lake in the park, couples were rowing small boats and smiling and laughing. Everyone seemed to be enjoying themselves.

But Alex had the feeling that there was something missing - that there was an undercurrent of uncertainty and tension. He felt as if the people were holding back some way. It was as if they had been told to have a good time, but don't overdo anything, don't litter, don't get too friendly with each other, don't mingle, and most of all, don't look like you're having a bad time. He chuckled to himself as he thought of a parallel. He saw Hitler saying to his people, "You will smile and enjoy!"

Around the square, cordoning off the area where the various groups were positioned, hundreds of soldiers in the dress uniforms were standing at attention - each about six feet apart. They seemed like statues as they faced the center of the square. On the perimeter of the square, the common people of Peking milled around, watching the various units perform. The alleys formed by soldiers on the inside of the square between each group were about fifteen feet wide. The precision with which each group worked within their boundaries was impressive.

Alex worked his way through the milling crowd outside the perimeter of the square toward the reviewing stand. He kept his eye on Wu Ting's group. At first he felt self-conscious, but as time wore on, no one seemed to be looking at him, and he felt confident his make-up job was convincing. It took him a long time to walk around the square to get near the reviewing stand. He saw Sz An on the stand in the last row of dignitaries. It occurred to him that there was a chance Sz An was in with Wu Ting. Alex was growing more and more wary of the plan.

"When does all this ceremony end?" he asked an old man standing next to him.

The old man didn't even look at him. "I am told," the man said in a cracking voice, "At precisely one o'clock. Then the Chairman has his meal."

Alex glanced at his watch. 11:45. He knew how to get Wu Ting out of the way, but, now, seeing the organization of each of the groups and the soldiers made his plan to make it look like Wu Ting shot someone was a suicide idea. He began to make his way back to the truck.

He stopped suddenly. His face lit up as he turned around and started back toward the square.

Alex worked his way through the crowds and got to the road beside the People's Hall just in time to see the closing ceremonies. At precisely 12:55 everything came to a complete stop. The last group had just performed in front of the reviewing stand. A hushed silence fell over the square. Then the trumpets struck up a fanfare and the entire mass of people, nearly a million and a half people, began singing the national anthem. The voices rose to a deafening roar as the last few bars were sung. Then silence. All eyes turned toward Mao.

The Chairman walked to the front of the reviewing stand. His aides and other dignitaries - Chinese Officers, Russian Officers, foreign representatives from many nations stood nearby but back about three steps from where the Chairman presided. Mao stood very still. The throng quickly quieted. He waited until not a sound except the wind could be heard, then raised his hand and waved.

A huge roar filled the air, the banners were waved, the flags were pumped up and down by those holding them and the cheers blended into a chant Mao the father, Mao the father!"

Mao stood perfectly still during the chanting then raised both his hands above his head and the chant broke into a cheer. He waited then raised his hand and silenced the people. He stepped to a microphone and delivered a short message. "People of China, we are progressing daily toward our goal of unity and dignity for each man and woman. But we have far to go. What we have accomplished this year must be surpassed next year. What we have gained by our work must be built upon. We cannot let our achievements cause complacency. We must rid our minds and our bodies of the past and go forward into the future. Our enemies are all around us, they must be detected, exposed and educated. We must never let our guard down. We must prepare for the future, for without preparedness we cannot hope to achieve success. You are the strength of China. It is your boundless creativity and energy that will make China the most respected of all nations. We, the Chinese people, have begun the long march again, but this time the trail leads to a lasting and joyous victory.

"To our youth let me say the our future is in your hands. You are the life of China, the destiny.

"To all who stand here today and to all of our people everywhere, remember, it is only through the unity of the People's Republic of China, and its Party officials that lead us, that we can achieve our goal of world dominance and power."

The Chairman took one step backward and a tumultuous cheer again rose from the throng. The band struck up a military-like march and the soldiers formed their ranks and began leaving the square.

All during the speech Alex noted that although everyone wanted to see Mao, no one pushed or shoved. And that during his speech, not a word was spoken by anyone, even, the babies seemed to sense the importance of the speech. It was truly an impressive display of mass control. Alex looked at his watch, it was exactly one o'clock.

As the crowds dispersed and the various units of citizens marched off in one direction or another, Alex waited and watched.

It was nearly one forty-five by the time he had walked around the square looking at the sights, watching the people and even buying a small lemon ice popsicle. He had seen thousands of people from every region of the country dressed in their native dresses all looking proud and content. They seemed to exude the feeling that it was a great honor to be there today. The only note of fear he felt was seeing the many bands of youths, each dressed in the blue pants and white shirts of the working class and each with different colored arm bands. They seemed very serious. Wu Ting's group - the *Shaunyandwei* - with their yellow arm bands seemed to be watching the people intently, as if they were police. He saw children marching along in formation carrying the familiar banner with the picture of Mao and smaller banners which had sayings imprinted on them, "China for the People, "Heed the words of Chairman"" Beware of the Enemy Within," "Death to the Imperialists', "All Reactionaries are Paper Tigers", and "Keep to the Party Spirit and the Party Policy."

As he made his way through the crowds, Alex tried to think of a way to get Wu Ting out of the way and get Walters. Everything he thought of involved a strong element of failure. He could shoot Wu Ting or hit him over the head, but someone would see him, and it would be all over. He had to think of a way!

Then he was surprised to see Wu Ting leave his group and go into the Great Hall. It came to him. The best way was to use the masses of people standing around the square and the Great Hall. If the people were as he sensed, sitting on a sort of time bomb, they might just be right for a riot. What would set off the bomb? He struggled to find the key to set off the fuse. As he made his way back to where he was to meet Sz An, his plan crystalized.

When he got to the steps in front of the Great Hall, Alex was pleased to see the area crowded with people all hoping to get a glance of the Chairman. And another stroke of luck - there was only a small band of soldiers, and they were far off to one side. Ideal. He looked at his watch, 1:55. If things ran true to course, the luncheon would be over in five minutes. He pushed his way through the crowd to the place where he was to meet Sz An. He had less than a minute.

As he came out the door, Sz An saw Alex and came down the stair to meet him. Alex whispered instructions to Sz An. The small boxlike face lit up like a Christmas tree. He nodded with enthusiasm at every instruction and then went back up to the top of the stairs and waited.

Alex moved into the crowd and stood there watching Sz An. At last Wu Ting came out of the entrance. Alongside him was Roger Walters. Roger looked a lot older to Alex, and much thinner, but he had that same arrogant smile Alex always hated. Alex began climbing the stairs through the crowd until he was only a few feet from Walters and Wu Ting. They were coming right toward him. Out of the corner of his eye, Alex saw Sz An duck inside the Hall for only a moment, then he came bursting out the door yelling at the top of his voice "The *Shaunyandwei* have just murdered Chairman Mao!" "They are murderers!" It took only seconds for this message to sink into the thousands of people gathered there. At first there was no reaction, and Alex thought it wasn't going to work, but a soldier standing near Sz An picked up his rifle and shot it into the air and yelled "Death to the *Shaunyandwei*!" The riot was on.

Alex reached Walters, grabbed his arm just as some of the people realized that Wu Ting was wearing the yellow arm band of the *Shaunyandwei*. They grabbed Wu Ting. Alex pulled the surprised Walters away and down the stairs as fast as he could. Roger was fighting him, but Alex yelled in English, "Come on, Roger."

Roger frowned. He was confused and tried to pull away, then realized he should go with the person, after all it was the plan. He couldn't make out who the person was who had a viselike grip on his arm. Together they reached the bottom of the steps only to run into a small group youths with yellow arm bands. They were confused. They were milling around looking for direction when a large mass of people spotted them and began rushing toward them. The teenagers raised their banners in protest but by that time they were overrun. Alex and Roger just managed to get out of the way and stumbled to a doorway for safety.

The word spread like wildfire out into the square. Shots rang out. The entire sea of humanity let out screams and moans of despair and in the matter of minutes the word spread like a wave across the entire square. Suddenly, more than a million people were on the move, running, yelling, attacking the bands of *Shaunyandwei*.

Alex and Walters hugged the doorway as the riot was in full swing. Moments later, Sz An passed them by. Alex called out. Sz An stopped and came back to them. When he saw Sz An, he realized what was happening and he said, "Sz An, you started this!" He started to take a swing at Sz An, but Alex grabbed his arm. He struggled and finally turned and faced Alex.

Alex held Roger's arm tightly as he spun Roger around. "Good afternoon, Roger," Alex said with a grin.

Roger was stunned. At first, he just looked at Alex not knowing what to say or do. Finally, he asked, "Alex? Alex Hunter?"

"The same."

"But how, why you?..."

"You know me Roger, I just couldn't resist coming and getting you, let's go."

"But wait..."

"No time, we have a date in Washington." Alex took one arm and Sz An took the other. The streets were crowded but the people seemed to be running away from the Great Hall, just the direction Alex wanted to go. He tugged and dragged Roger. All the time Walters was protesting, "Wait, wait, we forgot Wu Ting. I won't go without him." Walters struggled to a stop and tried desperately to get away. Alex pulled the .45 out from his belt and pushed it into Walters' ribs. "Now Roger, we need your cooperation. I don't want to have to kill you. Just come along."

"But Wu Ting... "

"You mean Wan Yu Tan!"

"Yes. No. I mean... " Roger looked at Alex. He knew he had made a serious mistake. Alex knew it too, as did Sz An. Sz An's eyes suddenly burned with hatred. "So, you were setting us up for a trap. You bastard!"

"What, what are you going to do with me?" Walters asked, fear overcoming him momentarily.

"For that neat little trick I should let you have it right here and now, but I have a deadline. Roger, my friend, I'm personally gonna take you back home to Uncle Sam and let him take you apart. Now move." Alex pushed Walters forward with the barrel of the gun and then slid it into his coat pocket. "Just move right along and follow Sz An. One little step out of line and you'll find yourself in a lot of pain."

With Sz An leading the way, they made their way through the back streets of Peking to the staging area for the trucks. As they rounded the corner, they saw that guards had been posted near the trucks and they were stopping everyone who entered the area.

"Oh, oh. Hold up," Sz An said and motioned for them not to come around the corner. We can't get to the trucks, the guards are too alert."

Alex looked at his watch - 2:30. The trucks weren't due to leave for five hours. What could they do during that time? They couldn't go to the house, because Wu Ting, if he survived the attacks by the people on the steps, would send police there right away. They were stymied.

All of a sudden, they heard screams and yelling. They turned and saw two young members of the *Shaunyandwei* running down the street toward them. They were being chased by a large group of people, some carrying clubs. They yelled to Sz An and Alex to stop the "murderers." Alex stepped out as if to stop them, but instead he told them to go around the corner. The youths did just as they there told. They ran around the corner and right into a group of soldiers who were standing by the trucks. The soldiers saw the two running toward them, then saw the oncoming crowd rounding the corner. The two looked back, the crowd was on their heels. They rushed the soldiers. The soldiers tried to stop them, but by then the mob caught up with them and there was a wild fracas. Alex, Sz An, and Walters slipped carefully by the melee and into their truck. No one paid any attention to them. The mob was too busy trying to kill the two boys, and the soldiers were too busy trying to protect them and quiet the mob.

As Alex closed the flap to the back of the truck, he heard three shots and the sound of a jeep wheeling into the staging area with it's siren going full blast. He peeked out the flap and saw three Army officers in the jeep. As it skidded to a stop, one of the officers with a loudspeaker demanded silence. He explained that there was no attempt on Mao's life, that the rumor and subsequent riot was started by a group of counter-revolutionaries whom they now had in custody. It was not the *Shaunyandwei*. They, he explained, are loyal to Mao and should not be harmed. The crowd was told to disperse immediately and go to their homes or to the various staging areas around the city. The celebration was over for this year.

The crowd broke up and went their separate ways. Alex and Sz An overheard the officers tell the soldiers to be prepared to move the convoy out of the city as soon as all members of the unit had returned.

At that moment, in the emergency room at the hospital, Wu Ting lay dazed on a stretcher. He had been badly beaten but was still alive. He was mumbling something about an escape but no one paid any attention to him.

Alex and Sz An sat facing Walters, who was huddled in a corner of the truck. Alex and Sz An had their backs to the packing crates that masked the rear of the truck. Alex held the gun on Walters. He and Sz An tied and gagged Roger. They waited.

An hour later, they heard footsteps, and they knew something was about to happen. The officers called the roll to make sure everyone was back. One of the officers told everyone to get in their trucks immediately. Sz An climbed out of the back and into the driver's seat.

Alex watched Roger. For someone in this much trouble, Alex thought, he is too calm. Then he remembered they had not searched him. He waited until the truck started up, then crawled over to where Roger was tethered to a rail on the side of the truck. He untied Roger's hands, but left his feet tied.

"Well," said Alex in a whisper, "since you pulled one little stunt and are not what I would call a good risk, I think we should just make sure you don't have something else up your sleeve. Strip."

Walters looked at him incredulously. "Strip? You mean all of my clothes?"

"Everything. Take them off one by one slowly and throw them over in that corner."

Walters did as he was told and slowly removed all his outer garments until he was down to his underwear. Alex inspected each garment before he threw it into the corner.

"I said everything Roger, that goes for those, too," Alex said pointing to his undershirt and shorts.

Walters protested as he took off his undershirt. "Surely you don't think… ,"

"I'm not here to think Roger. I'm here to do. Your shorts, too."

"I can't get them off."

"Right," Alex said. "Give me your hands." He tied Roger's right hand to the rail again. Untied his feet. "Now your shorts."

Walters began to sweat. He knew that the small transmitter in his shorts would be found if Alex looked carefully. "I won't. It's indecent."

"Shut up, Roger," Alex said. " Take off your shorts."

Roger did as he was told, but instead of handing them to Alex he threw them into the pile of clothing in the corner of the truck. Alex didn't examine them. He reached into a box and pulled out a jumpsuit. "Put these on. They may not be quite the right size, but make do."

They went through the routine of tying and untying hands and feet until Roger was dressed in the jumpsuit. Roger huddled back against the rail. He smiled to himself, at least they didn't find the transmitter, he thought, it'll just be a matter of time until my comrades catch up with these fools.

Alex checked his watch. 4:30.

CHAPTER FOURTEEN

By the time the doctors finally got around to treating Wu Ting, it was nearly 6:30. He had been in and out of consciousness for the past three hours. When the stretcher was placed on the emergency table, he was still unconscious, but after a shot of adrenaline Wu Ting came around. Once he got is bearings, he told the doctor he had to call Colonel Chin immediately. The doctor shook his head and said, "All in good time, Comrade, all in good time. You have a mild concussion and must rest."

Finally, after another hour, Wu Ting convinced the doctor to let him call. He was wheeled over to a phone, and he placed his call to the Colonel's office.

Colonel Chin had been a busy man himself that day, attending the ceremony, the luncheon and then finding himself in the middle of a major scale riot. His first thought, when he heard the news that Chairman Mao had been shot was to see to the security of his headquarters. He fought his way across the square to get to his building only to find the regular guards had been replaced. He then went through a series of difficulties getting admitted to his own office. By the time he did get in, he was worn out. He checked with the truck which was assigned to track Walters, and was relieved to find out that the signal was coming in clear and that the truck had passed out of the city and was heading south with the convoy. The tracking truck was trailing the convoy at a safe distance of twenty miles and receiving the signals well.

The phone rang. When he heard Wu Ting's voice, he sat up straight. "What are you doing calling me? You're supposed to be on that truck with Walters protecting him!" the Colonel screamed.

Wu Ting told of being caught up in the riot. He was very contrite. The Colonel sighed and told him that Walters was in the truck with the radio transmitter and that the tracking truck was following them at a safe distance. Wu Ting relaxed a bit at the news. They talked over a plan of action. Sz An and the American agent might have tortured Walters and made him tell about the trap. Since no one was there on the truck to protect Walters, they decided to act quickly to rescue Walters. He was too valuable to lose. The Colonel would radio the tracking truck to go on ahead and stop the convoy and search the trucks immediately.

Twenty minutes before Wu Ting finally got through to Colonel Chin, Sz An cut the ignition on his truck and pulled over to the side of the road narrowly avoiding a grassy ditch. The other trucks in the convoy sped on past him but the last truck, a repair truck, pulled over in front of Sz An's truck to help out. The driver of the repair truck was alone. Sz An got out of the truck and raised the hood and was looking inside when the repairman came up alongside of him.

"What's the trouble?" asked the repairman.

"A cracked distributor cap. The motor has been cutting out frequently for the past five miles."

"Let me see if I have one in my truck." The driver went back to his truck and searched through some boxes. Sz An took out a knife and cut one of the wires from the spark plugs so that the motor would not run smoothly. The driver returned with a new distributor cap and put it on himself. "Now get in and try it."

"Right." Sz An got into the cab and started the motor, but as he knew, the motor did not run smoothly. The driver of the repair truck listened to the motor for a few minutes and then came around to the cab and told Sz An to shut the motor down. Sz An got back out, and they examined the entire motor, but the repairman did not find the wire that was cut. "I am responsible for all of the trucks in this convoy. By the sound of that motor you will not be able to make it all the way to our destination. I cannot leave this truck here, and it is too far to the next city. However, I am sure it will make it back to Peking. I'll tell you what. You seem to know a lot about motors, why don't you take my truck and follow the convoy and I will take this truck back to Peking and fix it. With hard driving I will be able to catch up with the convoy late tomorrow morning."

When Alex heard this conversation, he acted quickly. He untied Walter's feet. He motions for Walters to stand up. Sz An heard the movement, but the repairman didn't. Sz An reacted quickly. "I will go back and check to see that none of the boxes have slipped as I went off the road. Then you can take the truck."

"Good," said the driver, "I'll get my personal things out of my truck." The driver went back to his truck, and Sz An ran back to the back of his truck.

"Satan," he called in a loud whisper.

"Right here," said Alex almost right on top of him.

Sz An unfastened the flap of the truck. Alex jumped down and pulled Walters with him. He half-dragged, half-shoved Walters into the ditch, put his gun at Walter's head and whispered in his ear, "Not one sound, don't move one muscle or you're a dead man."

Sz An was tying the flap again when the driver came up to him. "Ready?"

"Yes. All ready," Sz An said with a smile.

The repairman got into Sz An's truck, turned around on the road while Sz An gave him instructions so he would not drive the truck in one of the ditches on each side of the road. He waved to Sz An and drove off down the highway toward Peking.

At that very same time, twenty miles on down the road, the tracking truck was cruising along. The officer and the driver were laughing and talking about their families. The radio crackled. It was Colonel Chin. He gave them instructions to catch up with the convoy, stop it, and rescue Walters.

The officer in the tracking truck asked the radar man where the truck was now. He replied about fifteen miles down the road and it seemed to be stopped. The officer shouted to the driver to speed up and catch the truck.

The truck leaped forward, and they headed off down the highway toward Sz An's truck.

We are gaining on them very fast," said the radar man.

"Good," said the officer. "Quick, hand me the map, I want to see where we are so I can pinpoint it for the Colonel. The radar man searched around for the map but couldn't find it. Just then a truck passed by them. The radar man was still searching for the map. Finally, the officer told him to forget the map and tell him how far they were from the truck. The radar man looked at his tracking scope and couldn't believe his eyes. He looked again then he said, "We have passed it."

"Impossible!" said the officer.

"But, sir, I'm sure we've passed it. In fact, it is going away from us toward Peking!"

"Stop!" the officer commanded. The driver screeched to a halt. The officer got out of the truck, and looked back down the road to see Sz An's truck disappearing in a cloud of dust toward Peking. He wiped his forehead. He went back into his truck and looked at the scope. "You are right, comrade. Turn the truck around." The driver did so, and off they sped toward Peking following the signal that lay in a heap of clothes in the back of Sz An's truck. The repairman whistled as he sped along.

CHAPTER FIFTEEN

150 Miles South of Peking China, May 1, 1960

As soon as Sz An's truck was out of sight, Alex pulled Walters to his feet, and the three of them got in the front seat of the repair truck. Walter's hands were still tied, and he was still gagged. When they were on their way, Alex pulled the gag out of Walter's mouth, and Roger gave a big sigh of relief.

"What the hell is going on?" Walter's demanded.

"Just sit still and you'll see." Alex admonished him.

"Where are we going?" Walters persisted. By now, he was growing more and more aware that he was going to be successfully spirited out of the country, and he was afraid of the consequences. He knew that once he was taken out of the country and back to the states, he stood a good chance of standing trial for murder as well as a traitor. His hands were perspiring heavily, and he broke out in a cold sweat.

"Relax, Roger. This is what you wanted. Right? Back to the States?" Alex said. "I know this isn't exactly what you planned, nor for that matter what we planned, but I think things are going to work out all right after all," Alex smiled at Sz An, and he returned the smile.

It was dark by now, and Sz An stayed far enough behind the convoy so he could not be seen when he turned off the main road. When he reached the small road leading to the farmhouse, he turned off his headlights and made the turn. Sz An parked the truck in the shed and set off to cover the truck's tracks with the brush.

Alex led Walters inside the house and tied him to one of the pillars holding the roof.

"How are we going to get out of China?" Roger asked.

"Fly."

"Fly?"

"Just like the birds."

Sz An returned, and they went to the secret room and began opening the crates that held the modular glider. They carried the equipment crate by crate up from the cellar and onto the smooth field nearby. No one said anything as they worked. Walters watched as the crates were taken up the stairs each one in the order stenciled on the side of the crate.

Alex looked at his watch - 9:30. Eight hours and twenty-two minutes until the pick up. Plenty of time.

"What's in the crates, Hunter?" Walters finally asked.

"A sailplane."

"O.K., cut out the crap, I'm tied up. What's in the crates?"

"He just told you, you bastard!" Sz An said as he sorted two crates. "A sailplane."

"What in the hell are you gonna do with that out here? Fly back to wherever you came from?"

"Exactly my friend, fly back. The three of us." Alex replied.

"The three of us?" Sz An questioned. "But I still have work to do here."

"Sorry Sz An, but I'm afraid our friend here caught on to you and set us both up for extermination. You'll have to come back with us," Alex said flatly. "We can't take a chance on leaving you here."

Sz An sat down on the floor. He had mixed feelings about leaving his homeland even though he knew Alex was right.

"Besides," Alex said, " I'm sure you can tell our people a lot that they don't know about the operations you were involved with."

Sz An smiled weakly then looked at Walters. "How did you find out I was working for the Americans?"

"Come on, Sz An, you don't really expect me to tell you that do you?" Walters said, looking straight into Sz An's eyes. "You weren't a very good spy, that's all."

"Why you... " Sz An leaped to his feet.

"Easy, Sz An," Alex cautioned. "We need him in one piece back there. Don't let him get under your skin."

Sz An sat back down.

"Let's get to work. We have a lot to do before the plane comes."

"I thought you said you were gonna use a sailplane." Walters spoke up.

"Oh we are," Alex reassured him, "you see it's very simple. We put this sailplane, which was dropped to Sz An some time ago, together. We attach a lead line to it. Then we stretch a loop at the end of the lead line between two poles. Then, at dawn, a plane will come along with a hook attached to its belly, fly low enough to catch the loop with the hook, and wham, we're picked up off the ground and go sailing off to the good old U.S.A. Simple huh?" Alex smiled and walked over to one of the crates. "This one's next."

Walters shifted around. "Can't you just untie me and let me get comfortable?"

"Nope," replied Alex, "we're taking no chances with you."

Walters struggled to get his hands free but the ropes were too well tied. He settled down for a long wait.

The tracking truck spotted the truck with the repairman ahead about a mile. The driver sped up.

"We'll have to take a chance and stop the truck," the officer inside the tracking truck called out to his men. He armed his pistol, and the radar man picked up his weapon as well. The driver of the tracking truck sped up, passed the other truck then slammed on his brakes and forced the truck off the road. The truck turned over and burst into flames. The repair man was trapped inside. It took nearly an hour before the flames died down and the officer could approach the truck. He saw that the driver was dead. He searched but there were no other bodies inside the truck. The only thing that was alive was the radio transmitter which kept sending its eerie message all through the fire and even after.

After a thorough examination, the officer walked back to his truck and radioed Colonel Chin. "We have found the transmitter and an unidentified body of a driver but the transmitter was not on his body, it was in the back of the truck."

"Fools," the Colonel barked, "Get back in your truck and catch up with the convoy. You must find our man. Just one minute." The Colonel's radio went dead briefly and then he was back on. "I have just had word from the convoy that two trucks are missing. You have one but the wrong one. When you find the other truck take caution, Walters may still be alive. Radio me as soon as you have found it. Meanwhile, I will send additional troops to aid in your search."

The officer acknowledged and motioned for the other two to get back in the radio truck. They turned around and headed back down the road toward the road where Sz An turned off.

"The last section," Alex said to Sz An as they returned to the secret room. Almost all of the crates were gone. Alex looked at his watch - 4:52. Just two hours to pick up. "We'd better hurry and get the pole sections out to the pick up area and put them together. Sz An nodded and took one end of the crate, And they carried it out the door.

While they were gone, Walters continued to struggle with his bonds. He'd made some headway - they were looser. He had the ropes loose enough to freely move his wrists. He knew he could get his hands free if he was left alone just a few more minutes.

When Alex and Sz An came in for their last trip out with the poles, Roger was almost free. But Alex was a cautious man. He went over Roger and checked the ropes. "Almost got free didn't you, Roger. Shame on you." Alex said as he retied Walters' hands even tighter. Walters winced at the pain as the ropes nearly cut off his circulation.

"Ow! You son of a bitch! That hurts!" Roger yelled.

"Just want to make sure you don't leave our little party. What's the matter, scared of flying?"

Walters spat at him but his aim was off.

"One more little trick like that and you'll go in a blissful state of unconsciousness, friend," Alex said. "Come on Sz An, let's put those poles together and get the hell out of here."

Outside, Alex and Sz An began assembling the poles. The sailplane was already resting on one wing. It didn't take much to put it together. Three bolts held each wing in place. Four bolts for the rudder and four for the stabilizer.

Once the poles were assembled, Alex checked the controls. They worked perfectly. He checked over the assembly to make sure everything was put together perfectly. It was.

Sz An set the long poles into the holes they had dug earlier. He fastened the lead line to the nose of the sailplane. Alex looked at his watch - 5:32. Twenty minutes to go exactly.

"Now remember," Alex said, as they hooked the lead line to the pick-up line, "the plane will only make two passes, the first at 5:52, the second after he has turned around at about 5:55. If he doesn't make the pick up at that time, we're on our own because he has to be out from over the mainland by seven when the radar stations go on visual sightings."

Sz An acknowledged and hoisted the last pole. "We have plenty of time by my watch, almost twenty minutes."

At that exact moment on the highway, the radar truck sped by the small hidden road leading to the house at breakneck speed.

Alex fed out the lead line to the two poles and made the proper size loop as he had done many times in training. He pulled one of the poles over and attached the line to the top of it. Then he went over to the other pole and attached the line. Then they reset the poles until the line was stretched across them and outside the wings of the sail plane.

Alex looked at his watch again - 5:37. "No use rushing at the last minute. I'll check over the controls again. You go in, clear the house, and get Walters."

"Right Satan." Sz An indicated a thumbs up and ran off to the house. Alex climbed inside and rechecked the controls. The ailerons seemed a little slow in responding, and he climbed out and began tightening the control lines.

Sz An carried the last of the crates back into the house and into the secret room. He armed the booby trap. Covered the secret door and then he began sweeping the dust lightly to carefully cover all his tracks.

Upstairs, Walters listened to Sz An sweeping the floor. He knew that this was his last chance to make a move. In a few minutes it would be the first light of day.

Sz An climbed the stairs, went around in back of Walters and began to untie the ropes holding Roger to the post. As soon as he was free, Roger slammed into Sz An with his body forcing him against the wall. Walters' tied hands frantically groped for the gun sticking in Sz An's belt and found it. Blindly, he pulled the trigger wounding Sz An in the stomach and groin. Sz An slumped to the floor. Roger stood over him with the gun in his hand but his hands were still tied behind him.

Alex heard the shot inside the cockpit where he had just finished checking the controls. He leaped out of the cockpit, cocked his .45, and began racing toward the house. "God damnit! What happened?"

Walters dropped to the floor and tried desperately to get his arms down below his waist and around his buttocks they just wouldn't go, his hands were tied too tightly. He felt as if he were pulling his arms right out of their sockets. He strained and finally managed to get one forearm and then the other over his buttocks. Now he was bending his knees and trying to get his feet inside his arms, he was doubled over in a very tight ball.

Alex burst through the door. Roger, still in a very awkward position, rolled backward and fired. Alex instinctively dove for the floor but he needn't have, the shot went wild and through the ceiling. Roger was like a turtle on his back with no control over his body. Alex leaped on top of him and cracked him in the face with the barrel of his pistol, smashing his nose and tearing his lip. Alex grabbed the gun away from Walters and started to smash him again when he heard Sz An moan.

Alex went quickly to where Sz An lay in a slow growing pool of blood. Sz An was badly wounded and bleeding profusely.

"Go on without me Satan," Sz An gasped.

"Not a chance Sz," Alex said. He went over and checked Walters. He was out cold.

"Can you walk?" he asked Sz An. The pain was so great all Sz An could do was shake his head no. Alex picked the small man up and carried him out to the sailplane and lifted him into the cockpit. Sz An let out a scream of pain and then collapsed. Alex fastened his seat belt and ran back to the house. As he ran he looked at his watch - 5:47.

When he got back to the house, Walters was shaking his head and trying to stand. Alex grabbed the rope that held his hands and pulled him tip to a standing position. "Come on, you son of a bitch, we've got a date with a lot of people who want to see you." Alex pulled him unmercifully out of the house and toward the waiting sailplane.

Roger stumbled and fell a couple of times. Each time Alex was more angry. As they approached the sailplane, Alex stopped. He heard the sound of the plane approaching. Alex pulled hard on the rope and Walters stumbled forward. When they got to the plane Alex pulled Walters around in front and Walters stumbled again. He fell across the lead line. One of the poles came tumbling down, and the line fell to the ground. The roar of the plane grew louder and louder, and there was a deafening roar as the black, unmarked B-25 passed overhead.

Alex's mind kept screaming, "Got to get him back, I've got to! It's my duty!"

He cracked Walters over the head and knocked him out. He pushed him into the cockpit of the sailplane and sat him upright. He righted the pole and made the pick-up line taut. Then he raced back to the sailplane, climbed in, and fastened his seat belt. Sz An was awake now and Alex handed him his gun. "If he stirs, hit him," he said. Sz An nodded wincing with pain.

Alex watched as the B-25 made a slow turn and approached the pick-up zone. Alex started to close the canopy, when he saw the pole sway, then fall down. He threw open the canopy, hopped out of the cockpit, closed the canopy and raced for the pole. He got there, attached the line again, and set the pole upright. The line was once again stretched between the tops of the two poles. The roar of the approaching plane was getting louder and louder. Alex started toward the sailplane, then all of a sudden, he heard a loud crack, and the sailplane was jerked off the ground and was coming right toward him. Alex dived for the ground but the tip of the wing caught Alex in the ribs and threw him out of the way of the oncoming tail that would surely have decapitated him. Alex rolled head over heels. When he came to a stop, he looked up and saw the sailplane climbing in a wobbly fashion right behind the pick up plane.

Alex shook his head to clear it and watched as the two planes like mother and son disappeared off in the distance. The sound faded rapidly. He looked at his watch - 5:56. "Right on time," he said ruefully. Alex dusted himself off and stood. He was a bit shaky. He looked around, there wasn't a sound, just the wind whispering.

CHAPTER SIXTEEN

150 Miles South of Peking, May 2, 1960

As the two planes disappeared in the early morning sky, Alex sank down on his knees. Everything had gone so well until just minutes ago he thought. Why didn't I go back with Sz An? Why? He pounded his fists in the dirt and yelled, "You stupid bastard!"

Alex sat there on his haunches for a long time. He had a terrible sinking feeling in the pit of his stomach. He felt weak as a kitten. Nothing was coming to him in complete thoughts, only half thoughts, pieces of ideas, if only… why didn't…, damn Walters, he made it… what am I going to…? His lips tightened until they were almost blue and the veins on his forehead emerged in a twisted mass. He was so mad that if it were possible, smoke would have come out of his ears. He looked over at the fallen pole, grabbed a handful of dirt, and threw it at it. In utter frustration he fell flat on his face. He lay there trembling with anger.

Finally, after ten minutes, he sat back up. The dust fell from his face. His tears were outlined in trails of dirt running down his face. Alex felt hot and sticky all over. His eyes scanned the horizon. "Enough!," he said out loud and stood up, dusting himself off as he did so. "Okay," he muttered to himself, "no more self-pity, it won't do you a bit of good. It sure isn't gonna bring that plane back, and it damned well isn't gonna get you out of this mess. You've gotta do it yourself. Think dummy, think!" He stumbled over to the poles. The ribs on his right side where the tip of the wing had caught him ached, and every time he took a deep breath, he felt a sharp pain. He poked at the ribs; they didn't seem to be broken probably just bruised he guessed.

He snatched up the poles and carried them toward the house.

As the small truck carrying the replacement crew for the radar base at Po Hai pulled up to the front of the shack, they were almost blown over by the prop wash of the B-25 as it passed over them at about 100 feet. They strained to see what made the strong wind and caught a glimpse of the plane towing the sailplane vanish over the horizon toward the sea. They ran inside and cranked up the radar machinery but it was too late. The captain in charge immediately called his headquarters and gave them the heading of the B-25.

As he walked, Alex's mind began to clear. He remembered what Brady had drummed into his head, "If Plan A doesn't work, use Plan B. It's a good plan, too." He could hear Brady repeating over and over, "Plan B is your secondary escape plan in case things go wrong over there. We have to work as hard on this plan as we do on the primary one. You can never tell what you will actually run up against out there. Your first action must be to survey your position. This survey is as important as any subsequent action you take. It can mean the difference between a successful escape and an unsuccessful one. Look around, take stock of your position, your equipment, your physical health, and your mental state. If you are okay physically and mentally you can probably accomplish whatever you want."

Alex went into the house and was about to throw the poles into the secret room when he realized that he did not have the key. Sz An had it. He hid the poles as best he could and tried to cover his tracks in the dust as Sz An had. He went upstairs.

Alex felt okay physically, and he was coming alive mentally. He began taking stock of everything in the house. He retrieved the burp gun and the .45 in the main room and gathered up all the ammo for both weapons. He went into the kitchen and packed what little food and water remained. Sz An had left a pair of binoculars and a poncho behind and he took those, too. His mind was now clicking on all cylinders. Alex moved faster, his motions were more precise, and his attitude was determined. He took his "stash" to the truck in the shed.

When he finished loading the truck, Alex took one last look around to see if he had missed anything. He used the same rough broom Sz An had used to try and make the house look vacant. Confident he had done the best he could, he shut the door of the house, and began brushing away as many footsteps as he could find to make it look as of no one had been there recently.

Back in the shed, he was about to start the truck to back out when he heard the sound of a plane. He quickly shut the doors of the shed and ducked back inside. He saw a small light reconnaissance plane approach from the east, pass over the house, then bank and return to fly over again. The plane made six passes over the house before it disappeared over the horizon.

Alex sighed. They will want to search this house, he thought, and are probably on the way. If he was right, the soldiers would arrive soon. They'd also be blocking all the roads in the area. Using the truck was out, he had to go it on foot. He made a makeshift backpack, brushed away the footsteps in the shed and closed the door. If they do search the house and investigate, he reasoned, they may think that everyone got away in the sailplane. And if they find the door to the secret room - boom!

He closed the shed doors and looked around. He saw it. A cloud of dust was wending along the road toward the house. The cloud was about three miles away and growing. He estimated they would be there in five minutes. Alex gathered all his equipment, and headed out toward a stand of trees nearby. He walked backwards using the broom to cover his tracks in the dust. He made it around the house and into a small grove of trees just before the small reconnaissance plane came down out of the skies and passed overhead again. He continued to cover his tracks as he made his way through the small forest.

On the other side of the stand of trees was a large open field. He looked up through the branches for the plane. It was nowhere in sight. He started out to cross the field when he stopped suddenly.

He heard the roar of the plane's engine as it approached from the other side of the trees. Alex dove back under the cover of one of the trees hugging it for dear life. He had no idea whether or not the pilot saw him. Sweat was running down his cheeks and his heart was pounding. He watched as the plane banked to the left and turned away from him and again disappeared over the horizon.

As he debated with himself as to whether to chance crossing the open field, he heard another sound. Trucks! They were coming close to the house. He looked back. He couldn't see anything except the cloud of dust. Alex made his choice. He raced out into the open field dragging the broom behind him as he ran. There was a large wooded area across the field. When he was almost to the new woods, Alex heard, then saw, the plane off in the distance turning toward him. He put on a last burst of energy and raced into the woods. Winded, he dropped down behind a tree. The plane passed over the house, but not over the woods where he knelt panting and praying. Alex looked back toward the house. He estimated he was about a thousand yards from the house now. There was a cloud of dust coming down the road toward the house. He had to move. Alex used the broom once more to cover his tracks. It was only a few hundred more yards into the woods, and he stopped when he reached the first trees. He decided that if they were able to follow him this far in spite of covering up his tracks, he didn't need to take the time to do it anymore. Instead, Alex decided on a zigzag course through this woods. He took off at a left angle, then after several steps turned right. He continued this pattern until he came to a small creek. He remembered the old cowboy movies and walked into the creek and followed it. He stayed in the water and let the current wash away his tracks. The creek grew larger, and it was hard to get his footing. As he rounded a bend, he saw a stone hill. He climbed the hill to get his bearings.

When he got to the top, he could see the house, off to his left about a mile away. An army truck was stopped about fifty yards from the house. Three men, an officer, and two others, their guns in a ready position were walking around outside. He watched as the officer motioned to one of the men to follow him. They went out toward the pick-up zone. He could see the officer when he got to the pick-up zone, go down on one knee and look carefully at the ground. Then Alex saw another larger truck coming down the road raising a huge cloud of dust. He watched as several soldiers scrambled out of the truck and surrounded the house. The soldiers, on a command, rushed the house.

Alex saw another officer and soldier walk out to the pick-up zone to meet the two already there. They talked and one made a gesture with his hand to indicate a plane taking off. They looked around and then walked back toward the house. A soldier came out of the house and motioned for them to come. The two officers took off in a dead run. Suddenly it flashed in his mind. You idiot, he thought, why did you take the poles back into the cellar? If you would have left them, they might have believed everyone was on the plane - now... Alex kicked the dirt. He looked at the house again. No action going on. Maybe they won't find the cellar entrance. He had been careful to cover up the trap door with dust.

What are you doing standing here? He asked himself. No matter whether they find the poles or not, they're just liable to find your tracks and take off after you. Get going. Alex took off in a dead run down the other side of the hill and through the woods. As he came out of the woods, he suddenly found himself at the edge of another field only this time he could see several workers bending over picking cotton. Alex went back into the woods and out of eyesight of the workers. He was exhausted. He sat and drank some water and rested. A few minutes later, he took out the map Sz An had left in the cellar and began to study it. He estimated he was about five miles from the small city of Te about fifteen miles south of the Grand Canal. He knew that if he followed the Grand Canal Southward about 70 miles, he would come to Tientsin, the primary city in Plan B. He figured he would travel by night and sleep in the daytime. If he was careful, he would have enough food. The only thing he would need to do was replenish his water supply.

I can make it there in five days barring any problems and get to my contact before sun up the next day, he thought. Again he went over the various steps in Plan B. He could hear Brady going over it with him, "There are two primary contacts. Yin Chwan-Ti, a tailor. He is a slight-built man as you can see from this photograph taken just two years ago." The face on the slide flashed through Alex's mind. "Yin's shop is on the corner of Tai Shan Ti and Lyang Syin Lu. It is in the northwest part of the city about five blocks from the new highway. When you get there, knock three times, wait, knock twice, wait, knock three times. When he answers, you ask "Is this the house of Dzwan the Great?" If he answers yes, everything is okay, if he replies in the negative, you are to go on to the secondary contact, Madam Ying. She is a madam in one of the few houses of prostitution allowed to remain open by the government. She and her girls service the officers of the general staff and some high Party officials. Use the same knocking signal. The recognition sign and counter sign, however, are different. You say you have need of a special girl, one with special talents. She will reply, 'Is she of special birth?' You reply, 'Yes, very special, a contortionist.' If she invites you in, things are all right, if not, you have to get to Tsingtao for your next contact." Alex could see both of the contacts in his mind's eye. He remembered their addresses and instructions on how to get there - everything.

Colonel Chin was furious. Every officer in his conference room was a failure. They failed to find any new agents of America, they failed to protect Captain Walters, they failed to capture Sz An and the American agent, and they let them all fly away to Taiwan. He ranted for three hours.

Alex checked his equipment, food, forged identification papers, and directions. He climbed a tree and looked to see if he was being followed. He didn't see anyone or hear anything. He threw his makeshift backpack over his shoulder and set out toward Tientsin.

CHAPTER SEVENTEEN

Skies Over The Yellow Sea, May 2, 1960

Roger slowly opened his eyes. He was staring directly at the rising sun. He moved in slow motion as he tried to raise his hand to shield the blinding glare only to realize both his hands were tied together. He wasn't fully awake. His head ached and the back of his neck was numb. As his eyes focused, he could see the twin tail configuration of the tail of the B-25 some distance in front of him. He followed the line as it trailed from the tail of the plane to the front of the sailplane he was riding in. He shook his head to clear the cobwebs and got his bearings. They were flying high over the ocean. No one had hold of the stick, but the sail plane was flying level as it was towed across the morning sky. There was no noise, no sound except a low whistle of air. Slowly his memory came back to him - the fight at the house, the wounding of Sz An, and Alex Hunter's anger as he shoved him into the sail plane. Then he remembered the falling pole and Alex getting out and giving Sz An the gun. Finally, Alex hit him and he blacked out. Alex wasn't in the seat in front of him. He turned but was constrained by the seat harness. He could see Sz An directly behind him. Sz An was slumped over. A trickle of blood was coming out of the left side of his mouth. His eyes were glazed over and his eye lids were fluttering slowly. The .45 pistol was dangling from Sz An's hand.

Roger squirmed around to get a better look. Sz An seemed to come awake and tried to raise the gun, but he was too weak and sank further in his seat. The gun dropped on the floor. Roger wasn't sure whether he passed out or died.

His instinct was to get out. He saw the red release lever next to the seat in front of him, but he realized he couldn't fly the plane, he didn't know how. He peered out the cockpit window and saw, far in the distance the outline of land. What was he going to do? What was he going to say if he did manage to land safely. He was certain the Americans would want to know what happened, and if Sz An told them about his plan to lure an American agent into China to find out about other traitors besides Sz An, they might just kill him. And how does he explain the absence of Alex?

The last question was the easiest, he'd tell the truth and back up Sz An. Sz An, he thought, that's my real problem. If Sz An were dead, he could make up any story he wanted to, but if Sz An survives, there's no limit to the danger he could be in. He looked at the horizon, not much time until they make landfall. He turned again and reached for Sz An. Too far. Roger unbuckled his harness and reached back. He could get his hands on Sz An. Sz An offered no resistance. He felt for a pulse in Sz An's neck. It was there -- weak, but steady. He got up on his knees and faced the wounded man. Now he could reach him easily. He felt through his jacket and found a knife. He almost dropped it, but managed to balance it enough to grab the hilt. He sat back down and holding the knife between his knees, cut through the ropes. He was free.

The plane hit an air pocket and Roger was thrown forward and almost hit the stick, but he managed to narrowly avoid it. Back to Sz An. He got on his knees in his seat and examined Sz An. He was obviously either too weak to react or had completely passed out. Either way he wasn't going to resist. How to kill him without making it obvious he was murdered to whoever might examine his body. He decided to smother him by holding his nose and mouth closed. He had to be careful not to get any blood on himself that he couldn't explain. He reached over and pinched Sz An's nose closed. No reaction. He was breathing out of his mouth and he was making small gurgling sounds. Roger grabbed his chin on the side that was not oozing blood and forced his mouth closed. Holding his mouth with one hand, he again closed off his nose. Seconds went by then Sz An began to move, labored movements. His eyes opened wide. He tried to struggle, but he had no strength. As the seconds became minutes, Sz An passed out, then died. Roger checked his pulse. None. He pushed Sz An's body back in his seat and adjusted the harness to look as if he died peacefully. He retrieved the gun, wiped it clean with his jacket and stuffed it into his pocket.

Land was fully in sight. Roger had to see if he could land the sailplane. He squirmed his way to the front seat, buckled the harness and looked at the controls. A horizon gauge, altimeter, and airspeed indicator. The stick seemed to be flying the plane. The rudder pedals were small. Beside him was the release lever to release the sailplane from the mother ship. There was a pair of headphones hooked over a microphone to his right. He put on the head phones. He could hear something, but he couldn't make out what it was. It was static. He took the microphone off the hook.

What was he going to say? Play it by ear he decided. "Hey. Anybody there?" he said after pushing the talk button.

The static continued for a few moments, then a deep bass voice answered in his earphones, "Alex? What's happening?"

Roger took a deep breath and answered. "This isn't Alex. This is Roger Walters."

There was a long pause. He knew the person on the other side of the mike was trying to decide what to say. After a minute, "Walters. Where is Alex?"

"He's not on board. He didn't make it."

"Is he dead?"

"I don't know. I don't know what happened to him. I have Sz An's body in here with me."

"Sz An's dead?"

"Yes."

"How?"

"A long story. How do I land this thing?"

"Let me get our expert, Lt. Cummins."

After another minute the Lieutenant came on the headphones. "Sir, I'm going to take you through a few drills, after that, I'll talk you down. Don't worry, it's easy."

Roger smiled. Maybe easy for him. He performed the drills and actually felt somewhat comfortable that he could control the sail plane. They were ten minutes away from release. Roger sat back and tried to relax as the Lieutenant had suggested. His mind was filled with 'what ifs' and keys to withstanding interrogation that he, himself, had taught many of his Chinese agents. The real problem was Alex Hunter. Where was he, and was he on his way back?

CHAPTER EIGHTEEN

Tientsin, China, May 7, 1960

Alex found himself on the outskirts of Tientsin about three in the morning five days later. He knew he didn't have much time to find his first contact, and if no one was there, he'd be caught out in the open. He found a good hiding place for the night.

Alex waited until midnight the next night before setting out to find his first contact. He tried to picture the map of the city he'd studied many times. The streets were empty and not very well lit. It was like a ghost town. Alex winced at the sound of his own footsteps.

It took him longer than he thought to reach Tai Shan Road, and he half trotted toward the rendezvous with Yin the tailor. When he rounded the corner, his face dropped. The building that housed Yin was a pile of rubble from a recent demolition. "Thanks a lot Brady. You're really up to date on your intelligence information," he said under his breath.

A new fear struck him, what if the same fate awaited him when he got to his next contact Madam Ying's? He glanced at his watch. There was only about a half hour until sun up, and he knew the streets would then suddenly come alive with people.

He looked around to get his bearings and visualize the map once again. It was still all quiet. He searched his mind but he couldn't focus. Beads of perspiration dotted his forehead as panic raced through his stomach. His thoughts were jumbled. Got to get a hold of myself, he chided. Deep breaths. Take deep breaths. Where the hell is her place? Think! You knew the location the other day! Let's see, Madam Ying lives at 113... 113 what? 113 Tai Shan road. No, that's this place. Come on damnit think! Madam Ying lives at... what? His mind drew a complete blank.

Alex sagged back against the wall in the doorway of the building across from the remains of Yin's shop. He took a deep breath, closed his eyes and tried to imagine he was back in training. At first it was only snippets of images. They were somehow unrelated and out of focus. Then, slowly, in his mind's eye, he could see the room where they trained, the slide projector and the beam of light it gave off, then on the screen was a picture of Madam Ying's house. He could see it clearly. A smile spread across his face. He remembered. The number of the house is... is 1455. That's it, 1455 Lo Shan Chi Road. He looked at his watch, 20 minutes until sun up.

Alex started to step out into the street when he heard voices and footsteps. They were coming down the street toward him. He quickly ducked back into the shadows and looked around. The footsteps got closer, and he could faintly make out the voices of some men. Soldiers? What? He hugged the wall, hiding in the shadows. He could hear the men talking about the work they had to do in the factory that made bolts and screws. Then the voices began to fade. Alex peered out to see the last of the men going around the corner to his right. When they were out of sight, Alex took off down the street in the opposite direction. He arrived at Lo Shan Chi Road just as the first light of dawn was spreading tentacles of light through the still empty streets. He peered around the corner and his heart leapt. There, in front of Madam Ying's, a small group of four army officers were standing and laughing and joking with two pretty girls who were begging them to be quiet. When the girls went inside, the officers talked for a few minutes then said goodbye to one another and broke up in two directions. Two of the officers started walking straight toward his corner. He turned and began walking back in the same direction from where he came. Hiding in a doorway was out, the doors were all right on the street in this old section of town. A more menacing sound broke the stillness. The sound of a car. The car was coming closer, but from where? It was not coming down the street behind him nor from across the way. Then he heard the car slow down and stop. It was very close, near the corner. A voice called out. "Yung Chiang. What are you doing out here?" The car had stopped the two officers heading toward him. He could hear their conversation clearly. They couldn't be more than a few steps from him around the corner. One of the officers in a drunken slur managed to tell the driver he was just coming from Madam Ying's and was on his way home. Another voice told him to get in the car and bring his friend. Alex heard the car doors slam and laughter as the car's engine started up and the car sped away. Alex turned around and headed back to the intersection. He looked down the street and saw the back end of the car turning the corner. Alex ran across the street.

"The back door! Go to the back door!" he heard Brady saying. Alex went behind the house and into the alley. There was the familiar green enameled door. He looked around. No one in sight. He knocked three times rang the bell twice and knocked again three times.

Inside, Madam Ying was supervising the girls as they cleaned up the downstairs part of the house. Most of the girls were young, about eighteen or nineteen, dressed in the scanty apparel. Some wore sheer, see-through tops, others long feminine robes. They were giggling and having a good time as they polished the enameled tables and straightened up the few chairs scattered about the reception room. Madam Ying was flustered when she heard the signal knocks. It had been nine years since the code was given to her, and she had long since given up ever hearing it. One of the girls put down her cloth and started for the door. "I'll get it Su Lin" Madam Ying commanded in a voice with too sharp an edge. The girls immediately stopped their work and looked up. "It is one of my very special customers," she explained. The girls all giggled. The tension was broken. She started toward the door, then turned to the girls. "Now I want all of you to go upstairs to your rooms immediately. This man is very shy and doesn't want to be seen. He is very influential. We'll clean up after he leaves. Run along!"

The girls, glad to be free from the work, giggled and started up the stairs. Madam Ying waited until they were all out of sight, and the last one had shut the door, then she straightened her greying, hair and went to the door.

Alex was surprised ,when the door opened. Madam Ying was about five feet one, very slender and about 55 years old. She was much older then the picture he had seen. Her hair was grey, too. Alex hesitantly asked, "Madam Ying?"

"Yes, may I help you?"

"Possibly, I have need of a special girl -- one with special talents."

"Is she of special birth?" Madam Ying asked cautiously.

"Very special, she is a contortionist." Alex looked quickly into her eyes. She studied him for a moment then motioned for him to be quiet.

"Come in quickly, and don't make a sound," she whispered.

She shut the door and told him to wait until she checked the upstairs. Alex surveyed the room he waited in. It was the kitchen, with a large old coal burning stove, a sink with running water, an ice box from about 1920, and a large, wooden table scrubbed clean. Everything was spotless. On the stove was a large tea kettle with steam coming out of it. Madam Ying returned a few minutes later and motioned for him to follow her. Together they crept up the stairs to the third floor past several doors, all numbered. Madam Ying came to a door at the end of the hallway. She took out a key, opened it, and turned on a light. It was a small anteroom with another door. She shut the door behind them, locked it, and then unlocked the second door. She turned on the light and Alex cocked his head. The room had mirrors on every wall, the floor and the ceiling. Madam Ying shut and locked the second door. Alex gave out with a long low whistle.

"We can talk here, the room is sound proofed. It is for customers with… shall we say 'unusual' tastes."

"I'll say," Alex blurted out. Besides the many mirrors, there was only one other thing in the room -- a large round bed in the middle of the room. On the bed was a crimson coverlet of red with a dragon in gold brocade. Alex went over to the bed and sank down.

Madam Ying looked at him. He was dirty, needed a shave and his eyes were bloodshot. She went over to him. "You look very tired," she said in her clear, crisp, Mandarin dialect. "May I get you something to eat?"

"I'm really not very hungry, I had enough food on my journey from... "

Madam Ying put up her finger to her lips, "Please do not tell me anything about yourself. The less I know, the better it will be for me and my girls should you be caught."

"I understand," Alex nodded. "I ran out of water yesterday. Do you have anything to drink?"

"I will get you some hot tea and I will see if there is anything else in the kitchen." She went to the door, stopped, and turned to him. "I shall return shortly. I will lock the door from the outside, but do not fear, because I have the only key to this room. I must caution you not to make any unnecessary noise even though this room is sound proof, there is still the possibility... " He nodded agreement.

She slipped out of the room and locked the outside door. When Alex heard the lock, snap, for the first time in a week he felt a degree of safety. He laid back on the bed and looked up at the mirrored ceiling. "Strange tastes! I'd say... looks like someone doesn't want to miss a thing," he said out loud. He closed his eyes and a soft blanket of sleep enveloped him.

At the first sound of the key being put in the outside door, Alex snapped wide awake. He rolled off the bed, grabbed his pistol and aimed at the door. The inner door opened, and Madam Ying stepped in.

He relaxed, put his gun in his belt and sat back down on the bed. She brought him a small tray with a couple of bowls of rice and a teapot.

"The tea is hot, but I could not find anything to eat except some cold rice. I hope this will be satisfactory for the time being. I did not want to take any chances cooking at this hour."

"It will be fine, Madam Ying, just fine." Alex got up and took the tray from her and put it on the bed. She poured the tea. He took it from her gently and sipped it. It was hot and felt good in his stomach. It was the first hot food he had had since the morning he and Sz An went into Peking.

"Mmm, this tastes great," he said savoring the warmth.

Madam Ying watched him as he sipped the tea. After a few moments of studying him and watching his movements, she sat down beside him. "I'm afraid you cannot stay here too long," she explained, "we have too many soldiers visiting us each night for you to be completely safe. Also, I am certain that the few customers who prefer this room cannot be dissuaded very long from using it. It would be suspicious. Also, my girls will not understand why the room cannot be used."

"I understand."

"May I ask what you want from me?"

"Yes, of course. I have been told you can help me to get to Tsingtao where I can meet with...

She stopped him. "Please, I must ask that you not divulge any information that would be helpful to the authorities. Should either of us be taken into custody, I will surely be forced to give them all the information I know. It is important that I not know anything other than you want to go to Tsingtao." She poured Alex another cup of tea and started for the door. "I shall begin the preparations for your journey immediately. In the meantime I suggest you try to rest. The trip to Tsingtao will not be easy. I will return late in the afternoon with food and drink. Pleasant sleep... uh, what shall I call you?"

"You may call me 'Satan'."

"Satan, yes, it is very appropriate. Goodbye." Silently she closed and locked the door behind her. When he heard the click of the lock on the outside door, Alex gulped down the rest of his tea. He took off his clothes and laid down on the hard bed and again fell fast asleep.

Alex awoke and looked at his watch, it was about two o'clock in the afternoon. He had slept for nearly eight hours. He felt pretty good. Alex dressed, except for his shoes (he didn't know just how sound proof the floor was) and walked to one of the mirrors. What he saw, he didn't like. His make up was all smeared with dirt and his clothes were dirty. He estimated he had lost several pounds during the last five days. He really needed a shave.

Sitting on the edge of the bed, he assessed his situation. One thing in his favor was that he was thinking more clearly now. Alex began to piece together the events of the last few days, and he was thankful that he had gotten Walters and Sz An out. At least, he thought they were out. He accomplished that part of his mission. He wasn't physically hurt, and during his travels, he managed to successfully avoid any contact with people. The one thing he wasn't sure about was whether or not the soldiers back at the house knew that he was still in China. Was there a search party looking for him? Did they find his trail?

His train of thought was interrupted by the sound of the door being unlocked. Madam Ying entered with a tray of hot food and tea, and carefully closed the doors behind her. "My girls are still asleep," she said as she put the tray on the bed. I have some disturbing news. I talked this morning with some of my friends who will help you get to Tsingtao, but I am afraid you will have to stay here another day or so!"

"Do you think it will be all right, won't the girls question the use of the room?" Alex asked.

"Probably, but I will take care of that. You will be safe. The problem is the youth groups. They are causing much trouble. Today I heard that they have started checking and inspecting every vehicle entering or leaving the city. Just this morning I heard that they killed several intellectuals they felt were guilty of 'revisionism'."

"Revisionism? What does that mean?

"It means that those people were speaking out against Chairman Mao saying his memory of the past was faulty. The students are fanatical followers of Mao, and they become incensed over the doubts expressed by some of their teachers. Those teachers feel the Chairman is too old and growing too soft to keep the progress of the government and communism moving forward."

"So now he is encouraging the youth to overthrow all who do not think as he does."

"That is my understanding. The young people will fight for him and his ideas because that is all they know. They have been born, educated, and manipulated by leaders who insist that the Chairman's way is the only way to live. He is their father, their mother and most importantly, their god. The Chairman, in turn, supports the youth with all his strength because he feels they are the key to China's future. They say because of his strong belief that it is possible for him to create a 'controlled' civil war."

"Civil War? He's willing to risk that?"

"My friends say it is not much of a risk since he has the youth on his side, and he controls all arms in China. We have heard many stories that the things that are just now happening in Peking are going to happen everywhere. There is a name for this 'war' now being whispered and sometimes now even being shouted. They call it, 'The Cultural Revolution.'"

"But what good will this revolution do if it turns teacher against student, leader against leader?"

"We are told this revolution is not against the people, it is for the people. It is to awaken us and help us see that the way for China to be a good place for all people is to have all people think as one mind, as one person. The 'war' is against the reactionaries who question the Chairman's control."

"So Mao intends to use the youth to kill off his enemies," Alex said.

"I do not think so. Not the way I think you mean. I have heard that the Chairman is upset that people have been killed. He does not want bloodshed. What he wants is a reeducation of all those who do not think as he does. He wants the dissenters to face public criticism, to be humiliated and refuted by others, but not killed. They should be shamed and dishonored until, through criticism and self-criticism, they realize the errors of their thinking and return to a new life as a more complete member of the People's Republic. This is the purpose of the 'cultural revolution.'"

"You sound as if you feel this is a good thing."

"In many ways the Chairman has helped our country and our people. He has given us the one thing many of us have wished, hope --for a future of peace. But I think this will come with much suffering and hard work, and change."

"So his message is 'Do it my way or else'."

"Yes."

"And you are not afraid his way will hurt you?"

"I suppose I am. So far the government is allowing me to live pretty much as I did in the old days. Oh, I do not have as many material things as I once had, but I have the freedom to run my own business for the time being. I do fear that one day the government will decide my business is not suitable and will take me to work in the fields. My hope, however, is that men will always want my wares. "

"I'm with them. Do you think there will be a day when the Party will regard sex as a bourgeoises need?"

Madam Ying smiled a wicked smile. "Not so long as there are men."

They both laughed heartily. Then a pained expression crossed Alex's face.

"Is there something wrong Satan?" Madam Ying asked.

"Well, I guess I forgot to ask one important question. How do I… well, go to the bathroom."

"Oh, I'm very sorry," Madam Ying said, her expression changing from a frown to a smile. She got up and walked to one of the mirrored walls and simply pushed on the panel to reveal a mirrored bathroom. Alex instantly leaped up and made a beeline to the room. Madam Ying gathered up the dirty dishes and put them on the tray and made the bed. Alex came out of the room with a very relieved look on his face and slumped down on the bed.

"In the famous words of someone, 'thank's, I needed that,' " he said.

"I must apologize. It was an error on my part."

"Well, I'm just glad you didn't say 'hold it'."

They both laughed again. She walked to the door and stopped. "I must go now. I hope there is enough food and tea to last you for a while, I cannot return until tomorrow morning. Is there anything you want?"

"There is one thing," Alex said with a twinkle in his eye, "but I think that might be a little more difficult."

"Whiskey?"

"That's not what I had in mind, but it will do as a substitute."

Madam Ying gave Alex a sad look, "I understand. It must be difficult to be in a house of pleasure and not be permitted to indulge in that pleasure."

"War is hell," Alex said with a boyish grin.

"So it is," Madam Ying said as she closed the door behind her. As she started down the stairs, she heard the girls calling her. She put the tray down on a table in the hallway and hurried down the two flights of stairs to the front hall where she was met by three of her girls. They were dressed in the peoples uniform of white blouses and blue padded pants. A tall, thin girl with her hair tied up in a pony tail met her at the landing. "Madam Ying, I just saw a military car pull up in front. There are two officers at the door."

Madam Ying checked her appearance in the mirror near the door as a loud knock rang through the house. She was frightened, but she took a deep breath, asked the girls not to be frightened, and opened the door. Standing in the doorway was the large imposing figure of General Wan Tu-Yi. A mean-faced man with a long Manchu moustache and small eyes. In his hand was a black folder.

"Why General Wang, it is a pleasure to see you. Won't you come in?"

The general spoke quickly and in a deep voice but there was no mistaking his attitude. He was upset. "Madam Ying, this is not a social call."

"Oh, I could see that," she said with a grin. "You came to the front door."

The girls all giggled at the joke, but the General was in no mood for jokes. He glowered at them. They drew back and lowered their heads in fear.

"Quiet," Madam Ying said to the girls. She noted a slight smile on the other officer's face, a Captain, in reaction to her joke, but she turned back to the General with a serious expression to indicate he had won his point.

"Madam Ying, you are addressing a member of the general staff. Please keep your remarks on that tenure."

"I am truly sorry for my behavior and that of my girls, General. I shall do as you wish."

"See that you do," the general commanded. "Now, you have a girl here, a *da bidza*." Madam Ying winced at the derogatory nickname of *big noses* the Chinese officers used for the Russians sent to China to advise them. "Her name is Lan Yin?"

"Yes," Madam Ying said with a quizzical expression.

"Bring her here immediately."

The girls began to chatter and moved away from the door as the Madam went to the bottom of the stairs and called out, "Lan Yin, Lan Yin." She turned to the girls and motioned for them to be quiet with a devastating look.

In a few moments a girl appeared at the top of the stairs. She was not Chinese, although she was dressed in the clothing of the working people. She was a small, slightly built, Eurasian girl, with long blond hair and a sweet face. She wore no make up. "Yes, Madam Ying?" she said, then she saw the officers. She gripped the railing hard, so hard the knuckles of her hands became stark white.

"Lan Yin. Please come down here a minute, child," Madam Ying said in a calm reassuring voice.

Lan Yin hesitated, but seeing the Madam Ying motion, she slowly descended the stairs. The room was so quiet you could hear her footsteps on the carpeted stairs. When she got to the bottom of the stairs, the girls separated so she could walk up beside Madam Ying. The Madam took her hand and pulled her close to her.

The General watched her carefully. When Lan Yin was beside Madam Ying, he opened his black folder. "Lan Yin", he read "you have been found guilty of contributing to the revisionist thought movement by questioning the thoughts of our beloved Chairman. Because you are of Russian birth, we will not attempt to reeducate you to our ways. We do not want foreign aliens in our country.

We, therefore, hereby notify you that you will be returned to your homeland as soon as transportation can be arranged. You will no longer be permitted to spread your vicious ways upon our loyal officers."

Tears were welling up in Lan Yin's beautiful blue eyes. Madam Ying squeezed her hand.

When he caught the Madam's eye, General Wan spoke, "Madam Ying, until we can arrange to have Lan Yin sent to her politically confused homeland, you will keep her here. Under no circumstances is she to participate in the activities of your house. She is not to leave."

"Yes General," Madam Ying answered. She let go of Lan Yin's hand.

The general again faced Lan Yin. "You will do as Madam Ying commands until the time for your return is here."

"'Yes General," Lan Yin said, her voice cracking. The strain of the news releasing the tear. It ran quietly down her cheek.

"Madam Ying," the general spoke, "I leave this matter in your capable hands."

"Yes, General, thank you." She waited to see if he had any other matters on his mind and was visibly relieved when the general turned and walked down the steps. He stopped and turned. He looked at Madam Ying and gave her a look up and down, then winked.

"Come back soon General," Madam Ying called after him. "Unofficially, of course."

A slight smile broke out on his face and then he said, "Possibly." He got into the car and it sped away.

The girls then broke out in nervous laughter and, as a group, walked out of the hallway toward the kitchen leaving Madam Ying and Lan Yin standing alone. Madam Ying took her hand and led her back up the stairs to Lan Yin's room. They went in and the Madam closed the door. Lan Yin fell face down on her bed crying.

"What's the matter child?" Madam Ying asked, somewhat surprised at the girl's reaction to the news of her deportment.

"Oh Madam, I don't want to go back! I don't know anyone and everyone will hate me for being a prostitute of the Chinese Army. I will be ridiculed and given the lowest jobs," she said sobbing.

"Come now. It won't be that bad," Madam Ying said somewhat confused.

"It will! I know it will." Lan Yin's burst out and a new flood of tears filled her eyes. She looked directly into the madam's eyes.

"It happened to a friend of mine. We worked together in Wuhai. She was sent back. The government questioned her for days and days and then sent her to work in the potato fields in Siberia. She said in her letters that all the people hated her and no one would talk to her. She is miserable, and worst of all, the work has made her ugly and old. She says she has callouses on her hands and knees, and they give her no make-up or pretty clothes. Oh, Madam Ying, I don't want to go back. I'd rather die!"

"But my dear," Madam Ying protested, "I don't understand, Russia is your home."

"I've lived my whole life in China," Lan Yin interrupted. "My mother was Chinese. It's true that my father was Russian, and he did send me to Leningrad to go to school, but only for a few years. I hated it there, and I hated those people."

"But I understood that you had family there. Surely they will take care of you."

"I don't have... not any more. My uncle died last year and there is no one there for me to live with... I will be all alone." Again she broke down and sobbed.

"You are young and pretty, surely they will let you continue to work as you do here."

Madam Ying tried to console the girl.

"No," Lan Yin snapped. Her face was filled with tears, her eyes grew narrow. "My friend tried to do that, but they laughed in her face. They said that anyone who had serviced the Chinese must be crazy to think they could do the same for the Russian men. Then they sent her away... to her long death."

"Perhaps things have changed."

"You just don't understand Madam Ying, you just don't know those people as I do. Things do not change." The girl spoke positively. When there was no response for Madam Ying, Lan Yin looked away and started to cry again. Madam Ying did not know what to say. She looked at the girl on the bed and saw the agony she was going through so she decided to come back later and talk. She started for the door when Lan Yin's voice stopped her, "Oh, Madam Ying, please, please, you must help me."

Madam Ying turned around to see the girl kneeling in front of her, her eyes pleading. The tear stained face looked so sweet and innocent. Madam Ying reached down and took Lan Yin's hands and lifted her up.

Lan Yin was still pleading, "You can do something! Talk to the authorities. Use your influence -- something."

Madam Ying felt helpless. She liked the girl from the first day she came to her a little over a year ago. Her mother had died, and she was working in a house in Wuhai. There, she met Madam Ying who was visiting her friend, the madam of the house in Wuhai. When the house in Wuhai was closed. Lan Yin traveled from Wuhai on foot and sought out Madam Ying. Long an expert on beauty, Madam Ying saw the potential in the girl and allowed her to stay.

Now, Lan Yin was in trouble. What could she do? "Don't worry my child," she said, "I will think on this. You must stay in your room, however, from now on. Someone will bring you food. I will have to lock the door. Rest, Lan Yin, rest." She closed the door and locked it. Madam Ying went downstairs. She told one of the girls that she had to go out for a while and asked her to oversee things. She got her coat and went out into the street.

Alex was dozing when he heard the lock in the outside door click. He looked at his watch, it was too early for Madam Ying, she had said she wouldn't be back until morning. He picked up his gun and again crouched down behind the bed. He took careful aim at the inner door and waited.

"It is me, Satan," Madam Ying called out as she opened the inner door.

Alex lowered the gun and got up from behind the bed, "You're early, you said you wouldn't be back until morning."

"I know," she said, closing the inner door, "but something has come up, and I need to talk to you."

"What is it?"

"I talked again to my contacts this afternoon, and they told me that you could leave sooner than two days. In fact, tonight."

Alex's face brightened, "Tonight. That's great!"

"But… well, there is more to it than before."

"More what?"

Madam Ying studied Alex for a moment then spoke carefully, "Could you… could you take someone with you?"

Alex, surprised, asked her to repeat her question. When she did, he sat down on the bed slowly. He then looked up at her, "Where would I have to take this person?"

"Out of China, hopefully to America," she said very evenly.

Alex thought for a moment, why was she asking this? Did she want to go with him? Another spy? He decided the only way to know was to ask. "Frankly, he said, "I don't know. It would depend. Is it you?"

Madam Ying laughed, "Oh no. I am an old woman, I neither want to leave nor feel I could stand the journey. No, this person I think might be willing, and I know is able to make the trip. The question is, will you take this person?"

"Is this someone important, an official of the government?"

"No, I'm afraid in the scope of things this person is very unimportant but the need is great. In fact, you might say it is a matter of life or a fate worse than death."

"You make it sound very important. Is it important to you?"

"Yes. It is very important to me, her future depends on you."

"Her?" Alex said, "One of your girls?"

"Yes, one of my girls."

"Is she in trouble?"

"Yes, and time is short. I do not know how long you will have to decide. Will you help me? Will you take her with you?"

"I don't know, I just don't know, let me have a minute or so to think." Alex paced the floor trying to weigh the pros and cons of traveling in China with another person. He could hear Brady saying, "Remember Alex, if you get in trouble, try to get out of it by yourself. Don't depend on too many others, and if at all possible, try to travel alone. Each additional person with you increases your danger geometrically." Alex turned and looked at Madam Ying. Madam Ying was the one person who, so far, had helped him. Now she was asking a favor of him. He knew that his chances were better alone, but how could he turn down Madam Ying?

"O.K." he heard himself say, "O.K., if you're sure that it won't in anyway endanger you."

"Thank you, Satan," she said, "Have no fear, I will be all right." She went to him and took him by the hand, slowly knelt down before him. "I cannot tell you what this means to me, but let me just say that you have brought my heart more gladness than I have seen in many, many years."

Alex was taken aback by her actions, but when he saw her face shining up at him, he broke out in a big smile too. Madam Ying went to the door. After saying she'd be back soon, she closed the door and locked it.

Alex looked around at the mirrored walls and saw his face. "Who are you?" he asked out loud. "You committed yourself to taking a complete stranger along on the most dangerous trip you've ever taken. You idiot," he said to himself, "you get in water up to your neck and then you start making waves." He started pacing around the room. All he could see in the mirrors was the shining face of Madam Ying with a gun pointed at his head.

About an hour later, Madam Ying entered leading Lan Yin by the hand. The girl was very scared as the old woman pulled her into the room. The girl stood just where Madam Ying stopped her. She looked at Alex for only a moment then lowered her head and bowed Chinese style. When she raised her head, she saw Alex standing there with his mouth wide open.

Alex was overcome by two things, the beautiful Eurasian face and the soft blond hair. He had been expecting a hard looking Chinese girl. He looked quickly toward Madam Ying with a question written on his face.

Madam Ying just smiled at his reaction, "Satan, I want you to meet Lan Yin. She is part Russian and part Chinese."

Alex looked at the girl. "Hello," he said, in his best Chinese, a new shyness overtaking him. "Your name is Lan Yin?"

The girl bowed her head once again and said softly, "Yes, I am Lan Yin, sir."

Madam Ying led her over to the bed and sat her down. She turned to Alex, "Lan Yin was born in China of a Russian father and a Chinese mother. She was educated in Russia, but has lived most of her life here in China. Our government has accused her of being a "revisionist," and they are going to send her back to Russia."

"And she doesn't want to go back?"

"No," blurted out the girl emphatically. "I don't want to go back. Ever."

"But why?" Alex asked.

The girl just looked down at the floor. Madam Ying explained that the girl felt she would be sent to Siberia for serving the Chinese soldiers.

Alex nodded in understanding. "You want to go to America?" he said.

"No!" again the girl said, "I want to go to Taiwan."

"Oh?" Alex said. One thing was for sure, he thought, this little girl knows what she wants.

"Yes, I am Chinese. I want to be with my people." She said firmly. Then, suddenly, she realized her attitude was jeopardizing her case. She quickly flashed a smile at Alex and lowered her head again. "I'm sorry. I spoke too harshly. It's just that I am so unhappy," she began to cry softly.

Madam Ying comforted the girl as she explained what she knew about the short life of Lan Yin. She was born in China. Her father was a famous Russian fighter pilot during the Second World War, and her mother was a well-known actress in the Chinese Theater in

Peking. When Lan Yin was fifteen, her father was killed in a plane crash. She returned from Moscow where she was going to school for the funeral. Her mother was consoled by other Russian pilots, and she left Lan Yin by herself with one of her husband's friends. He raped her and turned her over to two drunken Chinese officers who raped her repeatedly. When her mother found her, Lan Yin was naked in the middle of the room, passed out and lying between the legs of one of the Chinese officers. They told her mother she enjoyed it. Lan Yin begged for understanding and told her mother she'd been raped, but her mother was shamed and disowned her. She threw Lan Yin out of the house.

Lan Yin wandered aimlessly for several days. She begged for food, but no one gave her anything. She finally offered what she had to give – her body. Within three months she discovered she was left pregnant by the rape. She came back to her mother's house and begged to be let in. Her mother finally relented just a few days before the baby was born. Because of Lan Yin's malnutrition, the baby survived only a few days. Her mother finally realized that her daughter had been telling her the truth all along, and in a rage she went to the home of the Russian pilot and tried to kill him. He killed her instead.

Lan Yin was left to fend for herself. She met a young girl her age, Pi Shying, who was working as a prostitute in Wuhai. Pi convinced Lan Yin to go with her and work in the house. Lan Yin, seeing no other way out, went with Pi. At this house, Lan Yin met Madam Ying, who was a friend of the madam in Wuhai, Li Fong Chi. Li ran an illegal house of prostitution. When the illegal operation was discovered by the police last year, Lan Yin fled to Madam Ying's. Madam Ying took her in and got the necessary papers approved to register her and make her work legal because of her influence with high officials.

Madam Ying also told Alex about the General's order that day. She said she did not know what the girl had done to get deported and neither did the girl, but that was the situation.

Alex listened to the story intently. He felt sorry for the girl, and vowed then and there to take her out with him and give her a start on a new life. He looked at her, her head buried in the lap of the old woman, and gently took her arm. Alex spoke calmly and quietly, "Lan Yin, is this true?"

She nodded, but kept her head buried in the madam's lap.

"Lan Yin, I have promised Madam Ying that I would take you out of China with me. I will. And I'll get you to Taiwan somehow if that's what you want."

The girl raised her head and looked at Alex, her simple "Thank you" was almost inaudible. She sat up, brushed away her tears, and turned away. He could see her in the mirror behind her and was amused as the girl looked at herself and tried to fix her face. All women are alike, he thought to himself.

"Satan, I, too, am very happy you will take her with you." Madam Ying spoke up. "I have grown to love this girl."

"What happens next?" Alex asked.

"I have arranged for your passage to Tsingtao as you asked. You will both leave tonight."

The girl turned back, surprised, "Tonight?" she exclaimed, "but I do not have much time to pack my things."

"I'm sorry child but I'm afraid you must not take much. It must look as if you broke out of your room during the night and escaped. I will get whatever you need. From now on you must stay in this room."

"But won't the girls miss her?" Alex asked.

"I have confined her to her room and instructed all the girls to stay away from her room. I do not think they will know what is going on until I tell them that she escaped. So, stay here, and I will return when it is convenient." Madam Ying left the room and locked the door behind her.

Lan Yin sat on the edge of the bed. There was a momentary silence as the girl watched Alex standing across the room then she looked around the room and saw that there was no other place for him to sit, so she moved a bit then asked, "Won't you sit down?"

Alex sat, not too near the girl. Alex began to feel somewhat ill at ease alone with the girl for the first time. He didn't know what to say and neither did she. Finally, he turned and looked at her and smiled. She was watching him intensely. She returned his smile. He tried to think of something to say to break the ice. She, too, was hesitant. Finally he said, "Do you speak English?"

The girl nodded, "Just a little. We were taught in Leningrad."

"You speak Chinese very well," she complemented Alex.

"Thank you, you are very kind," Alex said. "Are you hungry? I have food," he said.

"No, thank you."

Alex felt as nervous as a schoolboy on his first date. "Lan Yin, when you get to Taiwan, what do you want to do there?"

"I want to marry, but... " she hesitated. "But I am not worthy of marriage."

"I don't understand."

"It is very difficult to explain. You see, when I lost my child, or rather when she was born, I had a very difficult time. For a while the doctors thought I might die. Now they say I cannot have another child."

"I see."

"I feel a woman is worthless unless she can bear children."

"That's not always so, Lan Yin. Not all men want to have children."

"Is that true?"

"I know some men who are very happily married and who do not have, nor want children."

"Do you want children?" she asked.

"Yes. Someday."

"Are you married?"

"My wife died."

"Oh? I am sorry. How?"

"It's a long story."

"You needn't go on. I am sorry I made you think of sad times."

"Oh they weren't sad exactly, but thanks, I really don't feel like talking about it. Tell me, do you like being a... well... "

"A prostitute?"

"Yes," he said avoiding her eyes.

"I really don't mind it. Sometimes it is even fun. Most of the time I feel I am helping the men I serve. It can be rewarding. I like many of the men who come here, and they are very kind to me. In a way, I feel this has been my first real home."

"So you like Madam Ying."

"Oh yes, very much," she said smiling first to herself then to Alex. "She is like a mother to me. She is to all of the girls I think. She protects us, looks after us when we are ill, and gives us presents from time to time. She is very kind."

"Well, as they say in America, there is nothing like being happy in your work."

"Yes… yes, that is true." She laughed and he did too. Then she looked at him. "What is your work?"

"I help people buy and sell houses and farms."

"Why do they sell their land? Here everyone wants to keep their land."

"Oh, perhaps it is because they want to move to another part of the country or they want to buy a bigger house or farm."

Lan Yin was incredulous, "You mean they can move from one part of the country to another?"

Alex nodded.

"Doesn't the government get upset about this? Do they permit it?"

"In America, first of all, not all people own land or houses or farms, but anyone who has enough money can. They can own land in any part of America they want. They can own land in many parts of the country if they want, and some do. In America, a person or family can live anywhere they want."

"Anywhere at all?"

"Yes, anywhere."

"I see, I must think about this more. Can we talk about this later?" she asked.

"Of course," he replied.

"I hope you don't mind my asking questions."

Alex smiled, "Not at all."

Lan Yin went off to the bathroom for a minute or so, when she returned she stopped and stared at Alex. Alex was lying back on the bed with his eyes closed. He had heard her coming back, and when there was no sound for a long time, he opened his eyes. He raised himself up on his elbows and smiled at her. She smiled back then walked over to one of the mirrored walls and looked at herself and straightened her dress and ran her hands through her hair and flipped it back over her shoulders. She looked very innocent at that moment, Alex thought. Just like many of the girls back home, young, and full of life. He caught her eye in the mirror and smiled again. She returned the smile, then a small frown came over her face and she turned and faced Alex.

"May I ask you another question?" Lan Yin was very serious now.

"Sure."

"Why are you here in China?"

"Well, I'm afraid I can't tell you what I am doing here. I don't think it would be wise for either of us."

"Why? Is it something wrong you have done?"

"No, well at least not to my way of thinking, but there are many here who might feel I have... er rather am, doing something wrong. I guess it's a matter of personal belief. I felt it was my duty to come to China."

"And have you... done your duty?"

"If you mean have I done what I came here to do, the answer is yes."

"Still what you have done, did it hurt people? Chinese people?"

"No," Alex thought for a moment. "No, I really don't think that what I came here to do will hurt the Chinese people, nor for that matter the American people. In fact very few people will ever know what I have done."

"Was it a good thing?"

"That is very difficult to answer."

"Do you regret your involvement?"

"No, in fact, if I get out of here safely, I suppose I'll feel very good about it."

"You do not seem very sure. Were you forced to do this thing?"

"No... no I more or less volunteered to come. It was a job that had to be done, they said I was the best man to do it. I guess you might say I was honor bound to do it."

"Honor bound? What do you mean?"

"Well, to me it means to be loyal to a certain belief. The belief I hold is that a man should do whatever he can to uphold the principles his country stands for, and to do what is asked of him, if it is for the good of his country. In this case my country asked me to come to China, and because I love my country, I came."

Lan Yin frowned and lowered her head thinking. She was quiet for a long time. She walked about the room and Alex's eyes followed her. Then she walked over to Alex and looked down at him. Her face was calm. Her powder blue eyes were warm. "You are a very nice person I feel, you are a man. I..."

Her sentence was interrupted by the clicking of the lock on the outside door. Alex sat up. Frightened, Lan Yin moved around in back of him. The inner door opened, and Madam Ying appeared. She shut the door behind her. Lan Yin relaxed and Alex got to his feet.

"All the arrangements have been made," Madam Ying began. "The truck will be at our back door very early in the morning. The driver can be trusted. But let me caution you, you must do exactly as he says."

"We will." Both Lan Yin and Alex answered in unison. Then realizing what they had said they laughed and Madam Ying broke out in a broad grin.

"Now here is what we will do... " Madam Ying began.

CHAPTER NINETEEN

Tientsin, China, May 8, 1960

It was nearly dawn when an old, rickety truck coasted into the alley behind Madam Ying's. The bed of the truck was laden with old furniture and boxes. The driver quietly stopped the truck and left the motor running. He got out and went to the door. He knocked very softly. The door opened immediately. Silently, Madam Ying gave a small bow to the man and ushered Alex and Lan Yin out into the alley and quietly closed the door behind her.

Alex and Lan Yin both wore the blue pants and blue quilted coats of the workers and hats covering their hair. Alex carried a small satchel with food for the journey. They glanced up and down the alley and crossed to the back of the truck.

The driver, an old man with greying hair, scanned the alley time and time again as he stood guard. He avoided looking at them. Madam Ying whispered to Alex that the man did not want to see their faces so that in case they were caught, he could not identify them. The thin, bent old man of sixty plus years explained to Madam Ying where they were to hide in the bed of the truck. He quickly untied a couple of chairs and still with his back to Alex and Lan Yin motioned for them to get inside a box in the middle of the truck bed. Alex and Lan Yin climbed in and Madam Ying shut the flap on the box. The driver retied the chairs to the truck. He bowed to Madam Ying, got into his truck, and drove down the alley. Once the truck was out of sight, Madam Ying ducked back into the house and bolted the door.

Alex and Lan Yin were huddled together in the box which was just big enough for the two of them. The ride very rough, and they bounced into one another all the time. The truck drove through the city at a moderate speed. The truck hit a deep rut in the road and Lan Yin was thrown on top of Alex.

"Oh, I am sorry," she said.

Alex put his finger to his lips, "Remember what the old man told us. We are not to talk or move around unnecessarily and not even to breathe heavily while the truck is stopped."

"That's not easy to do," she whispered.

"You mean not to move around, I see what you mean," Alex whispered as the truck hit another bump and Lan Yin's soft body was once again thrown into him. Alex groped in the dark to help her get situated better. It was hot in the box, but all Alex could think of at the moment was the wonderful aroma coming from the girl. The truck lurched again as the driver downshifted to stop the truck. Alex and Lan Yin braced themselves and tried to get as comfortable as possible so as not to have to move. The truck stopped. They could hear voices outside.

"Your pass Li Po," someone commanded.

The old man reached into the seat and pulled out a document and handed it to the soldier.

"Here it is Comrade Chu," he said as he handed it to the soldier. While the soldier was reading the pass, two soldiers walked around the truck inspecting it. Then one of the soldiers spotted a small table. "Li Po," he shouted.

Li Po got out of the truck and went to the back see what the soldier wanted. The soldier pointed to a table in the middle of the truck and asked if Li Po wanted it.

"Comrade, you know I cannot sell any of this furniture, it is for the commune at Poshan. They have already paid for it," the old man protested.

The soldier climbed up onto the truck and examined it closely.

"It is too old and battered anyway," the soldier said as he started to climb down from the truck. His foot caught on one of the ropes and the soldier tumbled off the truck. Li Po dared not laugh. The other soldier helped his comrade up and motioned for Li Po to get back in his truck.

"Is he all right?" Li Po asked as he got back into the cab of the truck.

"I am fine old man," the soldier replied angrily as he dusted himself off.

Li Po started the truck and started to drive off when one of the chairs that concealed the box fell off.

"Stop!" commanded the soldier.

Li Po slammed on the brakes, and the truck jerked to a stop throwing Lan Yin on top of Alex and in a very uncomfortable position. Her knee was in his face and her elbow in his crotch. Alex grimaced with pain. They couldn't move.

Li Po climbed out of the truck again. The soldier had picked up the chair and was putting it back on the truck. One leg of the chair hit the box hitting Alex in the back. He fought his instinct to cry out in pain. It seemed to Alex like it took Li Po hours to tie the chair back on the truck and drive off. He was nearly drowning in his own sweat and about to pass out with the pain of Lan Yin's elbow. Finally, the truck drove off. When the truck shifted into high gear, Alex felt it was safe to speak.

"Quickly Lan Yin," Alex whispered, "Move your elbow."

Lan Yin struggled to get into position to move her elbow which caused Alex even more pain, then she shifted her elbow. Alex's pain seemed to increase even more, and he felt sick to his stomach.

"Are you all right?" Lan Yin whispered as her hand reached out to touch Alex. Her finger nearly went into his eye. He grabbed her hand and pulled it away from his face, "I'll be okay in a few minutes."

"I didn't know he was going to stop like that," she said.

"Neither did I," Alex managed to whisper.

"I'm so sorry. I'm certain that must have hurt a great deal."

"Yes. I'm certain it did, too."

The two of them were jostled around in the box for nearly nine more hours before the truck pulled off the main road onto a dirt road full of chuck holes. They bounced around so violently that they almost tore a hole in the side of the box. Finally, the truck came to a stop.

Li Po got out of the truck and untied the chairs and opened the box a little bit. He instructed them to get out of the box only after he had gone around to the other side of the truck. They waited another minute then crawled out of the box. Neither could stand up straight for a while once they got off the truck. Alex was sore from head to toe. Lan Yin complained of the many bruises on her.

Li Po told them to take the small map on the front seat of the truck and to go through the woods in front of them.

Alex opened it. "As you can see on the map," Li Po said, still hiding his face from them, "there is a small abandoned house near the road on the other side of the woods. It is about fifteen miles from here, I must go back now to the main road and make a stop in Huimin. I always stay the night there. They would think it strange if I did not. Then I must pass through the Poshan check point in the morning before I get to the house. You must get to the house and stay there until I arrive tomorrow."

"Will do. Thank you, Li Po," Alex said.

"Please do not talk anymore. Tomorrow, I will have the box open before you come out of the house. Now go!"

Alex gathered up the food bag, and they ran to the woods. They stopped and looked back. They watched as Li Po retied the chairs and drove off. Alex and Lan Yin walked with the setting sun at their backs through the woods and into an open field. The sun was going down rapidly as they climbed to the top of a grassy hill. According to the map, they were in the rolling hills near the Yellow River. Alex dropped to his knees and peered over the rise of the hill. He could barely make out a wooded area at the bottom of the hill. As they started down the hill, Lan Yin tripped and went rolling down the hill. Alex started after her and tripped too. They both rolled down the hill laughing. He helped her to her feet and went back up the hill for his satchel. They trotted off into the wooded area.

By this time it was nearly dark. Alex took his bearings and they began making their way through the woods. There was no moon that night and soon they were in almost complete darkness. Suddenly, they heard the sound of a truck or car. Alex walked forward just a few feet and found himself in the middle of a road, the truck's headlights flashed in the trees just a few yards away, he grabbed Lan Yin and pulled her across the road and into a ditch. The truck bore down on them going about fifty miles an hour and passed within about ten feet of them. Alex was covering Lan Yin's head and face from the light. He caught a glimpse of the satchel that had flown out of his hands when he grabbed her. It was sitting in the middle of the road. The truck put on its brakes.

"They must have seen the satchel." Alex said. He jumped up, raced across the road and snatched it up. Running back toward Lan Yin, he motioned for her to get up. The truck had stopped now and was beginning to back up. Lan Yin quickly got to her feet. Alex grabbed her hand and led her into the woods. She fell, dragging Alex with her. The truck stopped where the satchel had been. Two soldiers got out. They began searching the area. Lan Yin and Alex lay only about fifty yards away. Then one of the soldiers called to the other.

"You must be crazy," the soldier said. "There is nothing in the road."

"I am sure I saw something," the other said.

Alex was breathing heavily and Lan Yin placed her hand over his mouth.

The two soldiers looked around briefly then got back in the truck and drove away.

Alex and Lan Yin got up and again started walking. It was too dark to see, and after a couple of hours of walking Alex stopped. "I wonder where the hell the house is. We should have been there hours ago."

"Can't we stop and rest awhile?" Lan Yin pleaded.

"We might as well. I don't have any idea where we are," Alex confessed.

Lan Yin sat down on the ground and Alex sat with his back to a tree. They were both exhausted. When Lan Yin drifted off to sleep, Alex decided to let her sleep. We'll just have to wait until there is some light, he decided.

At the first sign of light, Alex roused Lan Yin and they trooped off in eastwardly direction. They were walking in another grassy field when they heard voices. They stopped dead in their tracks and dropped to the ground. The voices were far away. Alex looked around and saw no one. Slowly they crept along, the voices not seeming to get any closer. Then, all of a sudden, he came to a drop off. Immediately in front of him was a steep cliff and about a hundred feet below was a canyon.

He saw the house near a wooded area in the canyon. Alex shuddered. All around the house were Youth Groups. The Youth Groups were chasing each other and having a good time.

Lan Yin crawled up beside Alex and saw the problem for herself. Alex motioned for them to crawl back away from the edge. "What will we do?" Lan Yin asked, a small tear welling up in the corner of one eye. "They will hurt the old man."

"I don't think the Youth Groups are waiting for us, there isn't any sign of a trap or guards posted. It looks to me like they were just using the house for shelter last night. But I don't see any sign of any transportation. I can't figure it out."

"But what if our driver comes?"

"I don't know," Alex replied. "I'm not sure what direction he'll even come from. My best guess is from the north. Here's what we'll do. We'll make our way to the road south of the house. If he comes to the house and sees the youth groups, he'll probably drive on, and we'll flag him down after he is out of sight of the house." Alex motioned for her to crawl to the edge of the cliff again. He pointed out a wooded area that would be out of eyesight of the house. They crawled back and started to make their way down the hill to the woods. It took them about an hour to make it, but they found a spot where they could see the house and easily make their way to the road. They sat and waited and watched the youth groups. From time to time the young people would look down the road coming from the north, shake their heads and continue playing.

Alex and Lan Yin were both hungry and thirsty by now. When they saw the youth groups drinking from the well, they got even more thirsty, but there was nothing they could do. They waited all morning and until late in the afternoon. Just as they were about to give up, they heard the sound of a truck approaching. The youth groups gathered up their things as the truck pulled into view. It was a Red Army truck. The young people hailed the truck and yelled at the driver for being late. He explained that the truck repairs that he went off to get done the night before had taken longer than he expected. After a bit of grumbling, the young people climbed into the truck and it sped off.

Alex watched as the truck disappeared down the road then helped Lan Yin to her feet and the two of them made their way to the house. It's a damn good thing we didn't stumble in here last night, Alex thought to himself as he looked around the house. It was a traditional Chinese house with the main living quarters facing a courtyard. The house was built of grey mud brick with a tile roof and rice paper covering the windows, except for one window with wavy glass. As they went through the gate into the courtyard, Alex carefully surveyed the area. Lan Yin waited as Alex raced across the courtyard and looked in the glass window. He could see very little. There was no sign of life, and the utensils and tools lying around suggested that no one had lived here for some time. Alex checked the shed that made up the south wall. Inside he found rusty tools and stalls for cattle. At one end of the shed was a large door leading out to a corral type area. The one door to the shed was slightly off its crude hinges. He crossed to the other side of the courtyard and found another smaller house built into the nine-foot high wall. Inside was a single room on a stone slab floor. There were one or two pieces of crude furniture, a bench and a table with no chairs. One end of the room was a huge fireplace. Then he went back out to the courtyard and to the front door of the main house. He slowly opened the wooden door. He peered inside. The place was a shambles. There were food containers strewn around the place, furniture overturned and the room divider made of wood and rice paper had a large hole in it as if someone had been pushed through it. On the wall to the right as he went in was another huge fireplace with some wood still smoldering in it. He went across the room and pushed the divider facing him open. There was a large old-fashioned bed in one corner with wooden bed posts, a chest overturned with the drawers lying around the room. A crock had been smashed against the outside wall. A window had been smashed out. Alex went out into the main room and pushed aside the broken divider to find a large table with several backless chairs around it and food hastily left behind. He went back out into the courtyard and called to Lan Yin to come into the house, it was safe.

"There seem to be a lot of vacant houses in China," Alex remarked.

"Yes, there are a great many," Lan Yin replied. "The owners have been put in communal houses and farms."

"But, I thought the landowners were allowed to keep some of their land in the great land reform."

"Oh, they probably do have some land," Lan Yin explained, "but usually the government does not let them keep the land they originally owned. They would be too sentimental about it. These people were probably given some land nearer their communal farm. In that way they not only do not have to go far to work the land, but they also feel a part of the community."

"I guess that makes sense," Alex said.

"What happened to our driver?" Lan Yin asked.

"I don't know. Maybe his truck broke down or he heard about the Youth Groups being here. I don't like it, but I don't know of anything else to do but wait. If he doesn't come by morning, we'll have to try to get to Tsingtao by ourselves."

"All right," Lan Yin said. "I see they left some food here, perhaps I can make something for us to eat from this mess."

"Good," Alex said, "I'll go out and look for some water." Alex went out the door and looked around. It was rapidly getting dark. He found the well in back of the main house. The rope was old, but the bucket was still tied to it, and it looked like it had been used by the youth groups. He dropped the bucket and as the rope unwound he heard it hit water below. Well, that's one thing that went right for us today, he thought. He looked around the small field as he hauled the bucket up.

By the time Alex got back to the house, it was dark and he saw a dim light coming from the inside. When he opened the door, he was surprised, the house was cleaned up; at least, there was nothing lying about. He couldn't see too well in the dim light of one kerosene lamp. There was a small fire in the fireplace and a pot containing something hanging over the fire. Alex poured the water into another pot that looked fairly clean. He put the water over the fire to boil. Lan Yin was in the bedroom putting some cardboard over the open window. She was moving around the house straightening things and cleaning here and there.

"It sure looks like the owners left in a hurry," Alex called out, "There's a plow and a harness rusting out in back in the field. And only part of a furrow is plowed."

"Yes," Lan Yin said as she kept on working, "One day a truck just comes along and takes you off. You don't know when or where you are going. They allow you just time to take those belongings you really need or want." Lan Yin went to the fire and took the pot off, and then she got some pottery plates and dipped them into the boiling water. She took the plates and the pot to the table. He looked in at the dining area where the kerosene lantern stood. The table was set with utensils which Lan Yin also had dipped in the boiling water.

They sat down, and Lan Yin poured water from the old iron kettle into the cups. She dished out the food, sort of a Chinese slumgullion. They were both hungry and ate in silence as the evening shadows danced across the walls from the flickering light of the lantern.

"I must say the place looks a lot better now, almost liveable considering... " and he dropped the sentence.

"Considering what?"

"Well, considering you, well you, uh haven't had much experience keeping house."

Lan Yin looked at him and his eyes avoided hers. "You mean considering I'm a prostitute."

"That isn't what I meant," Alex protested, but when Lan Yin looked at him and raised one eyebrow, he fell silent again and looked away.

They ate in silence once again. Alex only picked at his food and Lan Yin watched him. "Don't you like the food?" she asked.

"I guess I'm just not hungry."

"But only a few minutes ago you said you were very hungry. If you don't like the food, perhaps I can fix something else."

"No, no it isn't the food, really." Alex was quiet for a moment, then, "Lan Yin."

"Yes?"

"I'm sorry I made that crack. It wasn't called for. I guess I'm a little edgy... not thinking."

"It's all right, I, too, am edgy."

Alex gave her a little smile, and she returned it. He leaned back and rubbed his neck.

"I know just what you need, Satan," Lan Yin spoke up with a lilt in her voice, "You need a back rub. I do a very good job and that will relax you I know."

She got up from the table, stood in back of Alex and began rubbing his neck. Her long delicate fingers became strong pincers probing the muscles and fibers of his neck, and he could feel the energy draining out of him as she worked deeper and deeper into his tension-hardened muscles. Her hands seemed to grow in strength as she pressed against the nerves running down his back. Then she stopped and began to rub his temples and forehead. The strong hands pulled gently at his skin.

"You've found my weakness," Alex said between moans of pleasure.

"Is it comfortable for you sitting here on this stool? I think not. Come and lie down on the bed. I have straightened it up some."

They walked into the bedroom. The overturned chest was now upright, and the drawers put in place. The bed, which was broken down, now had the mattress on straight, and Lan Yin had taken down one of the curtains and put in on the bed as a cover. It wasn't very clean, but better than before. Alex took off his jacket and rolled it up for a pillow and sat on the bed.

"Take off your shirt, it will make it easier. The house is warm now."

Alex obeyed. Some of the tension was gone now, and the lack of sleep was catching up with him. Lan Yin took his shirt and spread it out over the dirty curtain. He laid down on his stomach as she lifted his feet up onto the bed. She pulled off his shoes and placed them beside the bed. Lan Yin sat on the edge of the bed and slowly began to rub his shoulders and then ran her hands down his spine touching each vertebra with a firm yet gentle touch.

"Ah," he moaned, "You've got great hands. That feels so good."

"I'm glad you like it. You are very tense. I can feel it in your muscles," she spoke very softly now. Alex closed his eyes. "Try to relax, let your body go limp." She rubbed for a long time and felt Alex's body slowly relax. "What is America like?"

"What's it like? Where I come from – the state of Indiana, the countryside is very much like the country we walked through today; rolling hills and grassy fields. On a day like today you can see the birds flying up from the south and the trees and grass are turning green. It's quiet there – peaceful.

"Is all of America just like that?"

"Actually, America has almost every kind of terrain. In the southwest there are deserts and flat lands; there are mountains and rivers in the northwest, beautiful lakes, and in the center of the country are grasslands -- miles and miles of low rolling fields of wheat and corn and in the South – cotton. The cities are big and teeming with people. I think what make's America so great are the people. They come from everywhere, Europe, Africa, Asia; all kinds of people from all kinds of cultures. They live and love and work there side by side. It is a melting pot for the world, a place where people can do as they please and say what they please without fear... "

"But," Lan Yin interrupted, "don't you have many concentration camps and aren't the black people slaves?"

"I guess a lot of people would like the world to think so... actually it's not true. Oh, we do have people who are poor and feel oppressed and deprived of many things. We have people who go to bed hungry or cold from time to time, but in America even those people can work their way out of poverty - many do every day. It is a country where, if you are willing to work and put your back into it, you can get ahead. I know many who have. The problem, of course, is that all have not been able to do this..."

"But I've seen pictures of riots and people being murdered in the streets... " Lan Yin interrupted.

"Yes," Alex admitted "I know... "

"Were these pictures lies?"

"No, not all of them."

"Then how can you say it is a good country, how can you say people are happy?"

"Because," Alex said rolling over and facing her in the dim light, "for the most part the people are happy, and the country is good. By far, most of the people are happy, hard-working, and most importantly have their own self-respect. Many who are poor are not willing to work, not all, of course, but a lot live off the work of others and have to be given money. They do not want to do their share. Some are genuinely poor, with little education, they are the shame of America and no one is proud of them, but they are also the victims... "

"The victims?"

"Yes, they are suffering because others are unwilling to help them. They are also the victims of those who would use them for their own self-gain."

"Are these other people poor, too?"

"No. Many of those who use the poor are, themselves, rich. Some are very rich. Many times they will cause trouble by exploiting the poor. But Lan Yin, for all the bad that is wrong in America, you must know that the good far outweighs it. America is a place where a person from any background can strive for a better life, and he or she has the opportunity to succeed. The important thing is that he or she decides their own fate - no one makes the ultimate decision for him."

"But isn't it very hard for a person to live by his own destiny?"

"Yes," Alex answered firmly, "Yes. That is why America is great. It is man against himself. If the time should come when a man in America cannot decide his own destiny, then like many rich and powerful countries before it, America, too, will stop being great."

"You keep saying America is great, and yet I have heard so many bad things about it," Lan Yin persisted.

"I'm sure you have," Alex said, "and some of the bad things you have heard are true, I won't deny it, but they are neither as bad as you have heard nor as many."

Lan Yin looked at him for a moment then spoke, "Do you think I would like to live in America?"

Alex looked at her, a small smile creeping onto his face, "I think so Lan Yin. You are brave, and that is certainly one thing you must be to be happy in America. Yes, I think you would do well and be happy."

"You make it sound like such a challenge to live there."

"It is."

Lan Yin looked into his boyish face and felt his strength. Their eyes met and held for a while, then she too smiled. She motioned for him to roll back over and she began to rub again. Her face grew more and more serious as she thought of what he said. After a few minutes, she stopped and rubbed her hands. They were getting tired. Alex rolled over.

"Are you tired? Here," he said getting up, "I feel fine now, let me rub your back."

"But Satan," she said and a large frown came over her face, "Oh, I hate that name. Couldn't I call you something else? What is your real name?"

"The less you know, the better." Alex cautioned.

"All right, then I shall give you a Chinese name," she said. She thought for a minute and then, "I shall call you... Gau Shan... yes, Gau Shan."

"Gau Shan?" he said, "You mean tall mountain?"

"Yes, because that is what you are to me. You are tall and you have the strength of a mountain… yes," she nodded, "that is a good name for you."

"I think you may be overestimating me, Lan Yin," Alex said with a grin.

"No, no, I don't think so," she said, her lips tightening "Gau Shan is very suitable."

"O.K. Lan Yin, Gau Shan it is." He got up off the bed and motioned to her, "Now how about that back rub?"

She held her hand up in mild protest, but when he gave her a mock stern look, she smiled and laid down on the bed on her stomach. Alex sat down beside her and began to rub slowly, his powerful hands gently finding and smoothing out the tight muscles in her soft back. Lan Yin responded to his rubbing, and she, too, began to moan lowly and move rhythmically to his touch. He moved from the shoulders and neck to her lower back and her responses increased in intensity. Then he got his hand caught in her blouse. He untangled it and continued to rub now and then catching his fingers in the cotton material.

"Oh, that feels wonderful, Gau Shan, you are so powerful yet so gentle." Alex's hand was caught once again in the blouse. She got up onto her knees. "Just a minute." She unbuttoned her blouse and took it off. She wore no bra. She started to lie down again when she caught the very surprised look that was on Alex's face. She smiled. "I'm sorry, did I shock you? I didn't realize you would be offended. It's just that your hand was getting caught in my blouse so much that I thought it would make it easier for you to rub. Do you want me to put my blouse on again?"

"No," Alex said, just a little too quickly, "No, I don't mind. I mean, you don't have to put it on again. It's just that well, up to now I guess I've sort of thought of you as… well as child in trouble."

"I'm a woman."

"Yes," Alex nodded, "Yes, you are indeed."

Lan Yin looked at him, smiled and laid back down again. Alex began to rub her back again only now the warmth of her soft skin ran through his fingers, and he began to feel very warm. They both were becoming relaxed when all of a sudden Lan Yin's back began to tighten up. Alex felt it.

"Gau Shan?"

"Yes?"

"Do you think we will get out of China alive?"

"Yes," he said quietly.

"You say that so positively. How can you be so sure?"

"I just am, I don't know why," Alex replied as a calm came over his face. "It's just that I don't have time to get killed. I still have a lot of things I want to do… and I know I can. I guess I'm an optimist. I've never really thought of dying."

"Never? Never in your whole life?"

"No, not really." He shrugged, "Even in the heat of battle in Korea, I never thought I'd die. Oh, I saw other men die, and heard a lot of men talk about dying, but it never occurred to me that I'd be one of them."

Lan Yin turned over and looked at him. He seemed very calm. Tears crept to the corners of her eyes. She reached up and grabbed Alex around the neck with both arms and buried her face in his chest, "Oh, Gau Shan, I don't want to die, I'm so afraid… hold me, please hold me!"

Alex hesitated, then put his arms around her and pulled her close to him. He could feel her heart racing, and a cold a tear ran down his chest. He held her tightly for a moment then in a very firm voice said, "I've got you."

"But… "

"No buts. I've got you and you're safe. No one's going to hurt you."

"I can't stand pain."

"There won't be any pain Lan Yin. No pain, no death. You'll live to be one of the loveliest old grandmothers in the world." He relaxed his grip on her, and she looked up at him. He was smiling. Alex gently wiped a tear from her face. She gave him a half-hearted smile then she pulled herself back into his chest and clung tightly. "I need you. I need you!" she cried.

"I know," he said. "I need you, too."

She looked up at him again and then raised her face to his and gave him a soft kiss. He returned the kiss with more intensity as his body began to respond to a feeling he hadn't known for a long time. His kisses became more heated and his hands began to caress her. His hands ran slowly through her long blond hair and across the back of her neck. Her fingers tightened on his back as he slowly ran his fingers along the back of her neck and then across her cheek, the light, gentle touch raising goose pimples on her arms. Then he took her face in both hands and kissed her with an ever growing passion. He kissed her eyes and then her neck. Lan Yin slowly pulled him down on top of her. His hands moved to her soft breasts and his fingers brushed ever so lightly against her ribs and on down her stomach. She moved sensually to his touch, and her fingers tightened on his back as he found more sensitive areas. He ran his tongue around her pink nipples and kissed her breasts. She was breathing heavily now, and her hands began moving faster on his back. He kissed her on the stomach, and she uttered a low moan of pleasure.

"Gau Shan... Gau Shan," she whispered when he probed her body lower and lower.

Lan Yin guided him into her and arched her back as he entered. Their lovemaking became a symphony of rhythm and violent movements until at last they both collapsed in the final movement. They lay still for a few moments. He started to say something, but she put her finger to his lips and shook her head. Alex kissed her and she wrapped her legs around him. They both drifted off into the soft greyness of sleep.

Neither slept deeply, and at one time during the night, Alex awakened to see her looking at him. "Gau Shan, do you believe it is possible for a person to find happiness after they have lived a life of evil?" she whispered.

"Yes," he said softly wrapping his arms about her. "I believe anything is possible, if you just work hard enough for it."

She snuggled in close to him, their nude bodies entwined, "Thank you," she murmured. They drifted back to sleep.

An hour before dawn, Alex carefully slipped out of her embrace and slid out of bed. He dressed silently and went to the door, opened it and walked out into the courtyard. The moon was still high in the western night sky. The air was chilly, and he wrapped his coat around his neck. Alex opened the front gate and peered down the road. He was worried. Where was the driver? Had he been detained or arrested? What should they do now? Wait? What? He sat on the cold ground with his back against the gate and tried to think of a logical next step.

About a half an hour later, he'd made up his mind. He got up and went back into the house. Lan Yin was sleeping as soundly as a small child. Then he put his hand on her shoulder and roused her.

Lan Yin rolled over. Alex bent down and kissed her. As she watched him through half-opened eyes, he put his cold hands on her cheek. She jumped and shivered.

"Oh, your hands are cold. And you are dressed."

"Yes. We should leave before it gets light."

"Why? Shouldn't we wait for the driver?"

"No, I don't think so. I have a feeling we should go now."

Lan Yin got dressed in the cold room. The fire had gone out during the night. She gathered up the remaining food they could use in the dim light of the lantern.

"We'd better hurry," Alex said, a gnawing fear growing in him. Lan Yin was ready just as the first dim light of dawn crept over the hill behind the house. Alex looked over the house – too clean. He decided to leave the house as they found it. He turned over some of the stools, scattered things and messed up the bed. Satisfied the place looked right, they went out the front door and left it ajar. As they got to the front gate Alex motioned for Lan Yin to stop. "Quiet." They both stood at the gate motionless for a moment.

"It sounds like a motor," Lan Yin said as she started toward the door.

"Let's get out of here," Alex said as he grabbed her arm and half dragged her back toward the house.

"But why?" Lan Yin managed to ask just before she was pulled off by Alex. She resisted and tried to stop him. "It must be our driver."

"It's not," Alex said as he pulled her through the front door and toward the back door.

"But how?"

"Come on," he said, as they ran out the back door toward the wooded area where they had hid the day before. When they got to the edge of the wooded area, Alex stopped and picked up a leafy branch. "You head for those trees on the hill over there." He pointed as he ran back to the house and closed the back door. Alex covered their tracks leading into the woods. Suddenly he stopped. The sound of the motor was gone. He moved faster to cover the tracks, and as he got to the edge of the woods, he dropped the branch and ran up the hill to where Lan Yin stood. He grabbed her arm and led her on up the hill to a large tree, pulled her behind the tree and down on the ground. They waited only a couple minutes, then Alex pointed to some movement in the bushes next to the road about one hundred and fifty yards from the house. Even from as far away as they were, they could see soldiers dragging their driver who was tied by a long rope, as he stumbled and nearly fell. As the soldiers cautiously approached the house, they fanned out. The old man had been beaten and was bleeding.

The soldiers surrounded the house but did not attempt to enter. They dragged the driver to the front gate and prodded him with their bayonets. He called out several times. Lan Yin flinched as they beat him. Finally, the soldiers stormed into the courtyard and into the house. Seconds later, an officer and two soldiers came back out into the courtyard and tied the driver to a pillar holding up the roof of the porch on the main house. They beat him and yelled at him, but he just shook his head. Then the officer called his men together and talked to them. Afterward, they spread out and started looking for Alex and Lan Yin's tracks.

"We've got to move before they spot us," Alex said.

They got to their feet and crouching low began to make their way on up the hill. Lan Yin stopped as they were about to the top of the hill. She looked back just in time to see the officer put his pistol to the head of the old man and fire. She tripped and let out a gasp of horror. From the sound of the shot Alex knew just what had happened. He helped Lan Yin over the top of the hill. He looked back again and saw that the soldiers evidently had not found their tracks because they were still searching.

Lan Yin, out of breath, sat down. "Where do we go from here?"

"We have no choice, we have to keep moving. Our first problem is to find out where we are. Do you have any idea?"

"No, not really." She stopped suddenly and tugged at Alex's shirt. "I just remembered, didn't the driver say he had to go through a check point in Poshan?"

"Yes, he did say Poshan. Does that ring a bell for you?"

"Yes. One of the girls at Madam Ying's is from there."

"Have you been there?"

"No, but she told me that it was near the Yu Chi river."

"Do you know how far we are from there?"

"Not exactly, but I do know we are not too far from the river. I remember seeing it on our way to this house. It is north of Poshun."

"O.K., our first job is to find the river."

They started walking south avoiding the roads, villages and a couple of large communal farms. They kept as far away from civilization as possible. A day later, they came to the banks of the large river. They were both exhausted and hungry. Alex's three day beard was a definite hazard if they met anyone. By now the satchel of food from the house was gone. Somehow they had to find some food. They were still in the country, but from where they were standing, they could see a large railroad bridge spanning the river. "That is the Wu Hai bridge," Lan Yin said pointing to it. "I know because I have seen pictures of it. We must be near Poshan."

"Which way?"

"That way. The way the river flows."

Alex assessed the situation. There was a small village on their side of the river. They had to get across the river. He felt certain that late at night they could make their way across the bridge, but they were still faced with the problem of eating. Lan Yin was getting very weak from hunger. Alex sat along side her. "Do you have any money?" he asked.

"Yes, some."

"Lan Yin, we can't go on without food. The only way I know we can get some without running the risk of stealing it is to buy something in that village tonight. Now here is my plan. First, we have to disguise your blond hair."

They decided to stay at the edge of the village until the sun went down. At twilight, some of the villagers were still doing their evening marketing in the square. Alex checked her disguise. She looked fine. He crossed his fingers and sent her into the village. Hopefully, she could buy food at a small market without arousing suspicion.

Lan Yin started into the village. She looked back. Alex knew she was frightened, but she never complained about the risk. Lan Yin managed to get to the center of town where luckily the open air market was still thriving. One look at the food, the fish, the vegetables and the rice and her mouth began to water. She took a deep breath and plunged into the crowd. At the fish stand the proprietor was so busy that Lan Yin merely selected what she wanted and handed it to him, he grunted and told her how much and she paid without saying a word. It was a little different at the vegetable stand. She chose a stand in a corner of the village square in the shadows. An old woman waited on her. Lan Yin told the woman what she wanted but the old woman didn't understand the crisp Mandarin dialect that Lan Yin spoke and gave her a funny look. Lan Yin did not lose her head; she slowly pointed to the things she wanted and quietly asked the price. The old woman kept looking at her strangely as she went about getting the things together. Lan Yin understood her dialect enough to figure out how much to pay the woman, but just as she was leaving, the old woman motioned for her to stay. She went over to an old man running a stand with fruit. The old woman talked to the man in a very animated way. Lan Yin began to worry. She wanted to run, but she knew it would only look bad. She decided to wait and see. Glancing to her right, Lan Yin saw a soldier approaching the fruit stand. Someone called to the soldier, and he veered off in another direction.

The old woman took the arm of the old man and led him over to where Lan Yin stood. The old man spoke excellent Mandarin and greeted her with a smile. The old woman nudged the old man, and he told Lan Yin he was from Nankou just north of Peking. He wondered if she were from there. He explained that his son and daughter were still there and wanted to know if she knew his children. Lan Yin said that she had never been to Nankou that she was from Paoti to the southeast of Peking. The old man was very disappointed because he had not heard from his children in over three years. He thanked her for talking with him, thanked the old woman for trying to help him, and shuffled off to his stand. Lan Yin went over to his stand and bought some fruit, and then made her way back to where Alex waited impatiently.

By now it was very dark. They agreed that it was still too early to cross the bridge since so many people were milling about. They sat alongside a building where they could see the bridge and ate some of their fruit. Not long after they started eating, a train coming from the other side, crossed the bridge. They were both glad they had not started across earlier. They would have been caught in the middle by the train. As some of the people began to go to their homes then they noticed four or five groups of people were crossing the bridge. "Come on," Alex said. "We'll join the others on the bridge, and be a part of the group." They gathered up their things and started across the bridge. There were no lights on the bridge and at one time two teenagers ran past them surprising them both. They got to the other side and saw that all of the people were heading directly toward a large dormitory-like structure with a flanged roof. There was no other path, and there were people behind them. Alex motioned for Lan Yin to sit down. He bent down and looked down the bridge. There were two more groups of people coming. He started to take off her shoe, but Lan Yin stopped him. "We do not do that for women in China." She warned. Alex stood up and looked away as one of the groups passed nearby. He noticed that bringing up the rear was a man dressed as an official in a military uniform. He could hear the man telling the last group to hurry or they would be late for dinner. Alex's heart almost stopped. The leader would undoubtedly insist that they go into the building, and they would be discovered. He knew the officer had seen them by the side of the road. Then fate stepped in. One of the women carrying a large pot of some sort tripped and fell, breaking the pot. There was a commotion and most of the group including the officer stopped to see what was happening. Alex moved quickly. He grabbed the satchel Lan Yin was carrying, and pushed her off the abutment she was sitting on, over into some bushes. They broke her fall as she tumbled down the side of the bank of the river. He leaped over the abutment and followed her. Lan Yin had cried out in surprise when she was pushed, but her call was lost in all the commotion on the bridge. Alex managed to stop her before she went into the river and, helping her to her feet quickly, led her underneath the bridge. They hid under the bridge until the commotion was over above them and the group had gone into the building.

Alex insisted they wait about an hour until they saw all the lights in the building go out. When the lights were out and it was quiet, they made their way along the embankment and then up over the hill to the railroad tracks. Alex decided not to follow the railroad tracks to Tsingtao. He knew that the railroad ran south to Tsinan and then east to Tsingtao. He figured that if they went directly south, they would avoid the major city of Tsinan and run into the railroad line that led to their destination.

By the next afternoon, they had again come upon the railroad tracks that led away from Tsinan. By avoiding populated areas, they traveled unnoticed. They began following the tracks toward Tsingtao.

Late that night they came to a small train station. They started to go around it, when they heard a train.

Alex stopped Lan Yin. "The way I figure it, we are about two hundred miles from Tsingtao. It will take us days probably a week or so to get there walking all the way. I think we have to take a chance on the train, if it stops here."

They found a wooded area near the tracks a short distance from the station and decided to wait there. It was nearly morning when the train came to a stop at the station. It was a long freight train.

"Remember," Alex said, "we must find a full car large enough for us to get in. We don't want to have more things loaded in on top of us. In fact, if there is a full coal car we'll bury ourselves in the coal."

As they walked along side the many railroad cars, they checked each one. None was suitable. Not more than two hundred feet from the engine was a coal car. It was in the shadows and far enough from the engine they felt safe to climb on. They ran to it. Alex threw the satchel up on it, and helped Lan Yin up on the first step then climbed up behind her. They buried themselves in the coal and settled near each other. An hour later, the train started off and they relaxed. The ride wasn't comfortable but it was a lot better than walking. Alex's only worry was how they would get off undetected. If the train averaged thirty miles an hour, they would get to Tsingtao in mid day. He told Lan Yin his concern.

"I've come this way on a train to Tsingtao before Gau Shan," Lan Yin said. "We will know we are near when the train runs along the bay. As I remember, it is a very pretty sight."

"I hope it's so pretty no one sees us getting off," he said above the noise of the train.

Alex had figured it just about right. It was mid day when the train slowed down as it crept down a hill near Tsingtao. He peeked over the rim of the coal car and caught a glimpse of the bay. The train was going slowly through the hills. Alex decided to make his move. Because the long train was going around the hills, he knew they could jump and not be seen by either the engineer in front nor the brakeman in the rear of the train. He uncovered Lan Yin, and they got ready to climb down the ladder to jump. Alex saw a curve coming up. He tied the strap of his satchel around his arm and followed Lan Yin down the ladder as the front of the train started around a curve.

"Remember, bend your knees to break your fall but allow your body to roll." As soon as you stop, get under cover so the brakeman doesn't see you. Now when I say, jump. He looked ahead and saw the most likely place coming up fast. "Jump," he yelled and the two of them pushed themselves away from the car and hit the soft high grass and small bushes. They rolled to a stop. The end of the train was still not in sight. Quickly, they hid under some bushes as the rest of the train passed by.

When the train was out of sight, they made their way on down the tracks and around the curve. The city and the bay could be seen about five miles away. Alex guessed they were about two hours from the outskirts of the city. They decided to try to get close to the city before it was dark, but not to enter it until they were sure no one could see their faces. Alex laughed as he looked at her. There Lan Yin she stood. Her clothes were black from the coal dust and her face was smudged in a pattern that reminded him of Indian war paint. Her yellow hair was streaked with black.

"What is the matter?" she asked.

"Nothing, nothing, it's just that you, you look so different from the first time I saw you at Madam Ying's. You look like a poor beggar."

"Oh?" she said with a twinge of indignity. "You should see yourself. You look like a little boy who has been playing in the coal pile, except your beard of course." Then she began to laugh. They both laughed and sat down in the tall grass. A few minutes later, they began making their way down the steep hills toward the city.

When they came to the outskirts of the city late in the afternoon, Alex decided not to chance going any further. On a small knoll, out of sight of the railroad tracks, they looked out at the deep blue water of the bay and the city spread out below. The warm sun and the fresh sea air combined to make it a quiet, lazy spring afternoon. Lan Yin took out her handkerchief and using the water from the bag she had been carrying, used it as a face cloth and washed her face. She also took out a small mirror and looked at herself and began laughing again. Washing as best she could, she took off her cap and let her long blond hair fall about her shoulders, ran her comb through her hair, and generally fixed herself up. Alex decided to shave and get cleaned up.

"It was a good thing we found that stream back there," he said. "I was really getting thirsty."

Lan Yin watched in fascination as he lathered up the bar of soap he had in his satchel and smeared it on his face and using the small razor he carried in the bag - shaved. She laughed as she held the mirror for him. After he finished, she used the soap to wash her face again. They both felt better after they had cleaned up, and they laid back in the sun and relaxed. Alex fell asleep on her lap.

Lan Yin woke him just as the sun went down behind the mountain. They gathered up their things and started off.

"How well do you know Tsingtao?" he asked.

"Pretty well," she replied. "It is a resort city, and I came here many times with my father on vacations. The beaches are wonderful. Do you know where in Tsingtao you want to go?"

Alex racked his brain and recalled the instructions given him by Brady. "I want to go to the old church on the corner of Shin Yi Lu and Wu Pei."

"Oh, I know just where that is. I know how to get to Shin Yi Lu anyway. But it is very far from here. All the way across the city. It is in the middle of the port area near the bay."

"How long do you think it will take us to get there?"

"I really don't know, but I would think several hours."

"Well, we'll just have to try and make it before daylight."

"We must not be seen in daylight with these dirty clothes, it will raise suspicion. No one is allowed to be seen in dirty clothes on the streets of Tsingtao because there are foreigners here trading. They are very strict here."

They walked through the outskirts of the city avoiding street lights and made their way slowly toward the heart of the city. Alex noticed that all the houses were well kept up and even in the industrial areas everything was clean. It was slow going once they reached the more populated area because they had to duck around corners and hide often to avoid people. It took them most of the night to reach the inner city. They made their way to the dock area. Alex took careful stock of the area remembering that there was a contact in the fishing fleet. "But," Brady had warned him, "use that contact only as a last resort."

As dawn neared, Lan Yin became increasingly worried about their appearance. She knew that they were at least an hour away from the street they were looking for. When Alex noticed her anxiety, they decided to look for a place to hide.

In the predawn light they saw a large warehouse near one of the docks that looked deserted. Alex had her wait, and he crossed the street to check out the building. Just as he got close to the door it began to open, and he quickly hid in the shadows. A man pulled a truck out of the building and then closed the door behind him, but not quite all the way. The truck drove off. Alex looked in the warehouse and didn't see or hear anything. It was lit by a small light at one end of the huge storage area. Just to the left of the door, were some stairs leading to another storage area. Alex motioned to Lan Yin, and she ran across the street. They both crept into the building and looked around. There were all sizes and descriptions of boxes and packing crates stacked neatly in rows. The warehouse seemed to be empty of people, however. He looked at the stairs and motioned for her to follow him. The wooden stairs creaked. At the top of the stairs, he found three small offices with a work light burning in one of them. Further down the hall was a small storage area with packing crates and boxes. They walked past the offices and into the darkened area where the crates were. Just then, they heard the door of the building open and voices as the workers came to work.

"The workers are coming in," Lan Yin whispered.

"This early?"

"Yes, everyone begins work early in China."

Alex looked around for a place to hide. Then Lan Yin tugged on his coat. "These boxes say to 'hold until January'."

"Good, they won't be moving them right away." He looked at the boxes and saw that they were stacked nearly to the ceiling. There was space on top of them to hide. Even though they made noise, Alex and Lan Yin managed to climb to the top of the stacks of boxes. The activity below drowned out the noise. They laid down flat on top of the boxes. A little while later some men came up the stairs and into the offices. The warehouse was in full operation.

Alex and Lan Yin lay on the boxes all day. It was very hot, but they were safe. No one came into the area where they were hiding.

When night fell, the workers began leaving. Alex and Lan Yin waited until they heard no sounds for a long time. Then, quietly, they climbed down and started toward the stairs. All of a sudden Alex noticed that the lights were on in one of the offices, and he heard the sounds of a man closing his desk. The man opened the door just as Alex pushed Lan Yin behind a crate. He went down the stairs and out the door. They started to get up when Lan Yin whispered. "This crate is full of clothes, can we change so that we will not be noticed even if we are seen?" Alex thought it over and decided she had a point. The wooden crate was nailed shut. Alex looked around and found a hook used to move bales of cotton and pried the crate open. There were coats and pants and hats in the box all tied in neat bundles. They pulled out what they needed and changed in the dark. Lan Yin tucked her blond hair into a hat, and they pushed their old clothes under some of the clothes in the box. Alex shut the crate as best he could, then tapped it with the wooden handle of the hook.

A voice called out from below. "Who's up there?"

Alex motioned for Lan Yin to hide and stay still. They waited. Shortly, they heard footsteps on the stairs. Alex peered out from behind a crate and saw a man, obviously a guard of some sort, coming toward the open packing crate. The guard stopped only a few feet from Alex and looked at the open carton. Then he looked around. He pulled out a gun and started toward Alex. Lan Yin was hiding behind another crate. As he neared Alex, Lan Yin stood up. She had no top on. Startled, when he saw it was a woman, the man hesitated. His back was to Alex. Alex hit the guard with a sharp blow on the head with a board from the packing crate. He collapsed in a heap. They listened. No other noise. They ran down the stairs. Alex looked out the partially open door. There seemed to be no activity. He motioned for Lan Yin to follow and went out the door and around the building. They were safely out and on their way to Shin Yi Lu.

They stayed on the side streets and walked along at a fast pace. Two hours later, they came to Shin Yi Lu. It was a very busy street with shops and many people. The street lights were bright, and Alex decided that they should not walk down that street but go by way of side streets. Lan Yin told him the church was three blocks to the north.

When they arrived at the old church, Alex saw that it was exactly like the picture he'd seen during his training. It was made of stone and modeled after German churches that had been built there many years ago by German settlers and traders. Alex found a side door that was not locked, and they went in.

"There is supposed to be an old priest here called Father Grant who will help us," Alex whispered. "Let's hope they haven't decided to get rid of him."

"Gau Shan, I'm afraid again," Lan Yin whispered holding tightly to his arm.

"Me too," Alex said, patting her hand. He began walking through a darkened hallway. Lan Yin followed right behind. At the end of the hallway was a heavy wooden door. Alex opened it a crack and peered in. It was the sanctuary. It was dimly lit with candles burning at the altar. No one was in sight. He tiptoed out to get a better look when he was stopped cold in his tracks. "May I help you?" said a raspy voice in Mandarin Chinese.

Alex was startled. He turned around slowly and came face to face with a very short, white-haired, old man with steel-rimmed glasses and a chubby face. His black robe made him barely visible. His hands were folded in front of him. The priest stood silently waiting for Alex to speak.

"Are you... Father Grant?" Alex asked in his best Mandarin.

The old man nodded and looked hard at Alex.

"How is it the sea is blue?" Alex said.

"Blue is for tranquility," the priest said as he looked Alex square in the eyes.

Alex relaxed. The sign and counter sign were right. "My friend and I need your help."

"What can I do for you?" the priest asked. He was looking over Alex's shoulder at Lan Yin who had crept up behind Alex.

"I am an American."

"Yes." The old man raised an eyebrow and stared at Alex for a moment. "Is there another American with you?"

"No, she is Chinese." Alex turned and motioned for Lan Yin to come forward.

Father Grant looked at her for a moment and raised an eyebrow.

"I am Lan Yin," she said. "My mother was Chinese, my father was Russian."

"Oh, I see," he said. "Is there anyone else with you?"

"No," Alex said.

"It is not wise to talk here. Although I do not have many of my flock visit me anymore, you can never tell. Come with me." He pointed the way. They crossed to the other side of the altar to a small door. Father Grant led them down a short hallway to his study in the back. "May I offer you tea?" the Priest asked as he shut the door behind them. They both nodded. Father Grant went to a small hotplate on an old wooden table where a pot of tea was already brewing. He poured the tea as he spoke. "Please, won't you both sit down. You will be safe here for the time being. The communists haven't been here for many weeks." As he handed Alex his cup, he said, "I was very surprised at your coming. No one has passed through here in quite some time. I thought perhaps they didn't trust me or something. How did you know to come here?"

"I was given your name and address by some, shall we say... mutual friends. They suggested that if I found some trouble you might help me get out of the country."

"Are you in trouble here in Tsingtao?"

"No, I don't believe anyone knows I am... or rather we are here. We've come from another city."

"I see," Father Grant said, taking off his glasses. "It has been a long time since I performed such a service. It will be difficult to remember the proper people to contact, but I think I can be of service. The first thing we must do is get you to a place where we can be absolutely certain the communists won't find you. There is a small room in the basement I think you will find adequate. It is well hidden. Come this way," Father Grant said motioning for them to follow. Not far from his office was another door. Its hinges squeaked as he opened it. They followed him down a darkened stairway that reminded Alex of the dungeon stairways he had seen on old movies. They went through a storage area to a small door hidden behind packing crates. Father Grant opened the door and lit a candle revealing a small room. It had a couple of beds, a sink and a lavatory. There was a table in the middle of the room. It was not very clean, and he brushed away the cobwebs from the sink and turned on the faucet, after a little while rusty water came out then it became clear. "This room hasn't been used in a long, long time, but I think it will do for the time being."

"I can't thank you enough," Alex said in English.

"English," the priest mused, "It sounds so strange now. I haven't had the occasion to use it for many years," he said haltingly.

Lan Yin looked around, put down her satchel, and sat down wearily on the bed. A puff of dust rose in the stale air.

Father Grant looked at her for a moment then said, "Oh, I beg your pardon, did you say you have been traveling?"

"Yes, for many days," Lan Yin said.

"You both must be hungry. I was just about to have a bowl of my rather poor soup. Let me get some for you."

Father Grant returned shortly with three bowls of soup and a pitcher of water. The three of them ate the tepid soup. Lan Yin finished first, and laid down on the bed. She fell fast asleep. The priest noticed this and motioned for Alex to come out into the storage room with him. Alex followed. The two of them talked about Alex's trip from Peking. Alex was cautious not to mention any specifics of his travels as he was taught even though Father Grant often pressed for details. Finally, Alex said, "I think now you know pretty much of everything."

"Except why you came to China in the first place," Father Grant said.

"Well, I think that's better left unsaid."

The priest nodded in understanding. "Of course. I assume you want to go to Taiwan."

"That would be good. Whatever you can do, Father," Alex said. "We want to get out of China as quickly as possible."

Father Grant again nodded his understanding, but raised his hand. "Well, I'm afraid that isn't as easy as it sounds. You see, all of my contacts have either been killed or arrested, and I really don't know anyone right at this moment who can help. China is very difficult to leave these days. Even more so than three or four years ago when I last was able to help one of our friends. The police have tightened the security so much since then that I am afraid it is almost impossible but… well never mind, rest for now. I will try to think of something. I am sure that God will help us find a way."

"Thank you, Father," Alex said reaching for Father Grant's hand. The priest reluctantly shook his hand and Alex frowned. He saw the priest looking at his face and changed his expression to a smile. The priest did the same.

Lan Yin woke when they gathered up the dishes. Father Grant went to the door. "Good night and rest well, I will bring you food in the morning my children," he said as he closed the door.

Lan Yin ran to Alex and threw her arms around him. "Oh, I feel so much better now. I am no longer afraid. Oh Gau Shan, Gau Shan." Alex did not respond to her hug. She pulled back and looked at him. He was staring at the door. "Gau Shan?"

Alex didn't reply, and she tugged at his sleeve.

After a moment, Alex seemed to come out of a trance. "Huh?"

"You seem troubled. What is it?" she asked.

"I don't know," he said. He rubbed his face, looked at the door, and began pacing. Lan Yin frowned. She watched him for a while then grabbed his arm. "You need rest. You are very tired. Let your troubles wait until the morning. Come here," she said. She pulled his face to hers and kissed him. At first he was lost in thought, but her kiss aroused him and he kissed her back.

"Oh Gau Shan I feel so good. I just know everything will be all right now. We have help and shelter and food. Everything we need."

"Food," Alex murmured. "That's it. Father Grant said that his contacts were all gone and he didn't know who to turn to. I'll tell him about my other contact, the fisherman Yu Ling. Maybe he knows whether or not Yu Ling is trustworthy." Alex started toward the door.

"Gau Shan, can't that wait until morning? Besides, Father Grant told us to stay here and not go out of this room."

"I know, Father Grant said not to come upstairs, but," he hesitated, "Lan Yin."

"Yes?"

"Did you notice anything strange about the priest?"

"No. Of course, I really haven't known any men of God before."

"There was something about his manner that bothered me," Alex wrinkled his brow trying to conjure up something buried deep in his mind. Then his eyes lit up. "Lan Yin, did you see Father Grant pray before we ate?"

"No."

"Neither did I." Alex went to the door.

"Where are you going?"

"To tell him about the other contact. I don't like to leave things undone overnight."

CHAPTER TWENTY

Alex closed the door behind him and went upstairs to the Father's office. He was about to open the door when he heard him talking to someone. Alex turned the knob slowly and pushed the door open a crack. There at his chair behind his desk was Father Grant, talking on the telephone. "Yes, yes Captain, they are here now," he was saying. "No, there is no danger of them leaving tonight. They are in a room under the sanctuary, and there is no other way out except the one set of stairs. All right, I'll be waiting, but damnit be quiet. We can take them by surprise."

Alex quietly closed the door and quickly made his way back to the room. He burst in the room. "Quick, Lan Yin, we've got to get out of here, the old man is an informer. Leave everything. We've got to go now." Alex grabbed her hand and led her back up the stairs. He stopped at the head of the stairs. All was quiet. They started down the hall toward the sanctuary. Suddenly the door to the office opened flooding the hall with light. Father Grant stood in the doorway. "Wait my children. Where are you going? Wait!"

Alex and Lan Yin ran to the door of the sanctuary. The old man pulled a revolver out of his cloak and aimed it, "Halt, halt or I'll shoot!"

Alex got to the door and yanked it open. The first shot hit the door just above his head. He pulled Lan Yin through the door as the second shot grazed his arm. The fake priest was running down the hall and yelling. Alex dragged Lan Yin with him as they ran. They ducked behind pillars as more shots rang out. As they got to the main doors, the priest fired again. This time he hit Lan Yin in the back. She spun around and fell, Alex picked her up, but she couldn't stand.

"Oh, Gau Shan, I hurts. I hurt something terrible."

Another shot rang out.

"I'll carry you," he said as he began to lift her up.

"No... no you must save yourself I am hurt too bad." Lan Yin cried out. Another shot narrowly missed Alex. The old man was up the aisle toward them.

"But," Alex tried to protest, but Lan Yin put her fingers to his lips. Tears welled up in Alex's eyes, a mixture of anger and frustration.

"Please, go Gau Shan."

"But."

"I shall go to America in another life. Go." She slumped to the floor again. Alex dropped to the floor as he saw the old man round the corner and fire almost point blank. The bullet ricocheted off the floor near his hand. Alex leaped up and ran for the door. He pulled it open, ran out, down the stairs, and into a crowd that had gathered when they heard the shots. Just as he got into the crowd, a truck load of soldiers came around the corner. The priest stood in the doorway to the church yelling to the soldiers. "Get him, get him!" But the noise of the crowd was too loud for them to hear.

Alex worked his way through the people and cut down the side street that he and Lan Yin had come up. The truck stopped in front of the church and the soldiers jumped off but the scene was one of mass confusion. The officer with the soldiers ran up the steps to the priest. "Which way did he go?" the officer asked.

"I don't know. I lost him in the crowd. Come this way." The priest led the officer to Lan Yin who was laying in an ever increasing pool of blood. The priest picked her head up by the hair and shouted at her, "Where has he gone?"

"I don't know," Lan Yin replied. The priest slapped her. "He must have said something."

"No, no nothing. I hurt so much," she said with tears streaming down her soft white cheeks. "We didn't know where we were going, he just knew you had betrayed us."

"The truth," he said slapping her again. "Tell us the truth!"

"I am telling the truth," Lan Yin said as she struggled for breath.

"Let me handle this," the officer said as he pushed the priest away and knelt down beside her. "Is it true that you do not know where he has gone?"

"Yes," she said feebly.

"If you tell us you will not be harmed, and we will see to your wounds."

"I don't know."

The officer was angry and frustrated. "If you do not tell us immediately, you will suffer far more pain than you are in now." Lan Yin stared at the officer. "Now, tell us! Tell us now or you will suffer. Tell us!"

Lan Yin continued to stare. The officer yelled, but there was no answer. There could be none. She was dead.

CHAPTER TWENTY-ONE

Tsingtao, China, May 15, 1960

Alex was constantly looking back over his shoulder as he darted in and out of side streets avoiding as many people as he could. He could hear the sound of soldiers yelling far behind him. Suddenly, there was a loud clap of thunder quickly followed by large drops of rain. People scurried to find shelter making it easier to run. The sounds of the soldiers faded. In no time it was a full cloud burst. Alex pulled up the collar of his coat and kept running. In the pouring rain no one could tell whether or not he was Chinese.

It took Alex a little more than an hour to get back to the dock area where he and Lan Yin had been earlier that night. Alex no longer felt he was being followed. He felt safe for the time being. Needing somewhere to hide before sunrise, Alex looked up and down the dock area. He didn't think he should go back to the same warehouse they'd hidden in for fear they might have found the body of the soldier he'd killed. As he wove his way through the buildings, he didn't see anyplace that wasn't guarded or locked. He kept his cap pulled down over his eyes and kept searching the dock area. It was getting late, and he worried that someone might begin to suspect him if he wandered about the docks much longer.

Alex stopped in a doorway. He was getting cold, and he was soaked to the skin. He began to shiver not only because of the cold but because he could see Lan Yin lying on the church steps. He was furious at the priest or whatever he was. A lonely tear was indistinguishable from the rain drops as it rolled down his cheek. He swallowed hard and crooked his neck to relieve the tension. The church route was gone, but not the other alternative – the fisherman.

Alex wiped the rain from his face and remembered that gesture of wiping one's mouth was a technique Brady had taught him to help him remember specific things. "Clear your mind by rubbing your face. I know it sounds silly, Alex, but it works," he could hear Brady saying. Alex ran his hand across his face again. The voice on the training film echoed in his head, "Yu Ling is the owner of a small fishing boat that has a white dragon painted on the bow. He docks near the south end of the jetty," Yes. He could see the slide in his mind's eye, but he had no idea which way was south, but he turned right out of the doorway that faced the docks and began walking at a fast pace.

He passed several piers, but he didn't see any fishing boats, just some junks and sampans rolling in the stormy waters of the bay. It wasn't at all like Brady had described it. "The dock will be swarming with people and there will be hundreds of sampans and fishing boats. All you have to do is find Yu Ling, but remember we are not certain he is still on our side, so be careful."

After an hour of walking and not finding the boat, Alex decided he had to ask someone where Yu Ling's boat was. He saw an old man squatting beneath a canvas lean to weaving his fishing net. He was alone. Staying in the shadows as much as he could, Alex walked up to the man and asked the old man where Yu Ling the fisherman kept his boat. The old man didn't even bother to look up. He said that if Yu Ling was in the harbor, he would be docked about a half mile on down the dock past pier number 22. Alex looked around and saw that he was on pier 17. He thanked the old man and made his way along the dock toward pier number 22.

Minutes later, a large sampan blocked his view, but when he passed it, he could see several fishing boats rocking in the wind and rain. Some of the boats were small fishing trawlers, others Chinese junks. Alex wasn't sure what kind of a boat Yu Ling would have, but he decided just to go from boat to boat until he found the white dragon.

At last he found it. A Chinese junk with a white dragon painted on the bow. He looked up in the darkness to see an old man standing on the stern under an umbrella filling a long pipe. It was difficult to tell how old the man was, but he was a thin, wiry man with a long face and a white Mandarin beard.

"Yu Ling, is that you?" Alex called out.

The old man quickly put out his match and looked around. Alex motioned with his hands. Yu Ling ambled down the side until he came to the gangplank. He moved slowly. "Who calls?" he asked.

"Are you Yu Ling?" Alex spoke very deliberately.

"Yes, I am Yu Ling, who are you?"

"A friend."

The old man squinted his eyes and raised the umbrella to get a better look as he approached Alex. He stopped a few feet away. Alex walked toward him. "Who are you?" the old man asked again.

Alex could see Yu Ling's craggy, weather-beaten face by now, and he looked somewhat like the pictures Alex had seen; just as Father Grant had looked like his picture. He decided to take a chance and give the recognition sign. "Yang Fang."

Yu Ling immediately stopped and looked around. "Bai Fang," Yu Ling replied hesitantly. "Step closer so I can see you better."

Alex stepped out of the shadows.

"What is it you want?" Yu Ling asked. His voice dropped to a whisper. His dialect slightly more sibilant than the Mandarin of Peking.

"I need your help in getting out of China."

"What makes you believe I can help you?" the old man asked, as he looked around to see if anyone was near.

Alex saw some people coming down the dock toward them. "Can we talk someplace else in private?"

"I don't know. Perhaps if you come back tomorrow," Yu Ling said and started to walk away.

"But I can't tomorrow," Alex protested, "I am in trouble now. Both the army and the police are looking for me right now."

The old man stopped and turned toward Alex. "And how do I know you are worthy?" Yu Ling took a drag off his pipe and waited. Alex began to break out in a sweat as the group of men came closer. They were not soldiers, just working men, and they were laughing. They were getting closer and Alex didn't like it one bit. He turned so the men could not see his face. Yu Ling recognized them and waved. They returned the wave and kept on coming.

Yu Ling turned and looked at Alex with a broad grin, a sadistic grin, and saw that Alex was getting very nervous. He came close enough to Alex so he could see better in the rain. The corners of his mouth curled upward. "I must speak with my friends, if you don't mind. Perhaps, you had better wait on the fantail of my humble craft," he said nodding toward the gangplank.

Alex nodded and gratefully walked past Yu Ling and climbed on board the ship. He made his way through the rigging of the junk and up the stairs to the platform that was built out over the stern of the ship. From this vantage point, Alex could watch from the relative safety of the shadows as Yu Ling and the men, some old, some middle aged, engaged in a very animated conversation. At one point, one of the men pointed to the area where Alex stood and a cold chill went down his back. He wondered what they were talking about. He was growing more and more anxious as the conversation dragged on. He didn't know where to go if this last contact failed to come through. He felt trapped. He was scared. What was only a matter of a few minutes seemed like hours to Alex, but, at last, he could see the group breaking up, bowing and saying their goodbyes. Then, to Alex's amazement Yu Ling sat on a packing crate and lit up his pipe, leaned back and puffed contentedly. Alex didn't know whether to go down to the dock or wait on the fantail. He decided that since the old man had not given him a signal, he would wait on the fantail.

About a half an hour later, Yu Ling finally got up and slowly walked to the gangplank. When he reached the spot where Alex was waiting, he smiled, "Now, what were we talking about?"

"Helping me to escape I believe." Alex replied.

"Oh yes." Yu Ling sat down on a wooden barrel and motioned for Alex to sit beside him.

"I was just talking with my friends about this problem. They were most helpful."

Alex couldn't believe what he was hearing. The old man had talked to them about him?

Yu Ling went right on. "They tell me you are a notorious gangster from America. They say you have come to kill all the young people and organize unions and destroy our morals. It is all the usual propaganda. We enjoyed hearing about it." He smiled and took a long drag off his pipe. "What did you come to China for?"

Alex was taken aback. The old man's tone of voice changed drastically when he asked the question. Yu Ling's long, boney fingers accented the long pipe that was pointed directly at Alex's throat. Alex looked at the pipe then into the narrow, black eyes of Yu Ling. "You know as well as I that I cannot tell you. I will only tell you that I have already completed my mission and that I am on my way home. But, I need your help."

"Are you alone?"

"Yes."

"They say you were traveling with another. A woman of the flesh. Is this true?"

"What did they say about her?" Alex asked anxiously.

Yu Ling smiled an evil smile. "So, it is true."

"Yes. But she is not with me anymore."

"I know."

"How do you know? What have you heard?"

"My friends tell me a man of the turned collar shot her."

"Yes. Do any of them know how she is?"

"She is dead," Yu Ling said very evenly.

Alex's head dropped to his chest. He had been thinking about that possibility all the time he was running. He even felt he knew in the back of his mind, but now, now his fears were turned into reality. He remained very still for a long time. Yu Ling just watched and waited patiently. Finally Alex muttered, "She deserved better."

"That is true for all of us," Yu Ling said softly.

Alex looked up at the man. There seemed to be no emotion on his face at all. He was like a stone statue. His only movement an occasional flick of an eyelash. Alex took a deep breath and shook off his emotions as best he could.

Yu Ling continued to stare at Alex. Both men sat quietly, sizing up one another. Finally, Alex got up and walked over to the side of the ship and looked out at the darkened harbor. Only small reflections of lights flickered in the water. He felt sick at the death of Lan Ying. "If only I hadn't taken her with me, she might have… " his thoughts trailed off.

"Why have you come to me?" Yu Ling's harsh, high voice cut through the grey fog of Alex's subconscious. Alex thought for a moment then turned to face Yu Ling who had silently slipped up behind him. Alex was startled. "Perhaps you didn't hear me, I asked… "

"I know, why you?" Alex interrupted. "I came to you because your name was given to me by American Intelligence."

Yu Ling's eyebrows rose.

"They told me that as a last resort I might try you for help. They also said that you were not very trustworthy."

"Your candor is surprising, uh… " Yu Ling groped for a name.

Alex thought for a second and decided not to give his code name. "Gau Shan."

"Gau Shan. I see," Yu Ling said rubbing his chin in deep thought. He didn't believe Alex but he was interested in finding out more information. "So they feel I am not trustworthy… well, perhaps it is true. And where do you want to go?"

"South Korea, Taiwan, Hong Kong. Anywhere where I can contact our people."

"I see. It is possible to get you to a 'friendlier place' I believe, but let me ask you an old American question. What's in it for me?" His smile was broad now.

"Yu Ling," Alex looked him straight in the eye, "I gotta give it to you straight. I don't know what's in it for you. No one said, but, I can only promise you this, if I get out of China and back home, I'll do my damnedest to see to it our people find some way to repay you.

That's all I can do at the moment. I can give you what little money I have on me now, the rest you'll have to trust me for. We both know you're my last chance, it's up to you."

Yu Ling didn't take his eyes off Alex. He continued to stare at him as he thought about what Alex had said. "You are very frank, Gau Shan, I must say, but... " He stopped.

"But?"

"But you must realize that helping you is a treasonable offense. Not only would they be unhappy with me, but my family as well. We would be in great danger."

"I know. I know," Alex said looking away. "One person has already been killed because of me." He saw no reaction from Yu Ling. He pursed his lips, sighed and started walking toward the gangplank. "I'm sorry I bothered you."

"Wait," Yu Ling said, and in one quick catlike movement, he had hold of Alex's arm. "I didn't say I wouldn't. To the contrary, I find my life a bit dull at the moment."

Alex turned to see a big grin on Yu Ling's face. Two of his front teeth were missing, and he had a gold tooth on one tooth.

"I suppose I must blame the Americans for showing me all the excitement of my life. I could have been a simple fisherman, but during the great war, one of your American friends and I became close and I remember him often quoting a man, I think he was one of your presidents, Theodore Roosevelt?"

Alex nodded.

"He would say, 'Far better it is to dare mighty things, to win glorious triumphs even thought checkered with failure, than to take rank with those poor spirits who neither enjoy much nor suffer much. Because they live in the grey twilight that knows not victory nor defeat.' Yes, I can remember him shouting that saying many times when we were in trouble."

The old man leaned against a spar and drifted back in time to his youth, his eyes half closed, a warm smile on his face, and a relaxed posture. "Ah, that was a wonderful time. The excitement and the danger were powerful feelings. Feelings I liked very much." Yu Ling didn't say any more for a while, then he came out of his dream and looked at Alex. "I think I will help you, Gau Shan. Yes. It will be good for my blood. Come with me."

They walked back to the stern of the ship. On their way, the old man opened a hatch and yelled down at his wife to prepare food for his guest, a friend. Alex followed as Yu Ling led him down some stairs to a small cargo area filled with nets, hooks, etc. The old man pulled on the hooks that held the nets and the whole back wall folded down, exposing another small room. Alex followed Yu into the room and watched as he shut the door and lit a small kerosene lantern. The room was small with each nook and cranny filled with special equipment, scuba gear, a couple of automatic rifles, a radio, and a box of hand grenades. Yu motioned for Alex to sit on one of the boxes, and he sat across from him and talked in a low voice. "We will have something to eat soon, in the meantime, we will talk. You have come to me at a very favorable time, Gau Shan. I have permission to sail tomorrow night on a mission to North Korea for the People's Army. I must take some special messages to our military advisors in Pyongyang. I am the unofficial message channel for them."

Boy, would our people like to know that, Alex thought, and I'll bet for enough money or something we could probably get a peek at the messages through Yu. Yu's voice cut through Alex's thoughts.

"It would be very possible for me to take a somewhat indirect route to the south past a small island that is occupied by your American friends. You can swim I hope."

"Yes."

"Good," Yu replied nodding his head up and down. "I can let you off about four miles from the island, you will have to swim from there."

Alex nodded in affirmation, but thinking as he did so that he'd be swimming further than he had ever swum before.

"However," Yu Ling continued, "there is another problem. While I have the permission of the Army, the Navy is not told about these missions, it must appear as if I am going on my usual trip to North Korea. And the Navy knows, but has yet to prove, I smuggle things from time to time. It is possible that they will stop me and search my boat."

"And if they do?" Alex asked warily.

"Do not fear, I have a very good hiding place for you."

"Here?" Alex asked.

"No," Yu smiled, "They might find you here." He walked over to the scuba gear hanging in the corner, took the mask off its hook and held it up. "I have a rather unusual, but I think foolproof, place for you to hide. You see, under the hull of this old craft I have carefully attached a handle. Since she does not move too fast, it will be quite safe for you to hold on to the handle beneath, and I will tow you outside the harbor. Once we are safely beyond the harbor, you can simply climb back on board, and off we shall go. If by any chance we are stopped and searched, you won't be on board." He looked at Alex for approval and smiled. Alex stared at him for a moment then he too broke out in a wide grin, and the two men shook hands.

After they had gone over the plan several more times, Alex tried on the gear to make sure the straps were right. He'd never scuba dived before, but this seemed like a good time to start. Minutes later, Yu Ling's wife called them to dinner.

CHAPTER TWENTY-TWO

Tsingtao - May 17, 1960

After sweating out two days and nights in the small "equipment room" in the hold of the junk, Alex breathed a sigh of relief when the long, sleek junk slipped out of its mooring and moved out into the harbor. The night was dark, no moon. The junk was enveloped into the blackness once it sailed a couple of hundred yards offshore. Yu Ling opened the door and waved Alex out onto the deck with his scuba gear. They had agreed that neither of them would talk because sound traveled far over the water of the harbor. Yu Ling navigated the junk so that when Alex entered the water, the junk was between them and the shore. Yu Ling stopped the small auxiliary motor used to navigate in the harbor, and helped Alex over the side.

Even though he had a wet suit on, Alex felt the cold water engulf him as he dropped into the water. He was careful not to make any noise. He slipped beneath the water to prepare to put on his mask. He bobbed up to the surface, put on the mask and got his bearings from Yu Ling who pointed with a flashlight to the general direction of the handle. Alex ducked under the boat and felt for the handle. Since they did not want to risk a light, he had to find the handle by feel only. Remembering that Yu Ling had said that the handle was near the keel, almost in the center of the boat, he tried to dive lower, but he suddenly was confronted with an eerie feeling that he was suffocating. He had never used scuba gear, and in the dark water, he started to panic. He wanted to find the surface, but he was disoriented and was actually going deeper. It was as if the world was closing in on him. He thrashed in the water, flailing his arms and legs. He fought for self-control, and stopped moving. He let his buoyancy carry him up toward the surface. Then he bumped into the hull. He felt along the underneath of the boat and found the handle. A new calm came over him and he gripped the handle with all his might and rapped on the hull three times to signal Yu Ling that he had found the handle and was ready.

He heard the motor slip into gear and felt the sensation of moving through the water as the junk began to move toward the entrance to the harbor. It was pitch black in the water and he couldn't see a thing. The movement of the boat forced his body up against the hull. He was off on his strange ride.

Yu Ling was at the helm of his ship as it made its way into the channel at the mouth of the harbor. He was feeling good. It was the first time he'd ever made a trip whereby he could serve all three of his masters, China, the USA, and greed.

Just as he was about to pass through the mouth of the harbor, his happy thoughts were interrupted. Suddenly his boat was bathed in a harsh white light. At that same moment, he heard the screaming siren of a patrol boat. He turned to see a patrol boat steaming off his starboard side about 500 yards, its searchlight nearly blinding him.

"Attention!" a voice screamed out of a bullhorn, "Stop all engines and prepare to be boarded for inspection!"

Yu Ling was surprised. It wasn't because he had not been stopped before, it was because his friends in the Army told him they would prevent such a search because of his mission for them. He stopped his engines, and quickly ran through a mental checklist of all the contraband he had on board to make sure it was stored safely.

Alex saw the search lights as they streamed across the water. He couldn't hear anything, but a few seconds later he felt the boat come to a stop. Yu had warned him the boat might be stopped, but still Alex began to sweat in his wet suit. He didn't like the circumstances. It wasn't long thereafter until he felt a rush of water pushing him away from the junk, he gripped the handle tight. Alex realized that the hull of a boat was coming alongside the junk. He waited in the darkness.

The pompous Chinese naval officer followed his two deck hands as they boarded the junk. Two other members of the boarding party followed the officer. He greeted Yu Ling. They knew each other, and Yu Ling was comfortable with him. The officer motioned for the others to search the ship. Yu Ling smiled as the officer lit a cigarette.

"I hope you are not inconvenienced too much Comrade Yu," the officer said, "but we have orders to search each and every ship leaving the harbor. There is an American agent who escaped, and he might stow on board one of the ships. The officer took a deep breath, he was tired and he looked it. He sat on one of the hatches. "My men and I have just finished a three hour search of a tanker and… "

"Lieutenant," one of the men called.

The officer dragged himself to his feet and followed the man below decks. Yu followed.

When they got below, Yu was surprised to see that the man had found his hidden room. Then he remembered he had been careless when Gau Shan came up on deck. He had not secured the room. Another sailor was hauling automatic weapons and other contraband from the room and piling it on the deck. The officer shook his head in disgust.

"Yu, where did all this come from?"

Yu didn't answer. He knew he was caught. His head sunk to his chest.

Meanwhile, clinging to the handle, Alex waited. The light from one of the searchlights was dancing on the surface of the water which lit up the whole area below. It seemed the boat was stopped a long time, and Alex's curiosity began to get to him. He tried to talk himself out of it, but at last he decided to swim to the surface on the other side of the junk away from the patrol boat to see what the delay was. He swam silently to the surface near the rudder of the junk and peered around the stern of the boat. The lights from the patrol boat lit up both boats. He couldn't see or hear anything except the engine of the patrol boat idling. Then his heart sank as he saw Yu, and his wife, being led from the junk to the patrol boat, tied together. His first thought was that Yu may have told them about him, and that the patrol boat would probably send frogmen after him. The loud roar of the engines of the patrol boat being revved up changed his mind. He watched the men on the deck of the patrol boat secure a line from the junk to the stern of the patrol boat. They were going to tow the junk.

Not knowing where he was, and what direction land was, Alex decided to stick with the junk until he sighted land and then dive under, wait until the patrol boat was gone, then swim to shore. He clung to a bar supporting the rudder and went along for the ride.

After about thirty minutes, he saw the lights of the harbor in the distance. He rode along for a little longer then dropped off and watched as the two ships disappeared in the darkness. One thing was for sure, he thought, he did not want to go where they were going. He picked out a dark spot on the shore line and began swimming toward it. His judgment of distance failed him. He thought it was just a mile or so. It wasn't. After swimming for nearly an hour, Alex felt he wasn't any closer to shore than he was when he dropped off the junk. The scuba tanks were heavy. He had decided to keep them on so that when he got close to shore, he could swim under water and go ashore undetected. The weight of the tanks even in the water, however, soon got too cumbersome for him, and he dropped the tanks.

It seemed like forever to Alex, but actually it was about two and a half hours later when Alex could make out a spot to land. He was near a commercial area with lots of boats and docks. Alex was exhausted. He was now swimming ten strokes and resting, swimming ten strokes, and so on. He was getting so tired that during the rest periods he began to have trouble keeping his head above water. His whole body ached, and he felt numb from the cold water.

At last, the tide began to carry him toward shore. He chose what looked like an old abandoned dock, separated from the other docks, and swam with a last burst of energy underneath the dock and crawled up under the pier in the sand. He wedged himself in a small area protected from view by some pilings. He was so tired. He knew he had to find a safe hiding place, but he was too tired. His eyes closed and he fell into a deep sleep.

Hours later, high-pitched voices began to creep into his subconscious. He couldn't make out what they were saying, but they became louder and louder until Alex moved his head and bumped it on the piling. This woke him up. He heard the voices clearly now, and yet, he felt too tired and exhausted even to move his eyelids. They felt as if heavy chains were keeping them closed. Slowly he opened one eye and was immediately blinded by a flare from the sun. He moved his head slightly and opened the other eye and found himself staring up at a slit in the dock above him. The sun was so bright he turned away, and as he did so, he heard children's voices above him. He turned his head and saw a group of small children staring down at him. They were laughing and pointing at him. He smiled back at them weakly and said good morning. The children stopped talking immediately, and the smiles faded from their faces. Then they turned and ran away, laughing again. Alex shook his head trying to clear the cobwebs from his mind. He was lying on his right side, and he felt a cold chill race down his back. He tried to roll over but his right arm and shoulder were asleep. When he tried to move, pain shot through his cold, exhausted body. He managed to turn over enough to get the arm freed from under him and as he did, the pins and needles sensation began to increase. The pain was severe. Blood was slowly crawling back into his arm and shoulder and the sharp jabs of circulation really hurt. He laid there for a few minutes until the pain subsided. He started to get up, but hit his head this time on the planks of the dock floor. He was still under the pier. He sagged back and closed his eyes again trying to rest. He passed out again.

A shock wave raced through his whole body like a tidal wave starting with a sharp pain in his right foot. Instantly he was awake staring into the gleaming blade of a bayonet. The soldier holding the weapon had just kicked him on the bottom of his foot. Then he heard the shout of the soldier. "Janchilai, Janchilai!"

Alex quickly looked around to see several other soldiers, all with their weapons at the ready, standing in a semicircle around him. Not far from the soldiers were the little children standing silently in a group.

Things began to happen very quickly from then on. He was dragged out from under the pier and prodded to get into an army truck. He was pushed into the back where four soldiers guarded him as the truck sped off.

Alex tried to sit on the bench, but a soldier hit him sharply with the butt of his rifle and Alex was knocked out cold.

As the truck raced through the streets, Alex rolled and crashed into the sides of the truck bed and was kicked by the soldiers. When he was awake, he was either burning up with fever or suddenly being overcome by extreme cold.

He was pulled out of the truck and put on a stretcher when they arrived at the army hospital. Doctors looked at his eyes and his throat, took his temperature. They talked in hushed whispers on the other side of the room, but they never said a word to him. The ringing in his ears grew louder and louder until he passed out.

He tossed and turned in his hospital bed for several days half in and half out of conscience. His fever broke on the tenth day, and he was told he had pneumonia. From that day on no one talked to him. He kept asking about his health, his whereabouts but to no avail. Even the nurse who brought his food and the small, thin doctor who examined him daily refused to say anything to him.

He began to feel better and often sat on the edge of the bed. He was weak, but after ten days, he could stand and walk a bit. Then one day two soldiers came into his room and threw some clothes to him. Alex sat up on the edge of the bed, and after a bit of silent prodding by the soldiers, he dressed himself. He was marched out of the hospital. No one said anything, but the prodding of bayonets was all the instruction he needed.

Alex was driven across town to a prison building. He was led up the steps and into a large room with no furniture, only the one door and no windows. Only one lone bare light bulb burned brightly. The door was slammed shut and again there was silence. Alex walked around the room. After a while he became tired and started to sit down, but when he put his hand down to help himself sit, he got an electric shock. He quickly stood up again and looked around. The entire room was steel plated and painted a bright red. Curious, he walked to the wall and put his finger on the wall and again got a terrific electric shock. He looked around again. Then he looked down at his feet and saw that he had on thick rubber soled shoes. He paced around some more growing more tired by the minute. He bent down and tested the floor. Again the electric shock. He walked some more; he sat on his haunches, it seemed like hours since he was put in this room. Finally he stopped walking. He couldn't lean against the walls, he had tested them all, he couldn't walk any further. He squatted down and that was restful for a few minutes, but then his legs began to ache. He decided to test the floor again, but not with his bare hand, this time he knelt. The shock came right through his trousers, and he tried to get up but his legs were so weak that he had to put his hand on the floor again and the shock was very painful. He managed to get back on his feet. Time became his enemy. Alex paced around trying to think of something to shield him from the electric shock. He took off his shirt and folded it over several times and put it on the floor and then knelt on it. It worked. He knelt down and got as comfortable as possible and started to drift off to sleep. Suddenly the door opened and two soldiers entered and took his shirt from him. Then they threw him down on the floor. This time there was no shock but the men began taking off all his clothes except for his shoes. He was left completely nude, except for his shoes. He struggled as they were striping him, but in his weakened condition he was no match. When they left, they stood him up again. As soon as the door was closed, he started to sit down but luckily he tested the floor again, and there was his enemy the electric shock again. Alex was helpless against the room. He tried standing in every conceivable position to get some sleep but nothing lasted for more than a few minutes. Then he found a comfortable standing position, and out of exhaustion fell asleep standing up. But, with no support, he soon fell. The pain of being on that floor with the electric shock biting at his body was excruciating. He managed to get back up on his feet, but he was in tears and shaking from the pain and the shock. He staggered around the room trying everything to keep awake, singing, slapping his body, yelling, running, kicking the walls, but nothing could defeat the exhaustion and sleep that was taking over his body. He collapsed again and again, and each time the electrical shocks forced him to get back up off the floor, his falls became more frequent and the pain was unbearable. Finally he fell again and this time he couldn't, no matter how hard he tried, how hard he screamed in anguish, get up. Then like a miracle the electric shock seemed to go away. He dropped off to sleep.

Alex slowly awakened. His mouth was very dry, his body ached, but his mind slowly cleared. He rolled over and using his hands, pushed himself up into a sitting position.

"Ah, I see you are awake," came a loud voice from a hidden speaker. The voice, in a crisp Oxfordian English accent, was loud and clear and nearly deafening. "I hope we haven't inconvenienced you too much. On behalf of the people of China I welcome you to our humble school of human behavior. Stand up."

The words raced around the room. Alex shook his head to clear it. He didn't move.

"Come now," the voice said in a lower volume, "Stand up. You must learn that it is very impolite to disobey."

Alex heard the voice clearly, but he chose not to obey.

"I will give you the benefit of assuming that you did not hear or understand me. Please stand up," the voice repeated in both English and Chinese.

Alex decided he was in no position to fight what he could not see, and he didn't want to feel that electric shock again if he could help it. He slowly rose.

"Thank you. Now won't you please tell us your name?" The voice was clipped and not too deep, and Alex had the feeling he had heard it before. He racked his brain trying to determine where he had heard the voice.

"Come now," the voice interrupted, "I don't think that is such a difficult question. What is your name?"

Alex decided that if they didn't know who he was maybe he could get by with letting them force a lie out of him, but in any event he was sure he wasn't going to volunteer information.

"Oh come on now, even a soldier is allowed to give his name."

Alex shrugged, "Grant Williams."

"Grant Williams, how unoriginal. What is your real name?"

Alex repeated the fake name.

"We are by nature a very patient people, but we do not consider our time valueless. Please just tell us your real name and a few other things and you can get some rest and something to eat."

It wasn't until the voice mentioned food that Alex realized he was hungry. He knew he was tired and embarrassed standing there in the middle of the room stark naked except for his shoes. Thinking about himself brought on the exhaustion his body felt all along but did not transmit to his active brain. He sagged a bit but didn't answer.

"You must understand. Our methods of extracting information do not allow you to feel in any way you are in control of the situation. You must feel that you are winning by your silence. I assure you, you are not. We will get the information we are seeking and we will get it now. You have your choice. You can tell us or you can scream out the information. Now which will it be?"

Alex decided to test the voice. He had nothing to lose. His mission was completed. He could tell them everything. But Alex was a stubborn man, and he decided to find out what they had in mind.

"Your silence gives us the answer to our question," the voice boomed.

The door to the cell opened and a large steel chair was pushed in by two soldiers. The soldiers didn't say a word, but went right to their work. They pushed the chair to the center of the room and with a screwdriver forced open sockets in the floor. The legs of the chair were placed in the socket holes and then fastened by bolts to the floor so that the chair was impossible to move. Alex watched as they worked and looked at the open door. He made only one short move toward the door when another soldier stepped into the doorway.

After the soldiers had completed bolting the chair to the floor, they motioned for him to sit down. Alex hesitated but decided to sit. He was tired.

"Now, before we go any further, I most earnestly suggest that you answer my questions and make it easy for both of you and me. Tell me your name and why you came to China."

Alex remained silent.

"Very well," the voice said with a big sigh, "I shall return tomorrow, perhaps by then you'll be more cooperative."

"Go to hell," Alex muttered.

"I'm sorry, I didn't hear you."

"I said, 'go to hell'."

"Yes, that's what I thought you said." There was a click when the microphone was turned off. Alex waited, and the soldiers waited, for a long time. As the time began to drag, the anticipation of what was going to happen next began to make Alex edgy. "What's next?" he asked. Neither of the soldiers answered. Again the silence and the waiting. Finally Alex decided to get up. He started to stand but that was as far as he got. The two soldiers quickly fastened his arms and legs to the chair. All the time they were doing this, there was a total absence of expression on their faces. When he was securely fastened to the chair, they placed a metal band around his head and fastened it tightly and then fastened it to the chair so that he could not move his head. The door opened and suddenly as if a mirage, a very pretty Chinese girl appeared. When he saw her, his first instinct was to cover his nakedness, but, of course, he couldn't move his hands. She was dressed not in the blue cotton pants and shirt of the workers but in a very ornate, very feminine Cheongsam dress and high heels. She smiled and walked to him and stood only a foot away. Her hands were behind her back. Alex returned the smile and relaxed a bit. Then she brought out a long feather from behind her back and gently began to run it along his cheek. It felt soft and good, and he relaxed even more. Then she ran the feather lightly over his arms and neck. It tickled a bit, and he stifled a laugh. Then she ran the feather across his chest and down his body. It tickled, and he squirmed as best he could. He began to be aroused. She stopped and looked down then up at him and gave him a broad smile. His body tightened, and he became erect. She bent down on one knee and began to run the feather around his crotch then across his legs. By now he was really excited and laughing at the same time. Then she stopped and looked at him with a sensuous smile. His heart was beating fast and the blood began throbbing in his head. She stood up again and playfully began running the feather near his nose and beneath it. Alex sneezed. Her face lit up in a broad smile. The sneeze hurt Alex's head as he involuntarily strained against the head band. She didn't say a word in reply, but again began touching his nasal area with the feather and again he sneezed. Because his head was in a fixed position, he could not see the expressions on the two soldiers' faces standing beside the chair, but from her expression, he knew they acknowledged her smile. Again she touched his nose with the feather and again he sneezed. This time he felt a sharp pain in his chest. It lasted only an instant. "I really wish you wouldn't do that," but his sentence was interrupted by the feather again playfully touching his nose and another sneeze. The smile was gone from the girl's face, and Alex knew she was no longer playing, she was serious. She had been testing him to find an area of vulnerability. She had found it. The next ten hours became an increasing nightmare of pain and silence. The woman continued to make him sneeze varying the intervals between. His eyes were watering, he had urinated, his heart was pounding. It felt like a huge hole in his chest, and each time he sneezed, the pains in his chest grew more unbearable. Alex by now was screaming in pain each time he sneezed. He was cursing the girl, the world, and everything he could think of, but each time he stopped, the feather produced a new and more violent sneeze. His mind began whirling, he couldn't concentrate on anything but that feather. His nose was running and ached like no pain he had ever felt before. He begged her to stop saying he would tell all. At last he began shouting his name but the girl was now like an automaton - expressionless, relentless, and seemingly unaware of his screams, pain, and involuntary excretions. Finally, she stopped and stepped aside. Alex, through his tears, saw a man in a long white coat approach him. He was the doctor who had treated him in the hospital. He took Alex's pulse, put a stethoscope to his heart, looked at his eyes and throat. Alex kept pleading with him to make the girl stop. The doctor did not say a word. He then turned and walked away. Alex yelled after him, "Doctor please! I'll talk. I'll talk! Take her away! Please. In God's name make her stop!"

The doctor just kept on walking and suddenly Alex's view was blocked by the willowy body of the girl. She again produced the feather and, involuntarily, he sneezed again. Autosuggestion was taking over his mind.

After another hour of sneezing, Alex passed out from pain. He was revived with a bucket of water and made to sneeze two more times. He wasn't thinking of anything, the pain was too great. When he closed his eyes, all he could see were red blobs. Then the girl turned and walked away. He sank down in the chair as much as the restraints would let him and sobbed uncontrollably.

Three hours later, the girl again walked into the room. Alex was awakened from a fitful sleep by more water. When the girl put the feather on his nose, he sneezed again and the pain in his heart and chest caused a violent reaction throughout his body. It was as if he had been struck in the chest with a huge board. He screamed. Again she put the feather near his nose and again he sneezed. This time without the feather touching him. He screamed in agony. She stopped and walked away near the door. He sneezed twice more involuntarily.

"Good morning, Mr. Hunter," the voice cracked through the room, breaking the silence. "I understand you have changed your mind about talking to us. I am glad for your sake. The doctor tells me you probably wouldn't have lasted more than another day or so. Am I correct? Do you wish to talk to us?"

"Yes," Alex barely managed to get out.

"You'll have to speak up, Mr. Hunter."

Alex's throat was so dry and raw he couldn't talk any louder. He took a deep breath and with all his might yelled as loudly as possible, "Yes!"

"Very good. I understand you do have some trouble talking so we shall allow you a few days to regain your strength."

Again the ominous click of the microphone. The guards untied him, and he collapsed on the floor unconscious.

CHAPTER TWENTY-THREE

Tsingtao Prison, Tsingtao, China, May 30, 1960

Alex awoke from the long interrogation in a hospital bed. He was given the silent treatment again in the hospital, which he didn't mind too much. But, he knew he was becoming very depressed about giving them so much information. He was fed well and given excellent medical treatment, and he began to feel pretty good.

After ten days in the hospital, Alex was taken back to the prison and into an interrogation room in the basement of the building. It was dark and dank, and smelled musty. The room had unpainted bare brick walls, a well-worn metal desk and chair, a small goose-neck lamp on the desk and a straight-back chair. He was left alone for nearly an hour. When the door opened, a very small, slightly built man with steel rimmed glasses, a small mouth and narrow slits for eyes entered. His officer's uniform was starched and pressed, and he had a briefcase in one hand and a walking stick in the other. "I am Colonel Liang Cho Bing," he said in a very high pitched voice. He, too, spoke English with an Oxfordian accent. He appeared to Alex to be a very nervous and high-strung man. He motioned for Alex to sit as he walked to the desk, opened his briefcase, took out a writing pad and pencil and placed his walking stick on the desk. He began to close the briefcase, but stopped and pulled out a feather. Colonel Liang showed it to Alex then put it back in the case and closed it.

"Mr. Hunter," the colonel said, "I trust you are feeling, better nowadays since your ordeal."

"Physically yes," Alex answered sullenly.

"Good, very good. So I assume we can get on with things in a normal way. I ask the questions - you answer?" the Colonel asked as he peered at Alex over the tops of his glasses.

"Yes," Alex said.

"Very good. Shall we begin?"

Colonel Liang's interrogation lasted nearly five days. Every time Alex became resistant to a question, Colonel Liang would remind him about the lady with the feather. One time, she actually appeared. When she did, Alex began to have shortness of breath and started sneezing. His resistance to the use of autosuggestion (the feather) waned and soon he told the colonel everything he wanted to know.

As he sat in his chair the last day, Alex had the feeling the Colonel Liang was simply going through the motions - that he already knew the answers. He was able to get by with some lies about where he was trained and who the pilot for the mission was, but for the most part, he told the truth. He told them all he knew about his mission to get Walters back, and why he had come. Alex was as careful as he could be, but he told more than he wanted to. The threat of continued torture and his own physical and mental condition caused him to make grave errors at first, but when Colonel Liang asked a question a second or third time, Alex knew he was caught and changed his story to the truth. All of this depressed Alex to the point of actually thinking of suicide.

At the end of the last day, the Colonel stood and began pacing back and forth in front of Alex. "Now I suppose you are wondering what is in store for you for the future."

"I really don't care anymore," Alex said, his voice reflecting his mental depression.

"Oh, I'm sure you do. We all do," he said. "The instinct for survival is a most powerful one." The Colonel stopped pacing and looked at Alex who was staring off in space. "I am sure your wife felt it even as she plunged to her death."

"She committed suicide."

"Did she?"

Alex leapt to his feet and went for the Colonel, "What do you know about Crissy's death?"

The door burst open. Two guards grabbed Alex immediately and forced him back into the chair.

"I know many things. But that is for a later time. A time when you will understand."

Alex struggled to get free. "You rotten son of a bitch," Alex shouted, straining to get up.

Colonel Liang's eyes narrowed even more. "Well, I can see that your little feather escapade hasn't done much to curb your temper. You must learn self control."

"Screw your self control!"

"Mr. Hunter," the Colonel said with a sigh, "In order to exist in our country, and, of course, you voluntarily brought yourself into our country, you must learn to control your thoughts and your emotions. You must learn to take a hard look at yourself inwardly and examine your attitudes and experiences so that you may better yourself and contribute to the land you have chosen to enter."

"Contribute?" Alex said incredulously. "You've got to be out of your mind Colonel. I am not about to contribute to China in any way, shape, or form."

"That statement is precisely what I am talking about Mr. Hunter. You have just made an irrational instinctive remark without thinking, and without looking at the alternatives."

"That's where you're wrong," Alex said defiantly. "I have thought about it a long time. I thought about it before I agreed to do this job for my country, and I thought about it many times since I was captured. Sorry Colonel, I know a lot about brainwashing, and one thing I know, you can change everything about a man except his basic instincts and my basic instinct is for freedom. I know what it is, and you can't take that away from me. If you think I'll cooperate in any way, you're sadly mistaken. Oh, I'll do what I must to survive, and I know each man has his breaking point physically, but I won't cooperate with you, and I'll fight you all the way down the line."

"I see," the colonel said, pacing again.

Alex watched him moving in jerky motions across the floor.

"I think that will be all for today, Mr. Hunter. Thank you," Colonel Liang said as he packed up his writing tablet and pencil in his briefcase, picked up his walking stick and went to the door. "Just for your enlightenment, we don't call it 'brainwashing', we call it 'brain cleansing.'"

Alex was taken from the room and back to his cell.

Colonel Liang walked down the long corridor to a temporary office Colonel Chin was using in Tsingtao. He knocked twice and entered. Colonel Chin was standing at the window admiring the view of the harbor.

"Come in, Colonel," he said, his back still to the door. "Have a seat."

Colonel Liang entered and took a chair by the door. He nodded to the man seated in an overstuffed chair in the corner.

"I think you know Mr. Grant."

"Yes," Colonel Liang said nodding his greeting to Grant. "No priest collar today, Mr. Grant?"

"You have to admit, it worked. We captured the foreign devil, Mr. Hunter."

"Yes. I agree. It worked to our benefit. Frankly, I had thought that escape plan had been abandoned by the Americans years ago."

"I, too, Comrade, I was just about to stop playing that role when in they walked. Most fortunate."

"Most fortunate indeed," Colonel Chin interrupted. Colonel Chin walked away from the window to the desk and sat. "Well, Colonel Liang, what do you think?"

"My assessment of Mr. Hunter is that he is a very well-adjusted, well-educated man. He is an individualist and a firm believer in his country's political ideals. He reacts quite normally when put in a stressful position. He is adaptable and inventive and above all a tremendous challenge.

"And your prognosis for his future worth to the state?"

"I believe that because he is so determined and arrogant and because he is intent upon resisting that reeducation will take quite a long time, but," he leaned forward, "I believe that he is going to be very useful to you in the future. He will respond."

"If he is so independent, why do you feel he can be changed?"

"Because we have a weapon to change his mind about his country."

"Which is?"

"He still believes his wife committed suicide. We know different, and we know his country lied to him about it. It is his one weakness."

"Interesting. Very interesting. So how long do you feel it will take until we can safely use him for our purposes and propaganda?"

"I imagine it will take at least a year until we can use him in controlled situations and two to three years before we can safely take him before an open press conference for instance."

"And if we tell him the truth about his wife's death?"

"Probably sooner."

"I see," Colonel Chin mused.

"I feel I must say that although he is very difficult to work with, by the time we are finished with the initial phase, I believe you will have one of the most loyal and obedient comrades we have ever been able to turn out," Liang said with pride.

Colonel Chin raised an eyebrow. He looked over at Grant but got no response. He sat silently for a minute then turned to Colonel Liang. "All right colonel, he is all yours. You understand we would like to use him as soon as possible."

"Yes."

"You will begin right away?"

"I think we shall let him recover from his malnutrition and get all his strength back. I also think that we will move him to our control base in Palung."

"Oh? Tsinghai Province? Why?"

"It is in a remote location, and the people there have not seen an American for a long time. I think I can make use of this for the first part of his training."

216

"Is the first part of the training to be self-criticism?" Evans spoke up.

"In most cases that approach would be our starting point, but Mr. Hunter is unlike most of the subjects I've had to work with. He is totally dedicated to his country. He is not a defector nor an idealist. With that sort, we must break down the very moral and spirit of the man first, so that we can start with a more malleable subject. He is like cold clay, difficult to model, we must soften him up first. I have an old method I want to try first."

CHAPTER TWENTY-FOUR

Palung, China, June 3, 1960

Alex shuddered when he got off the plane in Palung. It was in the remote northwestern plains of China. The hills were brown and barren looking. Except for the city, the rest of the countryside seemed to have been forgotten by Mother Nature. There was not an ounce of breeze. It was very hot, arid. Almost desert. He was dressed in a cotton quilted uniform which he wanted to take off immediately as he broke out in a sweat. He looked around and wondered what he was doing here.

Alex was made to stand in the hot sun and wait for whatever it was they had planned for him. He could not take off his coat. He could not sit. He had to just stand there. It was an eerie quiet. No one said anything. The soldiers guarding him stood under the wing of the plane in the shade.

About an hour later he saw a strange sight. An old man prodding an oxen that pulled a wooden-wheeled cart was coming across the tarmac toward them. The cart had a crude, handmade cage on top of the bed. This strange procession moved closer and closer. Still no one spoke. Finally, the old man stopped the oxen not far from the plane. He took off his round 'coolie' hat and waited.

Colonel Liang emerged from the plane, came down the steps and walked over to the old man. They talked, but Alex couldn't hear what they were saying. The old man nodded several times. They walked over to the cage on the cart and the old man pointed at several things. Colonel Liang nodded. Then he turned and walked over to Alex. "Please remove your clothes," he said politely.

Alex gladly took of his coat. "Everything, Mr. Hunter," Colonel Liang said.

Alex looked at him. What a strange request. "Everything?"

"Everything. Do it now or I will have my soldiers 'help' you."

Alex didn't like the looks of any of the soldiers. They were not as well dressed as the other's he'd seen, and seemed to be sort of motley. They watched him, and he felt their anger. He decided to do as told, and he stripped. The tarmac was hot on his bare feet. He started to dance around when two of the soldiers grabbed him and dragged him to the cart. The cage looked like the cages wild animals were paraded in for the circuses. One of the soldiers put handcuffs on one of his wrists while the other climbed into the cage. A third soldier with a bayonet on the end of his rifle, prodded Alex to climb into the cage. Once in, the soldier raised his arms up and clasped the other handcuff on his other wrist but only after it was put over one of the bars on the top of the cage. Alex almost had to stand on his tip toes while his hands were cuffed. Afterward, he could stand, but very uncomfortably. Colonel Liang told the driver to go, and the wagon started up. Alex was caught off-balance and his feet slipped out from under him. The handcuffs tore into the flesh on his wrists. He winced in pain. Colonel Liang and another officer got into an army staff car and followed. The soldiers lined up on both sides of the cart and walked alongside.

Colonel Liang had done a good job of preparing the people of Palung. They were lined up all along the streets of the city screaming and shouting as the cart slowly wobbled along. Banners and slogans written on the walls proclaimed that the man in the cage was a "foreign devil" who had come to China and tried to assassinate Chairman Mao. The people hated him. As the cart was pulled slowly along the streets, the people ran along side the cage and spat on him, mocked him, and jeered him. There was no place to hide from the stares and jeers of the people as they paraded by him. He was an animal in a cage.

For nearly an hour the odd procession ambled along various streets of the city. The crowds chanted "Kill Him! Show Him No Mercy!". Alex was covered with spittle, embarrassed, angry and really afraid the crowd was going to lynch him.

At last, the cage was pulled into a large auditorium and parked right in the middle of the empty room. The crowd followed and kept on chanting and cursing him. The oxen were unhitched from the cart, and guards were posted at each corner of the cage. The room shuddered with the sheer volume of the curses and yelling mob. Colonel Liang's car pulled alongside the cart. He got out and using a bullhorn, he told the people to leave the auditorium. When they had gone, the two officers drove away and the door to the outside was shut. The guards sat down and talked.

Late that night, a doctor and a nurse came into the auditorium and checked him. He was given some medicine, a drink of water and the first food he had had since before he left Tsingtao. He was left hanging by his cuffs all during the examination and feeding. No one spoke to him. After the examination was over, one of the soldiers climbed into the cage, removed his cuffs and left. This examination was to become a part of his daily routine.

The next morning, Alex was handcuffed to the cage. The driver led the cart out of the auditorium and on to the road. Thus began Alex's two month existence as an animal in a zoo.

At first, Alex tried to keep himself mentally alert by thinking of any and everything he could that took his mind off the situation. He sang songs, repeated prayers, and poems he had learned as a child. Mentally he played hundreds of rounds of golf on his home course in Indiana, did math problems, counted the 82 bars in his cage over and over, counted the lights in the room, the doors, the people, memorized faces of the people who came to see him and gave them names and ages.

After a month of doing this nearly twenty hours a day, Alex grew tired of the mental games and began to have periods of blank thoughts. Two weeks later, he was in a perpetual daze. The people jeering him, their voices and sounds melted into a blur. His vision became poor, and he lost control of the muscles in his legs for long periods of time. The pain of the sores caused by the exposure and the sticks and stones became so intense from time to time that he blacked out. People began bringing him food during the second month so he would do tricks for scraps of meat and peanuts. He no longer could talk in coherent sentences or think about any one thing for longer than a minute. He was truly a broken man.

All during this time, no one engaged in conversation with him nor answered his questions nor paid heed to his pleading. By the end of the two months, he was a physical as well as a mental wreck. He couldn't think straight even at night. All the administering by the doctor each night managed to do was keep him alive and free from infection otherwise he was cut, bruised, and was covered by sores. He had gone through dysentery attacks, the chills and fever of the flu, and at one time, had to be treated for a circulation problem in his shoulders because his hands were handcuffed above him when he was in the cage on parade. In the second month, during the treatment for his shoulder his hands were finally untied, but by that time any instincts he had for covering himself up in public were gone. His fingers were numb, and he couldn't use them for a week. Just when he was getting used to using his hands again, he was retied.

Nearly 45 days after he had gotten off the plane, in a small town, Alex was taken to a large stone building and made to crawl down a long corridor. People lined the hallway laughing, and kicking him. He was stopped before a door. Two soldiers yanked him from the floor and made him stand. The door opened, and he saw Madam Ying. She was tied to a chair. She looked old and tired. She stared at Alex and bowed her head. Suddenly, a shot rang out. Her head snapped back revealing a face which was a blur of blood. She slumped over. For her a swift end had come. Alex blacked out.

Each night thereafter, in his dreams, he saw Madam Ying being shot again and again. He always awoke and found himself screaming at the top of his tired lungs. No one paid attention to him.

On a hot, humid August day, a week later, peasants planting rice stalks in the stifling heat of the day stopped their work to stare at the odd procession slowly moving up the old road to their village. In the front, an old cart with wooden wheels, pulled by an ox waddled up the old road. Atop the cart, in a crude bamboo cage Alex, naked with his hands handcuffed to the top of the cage, dangled and swung freely as the cart bounced around in the deep, timeworn ruts of the road.

The ox cart driver shuffled barefoot alongside the cart and occasionally flicked the ox with a long bamboo pole to keep it moving. He paid no attention to the man in the cage.

Beside the cart, on each side, three Chinese soldiers, their rifles slung over their shoulders, plodded listlessly along. Their boots stirred up small whiffs of dust. Their Sergeant trailed behind the cart. His burp gun was slung over his shoulder, and he squinted over the top of his wire rimmed glasses. Behind him, an olive-drab 1940 American-made Packard sedan with a red star painted on each of the front doors trailed the procession and bounced along in and out of the ruts. Inside the car, a stocky, rather bloated looking Chinese Colonel squirmed in the back seat of the car each time the car jolted back and forth as if he could never get comfortable. His thin, lanky aide, a Captain, sat beside the Colonel and stoically peered at the vast countryside of the rolling hills around them. The car's driver fought to keep control of the car as it veered from side to side.

Alex's hair was matted, his wrists were caked with dried blood, and his eyes were red and swollen. He had not been shaved since the ordeal began. He tried to see the ruts coming ahead in the road and brace for them, but he was simply too weak. Because his hands were cuffed to the roof of the cage, he could neither sit nor kneel. As long as he stood upright, the handcuffs attached to the roof of the cage didn't cut into his wrists, but if he slipped or began to pass out, the rough edges of the cuffs ground against his wrist bones and sent tremendous pain cascading down his arms and into his already beaten and bruised body. His lips were parched, and he was in great pain, not only from the sores on his wrists, but from the many bruises and lacerations on his sun burnt body. He winced with pain every time the cart ricocheted off a deep rut. His mind understood why he had to be alert and try to stay on his feet, but the exhaustion combined with the pain wouldn't let his body do as his brain said. Alex tried to think about something, anything, but his agony was too severe.

Whenever the cart crossed over a particularly rough spot in the dirt road, Alex would lose his balance, or slip on his own sweat or blood and would hang by his hands until he managed to get his feet back under him and stand again. But, from time to time, he simply could not get to his feet, and the more he struggled, the more the pain grew until he passed out.

Each time he passed out, the Sergeant yelled at the ox driver to stop. He ordered one of the soldiers to prod the man and determine whether or not he was faking. If he decided Alex was not faking, the Sergeant made two soldiers in the squad run to the back of the car and draw a bucket of water from the water barrel tied to the trunk. The soldiers doused the man in the cage. The shock of the water usually would arouse him. If it didn't, they would pour more water on him until he was conscious. Then the procession would continue.

This procession slogged its way through the sparsely populated back country of Shensi Province. The soldiers longed to come to a village where they could rest. On this day, as the cart topped a ridge, the soldier's smiled. In the distance was a village at the top of a ridge. They began talking and chattering as their spirits rose. They wanted the cart to go faster and urged the driver to whip the ox. The old man tried, and the cart sped up only to fall into a very rough section of the road. Alex screamed with pain as time after time he slipped and lost his footing. The soldiers laughed at him and prodded the ox driver to go even faster. The soldiers' high spirits climbed higher only to be dashed when the man passed out again. The procession stopped. The reawakening routine began again, but after three buckets of water were poured on the man, he was still unconscious.

The officers in the car watched as the soldiers poured more and more water on the man hanging limply by his wrists. When the man failed to respond, the Captain got out of the car, walked to the cage and looked at the man. He reached in, grabbed Alex's leg, shook it violently and screamed at him to stand up. Alex's body jerked involuntarily. The Captain repeated the procedure twice more. The captive stirred and opened his eyes. The Captain didn't say another word but just stared at the man.

Slowly, in extreme pain, Alex managed to stand again. He looked down at the Captain. He wanted to kill him and everyone in sight.

The Captain looked the man over carefully, assessed his condition, turned and walked back to the car. Before he got in, he commanded the procession to continue.

The Colonel moved over to allow room for his aide to get in. "And? Doctor?"

"He can survive one more stop," the Captain said.

Two hours later, the cart stopped in the square in the center of the village. The two hundred curious people of the village immediately surrounded the cart and peered in at the man hanging by his wrists. He tried to stand and slipped a few times before he regained his footing. The villagers began shouting and taunting him. They spat on him, threw rocks at him, poked him with sticks and called him vile names. He wanted to yell back at them, but he had no energy.

Alex was taken out of the cage and paraded down the main street with a chain around his neck like a dog. Women jeered him and made fun of his private parts and hurting them. They threw water on him and pretended to bathe him. The bathing was a real crowd pleaser.

The Colonel and the doctor got out of the car after about twenty minutes of observing this behavior. The soldiers put Alex back in his cage. As the officers approached the main square, the soldiers immediately made a path for them to the front of the cart. The villagers scampered out of the way.

When the Colonel held up his hands, the crowd immediately fell silent. He took off his high-peaked hat, wiped the sweatband with his handkerchief, and put it back on. The Colonel waited until he had the complete attention of every person in the village square. His small black eyes scanned the faces of the villagers to make sure they all were watching him. When the villagers made eye contact with the Colonel, shivers of fear trickled down their backs.

"Comrades," the Colonel began in a high-pitched, singsong voice, "this foreign devil snuck into our country to destroy our way of life. He is our enemy, as are all foreigners who come to China." He spoke slowly, in a crisp Mandarin dialect, and weighed the villagers' reactions as he parroted the party line. "We brought him to your village so you could see one of our enemies for yourselves. We also wanted you to see what happens to our enemies when they are caught. And I assure you, all enemies of the state are eventually caught."

Alex pretended to be unconscious, but he actually listened very carefully. Through a haze of pain and exhaustion, he interpreted every word into English.

"We will not execute this man, because as Chairman Mao says, most men are good inside. If they stray, it is up to the people to set them back on the right path. We believe this man can be reeducated and possibly become useful to the state. If not, of course, he will die. We will rest in your village. Make places for my men among you. Return to your homes."

The crowd quickly dispersed. Many of the villagers looked back at the man in the cage, shook their fists in anger, and kept on going.

The Captain ordered the soldiers to get the man out of the cage, wash him, and put him on a stretcher.

When he heard the Captain's orders, Alex whispered a quiet, "Thank you, God," and passed out.

Alex was tied to a stretcher and carried to a waiting plane. He saw little and eventually passed out. He didn't remember the plane trip at all.

CHAPTER TWENTY-FIVE

Four Miles Outside Wuwei, China, September 15, 1960

Alex awoke on a hard bed. His hands weren't tied, and there was a clean sheet over him. He sat up and began to focus his eyes. He was in a small room with no windows - only a bare light bulb dimly lit the room. He was dressed in loose-fitting clothes and his wounds and sores were treated. There was a wash basin and a commode in one corner of the room, and a small table with a writing pen and paper up was pushed up against the wall across from the bed. He felt his face. He had been shaved, and the hair on his head was shaved off. There was no sound at all in the room. He moved his fingers and arms. They ached tremendously. Alex did not know how long he had been there, but he knew he was very hungry and very thirsty. His lips were cracked from thirst. He noticed a pitcher and a cup on the table.

It took all the energy he could muster to crawl out of the bed across the concrete floor to the table and pull himself up into the chair. He looked into the pitcher and saw it was filled with water. He tried to lift the pitcher to pour the water but it was too heavy and his hands too numb. He cried. Then slowly he came out of his hysterics and began to think. He reached for the tin cup and hooked his finger in the handle and in a very shaky motion managed to dip the cup in the pitcher and get some water in the cup. Twice he spilled the water getting it to his lips leaving only a few drops to drink but finally, mustering up all the concentration he could, he managed to get a half a cup of water to his lips and he drank it in one gulp. Almost immediately he felt a sharp pain in his stomach. He fell off the chair with a cramp writhing in pain. "You stupid bastard," he said to himself, "drink slowly, drink slowly, think, think!" The pain slowly subsided and he began to sip the water. His body began to accept the water and he felt better. His eyes cleared somewhat and he could feel the chair on his bottom. His circulation improved by the minute until he could move his fingers and toes without too much pain. He was tired. Very tired. He hobbled over to the bed and sat down. He breathed a long sigh and toppled over. He was asleep before his head hit the pillow.

Over the next few days, Alex began to get better physically. A doctor came into his room each day and changed his bandages, checked his heartbeat and his eyes, ears, nose, and throat. The doctor never spoke, just jotted down a few notes and left.

Alex regained full use of his hands and legs. He was fed good food three times a day. He began to put on some of the weight he'd lost, and after two weeks he began an exercise regimen of sit ups and push ups. As he recovered, he thought about his ordeal in the cage. He was amazed at all the punishment his body had been able to withstand.

A piece of paper was slipped under his door a few days later. It was written in English and contained a list of instructions for keeping his cell clean, his daily hygiene, and how to return his dishes. Still no one had spoken to him. The only sounds he heard were when the food was delivered and when the doctor came by for his visits.

He could think more clearly now. He read his instructions about keeping the room clean and obeyed them to the letter, as much for his own comfort as to do their will. Then the doctor stopped coming. For the next few days the silence was deafening. He was beginning to get jittery - eager to hear a sound or to talk to someone. He sang to himself and talked out loud. He paced. He knew this was a form of brainwashing, but he didn't know how to combat the feeling of utter loneliness.

One day as he was reciting a poem, he stopped in front of the table and looked down at the writing paper and pen. He sat down and wrote out the poem and other thoughts that came to mind. That night he was awakened when a soldier came into his room removed the paper, and restocked the supply. The soldier left silently refusing to answer any of Alex's questions. Alex decided he wasn't going to do that again.

Since he now felt physically better, Alex's main problem was to keep control of his mind. He did physical exercises and talked to himself. He made up conversations anything to stay mentally alert, but one day he noticed something that scared him very much. At the sound of the slot being opened for his food tray, he began to salivate. He was being trained, even against his will, he was being trained. A cold chill went down his spine. Try as he might, from that time on, he could not stop the involuntary secretion of saliva at the sound of the slot being opened.

Alex had no way of knowing how long he'd been in the room, but it had been nearly three months. He found mental concentration becoming increasingly difficult. He often blanked out in the middle of a poem or prayer. He would shake himself and curse himself, but it happened over and over again. One day, in utter frustration he sat down at the table and took up the pen and tried to make a crossword puzzle. He couldn't. He couldn't write anything. He stared at the blank paper for a long time, then wrote 'Oh God, help me'. He looked at the words on the paper and picked up the paper and carried it around with him as he paced the room. Periodically, he glance at the words. After a long time, he went back to the table and wrote the first line of a poem he'd remembered as a child -'On the eighteenth of April in '75, hardly a man is now alive'. He stared at the words and remembered the rest and wrote it. Then another thought came to him and he began to write enthusiastically. He would write for a while, then get up and pace around the room and read what he'd written over and over. Afterward, he sat down and wrote more. Every so often, he'd wake in the morning to find his writings gone and a new supply of paper in its stead. He wondered why they took his writing, but of course, had no way of finding out.

One day, when he was writing, he thought he heard voices. He strained to listen. Sure enough he could hear voices, he couldn't quite make what they were saying but he knew he heard voices. Voices in English. All day long and for the next few days he strained to hear. He was getting very edgy now because the voices were continuous. He wanted to hear what they were saying. He cried out many times "Louder, louder, speak louder!" Still he could not comprehend what was being said. Then one day he caught a few words. Was it his imagination or were the voices louder that day? He began to write down the words he could understand. "Mistakes," "Selfishness"? "Errors." "Conceit," "Oppress", these words seemed to be clear while the others garbled. The words were repeated in sentences over and over again. They began to sink into his mind. He began to think now only about these words and how they related to him.

After a few days of hearing the voices, he heard a different voice saying different words and now and then phrases. As he strained to listen, the words became clearer in addition to the ones he first heard. Now it was easier to make out the words - "Your past was misguided," and "You cheated others," and "Your enemy was justice." Alex was frustrated because he could hear sounds in between these words but he couldn't make them out. What were they saying? What do they mean? He found himself writing down the words and phrases and posing questions beside them. Then he began relating them to himself, what mistakes did I make? who is oppressed? what is true justice? what about my past? He knew this tactic, too, was a technique of brainwashing, but he didn't care.

The day came when he first understood full sentences. They were his own questions being repeated back to him. They were using his own words to tantalize him. He found them monotonous. At first he couldn't sleep as the voice, in a monotone, droned his questions back to him. He spent many long sleepless hours. But in time, he dropped off to sleep with the sound of his own thoughts fading in his mind.

Soon the voice became as wearing on him as the silence had been, and he longed for quiet. The volume grew just a little louder every few days, and the dull, monotonous voice repeated the same questions over and over. It was driving him crazy. He couldn't think; all he could hear was the voice droning on and on. And there was the sound of the slot being opened to pass him food. He accepted his salivation and forgot about it.

Finally, the voice became so loud that he began shouting, shouting anything that came into his mind, but nothing he did would stop the voice. He held his ears, he buried his head beneath the covers but nothing could stop the pounding voice. He found himself screaming at the top of his voice "Stop it! Stop it! I can't think!" His food intake dropped off sharply; his stomach was tied up in knots. His throat was raw from his own shouting. He couldn't sleep. He was reduced to a sobbing shell of a man sitting in one corner of the room with all the blankets and even the mattress coiled around his head trying to keep out the sound. But the volume of the voice was too high, and he could still hear. At last he threw off the things around his head and just curled up in the corner and sobbed.

As quickly as it began, it stopped. The voice stopped. For two days the voice still rang in Alex's ears, but as the days passed, he slowly began to regain his sanity. Just when he thought he had gotten rid of the voice, he would hear it again repeating his questions, his thoughts. "What mistakes did I make?" "Who is oppressed?" "What is justice?"

The questions made him think about his life, his homeland, his family, his mission, in fact, he became obsessed with the questions. He said them out loud, he dreamed about them, he wrote them over and over as well as various answers he made up to them. The voice came and went sporadically. Alex was almost always caught off-guard.

Then two weeks passed without the voice. It was quiet. Very quiet. Alex became wary and for a while couldn't sleep, but as the days passed, he calmed down. He found himself yearning for fresh air, sunlight, the outdoors. He began to be claustrophobic. His heart raced, he was nervous, he couldn't sit or lie down for more than a few minutes even seconds. He paced wildly around the room and began his screaming again. He didn't know how long this lasted, but one day another voice was piped into the room. This time the voice had a more pleasant tone. The sentences were delivered in a sympathetic tone of voice. It was a fairly short speech which was repeated about every five minutes.

"Alex, this is a very important time in your life, and you are one of the few people in the world who have the time to reflect upon it and make good use of it. You have asked yourself many questions that only you have the answers to. To become a better person to yourself and all others whom you come into contact with, you should answer yourself. Be truthful and honest. Think over the questions and, if you like, write the answers down. It will be helpful to you if you write the answers down because we can help you, but only if we know what you are thinking. The first question you have asked yourself should be, what mistakes have I made in my life?" Think about that. Answer yourself. Look deeply into your life and find the honest answers. What mistakes have I made in my life?"

The voice stopped. Alex thought, not about the question, but why? Why? Why are they asking me to do this? It must be an advanced technique in brainwashing he decided. I can't let them get to me. I won't do what they ask, I won't let them use me. Alex tried to get the question off his mind. He thought about his mission, his family, anything to keep from thinking about the question. Five minutes later the voice came on again. "Alex, you must try to help yourself. Think about the question. Make a list. What mistakes did you make in your life?" Then silence. This routine continued for several days. Alex fought hard not to think about the question, but the voice interrupted at five minute intervals all day long, and all night long. The question was being burned into his mind, and he knew it, but he fought to suppress it. Always the same question. On the fourth day, Alex found himself at the table writing, not answers to the question but anything, to keep his mind active. All the time he wrote, the voice was silent, but whenever he stopped writing, the voice again pleaded with him to answer the question.

231

He wrote anything to stop the voice. He wrote down the Lord's Prayer, math problems, nursery rhymes, all the specifications on his plane, contracts for the sale of houses, anything to keep from hearing the voice. Try as he might, however, about a week later, he began to see his stream of consciousness appear on the paper, "I mustn't write about my mistakes, I must control myself, I can't let them get to me about my mistakes." When he first saw the word "mistake" on paper he broke out in a cold sweat, his hands began to tremble. He tore the paper up.

Periodically, usually when he was asleep, a guard would come in and take all of his writings and leave a fresh stack of paper on the table and newly sharpened pencils.

Three weeks passed by with the voice asking him to write about his own question when Alex finally began to write about what they were telling him to write about. At first, the mistakes he wrote about concerned the mission and his life in China including being responsible for the death of Madam Ying and the driver and Lan Yin, then he drifted off into the past. He wrote about his childhood, his life in the service, his business his family.

As the papers were taken from him and examined by an unknown someone, the voice became more specific about what he was to write down next; always in the context of the original question. They urged him to write about his family, his friends, the schools he attended, his life in the service, his politics, his beliefs.

The voice now did not begin whenever he stopped; it seemed to allow him time to think.

For nearly five months Alex sat in this small room, writing, documenting his thoughts, his history, and his belief. The voice now became a friend, pointing out what he had not covered, urging him to examine more deeply such things as his religious beliefs, his political beliefs, his government, his country. There were no lectures as such, just endless questions. As the months wore on there were more and more questions about his motivations, his drives, why had he come to China, why did he feel it was the right thing to do, what did he feel he had accomplished by getting Walters out of the country, who did he think benefitted from this action. Probing, always probing.

At the end of the five months, one morning, just after he had shaved and eaten breakfast, the door opened. He just watched, expecting the guard to change the paper on the desk and take out the tray of dirty dishes, but the guard motioned to him to come with him. Alex was very wary. Were they through with him? Were they going to kill him? He knew he was getting dry of thoughts. He had not written much for the past few days. The guard did not say anything to him just motioned to him. Alex drew back into a corner. The guard patiently waited. The guard wore no gun. He just motioned to Alex. Then another guard appeared at the door, and Alex gave a big sigh. He was trapped. He knew he would have to go with them. He didn't want to be beaten or put through any more pain, but he had no choice. Shaking with fright, doubts and anxiety Alex slowly walked to the door. The guard motioned for him to follow. They walked down a long corridor with many doors just like his with slots for food trays. He wondered who was behind these doors. Then they came to a door, and the guard opened it. The bright sunlight, which Alex hadn't seen in nearly eight months, blinded him. He squinted and covered his eyes. Tears welling up in them from the light. There was a warm breeze coming in the door - fresh air. He took a deep breath. The fresh air hurt his lungs. He coughed. Then the guard stepped aside and motioned for Alex to go on out the door. Alex looked at both the guards trying to see if there was something in their expressions that would tell him what he was about to face, but their expressions were blank.

Alex hesitated, then with a deep resolve to face what was out there, he slowly walked to the door. Now his eyes had adjusted to the sunlight and he could see grass and it was a courtyard. There was a concrete walkway and a well manicured flower garden in the center of the courtyard. He stepped out into the sunlight and felt it's warmth on his face. The door closed behind him and he was alone. He examined the courtyard. It seemed to be built in the middle of a large building complex. The walls were about two stories high and he could see the edges of the red tile roofs hanging down from all sides. There were no windows facing onto the yard. Just four doors, one to each building. All were solid steel. Then he was distracted by a sound high above him. It was a pigeon landing on a roof. In the middle of the courtyard which was about one hundred feet square stood a large tree with a bench beneath it. Alex began to walk. He had been confined to such a small space for so long he quickly grew tired, and he sat down on the bench. Then he walked some more. After a while the door opened again, and he was beckoned back to his cell. His exercise period was over. When he got back to the cell, he found a snack waiting for him - fruit and a chocolate bar. He savored each bite. Then the voice began:

"Well, Alex, I trust you enjoyed your first taste of freedom. It is nice isn't it? I feel I should tell you that you have earned this privilege by your cooperation. Now we want you to sit down at your desk and write us your life story once again. When you have finished, and we have read it, you will be notified as to its worth."

Alex was made to write his life story twelve times, each time he was criticized about the shortcomings of the one before. "Alex, we believe this last draft you gave us is far superior to the ones before it. Congratulations. You have just entered into phase one of your new life."

Alex felt strangely satisfied. He caught himself feeling this way and inwardly chided himself. But there was no doubt about it, he knew he was being controlled. "Now Alex, in order to progress into phase two, you must begin to learn about real life. Take your pencil and write down these words, "Even if we achieve gigantic successes in our work, there is no reason whatsoever to feel conceited and arrogant. Modesty helps one to go forward, whereas conceit makes one lag behind. This is a truth we must always bear in mind." There was a pause then the voice said, "I shall repeat this lesson."

The voice repeated the saying over and over until Alex had written it all down. Then another voice came on. This time a woman's. She repeated the quotation from Mao once every five minutes for the entire day. He was asked to write it down again and again. He did so as she repeated it slowly.

The next morning the door again opened, and again he went for his exercise period. When he returned, he found only blank paper. He was asked to write down the quotation, and hand it through the slot to the guard. He wrote down as much as he could remember. He handed it out. He waited and then it was passed back to him with corrections in spelling and punctuation and noting all the missing words. The woman again began to repeat the quotation all day long. He wrote it down. He went out for his exercise the next morning, took the test afterward and passed. A new quotation was begun and the routine of learning went on for three more months with surprise quizzes on quotes learned a long time ago until at the end of the three months he knew each of the quotations he had been asked to memorize by heart. His re-education was progressing well.

CHAPTER TWENTY-SIX

Diren Shou Fa Prison, Wuwei, China, March 1962

It had been nearly two years since Alex entered the reeducation center in Wuwei, China. He had been interrogated, educated, and analyzed a hundred times during this period. He was resigned that he would remain there for the rest of his life.

Alex was eagerly looking forward to his exercise period. He put on his heavy coat, which he had been given to combat the cold winds of winter, and stood by the door waiting for the guard to motion him out to the courtyard. The door opened, but instead of the guard standing there, it was Colonel Wang.

"Hello Alex," the Colonel said.

Alex was dumbfounded. These were the first words spoken directly to him in Almost two years. He didn't know what to say. He just stood there. His heart began beating faster and faster and he felt a wash happiness slid through his body. Wild thoughts of human contact and conversation began racing through his head. He felt giddy. Just as he was about to speak, another man, dressed as a worker with a chubby face, and a half-smile stepped up beside the Colonel.

"Alex? Aren't you going to say hello to Colonel Wang?" the man said in perfect English.

Alex immediately recognized the man's voice. It was the same voice he had heard too many times before over the loudspeaker in his cell. Alex tried to speak but the words stuck in his throat.

"Alex?"

Finally, after a few more seconds of staring at the men, Alex managed to say hello. He had tears in his eyes. He stood there shaken and trembling. His first communication after such a long time with another human being was unnerving. His mind, dulled by the months of rote learning and solitude, wasn't responding as he knew it should. He couldn't find the thoughts or the words to say, to start a conversation.

The two Chinese just stared at Alex - evaluating him. After a long time, or so it seemed to Alex, Colonel Wang spoke. "Mr. Hunter, Comrade Su An Chi happily informed me the other day that he felt this phase of your training had been successfully completed, and he felt you were ready to take on additional responsibilities. Would you like that?"

Alex couldn't think of what to say. He was afraid that what he might say would be wrong and they would send him back into that cell again, and no one would speak to him for another year. He tried to think of what to say. His mind was clear, he wanted to say "yes," but he didn't know if that was the right answer.

Neither the Colonel nor Comrade Su An Chi pressed Alex for an answer. They had been through this many times before. They knew that the best indicator of whether or not a subject was responding favorably to the retraining was to watch his eyes.

Finally Alex raised his head and looked them in the eyes and said, "Yes, yes, Colonel, I believe that I can rejoin the people, I have so much to learn."

Without hesitation Colonel Wang walked to him and nodded, "I, too, believe you are ready. Come with us.".

Alex walked beside the two men as they went down the long hall and out into the courtyard. They walked briskly across the courtyard toward the door directly opposite the one Alex had been coming out of for such a long time. He had always wondered what was behind that door. Near the door was a large tree. They directed Alex to the base of the tree. They stopped. Comrade Su An Chi spoke softly, "Alex, you are like this tree. This tree symbolizes your life. Like you, it was replanted. It had to adjust to a new environment. You, now, are just beginning a new, long and difficult journey to understand your new environment. Your learning has progressed and you have been re-planted so to speak. Now you must put down new roots. But you must always remember, as Chairman Mao has said so often, 'In times of difficulty, we must not lose sight of our achievements, must see the bright future and must pick up our courage'. You have achieved a very important first step. Do not let the next step be a strong wind which uproots your progress."

Alex looked at the twisted old tree for a moment. There was a hint of a smile as he pondered the advice. They led him to the door. He followed the men in the doorway and down another long corridor. They stopped in front of the door. Alex's nerves were tingling and his breath was coming in short pants. Colonel Wang opened the door. Alex stopped in the doorway and surveyed the room. There were four other men in the room, two were Chinese, one Asian, from where he did not know, and the other was Indian. The four sat in chairs in a semi-circle facing a blackboard. There were six chairs. The one in the middle and the one farthest from the door were empty. Comrade Su An Chi motioned Alex to sit in the chair farthest from the door. Colonel Wang said his goodbyes to Comrade Su An Chi and left closing the door behind him. Alex looked around. The room was small, maybe twelve foot by twelve foot. Two small windows, about chin high for him, were to his back. On the wall to his left several maps seemed to be pasted to dull green plaster. In front of him was a large blackboard and above it, the ever-present picture of Chairman Mao.

"Comrades," Su An Chi began speaking in precise Mandarin Chinese, as he crossed to the empty chair in the middle and sat down, "Today marks a step forward in your lives. Today you will begin your most important journey - your journey to understanding and knowledge. This journey is long and difficult, but it is rewarding." Su An Chi rose and walked over to Alex and motioned for him to stand. "This is Comrade Hunter. He is an American. Of his own will he chose to enter China on a mission to destroy our way of life. In the old days before Chairman Mao rose from the fields to lead us, he would have been put to death instantly. But our Chairman has led us wisely and shown us the way of education. He has taught us that our enemies can become our allies if we are patient, and give them the proper guidance. Comrade Hunter has shown us that he can be taught because he is an intelligent, resourceful, and practical man. Each of you possesses these qualities." He motioned for Alex to sit.

Su An Chi stopped in front of each of the other "students." The first was a Chinese man, Li Fung Cho, about thirty, wearing glasses and sitting very erect. His eyes were close together and very narrow. Su An Chi described this man as a professor at Peking University who had been found guilty of expressing ideas counter to the thoughts of Mao. Next was the Indian man, Namu Jandi, a thin, gaunt man who wore steel-rimmed glasses. He was an officer in the Indian Army and had been taken prisoner during the brief border war a year ago. The small Chinaman seated next to the empty chair was Shen Ti-Lyou, an atomic physicist who had defected from the United States several years ago and was working on many projects for the government when he was caught trying to send a coded letter to his cousin in Hong Kong. Finally, there was Hok Du San, a Filipino, who had asked for political asylum while he was visiting China. He was an economist from Manila. Each, Su An Chi pointed out, had been through the initial stages of "training" and had satisfactorily performed. Now they were gathered here together in one classroom to absorb and learn to apply the thoughts of Mao and the Chinese Communist doctrines.

Su walked to a table in the back of the room and picked up five copies of the small red book, Quotations of Chairman Mao, and handed each one of the students a copy. While Su An Chi spoke only in Chinese, Alex noted that his copy of the "Quotations" was in English. The stoic Chinese man, Chiang Po-Li, next to him got a copy in Chinese and so forth.

"This book will guide you through your training," Su said, "and by the time you have completed this course you will know and understand every passage in the book and be able to apply the Chairman's ideas to any situation. You must keep this with you at all times and study it carefully each time you have a free moment." Su then walked back to the table and picked up another stack of books and passed them out. They were copies of Karl Marx's Das Kapital.

"The force at the core, leading our cause forward is the Chinese Communist Party. The theoretical basis guiding our thinking is Marxism-Leninism. To understand our philosophy and actions you should first understand the basis. Therefore, you will read this book first, and we shall discuss it. Then you will read other books by Marx and Lenin until you fully understand their thinking. Then and only then will you understand how perfect are the thoughts of Chairman Mao."

Alex opened the red book of Mao's quotations and read the first quotation - "The force at the core leading our cause forward is the Chinese Communist Party. The theoretical basis guiding our thinking is Marxism-Leninism." A cold chill went down his back.

Su watched him as he read. Alex felt Su's eyes on him and looked up, "Yes, Comrade Hunter, I have already aptly applied the thinking of our leader." Su then took his seat and opened Karl Marx's book to the first page. "Now we shall all read together at a slow pace. Whenever you have a question or don't understand something, speak up. Do not be afraid to disagree, you will learn soon enough that Chairman Mao does not agree with all that is said in this book. The books were in Chinese and each person read the translation.

By the end of the first day, they had covered only three pages of the book and no one had questioned anything. They had been together in the room for nearly eight hours without speaking to one another. Alex could envision many months of classroom study without anyone talking except Comrade Su.

Comrade Su closed his book after properly marking his place and stood up.

"Please forgive me comrades, I have completely forgotten myself. I know you must all be very hungry and tired. Let us enjoy our meal." He motioned for all of them to follow. They went down the hall to a dining room set with three or four tables. One was set for six and, they were instructed to sit wherever they liked. Comrade Su at the head of the table and Alex at the foot. "You have all been very quiet today, and that is understandable for it is the first day for each of you, but I don't want you to think you are required to sit in silence. You may talk to each other at any time you wish."

They all sat there in silence for a while and Alex knew that all of them had been through a the same treatment - the period of silence. Each looked as if they wanted to speak, but were afraid. Alex felt the same way.

"Tell me Comrade Hunter," Comrade Su's voice cut through the silence, "Which state in America were you born?"

Alex was startled but recovered, "Indiana."

"Ah, as I remember my geography that is near the center of the United States is it not?"

"Yes. East a bit from the center."

They all sat in silence again. Comrade Su looked around the table then said, "Do any of you have any questions for Comrade Hunter about America or his home?"

The students lowered their eyes and gazed at the floor. Silence.

"Come now," Su An Chi chided, "surely someone is curious."

Jandi cleared his throat and haltingly asked, "Are there many starving people where you come from, Comrade Hunter?"

"No," Alex said too quickly, and he caught himself. "Well, I don't know of any."

"Then you must have been very rich," Professor Li Fung Cho murmured.

Alex smiled at the absurdity of the comment. "I think you have a lot to learn about the United States, Comrade."

"Tell us about your country, Comrade," Su spoke up, "and feel free to say what you truly feel, not, what you think we might want to hear. This time is as valuable as our classroom studies."

Alex began to talk about his home, his life and thus began a long conversation that lasted during the entire meal of rice, some kind of bean curd, and a tasty cream-like dish. He was interrupted from time to time by each person at the table with questions and comments. By the end of the evening, everyone was noticeably more relaxed.

After two hours, Comrade Su decided that they had had enough for one day. He led each one back to his individual cell, and locked the doors.

The "normal" routine was set the next day: breakfast and inspection of their living quarters early in the morning, then four hours of classroom study, one hour for lunch and conversation, four more hours of study, two hours for dinner and then another two hours of informal discussion and to bed. At the end of the first month the four hour study periods were broken up by half hour exercise periods where they learned the ancient Chinese Tai Chi.

Two months later, they were expected to have done their exercises before breakfast. The exercise period remained, however, except that now they were organized, the "students" could walk and talk freely under the watchful eye of Su An Chi.

Alex figured it took them thirty nine days to read through and discuss Karl Marx, another 49 days for Lenin, and then began the works of Chairman Mao.

"The application of the sayings of Chairman Mao is as important as learning the sayings themselves," Su began, "and I believe for this group there is a quotation quite appropriate to begin with, it is in Article 21, the last quotation. He began to read. "There is an ancient Chinese fable called the Foolish Old Man. It tells of an old man who lived in Northern China long, long ago and was known as the Foolish Old Man of North Mountain. His house faced south and beyond his doorway stood the two great peaks, Taidwo Shan and Wangwu Shan. These mountains obstructed his view of the sea. He had always wanted to sit on his porch and look out at the sea.

"One day. with great determination, he led his sons up the Taidwo Shan mountain and they began to dig away at the top of it to make it smaller. Another *lau tor* (old head), known as the Wise Old Man, saw them and said derisively, 'How silly of you to do this. It is quite impossible for you few to tear down these two mountains. You will never see the sea.' "

"The Foolish Old Man replied, 'Perhaps. But when I die, my sons will carry on; when they die, there will be my grandsons, and then their sons and grandsons, and so on. High as they are, these mountains cannot grow any higher and with every bit we dig they will be that much lower. One day one of my ancestors will sit on my porch and he will look out at the sea."

"Why did Chairman Mao include this story? To teach us many things. That time and patience can conquer even the most difficult task if we persevere. It teaches us that our goals can help others. It teaches us that we must not listen to those who detract from our goals for they are often wrong. And it teaches us that while one man may not be able to achieve his goal, by working with others the goal can be accomplished."

"I have chosen this work to begin our study for two reasons. One, to demonstrate that all tasks are simple in the long run. Your task of grasping the Chairman's way of living is a long and difficult task. It will take much time and perseverance. You must be like the Foolish Old Man and not like the Wise Man. You must see the future as well as the present. As you shall learn, "Your need is to maintain an enthusiastic but calm state of mind and intense but orderly work."

Everyone nodded in agreement. They knew it was a direct quote from the Chairman.

For the next four months the six men gathered each day, seven days a week in the familiar classroom. They read aloud and chanted the quotations of Mao. They discussed each saying until Su An Chi felt they had mastered not only the rote learning of the quotation verbatim, but the practical application of same. They were encouraged to say what they felt, to disagree, but as they all were to soon learn, disagreement was eventually turned into agreement.

Su An Chi also began a "self analysis" program involving careful criticism by the others in the group. Su An Chi usually began such meetings with a statement made by one of the group that day in a discussion of the quotations and practical history. For example, one day discussing the value of "correct political thought" Alex brought forth the comment that in the United States the people are encouraged to think for themselves and can say what they think on any subject, political as well as personal. Su copied down Alex's statement word for word. And that night he repeated the statement. "Comrade Hunter today you said, and I quote, 'In the United States every person has the right to say what he thinks about the government.' While you did not say it directly, the inference in the tone of your voice was that the people of China do not have this right. Am I correct?"

"Yes," Alex said confidently, "I did mean that."

"Do you know for a fact that the people are not allowed to freely express their opinions about the government?"

"The people in general? No. Although one of the people, whom I trusted while on my mission, suggested so much."

"And this person said that people are not allowed to criticize the government?"

"Yes."

"Did this person also say the people were not allowed to speak their minds on politics?"

"Yes. Well, not directly. She inferred… "

"You just took her tone of voice to mean that?"

"No, she," Alex hesitated, he realized he had given away the sex of the person and knew that would open himself up for further criticism. He glanced around the room. They were all ready to attack. Everyone knew the minute he said "she" that Alex had let his guard down and revealed a weakness.

"You said 'she', Comrade Hunter," Comrade Chen chimed in, "Who is this woman? Be accurate."

Alex spent the next three hours telling the group about Madam Ying, who she was, what she did, how she died, finally saying that she was allowed to operate her house of prostitution with the knowledge of top Party members.

With that news the others in the group fell silent, they saw a chink in the armor of the Communist Party, but Su stepped in immediately and brought out two of the quotations of Chairman Mao which spoke to this very point.

"Comrade Hunter, you have opened my eyes as well as the others with this information. It is good that you have done so because it is a just and fair criticism of the Party. But I must remind you of the words of Chairman Mao, 'The Communist Party does not fear criticism because we are Marxists and the truth is on our side as are the masses, the workers and peasants. We have the Marxist-Leninist tradition of criticism and self criticism. We can get rid of a bad style and keep the good. You must know that if we have shortcomings, we are not afraid to have them pointed out and criticized, because we serve the people. Anyone, no matter who, may point out our shortcomings. If he is right, we will correct them. Do you think it is right for the Party to allow houses of prostitution in this country?"

Alex thought for a moment. He was getting in deep and he wanted to make sure he got out of the circumstance correctly.

Su An Chi interrupted his thoughts, "Let me ask you, comrade, do these houses serve the people and the People's needs?"

"Possibly. Some people," he answered.

"Yes, you are correct, some people. But isn't the Party allowed to exist by the will of the people, all the people?"

"Yes."

"Yes, and would you say that these houses serve the majority of the people?"

"No, not the majority of the people."

"Then what is your answer to my question?"

"On that basis, no, I do not think it serves the people to have such houses."

"But there is another basis?"

"There is the moral aspect of the question."

"Ah, yes. The moral question. Is it right or wrong. Am I correct?"

"Yes."

"And who is to decide what is right or wrong?"

Alex was ready for this one. It was his way out. "The people."

"Very good. The people. So, we agree, but on two different levels. Now we must find a common meeting ground so that we can both accept the correct answer to the question. What do you suggest?"

"Perhaps," Alex found himself saying, "we should find a quotation from the Chairman which will help us find that common meeting ground."

"Very good, do you have one in mind?"

"Two actually," Alex was frantically searching his mind for the right ones, "In this world, things are complicated and are decided by many factors. We should look at problems from different aspects, not from just one. That I believe is one reason why we differ only in how we arrive at the answer. The other is the words of wisdom 'It is man's social being that determines his thinking.' I was brought up to believe that houses of prostitution are bad, therefore, that is what I believe. You may not have been brought up with this thought in your society, but as Chairman Mao has said, "We must learn to look at problems from all sides""

"Very good, comrade. I agree. Even though we look at the problem from different sides, what matters most is that we see the same solution."

Everyone relaxed as this point was finally resolved, but Jandi frowned, "Comrade Su," he spoke up. "While this is very enlightening in and of its self, but we have not discussed the main question as to free speech."

"True comrade. We must not become complacent over any success, as the Chairman reminds us. Now, Comrade Hunter, what did Madam Ying say that led you to believe that the people cannot speak out concerning the government?"

And so it went on into the night and the next night until Alex was beaten down, educated enlightened and thoroughly convinced that the people of China do have the right to speak out and criticize the Party. The only thing they do not have the right to do is to tell lies or incite to riot.

Professor Li spoke out against the Party. He was telling lies. After some discussion with a few Party members, he confessed what he had said and told how he was duped by others into believing false things about the Party. He had to admit to his wrong doing in the public square while tied to a chair with burning torches being waved very close to him, so close that he thought he was going to be killed. He said he was saved by a Party member who recognized him and was able to convince his captors and the people that he could become a valuable asset to the Party. He was sent here to be reeducated.

Each of the five members of the class was taken apart mentally, piece by piece, by the others in the group and Comrade Su. Each phase of their lives was examined and reexamined, criticized, discussed, praised when appropriate to the teachings of Mao, until each one felt as if he had been through a wringer. Alex, like some of the others, had begun to doubt the sincerity of many things, his wife's love for him, the usefulness of his mission into China, except as it pertained to his reeducation, the free-enterprise system, national goals set by Congress or a president, the right of a man to choose his own career or path of life. Religion was questioned - even the existence of God. All of these things were hard for Alex to defend or stand up for. Su and the others became very accomplished debaters and critics. Even simple questions from these people became difficult to answer. Questions such as: "Name one thing God has done for you," or "why should some people live in wealth and waste while others are starving?" or "who is your best friend and why?" These questions were discussed for hours on end until Alex's head fairly reeled. He found himself agreeing with some of the Communist philosophy not because he was forced to, but because he was convinced by the arguments presented. He found himself defending his point of view through the teachings of Mao which by now he could spout verbatim at will. He was frightened not of the others but of himself.

After the third month of criticism and self-criticism, Alex was drained. He no longer felt any urgency at all for defending his life before, he began to believe sincerely that he was wrong and that they were right. Su, he noticed, was not smug or arrogant about the change in Alex, in fact, Su seemed entirely sympathetic to his problems and helped him defend himself at times. He often felt that his only real friend was Su. He began to confide in Su and turn to him for help. The more he did so, the more he felt content with himself.

The class began to become involved in other things. They took turns making meals for each other, cleaning up the compound and were even encouraged to work in the fields alongside the peasants who provided food for the prison. They were allowed to talk freely to the guards, the other peasants, and the other inmates who were at their same level of "progress." Alex began to feel useful once again, as did the others, and life seemed to be on an upward trend.

They were taken into the town of Palung to see the various traveling plays based on political themes once a week, and they were allowed to participate in the political discussions with the townspeople. They were better equipped to relate the Red Book of Mao's Quotations to the discussions than the townspeople who had been indoctrinated slowly. After five months, they were free to walk the streets of Palung and talk with the people.

The final phase of their training was the application of all they knew about foreign affairs.

One day in the spring, nearly two years after Alex was captured, they were discussing the application of the teachings of Mao in foreign affairs and Su was saying, "We have been taught by Chairman Mao that it is inevitable that the people of China will become the center of all the earth and their ideas will prevail. We will be most suited to rule the thoughts of the world because we have the greatest understanding and ability to rule."

Comrade Shen interrupted and asked, "How soon will this come about?"

"Truly I do not know," Su said, "I only know that it will come about because we have on our side the most valuable asset known to man - time. We understand the value of time as no other people have before us, and we will use this precious tool to manipulate the minds of all men, white, black, red, and yellow. We will convince them that our way is the right and just path to peace and a useful life. But, before this life can be enjoyed by all men, we must dedicate ourselves, and the lives of our sons and daughters to teaching the ways of our beloved Chairman Mao."

Jandi spoke up, "I can understand how this might be accomplished in my country and other less wealthy nations where the oppression and poverty are so apparent, but what of the imperialistic peoples of the world? Won't these peoples fight against such teachings and possibly use force to prevent the dissemination of Chairman Mao's thoughts?"

"Yes, in many ways they have already," Su said rising and going to the center of the semicircle and facing them, "and it is possible, but only as a last resort, that we may have to resort to the use of force and war. But I believe that this will not be necessary. We are wearing down the imperialists slowly but surely. We will win their minds."

Hok Du San raised his hand, "This I both understand and agree with, but to get back to the question of Comrade Shen, how will we teach the imperialists like the United States?"

"Let's see what Comrade Hunter has to say about this. How do you feel we can best teach the people of your country comrade?"

"I will refer to the strategy that our beloved Chairman Mao used during the great revolution and point out that these same tactics can be used in America as well. We can break down the government by planting seeds of distrust... encouraging dissent... arm our friends with the logic and wisdom of the Chairman. We can find fault with everything, destroy the faith of the people in their government, make fun of national purpose and nationalism, undermine all authority and law, encourage the youth to revolt against the family and the system of government. As we do these things, the people will destroy themselves."

"Ah, that is very good comrade, but you have not included one important element, create apathy by pointing out the futility of doing anything. This is very good, but we must remember the story of the Foolish Old Man, this cannot and should not be rushed. We have time, and we must take time so that our efforts become a way of life even before they realize it. Remember what Chairman Mao taught us, 'To be superficial means to consider neither the characteristics of a contradiction in its totality nor the characteristics of each of its aspects; it means to deny the necessity for probing deeply into a thing and minutely studying the characteristics of its contradiction, but instead merely to look from afar, and take small steps to victory.'"

Comrade Su rubbed his chin for a moment then turned to Alex. "One of the things you mentioned Comrade Hunter that I found greatly interesting and worthy of further discussion was your statement, 'Encourage the youth to revolt.' In fact, Comrade, this is a very appropriate time for that to be mentioned. We have, waiting outside, another guest lecturer."

Su went to the door and opened it and walked down the hall. He was gone briefly. When he returned, he had with him an Occidental. It had been two years since Alex had come into contact with a white man except for the brief encounter with "Father Grant." The man was young, about twenty-five Alex guessed, with a blonde beard and long hair. He was Larry Neyer, a graduate student at UCLA. He had done his undergraduate work at Berkeley and had become involved with the Communist movement in his sophomore year. Neyer was admitted to a cell on campus and rose quickly to become a leader of the movement on campus. At the end of his junior year, he was sent, via a circuitous route, to Cuba where he was trained in the various techniques and tactics of the International Party. When he returned, he turned his work at Berkeley over to another student so he could concentrate specifically on recruiting and training young people in cover organizations. His mission was the same as those articulated by Alex earlier: create dissent, distrust and confusion.

"I am proud to report," Neyer said in his high whiny voice, "that our progress is greater than we could have dreamed. The students are apathetic and losing faith both in their teachers and anyone in authority. We are experiencing success and plan a fully executed full scale riot on campus. We led the students into armed combat with the police and got them so enthused that they burned the library. Many are joining our cause. They are excited about tearing down the traditions and beliefs of the intelligentsia. Their numbers are growing and many have left their campuses to spread our philosophy at other universities. The success of our work has been much more than we hoped for when we began in 1960."

"To what do you attribute your success?" Comrade Shen interrupted.

"I think it is due to the affluent society the students have been raised in. They have all the money they want and all the food, their minds hunger for challenge, and we are able to provide it to them. By doing so, we can control their minds. I truly believe that in my lifetime, barring any unforseen set backs, and by diligent and conscientious work, we will have control of America in mind and spirit and body."

Su interrupted, "Do you think there will be a war?"

"Frankly, comrades, I do not see the need for a war. We are educating the youth to believe as we do. In just a few years, they will be in influential positions and able to control the destiny of the United States. In fact, I would not be surprised if they opened the doors to the Party without the firing of one shot."

"Thank you," Su said, "We were just talking about war with imperialistic countries before you came."

"It is not my belief, nor that of Chairman Mao's, as I recall, to enter into armed conflict. As he said, 'We stand firmly for peace and against war'."

"Yes, but," Hoc interrupted, "the Chairman also said, "The seizure of power by armed force, the settlement of an issue by war, is preferable to not winning at all which is the central task and highest form of revolution."

"Ah, but I believe he was referring to when all else fails. I agree, there are times when war is necessary to accomplish one's goals, but I believe the American youth are so gullible that they will eventually, probably in my lifetime, accept peace at any price."

This discussion penetrated Alex's subconscious. Maybe it was because he was seeing an Occidental for the first time, or maybe it was because they were talking about war, or maybe it was the smug attitude and squinting eyes of Neyer, but Alex was beginning to focus again on the United States and his home, and he could, for the first time in many months, see the faces of the children in his neighborhood. He saw an angry, yelling child, and he didn't like it. He shook his head, and Su looked carefully at him. Neyer continued to talk about his cells and the goals they set for themselves and their accomplishments. Neyer left after about three hours. The group was excited and talked loudly and enthusiastically about what Neyer had told them and the possibilities for the future.

After three days of discussion on the lecture, they returned to their normal studies.

Alex began to drift back into his state of cooperation. Comrade Su, however, had taken a new interest in Alex.

CHAPTER TWENTY-SEVEN

Comrade Su reported his feelings about Alex to Colonel Liang. He told the Colonel that he thought Alex was reverting somewhat to his former self after Neyer's visit. The Colonel paced for a moment. He looked at Su and then said, "I believe it is time to sink the final dagger."

"The murder of his wife."

"Yes. We must tell him everything about the circumstances of her death. Everything."

"Do you believe this will completely win him over?"

"If it does not, he may not be of future use to us. You will tell him immediately."

Su nodded. He liked this idea.

Alex sat stunned as Comrade Su read the entire thirty page report. He couldn't believe his ears. Roger and Crissy on the afternoon of their wedding, and in Japan, and...his mind was overwhelmed. Roger had actually murdered Crissy?

For the next month, Alex was of little value to the group. Su witnessed the logical progression of Alex's turmoil over the murder of his wife. At first, Alex's anger was directed at Roger. It was logical, expected, and natural Su observed. He saw that anger and heard it in Alex's voice. Whenever they had a session alone, Alex wanted to know everything that Roger said about the murder and his relationship with Crissy. Comrade Su told him everything including the part about Crissy wanting to divorce Alex, and about the frequent sexual encounters Roger and Crissy enjoyed. Su said that Roger claimed he and Crissy were playing sex games when she fell over the balcony, but after intense questioning, he finally admitted that he threw her over the balcony because she was pregnant and was going to tell Alex.

Next came his anger at his government, the C.I.D., the C.I.A. and everyone who knew about the murder but didn't tell Alex. This included Major Brady and the people who trained him for the mission. He kept asking Comrade Su why they had not told him, and each time Comrade Su emphasized that they didn't care about the murder once Roger defected. They didn't care about Alex's feelings either. They moved on to other things and left Alex swaying in the wind.

The third logical step was for Alex to get angry at himself - to place at least part of the blame for Crissy's murder on his own shoulders. He started out that way, blamed himself for not loving Crissy enough, blamed himself for being apart from her so much, and so on. Slowly this attitude changed to self-pity. He hated himself for letting his feelings last for Crissy after she was dead, for not going on with his life and enjoying it. He began to wallow in self-pity and Comrade Su didn't like that. It meant that he was a weak man, but Su knew this wasn't true. Was Alex playing games? This was definitely not logical.

Alex was playing games, but even he didn't know it for a while. When his mind-set changed from anger at the U.S. to anger at himself, he felt justified in that feeling. He felt he had not loved Crissy as much as he should have, and he blamed himself for having her come to Japan, etc. But those feelings became muddled as the days went on. Alex couldn't pinpoint why he felt he didn't love Crissy enough. This, coupled with Su telling him that Crissy had an affair with Roger, made him wonder if it wasn't him but her. And, as he recalled, it was Crissy who wanted to come to Japan - he had actually discouraged this. Finally, during this self-questioning period, Alex suddenly came to the conclusion that he wasn't so bad after all. And, as he delved more deeply into his past, he realized he was being had. Alex knew that Su was looking at him oddly - as if he didn't believe Alex's behavior - which he didn't.

Alex pretended to slip more deeply into the pit of self-pity. He cried easily, and stopped taking care of himself. Alex was seemingly inattentive and unaware of his surroundings. He had 'dreams' in which he talked out loud about his failure as a man. He wasn't sure where this ploy would lead him, but he hoped it would offer hope for escape. He wanted out of there to pursue his real goal - to get hold of Roger and make him tell what really happened.

After two months of this behavior, Comrade Su was on to Alex. He'd seen this behavior before with other "students". He was certain Alex was faking. He discussed this with his superior, Colonel Liang and several other 'educators'. They all agreed that Alex was not following the usual behavior. A change of venue was in order.

Alex was called into Colonel Liang's office. The game of cat and mouse began. The Colonel could see the change in Alex's behavior. The Alex Hunter he had observed only a month ago was not standing in front of him. Instead, Alex was listless and anxious. He was apologetic for everything from standing incorrectly to forgetting a teaching of Mao's he'd known earlier. Their decision was correct. "Please, have a seat, Comrade Hunter," the Colonel said.

Alex hesitated then sat. "Thank you."

"I have just been going over the progress reports on you, Comrade, and I must say, I am very pleased."

"Thank you," Alex said, wondering what this was all leading up to. "As Chairman Mao says, 'Obedience and the gaining of knowledge of one's self and his duties serve to make the lives of all the people more fulfilling'."

"Very Good!" Colonel Liang said with a smile. "You are able to apply his teachings most aptly."

"Thank you," Alex said, almost as a robot. His mind was whirling, waiting for the other shoe to drop.

"In fact, comrade, you have progressed so well we have decided to let you take advantage of a more advanced school not far from here." Alex frowned. "We have given you the basics, but there your knowledge will be refined, and you will be more able to become a useful member of the world community." The Colonel stood up, walked around his desk and sat on the edge of the desk. "You will find this new environment much more liberal, and I know you will continue to progress satisfactorily. "Now," he said rising. "You will gather up your personal effects and go with Comrade Su. I wish you good fortune in your journeys." He shook hands with Alex. Alex was so taken aback by the western gesture, along with the news of his transfer, that he didn't react at all. He was numb.

Alex went out the door not sure what was going on. He saw Su standing nearby. They went to his cell where there was already a guard with a small leather bag. Alex packed his few belongings and together with Su walked to the motor compound. A truck was parked waiting for him.

"No one else is going?" Alex asked.

"Not at this time, perhaps later," Su replied. He walked to the truck and motioned to the driver. The driver handed him a piece of rope.

"Comrade Hunter, surely you know that I trust you completely, however, regulations in this case must be followed. During your transfer you must be tied. I hope you will not take offense to this gesture."

"I understand," Alex said. Now he was sure something was wrong. Why just me to a new school? Why alone? Are they going to kill me? Did they see the doubt I began to feel after Neyer came? Or was it about Crissy's murder? He was scared. Su motioned, and Alex put his hands behind his back. As Su was tying his hands Alex strained to separate his hands just enough so that when he relaxed the ropes were loose. Su helped him into the front seat of the truck alongside the driver, but then he tied Alex's feet so he couldn't move them. "Goodbye Comrade," Su said. "May you apply all you have learned here toward a successful and full life ahead."

Su stepped back, and the driver started the truck. For the first time in a long time, Alex felt very nervous. Something was definitely wrong.

The truck moved along the dirt road for about a mile until they came to a paved road. The compound was no longer in view and Alex immediately began to work on freeing his hands.

"What is your name?" Alex asked the driver as he edged his body into the corner of the cab of the truck so he could work on his hands. Alex looked carefully at the driver. He was about twenty, Alex guessed, with a baby face and small in stature.

Ling Chi, the driver, answered without taking his eyes off the road.

"Is Palung your home?"

"No, I am from Jining, it is east of here."

"Where is the base you are taking me to?"

"It is near Sining about 250 miles from here. We must go around the Koko Lake."

Alex relaxed a bit. The place they were sending him was not just a few miles away so he did have time. He needed to get out of the ropes and try to escape. His biggest problem was to pick the spot for his escape.

CHAPTER TWENTY-EIGHT

On the Road to Sining, China, April, 18, 1962

Two hours later, Ling was still driving along at a steady pace. He was very quiet and intent on his driving. They passed through several villages. Alex was trying to place the location of Koko Lake in his mind geographically. He knew it was in the interior of China, but just where he couldn't remember. Alex asked Ling what the countryside was like where they were going, but he didn't really know, he only knew about the territory near his home village. Ling had never been more than three hundred miles from home. By this time, Alex had the ropes loose, but he didn't want to untie them all the way for fear he might be discovered before he was ready to make his move. Ling did have a pistol on his side, and Alex didn't want to take any chances now. He waited.

Three hours later, at mid day, they came into a larger town, Chinghai. Ling stopped for gasoline, and Alex stayed in the truck tied up. Ling fed him some rice cakes and tea. Alex was told by Ling that the Koko Lake was just a few miles north of Chinghai. Ling got back into the truck and off they went through the town and out into the foothills of the Nan Shan mountains. The road was deserted, and there didn't even seem to be any farms for miles. Minutes later, they came to an intersection. Alex asked where the crossroad led to. Ling said Sining. Sining was a town that Alex remembered from his training. One of his professors in language school had come from Sining and had told of his life along the banks of the Hwang River.

Alex decided to make his move now. If he was successful, he would head toward Sining. At least he'd know where he was.

Alex chose to make his move along a flat stretch of road with open fields on both sides. He removed the rope, and behind his back, he tied a knot in the middle of the rope. All of this was done by feel since he couldn't see his hands. He felt for the ends of the rope and wrapped them around his hands making sure the rope wasn't hung up anywhere and was free. He asked about the mountains to Ling's left so his head would be turned away from Alex to give him the most time to slip the rope over Ling's head to strangle him.

"What's that mountain over there to your left, Ling?"

Ling turned his head slightly trying to keep one eye on the road, and Alex moved with all the speed in him. He flipped the rope over Ling's head in one motion and pulled with all his might, strangling him. Ling, reacted instantly by turning the wheel and trying to pull away. Alex's garrote was too tight. Ling struggled fiercely and finally took both hands off the steering wheel to try and pull the rope from around his neck. When that didn't work, he tried to reach the gun in his holster, but by that time, he was too far gone. Alex's mind, meanwhile, was racing a mile a minute. How do I stop the truck from turning over? How do I stop it? Is he dead?

The second he felt Ling sag, Alex let go. He knew if Ling was still alive, Alex was in trouble, but the truck was now careening through an open field bouncing and creaking. Ling's foot was firmly planted on the accelerator. Alex turned the ignition off, and the truck slowed to a stop. He reached over and got the pistol out of Ling's holster and then checked the body. Ling was dead. Alex looked out his window and could see no one. He untied his feet, got out of the truck and looked around. The truck was in the middle of a field, and there was no one in sight from any direction. He opened the door of the driver's side and Ling's body fell over toward him, but Alex caught it and pushed it over to the passenger's side. He got in, started the truck, turned around and headed back toward the road. When he got to the fork in the road, he saw a sign with arrows pointing toward Sining and another toward Lanzhou. He chose the road to Lanzhou.

Alex drove through three small villages then remembered Lanzhou was a large city. He turned off on a side road and headed back toward Sining. He passed through the same villages again, but with Ling's hat on and no stop signs, no one took notice of who was driving the truck.

An hour later the truck was climbing into the foothills of the mountains. Alex checked the fuel gauge and figured he would have enough to get over the mountains, but not much more. It was desolate mountain country. In some areas it looked like the surface of the moon. He came to the tree line and suddenly he was in a dark forest. The mountain was higher than he estimated, and late in the afternoon, he looked at his fuel tank. Not much remaining. Alex decided that he wouldn't have enough to get over the next mountain. He stopped on a curve and looked down. It was a steep cliff. He decided that the usefulness of the truck was at an end.

Alex changed clothes with Ling and tied him up just as he had been tied. He waited until dark. He hoped that if anyone found the truck they would think that he had died in the crash. Alex took everything he thought he might use: a water canteen; a pair of binoculars he found in the glove compartment, and, of course, Ling's pistol. He backed the truck up the road, opened the door on the driver's side, and started it toward the cliff. When it had enough speed, Alex jumped clear. The truck rolled over the cliff and was smashed to bits when it hit the first cliff jutting out several hundred feet below, and finally came to a stop in a ball of fire just at the tree line.

Alex carefully cleaned up his footprints around the area where the truck went over the cliff leaving the tire tracks, of course. He checked to see that he had left nothing as evidence, and walked on the hard surface of the road toward Sining.

CHAPTER TWENTY-NINE

Alex walked until dawn when he reached the turn in the road that started downward. He looked out over the vast expanse below. Using his binoculars, he saw the city of Sining far off in the distance. Leaving the road, Alex went deep into the forest. It was cold. When he felt he could go on no longer, he tore off some branches from small pine trees and made a bed. Laying on the soft branches, he covered himself with other branches. He fell fast asleep. Three times he woke in a panic. He was having nightmares about being recaptured. These fears were to haunt him each night as he traveled. He was happy to be free but scared of being captured and tortured again.

When dawn broke, he decided to travel south toward Burma. He had no idea where he was, but he felt that was the shortest route to freedom. It took Alex a full day to cross over the top of the mountain. As he started down, he looked out over the huge valley that lay below. Nothing seemed to be out of the ordinary. There was a small village tucked up against the south side of the hill across from him. Below were scattered fields of rice in the valley. He walked on until he came to a cave-like indentation in the side of the mountain and decided to make his camp there for the day. The area was too open and provided little cover for travel so he decided stay in the cave the day. He fixed himself cold tea and dried pork he had taken from Ling's lunch. Once inside the cave, he wrapped himself in his blanket and fell fast asleep

Alex woke just before sundown. He got up, stretched and walked out into the sunlight. He looked out over the peaceful valley below and saw, to his amazement, several trucks and a lot of activity, not far from the village. Curiosity got the best of him, and he retrieved his binoculars. He sat down and panned the binoculars down the road and focused in on a truck. It was a Red Army truck. The bed of the truck was covered with canvas. He panned ahead on down the road. The road ended in a clump of trees. He checked. The end of the road seemed to disappear. He panned back to the first truck and followed it with the glasses until it came to the clump of trees and then disappeared. Then another truck, then another. He was too far away to see where the trucks were going but it looked like they were going into the side of the mountain.

His curiosity was really aroused. He decided to investigate where the trucks were going. Alex gathered up his things, and under the cover of night, made his way down the side of the mountain. He was about two thirds of the way down to the valley floor when the sun rose. He began looking for a place to sleep for the day, when his eye caught a shining object about fifty feet in front of him. He walked to it and bent down. It was a wire. Just as he was about to reach down to pick it up, he heard voices. Alex scrambled back up the hill away from the sound of voices. He crouched down behind a fallen log and waited. The voices came closer, and he could make out what they were saying. "This is the third time this month we have had to come out and check the detection wire in this area," he heard one of the men saying with a slight Fukienese accent.

"Yes," said another voice, "and it was another tree branch."

"Comrades," he heard a third voice, deeper with a clear accent from Northern China. "It is this new magnetic field detection system. It is so sensitive that it picks up any object that comes within two feet of it and relays it to the detection center. And, until the object is removed, it will continue to show up on the board. We must remove these tree branches otherwise someone might cross over at the same point, and we would not know it. Our job is to keep the wires clear of foreign objects."

Alex peered over the log in time to see three soldiers walking on down the line now with their backs to him, their burp guns slung over their shoulders."But why couldn't we just trim the trees near the line or even chop them down so that this doesn't happen?" The voices faded out. Alex got up to one knee and watched the men disappear over a small rise. He decided to follow them for a while, so long as there was adequate cover.

About an hour later, he had trailed the men to a guard house beside a road. There were two guards outside the small house. They were talking to the three men. He noticed that each time a truck approached, the guards stopped the truck. They recorded information about the truck and inspected it. A small truck stopped, and the three men got in. They drove away toward the mountain.

Alex noted that the routine the guards used for each truck was always the same. The truck would stop at a line painted on the road. The driver and any other passengers would get out and walk over to the guards and show them their passes. One of the guards always had his gun at the ready. Then the other guard would inspect the truck, make his notations, and report back. They then released the driver and any other people and they would get back into the truck and drive off.

Scanning the area around the guard house Alex saw a clump of bushes not more than twenty-five yards from the guard house on his side of the trip wire. He made his way down the hill. When he was not too far from the bushes, Alex waited until the guards were distracted then rushed to the bushes. From there, he could hear everyone talk. Several trucks stopped and from the various conversations, he determined that each person had to give his name, rank, and section number to the guards. They checked them off from a master list.

He stayed for the rest of the day watching and listening. Only one car came through the check point. He made out two of the three names, a General Ching Yi and a Doctor Tsien. Something clicked in his mind when he heard the name Dr. Tsien, but he couldn't connect it.

After night fall Alex made his way back up the mountain to a safe distance, fixed himself some food and slept. The name of Dr. Tsien kept running through his mind, and he slept fitfully. He arose before daybreak and made his way back to the clump of bushes he'd used for cover the day before. It was easy to get to in the dark. He hadn't been there long when he heard the roar of several trucks approaching. Suddenly the area was bathed in the harsh blue white light of high intensity arc lights which the guards must have turned on. The first car came around the curve and stopped at the guard station. The officers in the car identified themselves and pulled on past the intersection and over to the side of the road. They got out of the car and stood beside it chatting about the nice weather, the long trip, suggesting that they were near the end of their journey, and how they would be glad to see their wives again. Then the roar of the trucks grew louder and around the curve came two large trucks moving at about twenty miles an hour, followed by a huge tandem truck carrying a large, covered cylinder about thirty feet long and about fifteen feet in diameter. Then another similar truck and another, four in all. As they passed into the light Alex could clearly see that they were sections of a large missile.

Then it came to him. Of course, Dr. Tsien. Dr. H. S. Tsien, a Chinese/American rocket expert who was kicked out of the U.S. in 1951 for being a communist sympathizer.

The last truck of the convoy passed through the gates and the lights were turned off. It was not yet light. Alex decided not to take a chance on staying this close for the entire day. He made his way back up to his cave, ate, and thought. "It looks like the Chinese are setting up a rocket center somewhere nearby," he said to himself, "I'd sure like to know where."

As the day wore on, Alex napped for a while then got out his binoculars and scanned the valley once again. When he first scanned the valley from near the top of the mountain, the valley had looked normal, except, of course, for the trucks seeming to drive into the side of the hill. Now, from his cave the valley looked anything but normal. The small village nestled up against the mountain was almost directly across from his position. Above the village was a well-camouflaged pillbox like complex in the trees about a half mile outside the village. Also, scattered about the valley, were several small outposts. The many farm houses dotting the valley seemed to be headquarters for the outposts. Near one corner of the canyon was a large rice field with several workers planting rice.

Periodically, trucks came into the valley and passed through it to the other side and disappeared into the side of the hill. It might be a tunnel, he thought, that leads to the other side of the hill another way out of the canyon. But when he started keeping track of the numbers on the trucks, he saw that the same trucks that went into the tunnel came back out again within an hour or so. It was strange. The rocket sections he saw earlier that morning were nowhere in sight.

All that morning and afternoon Alex debated with himself the pros and cons of trying to get into the valley for a closer look, not only at the tunnel but at other areas that were camouflaged. Right now he was free; he could continue his trek toward Burma and hopefully make it if he was careful. The question was, should he take a chance at getting caught just to see what was in the valley, or go on his way. His common sense and his instinct for survival told him to get out of the area, but something tugged at his conscience. It was his feeling that something was going on here that American intelligence should know about.

Once again his duty to his country won out over his duty to himself. He began planning. First, he had to test the warning system. It was mid-afternoon. He made his way down to the wire. Carefully, he selected a large dead tree branch. Using all his might, he managed to break it off the dying tree. He stood about ten feet from the wire on a rock, and using all his might, threw the branch across the wire. Then he quickly scampered up the side of the mountain to a preselected spot that overlooked the wire. He scanned the area with his binoculars. What he saw disheartened him. There, walking toward the wire about fifty yards in front of him, were ten soldiers. They formed a cordon and approached the wire. It had only taken six minutes for the soldiers to respond.

Three soldiers went to the wire and removed the branch while the rest stayed hidden among the trees. They didn't seem to be disturbed about it, and none of them went more than six or eight feet on the other side of the wire. They did look around a bit and one of them pointed to the spot on the old tree where Alex had broken off the limb. The soldiers shrugged and walked off after using a walkie-talkie to report to their headquarters. So much for trying to cross the wire.

Alex decided another approach had to be found. He had an idea.

That night Alex waited near the curve of the road not far from the guard shack. A truck, in anticipation of the guard house, slowed down as it approached the curve. Alex was ready to jump on the back of it when suddenly the flood lights came on. He was right smack in the middle of the area where the lights from the guard house lit up the approach. He had to jump back into the bushes to avoid being seen. He had miscalculated where to hitch a ride.

After the truck passed, the lights went out. He decided to move further around the bend and hide again. Less than five minutes after he arrived at his new hiding place beside the road, two trucks came by. Each was loaded with soldiers, no chance to hitch a ride on those trucks. The trick was going to be picking the right truck. He had only about three seconds to make a decision.

It was nearly two hours until the next truck came, and it didn't even slow down. Alex tried for it, but missed, and he had to hit the dirt when the lights came on.

He waited again. One hour. Two, three. Then he heard a truck approaching. He poised himself like a track runner shifting his right foot until it was firmly in place, and resting his left knee on the ground, his hands supporting his body, and leaned forward. When the headlights of the truck passed the bush he was hiding behind, he dashed out on the road. The truck was covered with canvas and the back flap was tied down, again he had to dive into the ditch to avoid the powerful lights. He lay in the ditch cursing his luck until the guard turned out the lights, and again he made his way back to the jumping off spot. He could have caught that truck if only the back flap had not been tied down. They say the third time's a charm, and in Alex's case it was true. Not only was the back flap not tied down, but the truck slowed even before it passed him. He made it to the back of the truck before the lights came on, and by the time the truck had come to a stop near the checkpoint, he was safely inside, hidden behind some boxes.

The powerful lights made the inside of the canvas-covered truck light enough to see the writing on the boxes. "Dr. H. S. Tsien, Top Secret"

The guard briefly glanced at the contents in the back of the truck. Alex ducked down behind the crates. Down behind the crates he read "Launch Sequence Mechanism." Any doubts he had had about what they were doing in the valley were gone now. This was a secret space center.

The truck picked up speed and passed out of the lights of the check point and on down the road. Alex had picked out a spot near a wooded area to jump off. He opened the back flap after about five minutes, only to see that the truck was already past the spot. He climbed out onto the tailgate and jumped into a rice paddy full of water. In the fall, he almost strangled himself on his binoculars. The truck didn't slow down so he knew the driver didn't see or hear him. Alex waited until the truck was out of sight. He picked himself up and smeared away the mud from his face and hands. It was very dark, and he couldn't see well, but he made his way out of the paddy to a wooded area nearby. His one fear was the wooded area might be a camouflaged outpost, but it wasn't. Alex decided that because there wasn't much undergrowth in the grove he would climb a tree and hide among the leaves. He picked a tall tree and made his way up it until he could hardly see the ground for the leaves. He wasn't sure about how much cover he had. He would have to wait until morning.

When the sun came up an hour later, Alex climbed a bit higher in the tree and checked out his position. It was a good position. He was in the middle of the wooded area far from where people were working. The woods were on the north side of the box canyon right in the middle of the valley. He could see everything clearly.

To his right, not more than two thousand yards, were the paddy fields and an outpost. To his left was the checkpoint he had come in through about three miles back. He was just where he wanted to be, directly across from the spot where the trucks disappeared. When he focused his binoculars on the spot, he let out a long low whistle. Nearly half of the hillside had been cut away yet it was well-camouflaged. It looked as if nothing had been changed. From his position, he could see that the camouflage hid a blockhouse, an assembly center, machine shops, a power plant and a large loading area capable of handling about twenty trucks at one time. Parked on one side under a camouflage net were the four trucks. Three of them had missile sections still loaded on them. The fourth was unloaded. The workers all wore yellow coveralls and hard hats. Some also wore masks. Alex wondered why.

He watched as the cover was removed from one of the missile sections. It was painted with a camouflage design. For two hours men worked around the section, then the truck drove out of the hidden area with the payload to a small wooded area not far from the center. What he saw next seemed like a part out of a science fiction movie. The truck stopped beside the wooded area and one of the trees began to move, it was a crane, well camouflaged. It lifted the section off the truck. As the crane moved, another tree slid along the ground out of the way revealing the first stage of the rocket already in place. A gantry was next to it and slowly the huge missile section was lowered into place. He could make out on the side of the second stage in large characters a warning, "Caution, Nuclear Warhead. Authorized Personnel Only."

"Nuclear Warhead?" Alex shook his head in amazement. Did this mean the Chinese were developing an atomic bomb? Did it mean they already had one? How? When? Did the U.S. know about it? What if they didn't? What if that rocket was heading toward America? Suddenly his need to get home took on a new and urgent meaning.

Alex spent the rest of the day planning his escape from the canyon. He waited until most of the lights in the Space Center had gone out and only a skeleton crew remained. He watched as the others went off to the village, which was primarily a housing unit for the scientists and workers in the center. About midnight, he climbed down out of the tree and made his way across the valley toward his camp. Alex moved very carefully. As he started up the mountain, he realized he didn't know where the wire was. He kept going until he stumbled over the wire. He started to run, then he regained control of himself. Quickly, he went back to the wire and covered his tracks as best he could. He heard a truck below him and soldiers getting out of the truck. He climbed up the hill, covering his tracks with a tree limb. After he had gone about 100 yards, he took off in a dead run.

He retrieved his things from the cave and set off up the mountain. Alex had a new mission, and it was urgent!

CHAPTER THIRTY

Near Sining, China, April 20, 1962.

Two days later, Alex finally relaxed. He had successfully gotten out of the valley and no one seemed to be after him. He was still headed toward Burma, but he was frustrated. The knowledge that the Chinese had an atomic bomb was constantly on his mind, and he was getting anxious to get out of China.

The grey light of dawn began to cut through the dark of night, and Alex had yet to find himself a suitable place to stay for the day. He was approaching a grassy plains-like area that seemed to be well populated. Alex had been traveling through hills and mountains where cover was easy to find, but open areas were too risky to travel in sunlight. As he climbed to the top of a knoll, immediately in front of him about a mile away, was a large compound of several houses surrounded by a low wall. There were fields all around. In twenty minutes or so they would be alive with people. He scoured the area and decided that his only chance was a small hill in back of him. He made his way to the bottom of the hill just as the sun suddenly burst over the fields. His long shadow made him even more conspicuous. Alex climbed to the top of the hill. To his left he saw a small river with trees lining it. Heading toward the river, he made his way carefully through the tall grass bending the grass back up behind him as he walked. It took him several minutes to reach the river. He scanned the area with his binoculars. No one was near. He picked out a large tree to climb which he felt provided sufficient cover. After he filled his canteen from the river, Alex climbed the tree and once again surveyed the area. He decided that continuing south was not practical. Too many flat areas from what he could see. North was out of the question - that was the direction he had just come from. West would probably lead him to the desert areas, so east it had to be.

After the workers left the fields, Alex climbed down and began his long journey eastward. In front of him were mountains, and he liked the cover they provided.

Alex walked for several days, eating off the land, and sleeping at night. The rigorous exercise and forced diet made him lean and hard again.

He passed near two towns, and took the chance of sneaking into one of them in search of food and shoes. His army uniform still looked all right, but he was wearing a big hole in his left shoe. The village was small, and he wasn't sure they even had a shoe store. He waited until twilight and slowly walked into the village. There were only two streets and the first was empty, but as he rounded a corner, there was a street market. He had walked right into the crowd. He bent low so he didn't tower over the others and kept his head down. He quickly scanned the street. There was a man selling shoes. Alex walked over to where the man was standing. He looked at the shoes on the table. Most of them were very small, but he saw the biggest pair right next to the seller's hand. He hesitated. The man, older, with a beard and beat-up hat, looked at him. He stared at Alex for a moment. Then, he began to smirk. "You are looking for something special?" he asked. Alex nodded. "A large size I believe," he said as he reached for the pair Alex had his eye on. "This is my largest size." His voice was high and yet very soft. "Ten Yuan." Alex reached in his pocket. He still had some of the money that the driver, Ling , was carrying. He looked at it. The man reached across the table, opened Alex's hand, and took some money. "May you travel a long distance in comfort," the man said as he handed Alex the shoes. Alex nodded again. "May I suggest one other thing?" Alex saw the smile on the man's face. He nodded again. "Strangers must beware of this village." Alex smiled as he nodded again and shuffled away.

Later that night, he slipped back into the village and stole small bits of food from various stands after the people had gone to bed.

Several days later, Alex reached the top of a hill and saw a city not far off in the distance. He panned his binoculars around and stopped. Did he see correctly? Was that a plume of smoke from a train? It was. He smiled. Maybe he could hitch a ride.

It took Alex a full day to bypass the city and get to the railroad tracks beyond. They seemed to be headed east. He decided to follow the tracks. Staying just far enough away from them that he could not be seen, he followed the tracks for two days. No trains came by. He kept walking.

Late that night he heard a train approaching. It was going fast. He watched the long freight train as it passed and let out a deep sigh. How many more days would he have to wait to catch a train? he wondered.

As dusk was coming on, Alex approached a town - Lungshi. He was surprised to see the freight train still stopped in the station. The end of the train was out of the bright lights in shadows. Did he dare? No time like the present he said to himself. He approached the train.

Suddenly, it lurched as the steam engine engaged the cars. Alex ran and ducked under the train and grabbed onto bar supports under the last car. He found a way to wedge himself onto a bar and hung on for dear life. The train began to move.

Several times he felt as if he was losing his grip, but held on. A few hours later, the train stopped again. The rear was out of the direct light again. Alex let himself down. His muscles were aching and he got the shakes for a moment as he lay beneath the train car. He had to find a better riding place.

He rolled out from under the train and stood up. He was on the side of the train away from the station. Listening carefully, Alex climbed up between the cars to the top of a cattle car. He peered in between the slats and saw it was empty. He was tempted to try to get in, but he wasn't sure he could get out without being seen.

The train lurched and Alex almost fell off, but caught himself. As the train began to move, he climbed onto the top and hung on. The ride lasted for two hours when dawn began to break. Alex knew he had to get off or be seen. As the train rounded a curve, Alex could see a large city. He had to get off now. He climbed down and as the train passed through another curve, he jumped and rolled over into a ditch. The train chugged on. Alex hoped the train passed through the city and out the other side.

It took Alex two days to get to the other side of Baoli. He was out of food, and worst of all, he was in a flat area with no place to hide. It was getting light. As he came to a ridge, he saw the train tracks not far away. There was a small shack nearby. It was his only cover. He ran to the shack, got the door open, and went inside. It was full of tools for repairing the road bed. He prayed the tracks were in good condition so no one would come.

Just as Alex was about to settle down, he heard a truck stop, then he heard footsteps approaching the shed. It sounded like only one man. Alex crouched down beside the door. He had his gun ready. The door opened, shielding Alex from the workman's sight. Alex stopped breathing as the man walked in, took a long pole and left without noticing him. He got back in his truck and drove away. Alex started breathing again.

Looking down the tracks, he saw that they headed up the mountain. He followed the tracks until he was out of breath. The long moan of a train whistle pierced the night air. Alex hoped his strategy of getting up high enough where the train would be forced to slow down would work. It did.

This time, Alex had his choice of open boxcars, and he jumped into one. He was off again in style. The car had boxes of food, fresh vegetables. He stuffed himself. He had to constantly keep on his guard for fear the train would approach a city, but as it wound its way through the mountainous passes, his fear lessened.

Just before dawn, the train started downward. Alex peered into the darkness and saw no lights. He fell asleep.

The train lurched as the engineer applied the brakes. The motion woke Alex. He realized the train was slowing down! It was daylight. Had they come to a city while he was asleep? He ran to the door and looked out. The train was passing over a river. There were several fishing boats below. After the train passed over the bridge, he looked out both sides of the train and saw nothing but fields and the river now running to his right side. The train began speeding up, as if to make up for lost time. He could get killed or seriously hurt if he jumped now. He kept watching for signs of civilization. It was nearly noon when the train began slowing. Alex saw that there was a curve ahead and buildings nearby. He decided to jump.

Alex landed on a hillside and cracked his arm against a large rock. When he stopped tumbling, he was glad to learn he had not broken his arm, but it was damned sore. He noticed several trees ahead of him and ran to them. They were at the river's edge. The shoreline was also covered with weeds and bushes. Great cover. Alex filled his canteen and sat under a bush. He could see the river clearly. A few fishing boats passed by. He felt safe, but he had no idea where he was.

When the sun went down, Alex began to make his way along the river bank. He stopped an hour later and watched as three fishermen tied up their boat and took their catch up a long, dusty road. The river seemed to flow east. He slipped into the water when the men were out of sight and swam to the boat and climbed in. The fishermen had left some food and water onboard. He untied the boat and let it drift away from the dock. It was motorized, but he didn't want to chance starting the motor because of the noise. Guiding the boat to the middle of the river by manually turning the rudder, the boat picked up speed when it got out into the fast-moving current.

The boat floated soundlessly by a small village where most of the lights were out and past a larger town. Just as he was going under a train bridge, the boat veered off to the right and got caught on a sand bar. Alex couldn't free it, and decided to swim to shore.

He no more got into the water than the boat freed itself and floated away from him. Alex swam to shore. He struggled up on the river bank and collapsed. He was very tired and knew he had to find cover. He knew he'd be found if he didn't. But his energy was gone. There was no moonlight, and he couldn't see anything. He managed to get to a thicket and crawl inside. He prayed hard.

He was about asleep when he heard the sound of a train whistle. It seemed to be coming right at him. Alex jumped up and ran forward only a few feet until he tripped over the train tracks. The train's headlight came into view. Quickly, he scrambled into the cover of some bushes and waited. He smiled a few seconds later when the engine passed him. It was going slow.

It wasn't a clean boxcar or a sanitary one. They'd probably just unloaded cattle. The smell was a familiar one. But it was a ride.

The train crossed over the river once again that morning and Alex could see a town on the horizon. The train slowed in anticipation of arriving at the station, and Alex, once again, jumped off. The foothills were covered with trees and Alex had no trouble hiding the rest of the day. That night, he started off to circumnavigate the town and catch the train on the other side. Only this time his luck ran out.

As he neared a clearing, a voice called out, "Halt. Who is there?"

Alex stopped dead in his tracks. If he gave the wrong password, the sentry would give the alarm. Alex thought and then began staggering toward the guard pretending to be drunk. "It's only me, friend," Alex said in a slurring voice. "Have you got any more wine?"

The guard stepped out of the shadows. Alex stumbled and fell. The guard, his bayonet fixed, approached cautiously. Alex began to cry. "My father is dead. My father is dead," he said through a flood of tears. The soldier didn't know what to do. He came nearer. Alex slumped as if he passed out. The guard prodded him with his bayonet. Alex didn't move.

He put down his rifle and tried to roll Alex over. When he did, Alex hit him in the throat with the side of his hand. The soldier immediately grabbed his throat. He couldn't call out. Alex kicked him in the stomach. He bent over, and Alex hit him on the back of the neck with both hands. The soldier fell to the ground. Out cold. Alex first instinct was to run. But which way? He backtracked, dragging the soldier behind him into the trees. He had to dispose of the man or he would regain consciousness and call out. He used the soldier's belt to tie his hands around a large tree root and gagged him. Alex ran back in the direction he had come from.

He had to see what was in front of him. He waited until it was light enough to use his binoculars, then climbed a tree and scanned the area. There was an army base right where he had planned to go. He picked an alternate route and managed to skirt the base by late afternoon.

But, when he got to the other side of the town, there were no train tracks. They just stopped at that town. He couldn't believe it. Having no real options, Alex set out toward the east on foot.

Eleven days later, Alex was standing on a plateau above yet another valley. The terrain was all beginning to look alike. He was tired, hungry and discouraged. It didn't seem as if he was getting anywhere.

Suddenly, he heard the whine of an engine and then its roar as a plane passed overhead about five hundred feet above him. It was a Russian Yak, CJ6, a low winged Russian-designed fighter with Red Chinese markings. Then another and another passed over, very low. They seemed to be coming from the west. Alex ran for the cover of a group of boulders and wedged himself in. He was forced to stay there for the rest of the day because each time he made up his mind to move, another plane would come swooping over. Were they searching for him? The same planes made several passes over the plateau. But they weren't circling or dipping their wings to indicate a search. He couldn't figure out what they were doing.

After nightfall, he went down the hill to a stream and cleaned himself up. Refreshed, he started back up the mountainside to hide for the day when he saw a road. Beside the road were several baskets of vegetables from the nearby fields. He took a few from each basket hoping no one would notice in the morning. An hour later he was into the rocks and underbrush of the mountain.

About four in the morning, Alex was still climbing. As he got to the top, he was knocked over by the prop wash and noise of a plane passing not ten feet above him. He rolled back down the hill. Whew, that was a close one, he thought. If that plane had been five feet lower his prop would have taken my head off! He brushed himself off and made his way back up the hill. Before he could get back up to the top, another plane passed over. He turned and watched the navigation lights make a left turn and fade into the darkness. This time when he got near the top of the hill, he crouched down and crawled the last few feet. He looked over the ridge and found himself staring right down the middle of a runway, complete with white runway lights and blue lighted taxi strips. The end of the runway was about a mile away, and he could see that the hill was about 100 feet above the runway. That meant that the pilots had to get the planes off the ground and climb quickly. He watched another take off toward him, the wings dipping and the landing gears staying down much too-long. "Trainers," he said, "practicing night takeoffs and landings."

Alex saw the stars were fading in the sky and surmised that he had less than two hours of darkness. He needed a place to hide out during the day, and he wanted to be able to get a good look at the airbase. By the time he found it, the sun was already up. It was a rock overhang in the side of the mountain. The front of the overhang was masked by several bushes. He decided to get some rest first.

Alex was awakened about nine in the morning by the sound of a Yak CJ6 fighter being started by a portable generator. He climbed back to the top and using his binoculars, he looked down over the airfield. It was large. He counted twelve barracks-like buildings, six large hangers, four small ones, four Administrative buildings and a large operations building with a tall control tower perched on top of it. All the buildings were painted grey on the outside. At the south end of the runway were parked 4 MIG 19 jet fighters, 2 ILS MIG 21's, a Russian IL 21 bomber and an old U.S. C-47 transport plane. All carried the markings of the Red Chinese Air Force. Near the hangers three more MIG 21's and a MIG 19 were parked in a line. At the other end of the main runway 27 Russian Yak CJ6 fighters were parked in neat rows. These were the kind of plane he had seen yesterday and last night. They were single seated, low winged fighters used at the close of World War II. They looked like British Spitfires. He saw three squads of men parading near the Yak CJ6s and a group of men standing around one of the fighters as a man with a pointer seemed to be instructing them. "No doubt about it, this is a training base," he said out loud. He watched all day as various flights took off and landed, the beginners in the Yak's, the advanced in the 19's, and the ones near graduation in the 21's.

The main runway ran east to west and a taxiway ran parallel to it. There was a north/south runway at the west end of the east/west runway. The bunkers that protected the 21's were inset in the side of a hill near the main runway. The other planes were just parked on the apron of the taxiway.

"Walking out of here is one thing," Alex said aloud, "but riding out is another. The only problem is how to get aboard my transportation." Alex surveyed the field carefully and made a map of the field on the ground. There were two possibilities. One was to break into one of the bunkers and try to get a 21. The problem with that was how to get it started without a generator, and whether he could fly a jet. He'd never flown one.

The second possibility was the Yak CJ6s. They were parked along the side of the taxiway and sitting out in the open. He didn't see any guards. At night he could slip down and make a try. Again, he would have to find a way to get one started if it wasn't equipped with an electric starter. But that was a chance he'd be willing to take. Then his hopes were dashed. Just as the sun started to go down, he saw a truck pull out on the apron of the taxiway, Several guards with dogs got out and positioned themselves near the planes. The same thing took place at the other end of the runway by the jet bunkers and hangers. Alex sagged back and heaved a great sigh, "It looks like you'll be walking, my friend," he said to himself. He decided he'd better get some rest.

At nightfall, he woke from his nap and packed his things for another night's march. He had picked out a land mark before he went to sleep and started off toward the western end of the airfield. He had to skirt the airfield to avoid detection. He was about a thousand yards from the runway on a small rise when the runway lights went on. The white light of the lights lit up the whole area. He climbed higher up the hill into the shadows to avoid being seen. There was a chilly wind blowing down the valley from east to west. He heard the sound of engines starting. It was the sound of the propeller-driven Yak fighters. He looked down the runway, and at the far end of it, he saw landing lights from three planes as they taxied out onto the taxiway and headed in a line toward his end of the runway. As the three planes got to the end of the runway, they stopped on the taxiway just below where Alex was hiding. The first one revved up his engines, checked the magnetos, and then taxied onto the runway and took off. The plane circled the field and made a touch and go landing, then another, and finally a third before it then landed and taxied back to the parking area. When the first plane reached the parking area, the pilot got out of the plane, and another pilot took his place. Then the new pilot taxied down to the end of the runway to take his place in line. For the duration of the practice, Alex observed that there were always two planes waiting on the taxi strip and one doing night landings and take offs. Alex watched for a few minutes, and slowly an idea was born. "If there aren't any guards out on the taxiway," he surmised, "And if I could get up on the wing of the last plane in line, which he could see sat in almost total darkness, except for its own landing lights, and if the pilot kept his canopy open as those pilots are doing right now then, I might be able to get the pilot and steal the plane. It's a hell of a lot of ifs, but maybe."

He rechecked the area where the planes were waiting to take off. He couldn't see any guards through his binoculars, but it was possible, since the night was very dark, that they were in the shadows. He had to make sure. Alex left his satchel and made a wide sweep around the bottom of the hill onto the flats. He crawled through the tall grass toward lights of the runway. He stopped about 500 yards away from the planes and waited and watched. The only guards he could see were nearly a half mile from the planes, near the jet bunkers, and he could only see them when the landing lights from the practice planes hit the area. As far as he could make out, there weren't any guards walking the perimeter. One "if" down, two more to go. The next problem was much more complicated. How to get near enough to the plane to get on the wing without being seen. He couldn't just run up to the plane from this distance. It would take too long and the chances of his being seen running by the pilot and possibly even the guards was too risky. He could crawl his way up, but it would take too long. The next plane's landing lights would be sure to see him. But, if he could get on the wing undetected, how was he going to get rid of the pilot? From his vantage point, Alex saw that all of the pilots had their canopies open until just before they took off. Once on the wing he could get to the pilot. However, the big problem remained, how to get close enough to get on the wing quickly.

He was just about to go back behind the hill where he left his pack and other things, when he noticed that no plane came up to replace the last one that took off. He decided to wait and see the last plane take off. He did. After it landed and went to the parking area, the lights on the runway were shut off. It was totally dark now. It was so dark that he could practically walk to the planes, he thought.

Crouching low, Alex made his way toward the runway. He was almost up it when he stumbled and fell into a ditch. He let up a yelp. Rubbing his leg, Alex laid perfectly still, listening to see if anyone heard him cry out. There were no sounds except the wind and some noise of mechanics working in a bunker across the way. He laid there for a few minutes thinking, "If I can get into this ditch and camouflage myself before the runway lights come on... That's it. I'll try it."

Alex went back to his hiding place under the overhang on the side of the mountain and began planning. He had to eliminate as many elements of chance as possible. The first thing he decided to do was to get his bearings and see what the landscape around the field was like, so that he could take advantage of any cover he had not used in getting to the runway ditch that night. He'd sleep on it.

By midday the next day, as he was surveying the area, he noticed something that had not occurred to him. The wind had changed. It was now blowing from west to east just the opposite from the last night. From what he knew of meteorology and just plain common sense, it was more likely that that would be the direction the wind would blow most of the time. It meant that the planes would probably be taking off from the other end of the runway. He focused on the other end of the runway and through his binoculars saw the ditch ran alongside the taxiway at that end, too.

As he was making notes, he watched three MIG 19s taxi out and toward the east end of the runway to practice daylight take offs and landings in just the same fashion as the propeller planes had done the night before. As he watched he noted that there was one advantage if the planes took off from the east end of the runway - not too far from that end of the runway the ditch was deeper. Another factor that concerned him was the terrain around the air field. Once he took off, he wanted to fly under the radar. Was that possible? He was too far down the side of the hill to see very far. He decided to climb to the top of the hill and take a good look, but he couldn't do that in the daylight. He'd have to climb up at night, see the situation and climb down the next night. The trip would cost whole day. He decided to do it anyway. He also knew he had to check out the amount of time he would have between the time a plane pulled up last in line, and the time the next plane's landing lights lit up that plane. He could only do that by observing the actual Russian Yaks. He devised a system for measuring time since he had no watch. He simply counted in a straight rhythmic cadence. The jets took off to a count of 655, on the average. It took a count of 1,500 for a plane to take off, practice, land, change pilots, and get to its place in line again. Alex practiced all that day counting in a steady rhythm, mentally timing the interval. The last problem was how to kill the pilot, get him out of the plane and into the ditch. The weapon he chose was the garrote again. He had been successful before and the pilot couldn't talk or cry out. He took a small piece of rope about two feet long from his kit and tied a knot in the center of it just as he had done when he killed Ling. Instead of wrapping the ends of the rope around his hands, he fashioned handles at either end so he would have a better grip. He spent hours practicing looping the rope around the stump of a small tree so that he could do it in the count of two. He watched as the pilots climbed into their planes, fasten their seat belts and shoulder harness. He was too faraway to see exactly what kind of fasteners they were using, but he thought he knew where the fasteners were by the position of their hands as they buckled up. He reasoned he might very well have to do it in the dark, and so he closed his eyes and imagined everything step by step. That evening before nightfall, he climbed to the top of the hill. As far as he could see it was flat or rolling plains to the east. The hill at the west end was high, but not too high to climb over. What was beyond his eyesight was anyone's guess.

Throughout the next day he surveyed the area and practiced counting and looping the garrote. Alex made a grass mat the length of his body out of straw. When the sun went down, he made his way down the hill and into the grassy area. He watched the guards near the Yak CJ6s. He was closer to them than he had been to the ones guarding the jet fighters. One thing was the same - the guards didn't move from the tie-down area. After watching for over an hour, he decided to take a chance and sneak into the ditch before the runway lights came on. He gathered up some tall grass, like that around the concrete runway, and stuck it into his shirt and pants. Slowly he made his way to the ditch. He laid down in it just at the turn in the taxiway so that the landing lights would sweep across him but not dwell on him. He hoped the pilot would be too busy watching where he was going to notice anything in the ditch.

Alex laid in the ditch for an hour waiting for the runway lights to go on. When they did, the whole area was so bright he was sure everyone in the world could see him, but as his eyes got used to the glare, he saw that it was darker than he first imagined. And he was in the shadow of the wall of the ditch. Not long after, the runway lights came on, he heard the whine of the engines starting up. He covered himself as best he could with the grass mat. The roar of the engine of the first plane coming toward him grew deafening. As the plane's landing lights swept across him he lay perfectly still.

He should have anticipated what came next - the prop-wash from the plane's propeller nearly blew his grass mat away. He held on to it for dear life. Some of the grass had blown away, and he began to worry that as the night wore on someone would surely see him. Even in the cool night air, sweat trickled down his temples and his back. Because of the runway lights, there was no way to get back to the woods without being seen. He would have to wait it out.

After six or seven planes had passed by, he began to think more clearly and began counting. He timed the intervals between when the landing lights swept over him from one plane to when the lights of the next plane swept the ditch. The interval was much shorter, averaging a count of 430, he would have to be able to do everything much faster.

Finally the planes stopped coming, and the runway lights were turned off. Totally worn out from the worry as well as the counting, he made his way back to his camp. The next day, under the cover of some bushes he again timed the intervals. In between time he tried to remember his Chinese geography. He figured he was about 900 miles from the Formosan straits. He estimated the Yak CJ6 air speed at best was about 285 MPH, making it about four hours flying time to the coast. Alex knew all of this was guess work, but he had to take the chance. He decided to get some rest before making his move. He laid down under the rocks, pulled his blanket up and fell asleep.

When he awoke, it was much later than he had planned. The sun was low in the sky. He checked his equipment, his pistol, his binoculars, his garrote. He had also woven more grass into the mat he'd been using for cover. His mind was racing with details. Through his binoculars he checked the wind sock on top of the control tower. The wind was from the west to east. Alex was all set. As the sun dropped below the horizon, he made his way down the hill toward the spot he'd picked out to wait. He was nervous as a cat.

CHAPTER THIRTY-ONE

Near Changchih, China, May 13, 1962

Alex bent low and made his way toward the ditch. It was pitch black out, a perfect night. When he got to the ditch, he took his bearings and moved to his position just opposite the turn in the taxiway that led to the runway. He laid down and covered himself with the grass mat. It was a perfect cover. He waited.

Two hours later, the runway lights went on. He steeled himself for the task before him. He had practiced getting out from under the blanket in a five count. He was ready. The sound of the engines starting began only a short time later. "The first plane should be coming any moment now," he nervously murmured to himself. Then, to his dismay, the sound of the engines began to get fainter. They were taxiing to the other end of the runway! "God damnit!" Alex said, "the wind shifted." He was right.

Alex spent the rest of the night watching the planes climbing over his head. When the runway lights went out, he returned to his encampment on the hill disgusted and tired. "I've got to think positively," he chided himself, "I got in a lot of practice counting and thinking. I'll be ready tonight." He went to sleep.

He made two trips down to the runway again that night. No flights. The next night, no flights. By now he was getting worried. Were they through with this training? He was running-out of food and water and becoming very tense and jumpy.

The fourth night, Alex again went down to the ditch and waited. Nothing for a long time. He prayed for a chance, but it looked hopeless again that night. Then, as if God had heard him, very late that night the runway lights went on.

"Dear God," he prayed, "Don't let the wind shift again." The sound of the engines starting was music to his ears, and when the first set of landing lights crossed over him, his heart began to pound furiously. He couldn't think, he was paralyzed.

After four planes had taken off, Alex began to settle down. He began counting… the first interval, 456, the second, 421, the third, 440, and so on. His rhythmic counting getting a steadier beat as time passed quickly by. As the light from the next plane swept past him, he looked out from under the blanket. He could see the pilot sitting in the cockpit about forty yards from him. He took off the binoculars from around his neck--they might get in the way. He retied his shoelaces. He counted … 451, 422, 500! Time was running out now, he must make his move. The next plane. The landing lights of plane number 084 swept over the blanket. Then it was clear. Alex flipped the blanket off and, in a low crouch, ran up beside the plane. The pilot was stretching his arms up in the air and looking about.

He planted his right foot on the wing. He kept low, the garrote in his right hand. As soon as he put his other foot on the wing, he grabbed the other end of the garrote with the other hand and made a loop. Then he stood up facing the cockpit. The pilot was turning to face him when Alex slipped the rope over his head. Both men knew what was going to happen. Alex pulled, 98, 99, 100, 101…

The pilot instinctively reached for the rope, but the knot was in perfect position … his neck was broken. Alex checked to make sure he was dead then reached in and quickly found the buckles for the seat belt and the shoulder harness and unsnapped them. 153, 154, 155…

Alex removed the pilot's helmet and unplugged the radio wires, noting where each came from and tugged on the lifeless body. He was heavy but Alex managed to get him up onto the edge of the cockpit. His leg was caught. It was being held by one end of his seat belt. 223, 224, 225… Alex gave a mighty tug and the pilot fell over onto his shoulder. Alex climbed down, carted him to the ditch and dropped him in. Quickly, Alex covered the body with the grass mat and ran back to the plane, 310, 311, 312... When he put his foot on the wing, he heard the engine of the plane in front of his rev up. He pulled himself onto the wing and into the cockpit and looked around. The landing lights of the next plane were moving toward him. He started replacing the wires one by one. 397, 398, 399, 400... His thoughts were interrupted by the noise of the plane in front of him revving up his motor, and moving up in line, as the front plane taxied out onto the runway. Alex pulled the helmet on his head. It was a tight fit, but it'd have to do. He plugged in the last two wires, and he heard a crackling of a radio in the earphones in his helmet.

The calm, steady voice of the ground controller in the earphones giving his instructions in his clear Mandarin dialect was crisp and clear. "081 you are cleared for take off, wind is from the west at 6 li, altimeter setting 3019. Call on base leg."

"081, Roger."

Alex struggled into the shoulder harness and fastened it.

"084, 084, this is Wu Hai, do you read me?" the controller asked.

Alex panicked. What was his plane number? He had checked, what was it?

"084, 084, this is Wu Hai over."

"084, that's me," Alex remembered. Now came the crucial test. Would they recognize his voice as not being the other pilot's? Alex found the microphone and took a deep breath. He pushed down the switch, and in a high-pitched Mandarin voice said, "Wuhai, Wuhai, This is 084."

"084, you are not up close enough to 076, move up."

"084, Roger." Alex was now sweating profusely. "Move up he says." Alex scanned the instrument panel. The dials were all lit up in red lights so as not to impair a pilot's vision in night flying. There were the familiar turn and bank indicator, fuel gauge, and oil pressure gauge. The instruments were labeled in Chinese characters, but he knew which was which. He found the throttle and put his feet on the rudder pedals. He pushed down and the brakes came unlocked, but the plane lurched forward because the throttle was too far forward. Alex slammed his feet down on the rudder pedals and fortunately hit the brakes. The sudden stop threw him forward, but he was held in by the shoulder harness. "Damnit Hunter," he cursed to himself, "be careful!"

"084, 084, are you in trouble?" the voice crackled over the radio.

"Wuhai, this is 084, no trouble."

"084, 076 reports you almost ran into him. You must be more alert."

"I know, I know," Alex said to himself under his breath. "Wuhai, 084, Roger."

Alex began to relax more after the initial test, and he felt more secure. "At least they didn't know I wasn't the pilot by voice," he assured himself. Alex went down a take off checklist out loud, "Inch the throttle forward until it is three quarters of the way open, leave yourself a safety valve of power, keep the tail wheel on the ground until you feel you can't hold it, then lift it off and get up to... up to what speed! I don't know the take off speed of one of these things! I'll just try to feel it. Once you are off, pull up the gears... where's the lever for the landing gears and the flaps." He looked and saw two levers. He couldn't decide. "Just won't use the flaps until I'm airborne and I try one of these levers."

"Keep the rudder pedals even... "

"076, 076, this is Wuhai, you are cleared for take off, the wind is from the east at 8 li, Altimeter setting 2019. Call on base leg."

"076, Roger."

The plane in front of Alex moved up and turned onto the runway. It stopped, revved his engines, released his brakes, and shot off down the runway. Alex moved up again, this time a little smoother, although he again jerked to a stop. He checked and rechecked everything. Then he waited for the other plane to make its practice take offs and landings. The time seemed endless. Nervously, he fiddled with the stick, and wiped the sweat off his hands. He kept his feet firmly planted on the brakes. Finally 076 made its final landing and taxied off the runway toward the parking area.

"084, 084, this is Wuhai, you are cleared for take off. The wind is from the west southwest at 6 Li. There is a slight cross wind so you must compensate. Altimeter setting 3010. Call on base leg."

"084, Roger," Alex blurted out in his best Chinese. He released the brakes and taxied shakily out onto the runway. He tried to line the plane up in the middle of the runway. He was very nervous. He closed the canopy, wiped his hands on his pants, and quickly rechecked all the instruments. Then, after hesitating for a moment, he gripped the stick firmly and pushed the throttle forward. The plane shuddered as the engines wound up, and he held down the brakes until he felt he could hold it no longer. He released the brakes, and the plane fairly leaped forward. It was all he could do to hold the plane in a straight line as he began to roll down the runway picking up speed every second. Finally, he got lined up and was rolling straight. He looked at the airspeed indicator 120 MPH, he slowly pulled back on the stick, eased the throttle forward and the tail-wheel lifted off. 150, and then he eased back on the stick a little more and "Hurrah!" he yelled as the plane lifted off the ground and began climbing rapidly. He could hardly contain himself. The excitement was welling up inside him. He fought to control of himself. "Steady boy. Steady, you're not home yet." Alex looked at the instrument panel. The altimeter read 700 feet. He eased back the throttle, reached down and pulled on a lever. Suddenly the plane began to shudder, "Goddamnit, that's the lever for the flaps," he yelled. There was an empty feeling in the pit of his stomach as the plane suddenly dropped right out from under him. In one motion he pushed the lever back down and pushed forward on the stick. "We're stalling, damnit!" He felt the stick begin to respond and he pushed the throttle forward and pulled back on the stick. Once again he began to climb.

"Now let's try the other lever, this must be the wheels." He pulled on the lever, and felt a rush of air under him and soon the dull thud under him as the wheels found their place in the wheel wells. The plane immediately began to nose upward. He eased back on the stick, and looked at the altimeter, 1,200 feet.

"084, 084," the voice of Wuhai cut in, "You are too far out and too high for this exercise. Turn left and return to the pattern."

"084 to Wuhai, Roger," Alex replied. He turned left and began to lose altitude.

"084, that is better, call on your base leg."

"Wuhai, 084, Roger."

Alex made a slow turn to the left and watched the compass, 60, 70, 80, 90 degrees. 90 degrees due east. He straightened out and began losing more altitude, 500, 400, feet.

"084, 084, what is that matter? You are too far east of the pattern, and you are dropping off our scope, are you in trouble?"

Alex didn't reply for a minute, he was thinking, then a small grin spread across his face.

In a very high panicky voice Alex suddenly screamed into the mike, "Wuhai, Wuhai, I am having engine trouble, I can't control the plane!"

He nosed over and started a dive but began pulling out immediately.

He pulled out at 100 feet and leveled off.

"Wuhai, Wuhai this is 084 I am out of control. He pulled out the plug to his radio microphone.

"084, 084, what happened? 084 do you read me?"

Alex laughed out loud for the first time in a long time. The laugh became uncontrollable. The plane dipped, but he managed to recover just in time. The altimeter read 100. He pulled up to 200 feet and sat in a pool of sweat. "Wow, I almost laughed myself to death."

The radio crackled from Wuhai, "084, 084, where are you? Does anyone see anything? 084, 084, come in!"

Alex settled back carefully watching the altimeter and headed due east.

For the next fifteen minutes the desperate calls from Wuhai continued pounding in Alex's ear. He just whistled along becoming more and more relaxed.

Suddenly out of nowhere a hill loomed in front of him. He pulled back on the stick hard, and the plane nosed upward, narrowly missing the top of the hill. The plane was getting near the stalling, point, and Alex dropped the nose, but then another hilltop flashed by on his right side, instinctively he rolled the plane over on its left side only to see another hill directly in front of him. He pulled up again. Now he was really scared. All of a sudden he was in hilly terrain and up to 2,000 feet. The perspiration was rolling off his forehead.

"Damnit, Damnit, Damnit! What the hell is this? Where did these hills come from?" Alex yelled out. Then again, like a huge black ghost, another hill came racing toward him from the left side. He rolled the plane over and pulled up again. He felt a bump as the tail wheel hit the top of the hill he narrowly missed.

The altimeter was climbing to 4,000 feet. As he climbed out, he looked back, "Someone has got to have me on their radar scope by now, I've got to get down below 300 feet." He decided to drop down slowly. The plane started downward, suddenly another mountain loomed up just in front of him, Alex pulled back with all his might on the stick and banked to the right, narrowly missing the mountain, only to see another peak just to the right, he kicked the left rudder medal and yanked the stick over, "I've got to see better. It's pitch black out." Alex turned on his landing lights and his heart sank. All around him were hills and mountains. "Christ! I'm right in the thick of a mountain range. This is stupid as hell, I'm gonna wind up smeared along the side of some hill."

Frantically he pulled back on the stick to avoid yet another hill just in front of him, and took a deep breath. He put the plane in a steep climb. "I've got to get up over the top of this mountain range, and just take my chances with the Chinese radar."

"084, 084, this is Wuhai, our radar shows you 110 li due east of our base, acknowledge," the controller's voice fainter now.

"Well, at least I'm still on course," Alex said to himself.

Alex leveled off at 9,000 feet and got back on his heading of 90 degrees. He wiped his sweating forehead with a shaky hand and saw it trembling. "Control boy, control."

"084, 084, this is Wuhai, return to base, repeat, return to base."

Alex pushed the throttle forward and trimmed the tabs for maximum speed. For the next ten minutes, there was silence as Alex settled down, the shaking stopped. "O.K. bright boy, you're in one hell of a fix now, you don't dare drop down because you don't know what's below you and you know they have you on radar. What's their next step?"

Alex figured that he still had nearly 800 miles to go and at 280 miles an hour that would take nearly three hours. He knew that now that they could see him on radar he would surely be intercepted and shot down. A cold chill ran down his wet back and he shivered involuntarily.

Suddenly his earphones crackled again with a new voice, "084, 084, this is Chi Tan Control, This is Chi Tan Control, do you read me, over?"

The new controller's voice was much louder and clearer.

"084, 084, this is Chi Tan Control. Be advised we have you on our scope, altitude 9,000, heading 090, speed 305."

"305, hummm" Alex thought, "I'm doing better than I thought."

"If your radio is not able to transmit, acknowledge by changing to altitude 8,000, repeat, 8,000."

Alex hummed along. "Maybe they think I'm just lost and the radio is out, I'll just play out the string... "

Alex dropped to 8,000 but did not acknowledge any of the repeated radio transmissions by Chi Tan Control and continued on his same heading.

The low drone of the radar was all but drowned out by the crackling of radio transmitters in the small concrete radar shack just three miles outside the city of Wuhan. Inside, peering at a small blip on the radar scope, two Chinese soldiers watched intently. Seated in front of the scope was a young man about 22, slight in stature, his brown eyes focused on the sweeping line as it passed over the blip. Behind him, standing, was an officer of about 33, tall and heavy set, with steel rimmed glasses. His stern look nearly cut holes in the radar screen. Impatiently he grabbed the microphone laying on top of the radio set and in a voice fighting for control he repeated, "084, 084, this is Chi Tan, return to base, repeat, return to base."

The only sound coming out of the speaker above the scope was the crackling of static. "He is still on the same heading Major," the soldier said quietly.

"Yes, yes, I know," the major said. He walked away for a minute rubbing his forehead. Then he stopped and walked purposefully back and picked up the microphone.

"084, 084, this is Chi Tan, return to base immediately. If you do not acknowledge within one minute, we will intercept, repeat we will intercept."

The soldier looked up, saw the stern face of the major, and immediately went back to the scope.

"Ring Colonel Sung's house immediately!" the major yelled across the room to a girl sitting at a small switchboard.

"Do you think he is trying to defect, or is he just lost?" the soldier at the scope asked, his eyes still watching the scope.

"He is not lost, he would be changing his heading if he were, even if his radio is out."

"On this heading he is just going toward the open sea. He is too far north for Taiwan and too far south for Japan."

"I don't know what his plan is, all I know is he is taking the longest possible route to the sea. Perhaps he wants to be shot down. I just don't know."

Alex was much more calm now and concentrating on his flying.

He had been airborne now for nearly an hour and a half and was making good speed. It was still pitch black out, and since he had turned off the landing lights, only the glow of the red lights on his instrument panel reflected on his face. The steady drone of the powerful engine was enough to lull him to sleep, but he was too keyed up. His eyes searched for a horizon line, some sign of light. It's not too long until dawn, he thought, "what then?"

In the radar shack the major hung up the field telephone next to the radar scope. "You're sending up a training flight to intercept 084?" the soldier questioned.

"Yes, Kiang, a training flight."

"But, well... I am not experienced in these matters, but shouldn't we send up a flight of trained pilots to intercept 084?"

"Kiang, we have an opportunity to give some practical training to our younger pilots. If the plane were armed, and if it were a jet, Colonel Sung and I might have elected to send more experienced pilots, but if he stays on the same heading, and we have no reason to believe he won't, it will be light long before 084 reaches the coastline. Then, if he does not respond to our visual signals to land, our young pilots will get some practical gunnery practice."

"Oh," the young soldier said with a broad grin.

"Besides, the flight leader is a veteran of the Korean War, should the younger pilots miss, there is no doubt he can finish the job."

"And," the younger man picked up on the plan, "since our planes are MIG 23's, it will be a greater challenge to the young pilots to deal with the slower moving prop plane."

"Exactly Kiang, all the better practice. As Chairman Mao points out, 'practical experience is the perfecter of theory'."

CHAPTER THIRTY-TWO

Skies over China, May17, 1962

Alex's hands began to shake. Something was telling him all was not well. It wasn't anything he knew, but he sensed it. His instinct was confirmed as his head phone cracked, "Chi Tan Control, Chi Tan Control, this is Hung Gou Leader, this is Hung Gou Leader, do you read me? Over."

The new voice was a sibilant accent and muffled. Immediately Alex knew a throat mike. Hung Gou was another plane.

"Hung Gou Leader, Hung Gou Leader, this is Chi Tan Control, I read you very clear. How do you read me? Over."

"Chi Tan this is Hung Gou, I read you loud and clear. Standing by for instructions."

Alex listened carefully. Beads of perspiration again popped out on his forehead.

"Hung Gou, this is Chi Tan. We have a possible defector flying a propeller driven aircraft, Yak 6C. Aircraft number 084. His heading is 090. Speed 295. We have you on our scope now, climb to an altitude of 12,000 feet, heading for interception is 130. 084 now approximately at position 427 on grid. It is possible his radio is out of commission."

We will advise further instructions when you are in visual contact. Over."

"Hung Gou, Roger."

The radio fell silent.

"O.K. now I know," Alex said to himself, "the question is what do I do? If I drop down, chances are I'll stack up on some hill, I can't climb much higher because I don't know how to turn on the oxygen. Besides, with me on their scope, they'll know every move I make. I'm gonna sit tight and wait for their next move."

It was fifteen minutes later when the radio crackled again. "Hung Gou Leader, Hung Gou Leader, this is Chi Tan, Over." "Chi Tan this is Hung Gou Leader, go ahead."

"Hung Gou you should be in position to gain visual contact within one minute. 084 is below you and to the right. Altitude 8,000. Report when you have made contact."

"Roger, Chi Tan."

"Visual contact, huh?" Alex quickly found the switch for the instrument lights and turned them off. "Now try to see me you bastard!" Alex strained to see if he could see them above and to the left of him. Then he saw them, the navigation lights of six planes approaching rapidly, they flew almost directly above him. He heard them talking.

"Do you see him, Hung Gou?"

"Negative Chi Tan!"

"'Hung Gou you must have passed over him, you are two miles past him, turn to a heading of 320, repeat 320."

"Hung Gou Roger 320."

Alex laughed. "Thank goodness there's no moonlight."

"Hung Gou Leader, this is Chi Tan, you are approaching 084 again, and he should be directly in front of you."

"I don't see anything, Chi Tan."

"You are less than a mile, do you see him?"

"Negative!"

"Hung Gou you have passed over again, suggest you reduce airspeed to the minimum and approach again, new heading 100."

"Roger 100, am reducing airspeed."

"Hung Gou, this is Chi Tan, reduce altitude to 10,000."

"Roger, 10,000."

Alex was getting a big kick out of the chatter on the air. He decided to try a maneuver of his own.

"Hung Gou to Chi Tan, on heading 100, altitude 10,000."

"Hung Gou, he should be directly ahead of you. Keep a sharp eye out."

"Roger."

Alex suddenly banked sharply and headed right for the oncoming planes. In less than four seconds he felt his plane shudder as they passed over him slightly to the right."

"Do you see him, Hung Gou?"

"I have him on my scope. He is changing course!"

"Hung Gou. We will figure a new intercept course for you." The major failed to close off his mike and over the radio Alex heard, "Quickly Kiang, what do I tell Hung Gou?"

"Chi Tan, Chi Tan, this is Hung Gou. I would like to try a different tactic. We will spread our formation on the next pass so that any maneuver he tries, one of us will see him. Obviously he has turned out all of his navigation lights and instrument lights but we can probably see the flames from his exhaust."

"Hung Gou this is Chi Tan, permission granted."

"Hung Gou flight, this is Hung Gou Leader, execute spread formation... Good. Chi Tan what is the new intercept heading?"

"Hung Gou, the new heading is 085, repeat 085."

Alex quickly changed course.

"He's changed course again correct to 100, repeat 100," the radar man was heard to say.

"Chan to 100, Hung Gou Leader."

"Roger, 100."

The planes were closing in fast now, and Alex knew he was trapped, but he had to get back on his course toward the sea, he turned until the compass read 90 degrees. He shoved forward the throttle.

"Hung Gou Leader, this is Hung Gou 2, I see him, I see him straight ahead, just the light from his exhaust."

"Roger Hung Gou 2, decrease speed and try to stay with him. Chi Tan, Chi Tan, we have visual contact, do we destroy?"

"Negative Hung Gou Leader, Negative. We may be able to force him to land. Circle, 084 until daylight and then signal him visually to land."

"Hung Gou Leader to Chi Tan, Roger."

"Circle and play cat and mouse you bastards!" Alex cursed out loud. "Time's running out. I've got to think of something, but what?" Alex racked his brain for a way out of his predicament but nothing came. He finally just sat there and waited for the inevitable.

"Hung Gou Leader this is Chi Tan," the voice was noticeably weaker, "You are moving off our scope, we are turning you over to Syi Yao Control, switch to Channel 3, repeat switch to Channel 3. Acknowledge."

"Chi Tan, this is Hung Gou Leader. Roger, Switch to Channel 3." Alex heard a click and then nothing. Alex looked up to see another MIG fly past him, the navigation lights shining brightly in the pitch black sky. "I've got to know what they are saying about me." Alex switched on the instrument lights and checked the radio receiver. There were three switches on the radio marked one, two, and three. The switch was down on Channel 1. He flipped the switch up and pushed down the switch for number three."

"Altitude 8,100, speed 300, heading 090. I have you both on the scope clearly, over."

It was another new voice.

"Roger, Syi Yao Control, over."

"Hung Gou Leader this is Syi Yao Control, continue present maneuvers until daylight. Call when you have clear visual contact."

"Syi Yao, this is Hung Gou Leader, Roger and out."

"I can't just sit here and do nothing!" Alex slammed his right fist on the canopy window. His frustration was agonizing. His lids tightened, his mind spinning with thoughts and ideas but so many he couldn't concentrate on one. He shook his head, told himself to stop, to think clearly. After a while, his mind cleared. He considered the facts and finally made a decision. He looked at the radio. "Well, I've got nothing to lose, I'll ask for help, at least it's better than nothing" Alex looked at the switches. He pushed down switch number two. Slowly he reached for the microphone. He gripped it tightly and brought it up to his mouth. He pressed the button, "Friendly forces, friendly forces, I am an American, I am an American, code name Satan, repeat code name Satan. Do you read me? Over." He released the button and all he heard was the crackling of static.

"Friendly forces, friendly forces, I am an American, code name Satan, do you read me? Over," he repeated.

Still nothing.

"Friendly forces, friendly forces, I am an American, code name Satan, I am somewhere over China in a Chinese fighter, altitude 9,000 speed 300, does anyone hear me? Over."

Donald B. Watson, Airman First Class of the USAF was bored stiff at his late shift monitoring frequencies on VHF. He was slowly turning the dial on his receiver, and his headset was propped back off his ears as he worked a difficult crossword puzzle. He was turning, the dial slowly and mechanically with his left hand as he tried to figure out a seven-letter word for a comical old world duck on his crossword puzzle. 31 down. Suddenly he heard a faint voice for an instant. "… Forces I am… " The voice faded. He stopped turning the dial. There was a puzzled look on his face. He put his pencil down and turned his attention to the dial. He used his right hand and slowly turned the dial backward. Nothing. Then back forward again. Nothing. He was scanning between 75 and 90 kilocycles. He shook his head and looked at the puzzle then back to the dial. He tried once again, back to 75. Nothing, then forward again inching along. There it was again. "… Forces. Friendly forces, I am an American, I am an American, Code Name Satan, Code Name Satan, I am over China somewhere. Please acknowledge."

The voice was faint but unmistakably readable. Watson pushed back his chair and called to the officer seated with his head down on his desk. The desk light was throwing weird shadows on the ceiling.

"Lieutenant. Lieutenant Moyers."

The officer raised his head up. "What is it Watson? Need my help again on that puzzle?"

"No sir, I've got something very strange on 82.5. It's a clear voice transmission."

The officer got up slowly from his desk and ambled over to where Watson was sitting. "Turn on the speaker, let's hear it."

Watson turned on the overhead speaker. The static was heavy, but in a few minutes Lieutenant Moyers heard the faint voice too, "Friendly forces, Friendly forces, I am an American, I am an American, Code Name Satan, Code Name Satan."

At that same time, in the radio shack of the destroyer Anderson, Seaman Second Class Geno Cimaglia was listening to the same transmission for the third time and taping it. The door burst open and a young Ensign leaned against the doorway, "O.K. Cimaglia, what's so important I couldn't finish my coffee?"

"Listen sir." Tony played the tape back and the lieutenant listened carefully. He played it again.

Alex kept repeating the same message over and over again. But there was no reply, just static.

Meanwhile, 15,000 miles away, in the Pentagon, Major General William Horton, chief of intelligence for the USAF, was just cleaning up some last minute paperwork before he headed home. It had been a long tiring day, and the 53-year-old General could almost taste the martini his wife would have for him when he walked in the door at home. The buzzer on his desk went off and startled him. He pressed the button. "General Horton? This is Colonel Layman in the code room. We have just received an unusual message from Taiwan, think you'd better have a look at it."

General Horton heaved a great sigh, "It never fails, something always comes up at the end of the day," he said to himself. "I'll be there in a minute Colonel," he replied into the intercom. He gathered up the papers he had on his desk and put them into his briefcase, locked his desk, got his coat from the closet, and walked down the long corridor of the east section of the Pentagon to the code room. The Marine guard at the door opened the door for him.

The young 32 year-old Lieutenant Colonel was standing by one of the many decoding machines reading as he entered. "What is it Colonel? The Colonel looked up and immediately handed the message to the General. He read the message twice. "What do you make of it Harry?"

"I don't know sir, I have the code name Satan being traced at this minute by the FBI, the CIA, and all the military intelligence headquarters. To me it sounds like a hoax. A guy, claiming to be this "Satan" character broadcasting in the clear on a Chinese military frequency sounds pretty fishy."

"It does to me too, I don't see... "

The General was interrupted by the ringing of the phone on the Colonel's desk. The Colonel picked it up. "Colonel Layman. Uh huh, I see, and when was this?" Just then a teletype machine in the corner, began clacking off a message. The General walked over to the machine and watched as a series of numbers in groups of four were rapidly being imprinted on the multi-carbon paper. A young Staff Sergeant walked over beside the General and watched also.

"O.K. Captain," the Colonel said into the phone, "get the file and bring it over." He hung up the phone.

The teletype machine stopped and the Sergeant tore the message off.

"It's from Taiwan sir."

"Have it decoded immediately."

"Yes sir," the sergeant said, and he went to one of the decoding machines and began working.

"General, that was Captain Toski in the file room. It seems we have used that code name, but the last man to be given it, was reported missing over two years ago. Toski's bringing the file in." The phone rang again.

"Colonel Layman, Oh, yes, Commander." The Colonel talked for a few minutes and then hung up. "That was Commander Matich of Naval intelligence. They, too, have just received a message from one of their destroyers reporting the interception of the same broadcast. He's passing it along to Admiral Benson."

"All right, Colonel," the General nodded. He walked over to where the sergeant was decoding the message. "Do you have it yet, son?"

"Just a minute, sir." They all waited. The General paced back and forth. "Here it is sir," the sergeant handed the message to the General. The General read it and handed it to the Colonel. "Radar's picked up seven bogies about a hundred and fifty miles inside China. They are heading due east. Radar says six of them seem to be circling one plane." The General frowned and shook his head.

"Colonel Layton," a balding Marine said as he entered the code room. "Here is the file on the Satan mission."

Alex was getting panicky, and yelling into the microphone, "Friendly forces, friendly forces, I am an American, code name Satan, repeat code name Satan, please acknowledge, please acknowledge." The sweat was flowing down his back now, and he kept his eyes fixed on the horizon for any sign of light.

The long-stemmed glasses clinked together as the champagne swirled in the fine crystal. "To our wonderful twelve years of marriage, Miriam," Hiram Brady said lovingly, and they entwined their arms and drank the toast. Miriam was still one of the most beautiful women in Washington, and Brady marveled again at his good fortune in catching her. A couple at the next table smiled.

"Major Brady?" a waiter interrupted.

"Yes," he said looking up.

"There is an urgent call for you, shall I plug in the phone here?"

"Oh no, not tonight," he said under his breath.

Brady just shrugged and said okay.

"Brady, Horton here," the voice explained, "you've got to get over here to my office on the double."

"But General, tonight's... "

"Now Brady!" The phone went dead.

Hiram took a cab and let Miriam take the car home. He was in the General's office in twenty minutes. After he had read the message, he looked up.

"Well, what do you think Hi?" the General asked. Colonel Layman looked on.

"General I don't know what to make of it. I thought he was dead. We know that he was captured in Tsingtao 22 months ago. It's possible he might've escaped. On the other hand, it could very well be a trick."

"Shit, Major don't give me 'on the one hand or on the other hand', give me something I can go on."

"Well, there is one thing we can do, General, we can contact him and give him some questions to answer that might help to identify him."

"Okay. Write up the questions, we'll have them encoded and sent right out."

"General if what you tell me is true, and it's going to be daylight out there in a half an hour, I suggest we contact Taiwan in the clear. It would save a lot of time. If I know anything about the Chinese, they are circling and waiting for daylight to try and force him down. Every minute counts!"

Alex was getting hoarse by now. To save his voice, he was transmitting about every five minutes. Wearily he again pushed down on the button, "Friendly forces, friendly forces, I am an American, I am an American. Code name Satan," he coughed, "Code name Satan, please acknowledge."

Silence. Alex waited. He looked at the navigation lights on the planes circling him and then he thought he could make out a dim silhouette. He knew it couldn't be long until daylight. He clicked on the microphone again, but before he could speak, the static broke and in a loud clear voice he heard, "Satan, Satan, this is Friendly, this is Friendly, do you read me? Over."

Alex's heart jumped, his mind leaped to attention. Quickly he pressed down the button, "Friendly, Friendly, this is Satan, this is Satan. I read you loud and clear, loud and clear. Over."

"Satan, this is Friendly, this is Friendly, We'd like an identity check. Please give answers to the following questions. What is your real name? Repeat. What is your real name?"

"Friendly, this is Satan, my real name is Alexander Ingersoll Hunter, repeat, Alexander Ingersoll Hunter."

"What is your social security number?"

"Friendly, it is 310-39-3390."

"Satan, this is friendly. One more question. Identify the registration number of your private plane. Repeat. What is the registration number of your private plane."

"That's easy, that's easy," Alex said in a voice filled with a mixture of excitement and tears, "the registration number of my private plane is 866 Bravo, repeat 866 Bravo."

"Satan this is Friendly, please stand by, repeat, stand by."

"But Friendly, you don't understand, there are six or eight enemy planes circling me right now, jets, and I'm in an old Russian Yak 6C. The best I can do is 300 mph. I need help!"

"Satan, this is Friendly. Stand by."

Alex wanted to cry out, but he held back. He was very nervous and getting sick at his stomach from the strain and frustration. He fought himself for control over his body and his mind, "Stand by. They said stand by. Got to, I've got to."

The radio operator at Syi Yao Control had been listening to Alex's conversations with Friendly for some time. Worried, he informed Major Cho, the commander of the control station. Cho smiled, "Don't worry sergeant, they can have all the conversations they want, but the traitor is too far from international waters. He'll never get out of China alive."

Alex looked out to see that the MIGs were now clearly outlined against the pale blue of the sky above, daylight was here. He could see them, and they could see him.

"Syi Yao Control, Syi Yao Control, this is Hung Gou Leader, this is Hung Gou Leader, do you read me, over."

"Hung Gou Leader this is Syi Yao Control, we read you loud and clear."

"Syi Yao Control we have 084 in visual contact. Repeat, we have 084 in visual contact, standing by for instructions, over."

"Hung Gou Leader this is Syi Yao Control, it is possible the defector will land on his own accord. Can you signal him visually to land? Over."

"Syi Yao Control, will do."

The leader banked his plane and dove down toward Alex's plane. By dropping his flaps, he managed to slow his plane down to fly just about as slow as Alex. He worked his way close to Alex's plane and looked over.

Out of the corner of his eye, Alex saw the sun flare off the shiny metal jet as it pulled along side. He looked over and the pilot was signaling with his hands for Alex to land. Alex nodded and smiled at him as the plane pulled on by.

"Satan, Satan, this is Friendly, this is Friendly, over."

"Friendly, this is Satan, Go ahead."

"Satan, this is Friendly. Nice try. Your little trick didn't work. Better luck next time. Friendly out."

Alex was stunned. He grabbed the mike and yelled, "Friendly, this is Satan, I'm not Chinese, repeat not a Chinese, I'm Alex Hunter. This is no trick, repeat, no trick, I have valuable information, please, help me, they're gonna shoot me, down." Tears were streaming down Alex's face. He was shaking like a leaf, and urgency streamed out of his voice, "Friendly, please, come in. Friendly!"

"Hung Gou Leader, Hung Gou leader, this is Syi Yao Control, we have intercepted an English voice transmission from 084. The pilot is not, repeat, not one of our pilots. He is broadcasting on Channel two, repeat broadcasting on Channel two."

"Syi Yao Control, this is Hung Gou Leader, understand, 084 is not one of our pilots. Repeat. Not one of our pilots, over."

"Hung Gou Leader this is Syi Yao Control. It is important this plane not escape. Execute alternate plan 7. Repeat, execute alternate plan 7."

"Hung Gou Leader, roger. Understand execute alternate plan 7. Hung Gou flight, Hung Gou flight, this is Hung Gou Leader, did you copy Syi Yao Control instructions? Acknowledge,"

"Hung Gou Leader, this is Hung Gou 2, understand alternate plan 7."

"Hung Gou Leader, this is Hung Gou 3, understand alternate plan."

"Hung Gou Leader, this is Hung Gou 4, understand alternate plan 7."

"Hung Gou Leader, Hung Gou 5, understand alternate plan 7."

"Hung Gou Leader, Hung Gou 6, understand alternate plan 7."

"Hung Gou Flight, form up on me, repeat form up on me."

Their red stars shining in the clear blue sky, the formation began to maneuver. Alex watched as the six silver fighters slowly flew into formation in the early morning sun, a few miles ahead of him and began to climb as one.

Suddenly, Alex lost the planes, they disappeared. His eyes searched for them, "Where are they? What the hell are they doing now?"

"Hung Gou Flight, Hung Gou Flight, this is Hung Gou Leader, today you have an opportunity to put into practice all the training you have had thus far. Execute the spread formation. Good. Now test your guns."

The voice of Hung Gou Leader was crackling loud and clear in the radio room of the destroyer Anderson. Listening intently were the radioman, Lieutenant Junior Grade Bill Hunsucker, and the skipper of the Anderson, Lieutenant Commander Harold Ello.

"Where are the bogies now Cimaglia?" the skipper asked.

The young radioman looked at the scope, "About twelve miles in front of our man sir, altitude 40,000 flying in a spread formation."

"That poor son of a bitch," the skipper mumbled under his breath.

From a second speaker rigged up on top of the main speaker Alex's voice cut in, "Friendly forces this is Hunter, Alex Hunter, my God, please help me! There are six MIGs out here. I'm unarmed. Please help me!"

"What are we gonna do, Skipper?" Bill Hunsucker asked.

The Commander tilted his cap back on his head and looked at the young Lieutenant, "Bill, that decision is up to the top brass. Probably Washington."

Alex searched the sky above and below him for any signs of the MIGs but couldn't see anything. One good thing he did see was that he was out of the mountains and over the flat lands 8,000 feet below. The almost perfectly checkerboarded squared fields with various shades of green seemed so peaceful and calm. The sun was at about eye level now, and he could barely see the sea in the distance. I must get there, he thought. He shaded his eyes from the blinding sun but could see very little. He blinked his eyes and looked around avoiding the sun. Alex saw that the fuel gauge read less than a quarter full now. "Fuck, they seem to have completely disappeared. What the hell are they up to?" He looked and suddenly a cold chill ran down his back, there they were flying in formation passing over him at least 20,000 feet above. He tracked them until he could bend his head no more, and they were out of sight.

"Hung Gou Flight, this is Hung Gou Leader, we are now in the proper position for attack. On my command, peal off in intervals of two seconds and make your first pass. Remember his airspeed is far less than yours and will be at the bottom of your dial. You must compensate, I will fly top cover. Lyou Chi, you will be last, I expect a strike report from you."

"Lyou Chi, Roger."

"Good hunting. Attack! Attack!"

"Sir, can't we at least give him a warning? They're coming down his back?" the radioman asked.

"Sorry, Geno, you know the orders as well as I."

Alex picked up the mike again, for his seemingly hundredth time, and pressed the button, "Friendly forces, this is Hunter. Please believe me, I am not Chinese, I am an escaped American agent, I have…" Just then one of the MIGs passed in front of him and the sound of his gunfire caught up a fraction of a second later. "Jesus Christ, what the... they're coming in for the kill!" he yelled, the mike still open. Two tiny holes snapped into his right wing as the next MIG passed in front of him. "God damnit!"

Alex shoved down on the left rudder pedal and pushed the stick forward, a second later he was on his left side and diving. The third MIG wasn't visible to Alex nor the fourth, but the fifth stayed on his tail and a line of holes ripped through the fuselage. "Where the hell's the sixth?" Alex said to himself straining to see behind him. Alex pulled up and got back on a heading of 90 degrees.

"Hung Gou Leader this is Lyou Chi, I think Hung Gou 3 and I hit him but there is no apparent serious damage."

"Understand Lyou Chi, form up and make another pass."

"Lyou Chi, Roger."

"Shit, sir, we can't just sit here like this and let that guy buy it," said Airman Watson. The Quonset hut on Taiwan was filled with men listening to the speaker. The heat in the room was about 100 degrees, but no one complained. They just sat there solemnly listening.

"They're forming up again sir," said Airman Second Class Stephen Jones, watching the radar scope at the other end of the Quonset hut.

"What's his position now, Jones?" asked Lieutenant Moyers.

"68 miles from the coast, Sir."

In one corner of the room a Puerto Rican airman was saying his rosary and another boy prayed out loud. "Help him out, Lord, help him."

Alex was twisting and turning in his seat trying to find the planes again but to no avail. But, just at the last moment, as they began to peel off, Alex caught a glint of the sun reflecting off the silver planes. "A sitting duck. Just a damned sitting duck," Alex muttered and pulled the shoulder straps tighter, "I hope this old trick I saw in a movie once works." He looked back to see the five planes coming down at him. He reached down and pushed down the flaps and lowered the landing gears at the same time. The plane shuddered and nearly stopped dead in mid air.

"Lyou Chi, this is Hung Gou Leader, strike report.
"Hung Gou Leader, this is Lyou Chi, we all missed that time, he drastically reduced his air speed."

A cheer went up on both the USS Anderson and in the Quonset hut in Taiwan as the interpreters gave the men the translation of Lyou Chi's report!

"Friendly, Friendly! This is Hunter. Help me! They're attacking now and I'm unarmed. Please, for God's sake, help me!" Alex was yelling now. He had tears in his eyes and sweat pouring out of every pore in his body.

"Lyou Chi, this is Hung Gou Leader, you have all learned one of the basic tricks in air to air combat, the use of airspeed as a maneuver. You are all flying too close to allow yourselves a chance to recover and react to the maneuvers of the enemy. Keep your distance of two second intervals and talk to each other. Reform and make another pass, time is growing short." There was a growing sense of impatience in the leader's voice.

"How far out now Jones?"
"55 miles from the coast sir."
Alex pulled up the landing gears and flaps and the plane leaped forward once again. He searched the sky for signs of the attacking planes once more.
"A-Ten-Shun!" the sharp command came from Lieutenant Moyers as he saw a three star general enter the Quonset hut."
"As you were men," the General said. "Lieutenant, what's the status?"
"Hunter is about 50 miles from the coastline now sir on his present heading. The bandits have made two passes so far and only slight damage to Hunter has been reported."

"I see," the General said. His thoughts were interrupted by the voice on the radio. "Hung Gou Leader, Hung Gou Leader, this is Lyou Chi, we are in position again."

"What the hell is that little chink saying, Lieutenant?" the General barked.

"He says they are commencing their attack again, sir," called out a voice near the speaker.

Alex pushed hard on the right rudder and the plane turned to the right. He looked hard over his right shoulder and saw the MIGs approaching once more. "O.K. you bastards try this one on for size!" He pushed the stick forward as far as it would go and the plane went into a steep dive. The first two MIGs were too close to follow, but the third reacted, and started down after him guns blazing. Alex heard the "tinging sounds" of the bullets as they pierced the skin of the plane. The third and fourth planes passed him up and pulled out below him, the fifth was following him down. He was now going 430 MPH, and the Yak began to shudder. He knew it wasn't built for that kind of stress. Alex could feel it about to come apart and he began to slowly pull out.

"Lyou Chi! Don't try to follow him all the way down; you cannot recover in time!" yelled Hung Gou Leader and the last plane broke off but not without scoring more hits on Alex's plane.

Alex pulled out of the dive at about 500 feet and quickly wiped the stinging sweat out of his eyes with his shoulder. Now the sun was higher in the sky and he could see a long distance in front of him. Still no ocean.

"Lyou Chi, this is Hung Gou Leader. Do not reform. Continue to engage. Time is running out. Repeat, continue to engage."

In the Quonset hut, the interpreter was translating almost simultaneously. "Looks like they're going in for the kill!" said a boy leaning up against a file cabinet.

"Radar man, what the hell is his position now?" the General snapped.

"46 miles from the coastline, sir."

Alex pulled back on the stick once again. I've got to get some altitude for maneuvering, he thought to himself. He decided to try again. "Friendly. This is Hunter. Help me. I don't know where I am. All I can see are fields below, help me."

"Can you plot me a course that will take him to the water faster Lieutenant?" the general asked.

"Yes, sir, we have a chart right here," The young officer said as pulled out a chart from the slots below the desk.

Alex was climbing steadily now, 2,000, 2,500, 3,000, suddenly, out of the corner of his eye, he saw a MIG heading right for him on the left side, he kicked the left rudder, but it was too late. Six 50 caliber bullets crashed into the cockpit smashing his bank indicator and a couple of other instruments. The last bullet tore a gaping hole in his left calf. His foot was thrown off the rudder pedal and the plane began to bank steeply. The wound felt as he had been burned by a cigarette. The pain was intense, but he was so busy trying to fly the plane that he couldn't see or do anything about it. Another MIG passed overhead, its shells tracing a neat line of holes in the aft fuselage and rudder. Alex's plane was nearly out of control as he fought to make his left leg work enough to work the rudder pedals. The plane responded as he pushed the stick forward and to the right. The other three missed with their passes, but Alex felt the stick getting mushy. His plane was not responding to his commands. Alex watched as the last MIG passed by in front and below him. He fired up the radio, "Friendly! That's a laugh! Okay, this is Hunter, I've been hit. My plane is damaged - hard to control. This is my last transmission. It can't take another pass. I've got to pass this on. I saw... "

At that moment two MIGs passed by almost hitting his plane head-on. His plane began twisting as the turbulence from them caused his plane to nearly stall. "You're gonna give it to me in the back aren't you, you chickens. Well, come on. Come on, lets get it over with!" Just then a thin trail of black smoke began seeping out of the engine cowling and oil was racing along the sides of the plane. He laughed. He laughed as the tears were streaming down his cheeks.

"Hung Gou Leader, this is Lyou Chi, he is smoking."
"I see, Lyou Chi, I see. There will be a medal to the one who serves Chairman Mao and downs this enemy."

"Those bastards! Those fuckin' yellow bastards!" yelled Seaman Cimaglia. Several men in the Quonset hut were crying openly now. The General, who had been talking on the phone, dropped it slowly as the translation of the last message was given.

Alex crouched low in the cockpit. He would try to zig zag and maneuver as best he could but he had no idea how well the plane would respond. He prayed. "Dear God, thank you for my life and all the good things you have given me." He looked up again and saw a glint in front of him. Then a tiny speck on the horizon, it got bigger and then became four specks. "They've called in help, those bastards. Can't get me with just the six MIGs." he said with a smile. He looked behind him and saw two MIGs closing in on him. He nosed the plane over. The four planes in front of him were heading right for him.

"Sir, new bogies on the screen," yelled Seaman Cimaglia, the same words came from Jones in the Quonset hut at the same time.

"Hung Gou Leader, there are four planes coming head on at us."
"Where Lyou Chi?"
"6 o'clock!"

Alex couldn't believe his eyes, they were heading right at him, they were going to ram him! A second later they passed by him, and he stared in amazement. Then he screamed, "They're Americans! American planes!" His heart began pounding in his chest, and he wept.

"Lyou Chi, Lyou Chi, they are enemy planes, break off, break off!" Hung Gou Leader yelled into his microphone. "Repeat, break off!"

The cheers were thunderous in the hut and in the radio room of the USS Anderson.

"Hung Gou Leader, Hung Gou Leader, this is Syi Yao Control, four enemy fighters approaching you from the east. Four, repeat, four can you identify?"

"Syi Yao Control, this is Hung Gou Leader. They are American Phantom jet fighters in close formation. I have given orders to regroup, shall we attack, repeat, shall we attack?"

"Hung Gou Leader, this is Syi Yao Control, stand by."

"Blue Leader, this is Blue 4. The five bogies seem to be regrouping with top cover," cracked out of Alex's radio.

"Roger, Sam, I see them. Let's let them make the first move."

"Roger, Blue Leader."

Alex tried to pull the nose up, but the plane responded only part way. He was in a downward glide.

"Hunter, this is Blue Leader, do you read me, over."

"Blue Leader, this is Hunter, I read you, I read you loud and clear!" Alex said his voice cracking with emotion.

"Hunter, what is the condition of your aircraft?"

"I don't know, Blue leader. I'm smoking but I don't see any flames as yet. The oil pressure is dropping but very slowly. I can't maintain altitude."

"Roger. Understand. Turn right ten degrees to course 105, repeat 105."

"Roger, 105."

"Hung Gou Leader, this is Syi Yao Control. Do not engage. Repeat. Do not engage. Continue to follow and stand by for further orders."

"Hung Gou Leader to Syi Yao Control, I'd like to try a pass at 084, I'm sure I can down him."

"Negative Hung Gou Leader, stand by."

"Roger." Hung Gou Leader said, disappointment evident in his voice.

"Blue Leader to Blue four, Sam, you take Charlie down with you and give a look see at Hunter's plane. Bill and I will fly top cover."

"Blue four. Roger."

Alex was busy trying to keep his plane in the air. The controls were very mushy, and he was losing attitude at the rate of 100 feet every minute or so. His leg was throbbing, and he was losing blood. His eyes were red and sore as the sweat from his forehead flowed down his face. His stomach ached, and he was miserable, but happy.

The two navy blue phantom jets their flaps down, glided down beside him. One of the planes went underneath and took a look, the other stayed on his right wing. Alex looked over and saw the pilot giving him the thumbs up. He returned the gesture and heaved a big sigh.

"Hunter, Hunter, this is Blue four. How is your oil pressure? Over."

Alex looked and his face became taught. "Oil pressure is dropping much faster now."

"Hunter, this is blue four, you've taken a hit in the oil pan and that's what's causing the smoke. Just try to keep her up. You keep drifting to the left, try to keep, on course, it's the shortest distance to the coast."

"I've been hit in the left leg, and I can't hold it on the rudder pedal too long without a lot of pain."

"Hunter, can you put a tourniquet on it?"

Alex looked around, and there was no medical kit, then he remembered the garrote somewhere on the floor. He found it and tied it around his leg above the knee. He was getting dizzy now.

"Blue four, how far is it to the coast?"

"Hunter, this is Blue Leader, we can see the coast from up here, you are about twenty-five miles out. Stay with it. If you drop on the mainland we can't help you any more."

"Hunter to Blue Leader, I'll try." Suddenly the plane dipped again and Alex fought the controls and managed to get the nose up a little.

"Hung Gou Leader this is Syi Yao Control, return to base, repeat, return to base."

"Syi Yao Control, this is Hung Gou Leader, I know I can slip down there and get him. Request permission."

"Hung Gou Leader, this is Syi Yao, return to base!" It was a new voice and a very strong one this time. "We cannot jeopardize the new fighters, return to base."

"But, Syi Yao, if I had only known sooner."

"They came in under the radar, it is too late. Return to base."

"Syi Yao, this is Hung Gou Leader," his voice now very listless, "Roger, return to base."

"I see it! I can see the water!" Alex yelled, he was now only about a thousand feet above the ground.

"Sam, get out from under him."

"Roger, Blue Leader."

The phantom jet slid out from under Alex's plane and came up on his left wing. The two jets escorted Alex out over the pale blue water of the Yellow Sea. Alex's plane was losing altitude rapidly.

"Hunter, this is Blue Leader. How much longer can you keep her up?"

"Blue Leader, this is Hunter, not much longer. There is no oil pressure now and the engine is sputtering a little."

Three minutes later, Alex heard, "All right, we're over international waters now. While you have a little power, I think you should ditch. Have you ever ditched in the sea before?"

"Negative."

"O.K., listen carefully. Check your shoulder harness and make sure you know how to get out of it quickly. Now, the sea is reasonably calm today. Keep your gears up and lower your flaps."

Alex began to lower the flaps and the nose took a dip.

"Pull the flaps up Hunter, you haven't got enough power to hold it! Pull 'em up!"

Alex did so immediately and the nose went up.

"Good. Now can you get the nose up at all to stall it?"

"I don't think so."

"Hell, you have to. Don't do it now, but then you get about 20 feet off the water, cut the engine and pull back of the stick as hard as you can. Now, open your canopy as wide as you can get it."

Alex struggled, his strength was ebbing. With his last ounce of energy he pulled the canopy back. The wind rushed in and the cool air was like a good slap on his face. He was more awake now.

"O.K., the canopy is open."

"Good, now drop her nose and pick up some speed, then flare out and let her drop."

Alex pushed gingerly on the stick and the nose dropped slowly.

"Good. Remember, when you hit the water, it will feel like a rock. Don't worry about that. As soon as the plane settles, get out of that harness and out of the plane."

"Roger." Alex said evenly. He was trying to concentrate, but his mind kept wandering. "Can I get out at all? I can't think, what if I drown? I don't have a life jacket or a raft. What can I... "

"O.K. Hunter, pull the nose up, as much as you can," Blue Leader cut in.

Alex pulled back on the stick, and the nose came up, but not as much as it had before. It looked like he was going to dive into the sea.

"O.K. Hunter, good luck. Cut the engine and pull back hard on the stick."

Alex cut the switch and with both hands he pulled back on the stick, no response. Still no response. He was diving into the sea. Then, as if someone was under the plane and pushing up, the nose began to rise. Suddenly, Alex could only see the sky and the horizon disappeared. Then he hit the water. He was thrown forward but stopped by the shoulder harness. The plane bounced twice then slowly settled into the sea. When he knew he was stopped, Alex quickly undid his harness and seat belt, and then tried to lift himself out. A jet went screaming over him. He pulled off the helmet and pulled out the wires. The sea was rolling the plane, and he felt the plane slowly sinking. He could see water washing over the wings.

He struggled, but without the use of his left leg, which now just hung there, he couldn't get out of the plane. It seemed like hours, actually it was only a minute until he finally managed to pull himself up on the edge of the cockpit. He fell over backward and hit his head on the wing. He tried to move as the water rushed over him but he was too exhausted.

"Move, move it you son of a bitch," he was telling himself, "get off the plane, it'll drag you under!" He was screaming at himself, but try as he would, he couldn't move. His hands slid out from under him and he fell back and looked straight up. Directly overhead a U.S. Navy rescue a helicopter was dropping three paramedics. He heard them splash into the sea around him.

Alex blacked out.

CHAPTER THIRTY-THREE

Taipei, Formosa, May 20, 1962

Alex yawned as he woke from a long, deep sleep. He felt spaced-out. He was very thirsty. His lips were cracked and dry. He opened one eye to see where he was. It was a very bright room. The walls were white and the ceiling was checkered with little holes. He realized he was flat on his back, and when he started to turn over, a pain shot through his left leg. Alex raised his head and saw his leg was elevated by a rope contraption of some kind. Out of the corner of his eye Alex saw a nurse sitting in a chair in the corner. She was reading a magazine. The door was closed, and there was a dresser across from the foot of the bed with flowers on it. It seemed like a normal hospital room - he wasn't used to a normal hospital room. "Nurse," he called. "May I have a drink of water?"

The nurse looked up and smiled. She had a black stripe on her nurse's cap indicating she was an R.N. She got up and came to Alex's bedside. He noticed she wore Captain's bars on her lapel. "First let's see how you're doing," she said as she pulled a thermometer out of her pocket, shook it down and stuck it in Alex's mouth.

She was a tall woman, Alex guessed she was in her mid-thirties, with a trim figure and red hair. As she approached his bed and began to take his temperature, Alex noticed she had green eyes and a smile that was warm and friendly. The nurse removed the thermometer and looked at it. "Fever's gone. Pulse is good. I think you'll live," she said with a grin. "I'll get the doctor." As she walked away, Alex noticed she had a great figure.

He sagged back on the pillow, which smelled like soap, and relaxed. Closing his eyes, he flashed back to the last thing he remembered, the guys jumping out of the helicopter and splashing only a few feet from him as he clung to the wing of the sinking plane. He shook his head in disbelief as the ordeal of flying out of China replayed in his mind.

His recollection was interrupted. "Good morning, Mr. Smith. I'm Doctor Rolands. I tried to fix up that leg yesterday. Sorry we had to knock you out for so long, but we felt you needed your rest." The doctor was a long, tall skinny man with a bald head and no eyebrows. He had a space between his front teeth and his coat was wrinkled. The oak leaf on his lapel identified him as a Major. "How are you feeling?"

"Well, first I'm not."

"For our purposes you are Mr. Smith. Now, I repeat, how are you feeling?"

"I'm not sure," Alex frowned. "I feel kind of numb all over and sore."

"Part of that's the anesthetic, and the other probably as the result of the buffeting you took during your arrival. You had quite a few bruises and cuts in addition to the leg wound. Which, by the way, wasn't too bad. The bullet went all the way through your calf and didn't seem to do too much damage. We'll have you up tomorrow."

"Tomorrow?"

"You'll be sore, but you'll be able to manage. Now that you're awake, we're going to do a few tests, blood work, the like. Want to make sure you're okay to travel."

"Where am I going?"

"Don't know. My instructions were to get you ready to move, and that's all I know."

The nurse pushed in a wheel chair as they were talking. "Nurse Gilroy will take you on your rounds. I'm going to undo your leg support, and it may hurt a bit, but we've got to get you going. I gather there's some urgency. By the way, there's a Colonel waiting outside who wants to talk to you, but I told him no go until we finish the tests. Okay, let's do it."

It was painful, but with the help of the nurse and the doctor Alex was soon sitting in the wheelchair. Gilroy pushed him out the door and past the Colonel who was in his dress greens. "Mr. Smith."

"Lay off, Colonel. He's ours right now," Dr. Rolands said as he accompanied Alex and Nurse Gilroy down the sterile hall to an elevator. The Colonel nodded.

The tests took three hours. When they were finished, Alex was wheeled into another examining room. A few minutes later, Dr. Rolands came in and gave Alex his report - everything was good. The leg wound was doing fine, and he should be able to travel in the morning after a good night's rest. "I've talked to them and they sent the Colonel away for now. Get some rest and I'll see you this evening."

After the doctor left, Alex lay on his bed trying to make sense out of what had just happened. Obviously whoever 'they' were didn't want anyone to know his real identity. He guessed that the incident over China was probably drawing a lot of attention and he supposed that had to do with security and foreign relations. He was sure something was up because when he was taken back to his room two big Marines were guarding the door.

He was tired and his body felt like one big bruise. He fell asleep.

Later, Alex remembered being wakened by Dr. Rolands and that he gave him a shot. Then softly everything went black. He curled up in a ball and stayed that way the whole night.

Alex was awake when Dr. Rolands came in the next morning. The doctor gave him a checkup, redressed the wound on his leg and pronounced him fit to travel. He was given civilian clothes and wheeled out of the hospital to a waiting limousine. When he got in, he wasn't surprised to find Colonel Brady in the back seat.

"Morning, Alex," Brady said.

"Morning, Colonel. You get that promotion for sending me to hell and back?"

"Probably." Brady nodded to the driver, and Alex noticed a Marine in the front seat with the driver. "I know you want to talk, but I think it's best we not do that here. Sit back. The ride isn't long."

Alex noticed that Brady was much more aloof than he was before Alex left. He seemed to be angry and irritable. He didn't look Alex in the eye and he seemed to move away from Alex in the seat. Alex was sure something was up besides security. He'd have to wait and see.

They drove through the city of Taipei. When they arrived at the air base, they went directly to the tarmac where an RB-50 transport was waiting with the engines turning. The Marine opened the door and Alex, using his crutches, got out and followed Colonel Brady up the stairs. The crew chief immediately shut the door. Alex was led to a seat opposite a table in a plush cabin inside the plane. Brady settled into the seat opposite him. The plane started rolling immediately.

Brady ignored Alex during take off. When they reached the cruising altitude, a steward came in and asked if they wanted anything. Alex smiled. "A Coke. I haven't had one in a long, long, time."

"Yes, sir," the steward said. Brady ordered coffee.

When the steward returned with the drinks, Brady ordered him to shut the two doors on either end of the special cabin and not disturb them for an hour. The steward did so.

Brady rubbed his chin and leaned back. "Alex, what happened over there?"

"Everything went okay until we found out about Walter's plan to trap us. Then we had to improvise."

"Trap? What trap?" Brady asked as he leaned forward.

"Didn't Sz An tell you?"

"Sz An was dead when we got to them."

"I didn't think he was wounded that badly."

"He's dead."

"And Roger?"

"He's okay."

"What do you mean 'okay'?"

"Okay," Brady said curtly looking hard at Alex. "He managed to get the sailplane down in one piece. Why did you shoot Sz An?"

"What? I didn't shoot Sz An. Roger did!"

Brady eyed Alex out of the corner of his eye, hesitated for a moment and rubbed his chin. He seemed to be pondering Alex's response. After a few seconds, Brady asked, "Roger? Why would he?"

"Because he wanted to escape. He had no intention of defecting. His plan was to get me or someone over there and then use them to ferret out other agents."

"You've got me confused. He wanted to use you to get to other agents? Did he know about Sz An being our agent?"

Alex nodded. "I think he'd known it for a long time and used Sz An to get to... "

"Us," Brady interrupted.

"Exactly. And his plan worked until we captured him, and sent him to you. That was his worst nightmare."

Brady looked down at the floor for a moment. "So he didn't come over voluntarily."

"He jumped Sz An, that's how he got shot. I overpowered him, got him into the sailplane and got Sz An in, too. Sz An was wounded but I thought he'd get fixed up once he was in your hands." Alex suddenly stopped talking. "Wait a minute. You think I defected, and Roger's the good guy?"

Brady heaved a big, long sigh. He unbuckled his seat belt and walked over to the door and made sure it was closed. "We let him believe that's what we thought. In fact, only three of us guessed what now turns out to be the truth." He laughed. "You have no idea what havoc your turning up is going to cause," he said chuckling more. He leaned back. "Alex, we've kept your return from Roger, and everyone else who sided with him. I know I'm supposed to be debriefing you, but I want to tell you what's going on before you botch it up."

"When Roger and Sz An were rescued, we were all shocked you weren't with them. Roger said you had defected, and he and

Sz An had a fight with you and they won. He said you shot Sz An and so forth. Nancy Clark and I were, to say the least skeptical. In secret, we had an autopsy performed on Sz An and found that he had been smothered to death and did not die of his bullet wounds. The blood in the cockpit confirmed that he had been alive when he was put in the sailplane so the only conclusion was that Roger killed him. Now we were faced with a dilemma. If we confronted Roger with our findings, he would be on his guard, hard to interrogate, uncooperative and probably of little use to us, so we didn't tell him. In fact, we told him the opposite. We cursed you and patted Roger on the back. We frankly thought you might be dead, and as the months went by, we were sure of it."

"In the meantime, we debriefed him, and true to any spy, he told us the truth about some things and not others. He gave us his 'insight' into the Chinese intelligence community and some names of the higher ups. He gave us names of a few agents in the U.S., and we took them into custody. But, we already knew most of them. Now before you jump ahead, we did talk about his murdering your wife, Crissy."

"He admitted it?"

"No, of course not. He said it was an accident, and that they were just playing around when she fell over the balcony rail."

This information coincided with what the Chinese told Alex.

"We swallowed it, and said we had come to the same conclusion. A lie, but a useful one. He seemed to relax, and we pretended to as well. When there was no word about you for six months, we decided you were dead or at least in prison for life. We declared the debriefing over and asked if he would like to work with us. Now here's where the tricky part came in. Since only a few knew he was still on their side, we had to let the C.I.A. in on it without blowing our cover. They took him on staff, but during the physical exam they found a cyst and had to operate. There was no cyst, but there is an implant that can be monitored. It was the first one we experimented with. It works. Roger's whereabouts are known at all times even though he thinks he's free. His apartment is bugged and so on. It took him nearly a year to get bold enough to act. He contacted some people whom we found out were agents and has been exposing their network in dribs and drabs for nearly seven months. He's been very useful to us. That's why I didn't want you to walk up to him and kill him - which, I'm sure, you want to do. You'll have your day, Alex. You deserve it. Patience." Brady leaned back and studied the wheels turn in Alex's head. "I'm sure you have questions, but hold on to them. We have work to do first. I'm taking you to a debriefing safe house. Several people are very anxious to talk to you about the last two years."

Alex shook his head. "There's something I must tell you first. It's more important than I am, or Roger or anything. The Chinese have an atomic bomb."

Brady sat up as if pushed. "What?"

"I saw it and a rocket they have they can launch to carry the damned thing."

"You saw it?"

"Yep. It's a long story, but I saw the missile and the place where they made the bomb. They have one of our top nuclear scientists working on it. Dr. T.S. Hsien."

"Hsien? The guy who disappeared from Los Alamos four years ago? You met him?"

"No. But his name was all over the crates the missile came in. And I saw him at a guard gate near the base when he gave his identity papers to the guard."

"Jesus Christ! Are you sure?"

"I'm sure."

"When do you think they'll attack?"

"I don't think they're going to attack. China isn't in some military mode. Everything seems to be going normal, but I do think that they're going to test something soon. Maybe the bomb, maybe the missile, I don't know what. I don't know when. I do know this is important."

"An understatement, Hunter. I'm pretty sure no one at the C.I.A. or N.S.A. know anything about the Chinese having an atomic bomb. Fuck the rest of this debriefing, I need you to tell me every detail of what you saw, where you saw it, and when." He went to the door and opened it. "Where's that map of China I asked for?"

Moments later the steward brought Brady the map and left the compartment. Brady spread the map out on the table. "Any idea where this place is?"

Alex turned the map around and studied it for a long time. He had an idea in his mind, but he couldn't be certain where it was. He knew it was in the western part of China, but that was a lot of area. He ran his fingers along a line looking for a name, a road, anything that would give him a clue where he was when he discovered the secret base. He was at a loss.

Brady came over and stood beside him and pointed to the southern coast line of China near Formosa. "You ditched here," he said. "100 Kilometers north of Fuzhou. Let's try to re-trace your escape. The range of the Yak C-6 is approximately 500 miles. If we make an arc 500 miles from the place where you ditched it will give you some idea where you stole the plane." Brady used the mileage projection on the map and drew the arc. "Anything?"

Alex looked at the areas near the penciled arc. He shook his head. He studied the map more closely tracing the arc with his finger and stopped. He pointed to a spot on the map. "I think I crossed the Yangtze River here."

"Good. Use that as a reference point and study the map some more," Brady encouraged Alex.

Alex squinted and turned the map several times. He wasn't sure. Brady watched. Alex studied. Then Alex looked closer. He ran his finger near the arc and stopped. He sat back for a moment then returned to the map. Again he ran his index finger along the arc and stopped at the same place. "I think this is the location of the airfield. Sorry I can't be more definite."

Brady looked at the place where Alex was pointing. He rubbed his eyes. Then he snapped his fingers. "Be right back," he said as he went forward to the cockpit. He returned a few minutes later. He came back with another map. He put his finger near Yichang. "You were right. Our navigator recalled a training base here. 50 miles West of Yichang."

"In a valley?"

"Let's look." The relief map confirmed the location. "Good. Now let's try and figure out where you were and where the damned missile site is. Tell me about your escape from the prison."

Alex explained that they were moving him from the prison to Sining. The truck went south and passed through the one town's name Alex could remember - Yongdeng - which is where the driver filled up with gas. It was during that stop that he got free, and he killed the driver between Yongdeng and Hekou. He then drove west into the mountains and until he nearly ran out of gas. There he changed clothes with the driver and ditched the truck off a mountain cliff.

Pointing to the map, Brady figured that he ditched the truck in the Migang Mountains.

Alex started walking south through the rough terrain of the mountains. He walked for five days until he came to the valley where the secret base was hidden. They guessed that it was somewhere near Sining. After he discovered the base, he started walking east. He walked for nearly four days then hopped a train. When the tracks ended at a city, he walked east again. It was rough going in the mountains and crossing rivers and streams. He saw the airbase near a large river - possibly the Yangtze - converging with two other rivers. There were several villages along the river and a town in the basin. After studying the map, Brady guessed the airbase was at Yichang.

Alex told him about how he stole the plane in the dead of night and got airborne.

"We know the rest of the story."

"Why didn't you help sooner?"

"A long story. Right now we need to get this information about the bomb to the right people. I'm going up to the cockpit for a while. Why don't you write down all you can remember about the missiles, the tunnels, etc. and any clues to help us find the place. I'll be back soon." Brady left.

Alex sank back in his seat and closed his eyes. He was happy Brady had believed him about the bomb, and that it was important, but what he was most happy about was being back among friends. A soothing calm washed over him, and he felt warm and safe. He was going home. He tried to imagine what his office and apartment looked like after two years. Then he saw her - his secretary, Ginny. What must she have thought on that day when he left without a word?

Alex dozed off for a while. In his dream he remembered his apartment and saw in his mind's eye his dresser with the picture of Crissy in the middle. Poor Crissy.

Then, suddenly, Alex woke and sat straight up. It was as if a door had been opened and he had walked through, he realized her death wasn't his fault. He wasn't the cause of her death. It was Roger. It was like a huge weight had been lifted from his shoulders. He was free - really free - for the first time since Crissy died. He sat up straight and opened his eyes. A shiver went down his back as he felt like laughing for the first time. A smile crept across his face which turned into a grin which became a laugh - a laugh out loud. It became more and more uncontrollable until he lost control and fell off the chair. The fall hurt his leg when he hit the floor. But it didn't matter, he sat there in a pool of joy.

After a minute, he regained his self-control and started to get up. When he reached for the table to help himself up, his hand slipped and one of the notes Brady was taking fell on the floor. Alex reached for it and sat back down on the floor and read, "Alex is having trouble with reality. His handling of his wife's murder is atypical of normal behavior. Dr. Newfeld?"

Alex studied the paper for a while then put it back on the table and pulled himself up into his seat. He looked out the window at the darkening sky. He could see his reflection in the window. He was a changed man. His hair was almost grey, his eyes looked like two sunken holes, and he had wrinkles on his forehead. He looked sad even though he felt happy. Maybe Brady is right, he thought. Maybe I have lost it.

Brady returned and sat at the table. "Alex, there's been a change in plans. We are going back to the place where you trained. For now, we're skipping the usual debriefing. Several people are flying in to talk to you about the bomb and your observations of the activity. I cannot tell you how important this is, and how important it is to keep this information under wraps. We'll be there in six hours. During that time, you have to help me figure out the most likely place for this secret base. Are you with me?"

"Of course," Alex said but thought it was a stupid question.

CHAPTER THIRTY-FOUR

Near Waco, Texas, May 22, 1962

When the plane landed in Texas, at an auxiliary training field, it was met by five cars. Alex and Brady were shuttled into one of the cars and the caravan sped off in the morning sun.

Alex recognized the house from a mile away. He could hardly believe that it was more than two years ago that he began his journey through hell in that very house.

For the next ten days, Alex and at least twenty experts hashed and rehashed everything Alex told them. Within two days, there were high-altitude photos of several possible sites. By day eight, the long table in the situation room was filled surveillance photos. The blowups, confirmed by Alex, pinpointed the secret base thirty-two miles southwest of Yichang. In several of the picture blowups, trucks could be clearly identified, and the entrance to the cave was pinpointed. As for the other information on people, what he saw, the size and description of the missiles, etc., each detail was dissected to the finest point. Alex was thoroughly exhausted. The only thing that went well for Alex was the presence of Lieutenant - now Captain - Nancy Clarke. She could confirm some of the things Alex told the group of scientists, military engineers, intelligence and logistics specialists gathered at the house.

Just before noon on the tenth day, Brady sent Alex out of the room. The consensus of the group was that they had all the information they needed. They expressed their profound thanks to Brady for saving Alex and for sending him over there in the first place. Brady called Alex back into the room. When he entered, the applause was enthusiastic and genuine. Brady then gave a farewell message to everyone in the room, and reminded them that no one was to talk about any of this except to those high up in the Atomic Energy Commission and the White House.

Alex, Nancy and Brady had a leisurely lunch on an outdoor patio that Alex didn't even know existed. Brady told Alex that he knew he was exhausted, but before they left, Alex'd have to be completely debriefed by a team from N.S.A. and the C.I.A. That team arrived the night before.

The two-week debriefing was painful for Alex. Reliving the murder of Lan Yin and the tortures and solitary confinement, and of course the endless 'indoctrination'. He told them that he did not resist once the physical torture was over, and that he found many of their doctrines good - good for him, good for the people. He said that he might have stayed in China had it not been for the one mistake that Comrade Su made of assuming that Alex would believe the U.S. would welcome Roger with open arms. Several strange looks crossed in back of Alex when the debriefing team heard that. Alex noted that when he talked about Roger, a couple of people took long notes. They frowned a lot, too, he noticed.

He also noticed at there was a 'good cop/bad cop' ploy working during the debriefing. Brady was the 'bad cop' asking all the hard questions, and Nancy was the 'good cop'. She would take Alex on long walks and rides in her convertible. They'd chat about everything, but Nancy managed to get in her questions as well. Alex knew all of this was going on, and he used his experience both from his work in intelligence in the Air Force, and from the 'education' techniques that Chinese used. He wasn't fooled. He'd laugh at night about all the hoops they seemed to jump through to get information from him - which, ironically - he was glad to give them. He had nothing to hide.

The next step in his 'return to normalcy' was anything but normal. They finally got around to Roger. What Alex heard, he did not like.

CHAPTER THIRTY-FIVE

Alex knew the formal debriefing was over when none of the 'debriefers' showed up for dinner. It was just Brady and Nancy Clarke. The rest of the small dining room was empty. Alex took his seat, glanced over his shoulder and said, "Something really good on TV I didn't hear about?"

Nancy laughed and Brady raised his eyebrows. Alex waited. "They had to go home, the street lights were on," Brady said. Everyone laughed. They had cocktails, ordered their dinners and made polite talk. The longer this went on, however, the more edgy Alex became.

"Enough," he finally burst out. "Where is everybody, and what's going on?"

The waiter was just coming in with their dinners. "Before or after dinner, Alex?" Brady asked.

"Before."

"Please keep our dinners warm and don't disturb us until we call," Brady told the waiter. He nodded and went back out with the plates of food.

Brady nodded to Nancy. She returned the nod. "Alex, the formal interrogation is over. We all believe there would be no purpose in continuing. You have been very cooperative and extremely helpful - especially when it came to the atomic bomb information. You have done a great service to your country," Nancy said in a well-rehearsed speech.

"But?" Alex said.

"No buts about your debriefing, Hunter," Brady said. "We all know you've been through a hell of a lot over the past two years. No one intended for that to happen to you. But it did, and it's in the past. Frankly, you amaze me. For a person so reluctant to take on this mission, you turned out to be terrific. Now," Brady said as he pushed back his chair and lit up a cigarette, "It's the future we're concerned about. We're anxious because we want you to stay involved, and we're not sure you will. It would be on a strictly volunteer basis. We all feel we can't order you to do anything against your will. But before you say 'no', please listen. What I'm about to tell you must never be revealed to anyone outside this room. Nancy and I and a few of our intelligence people are running another mission. We started it the day we got Roger."

"When they were rescued, and you weren't aboard we were immediately suspicious. Thus the autopsy, and thus the findings. But that's not what we told Roger. We told him Sz An died of complications to his wounds and left it at that. It was the consensus of the team that Roger was still a traitor and that we should use him if we could. His debriefing was tough. He was confronted with the evidence of his involvement in your wife's death. He didn't admit anything, and we pretended to accept his story."

"What do you mean 'pretended to accept his story'? They told me, when I was a captive, that Roger admitted he pushed her over the railing."

"He denied telling the Chinese anything about his involvement with your wife."

"That's not what they told me," Alex said.

"The fact is, Alex," Brady went on. "We suspected he murdered your wife within a few days of her death but were having a hard time proving it until we put the pieces together. By that time Roger had defected and we didn't want, wrong as it may have been, to get you all worked up again about her death. On hindsight we should have told you, but the irony is that because you didn't know for sure he killed Crissy, you were able to complete your mission. We were afraid that if you knew, you'd kill him on the spot, and we wanted him. So much for confession time. All that's water over the dam."

"You knew?" Alex asked incredulously.

Brady nodded, "Yes. The C.I.D. did. It wasn't until Roger announced he wanted to defect that they briefed me and a few other people about Crissy's murder and Roger's involvement. Nancy didn't know until we debriefed Roger."

"I still don't understand why they didn't tell me."

"I'll put you with the C.I.D. man in charge. He knows a lot more about that than I do."

Anger welled up in the pit of Alex's stomach. He fought for composure. Finally, in a soft, even voice he said, "I want to talk to Roger."

"We thought you'd say that, and believe it or not we want you to, but not for the same reasons you think. We want you to support Roger."

"What?"

"Hear me out before you fly off the handle. Roger is free to come and go right now. Why? Because we are using him and have been for the past year and a half to break up and identify Chinese agents and cells. All this without his knowledge - or at least we think so. It has netted us several agents and one cell at M.I.T."

"You actually think that Roger is helping you? That's not the Roger I know. He's much more cleaver than that. The trap he set for us backfired on him. He never intended to leave China. But, since he was forced to come over, my best bet is that he is using you - not the other way around."

"You may be right. And we considered this before we let him loose. We don't trust him, either, that's why we implanted the tracking device behind his ear. We haven't lost contact yet."

"Do you think he knows about the device now?"

"No."

"You sure?"

"There's no way he could have found out. He was under sedation when it was implanted and not wakened until the wound healed. I really don't think he knows about it," Nancy interjected.

"Could be, but I wouldn't put money on it. Does this device have an audio signal?"

"No."

"So you can see, but not hear."

"The research hasn't perfected the audio signal yet."

"Well, at least he can't defect, you hope. So, what is it you want me to do? "

CHAPTER THIRTY-SIX

Washington, D. C., June 23, 1962

Alex's plane landed at Washington National Airport on a hot and humid, rainy morning. He was alone. He took a cab to Georgetown and got out in front of a modest two-story brownstone apartment house.

Alex climbed the stairs, took out a key and entered. The apartment was sparsely furnished. He went upstairs to the bedroom, unpacked his few belongings, and sat down on the bed. He looked at the 'instructions' Brady had given him. He wasn't sure he wanted to do what they asked, but he did want to see Roger. He wanted to see Roger very much.

A few hours later, he burned his instructions in an ashtray, checked his Smith and Wesson .38 pistol, and put it into his shoulder holster and put the holster on. He grabbed his new sport coat and put it as he walked out the door. The special cab was waiting. Alex gave the driver an address and sat back. He was still unaccustomed to his freedom. He frequently checked to see if anyone was following him. His hands shook and sweat poured down his back. He kept remembering Comrade Su telling him about how Roger described Crissy's death. He stared out the car window without seeing anything.

When the cab driver told him they were at their destination, Alex was shocked at how few minutes it took to get to the restaurant. Instinctively, he reached for his wallet to pay the driver. The driver turned. He was one of the men at his debriefing. "It's all part of our full service plan, Mr. Hunter. Just look for this cab whenever you want to go someplace. We'll be nearby."

Alex got out and walked into the restaurant. It was a small, Italian place with white tablecloths and candles on each table. It wasn't crowded. It was only a few minutes after five. A waiter came up to him and motioned to him, "Sit anywhere, fella. It's early yet."

"I have a reservation."

"So?"

"I think it said what table I was to sit at."

"Oh," the waiter grumbled and reached behind the bar and took out a reservation book. He looked at Alex, "Name?"

"Hunter."

The waiter looked at the book, then frowned. He looked again, looked at Alex, slammed the book closed, and waved to Alex. "You're early. Right this way, Mr. Hunter." His attitude had changed dramatically. The table was in the corner of the room with a view of the entire room. Alex sat with his back to the wall and ordered a coke.

By six thirty, the place was full. Every table was taken. The crowd at the bar was loud and noisy. Alex had hardly touched his spaghetti and meatballs. He toyed with them as he watched the door. It was seven forty-five when his vigil ended. Roger came in with a beautiful young woman. The waiter greeted them as old friends and took them to a table that was being cleared. Alex covered his face with his napkin as they passed in front of him. His hands began to shake and his stomach was tied up in knots. He knew he didn't have a hard job this first night, but he was becoming frightened. He had to go to the bathroom. He would have to pass near their table. He couldn't wait. Crossing the room, he avoided eye-contact with Roger. He needn't have worried because Roger and the girl were in heavy conversation. When he returned to his table, he managed to keep his back to them.

Alex sat there a long time. He knew he had to get Roger's attention, but it took him time to gather up his courage. Finally, he paid the bill and stood up. As he stood up, his chair fell backwards making a loud noise. Many in the room looked at him. Roger was one of them. Alex replaced the chair and left the restaurant without looking back at Roger. His cab pulled up in front of the restaurant, he got in, and it immediately sped away.

Roger watched Alex's exit. He wasn't positive it was Alex, but it certainly looked like him. How did he get back? The last time he heard Alex was being reeducated. His thoughts were interrupted by his date who tugged on his jacket and urged him to sit down, people were staring at him. Roger sat.

"You look like you just saw a ghost, Roger," she said.

Roger looked back at her. "I did."

Alex laid down on his bed and looked at the ceiling. It was all so very strange, he thought. Three months month ago I was sitting in a cell in China. I actually felt safe, and now here I am back in America and I'm scared. He got up, went into the bathroom and began brushing his teeth. When he looked in the mirror he wondered if Roger even recognized him. His hair had touches of grey, his face was thinner, and he'd lost a lot of weight over the past two years. He should have looked back at Roger, he chided himself. It was important Roger see him - thus the ploy with the chair. He ran his hands through his hair and resigned himself to the fact that the first contact may not have worked. He climbed into bed and stared at the ceiling until he fell asleep.

Alex stayed in his neighborhood for the next two days, but on the morning of the third day the cab was waiting outside promptly at nine. Alex was surprised at the change in the weather. It had been cold and rainy since he got to Georgetown, but this morning it was warm and sunny. He felt in good spirits when he got into the cab. "I'm to tell you that you did a fine job the other night. The fish took the bait," the cab driver said as he drove away from the curb.

The cab pulled up in front of a three-story stone building on "H" street. "Room 310," the driver said. "Back at two."

Alex nodded.

The building was being remodeled, and there were painters in the hallway on the third floor. Alex knocked at 310 and entered. A secretary sat at a desk reading a magazine. She tipped her head toward the inner door. Alex entered. Brady sat behind a tattered desk. "How ya feel?" he asked as Alex put his coat over a chair and sat down.

"Okay."

"Good. I'll bet it was pretty hard on you."

"You might say that."

"Well, you lost your virginity. Now it's time to get to work, Alex." Brady sat up straight in his chair. "From now on you're going to be more or less on your own. We'll try to back you up, but you shouldn't rely on us. Understand."

"Yes."

"As our little drama plays out, if you have a question or want to quit, call up on a pay phone. It's a special number that you won't forget. 555-5555. Someone will be there all the time. You remember the plan?"

"I know what I'm supposed to do, but you didn't give me any specifics."

"They'll come as time progresses. The cab driver will know. I called you here today to ask if you want to go on with this."

"Yeah, I do."

"I thought you would. Roger looks pretty good doesn't he?"

"I didn't notice."

"Really. Were the stripes on his blue suit blue or grey?"

"Neither, and it was a brown sport coat."

"So much for not noticing. Okay. I can't tell you what to say when you two meet, you'll just have to follow your instincts, but we're more interested in what he says. You've got a cover story, you can tell him we told you his. Aside from that, let's see how things play out." Brady stood. "Watch your back, Alex. Both figuratively and literally. We won't be close enough to help immediately although we'll keep his tracking device working day and night. Good luck," Brady said as he held out his hand. Alex nodded. He left without shaking Brady's hand.

When the door closed, Brady picked up the phone and dialed. When the other person answered, he said, "Keep everyone out of sight. I think he's going to do it."

Alex waited in the shadows of the Mayflower Hotel entrance. He knew Roger would be along any minute. He shuffled his feet nervously as he watched the revolving door. Minutes later, Roger came out and looked around. The doorman was busy unloading a car and there were seven other people waiting in an ad hoc line for a cab. Roger started to go back inside but changed his mind and began walking in Alex's direction. Alex stepped out of the shadows and headed straight for Roger. A car horn sounded, and Roger turned in the direction of the sound. He turned back to see Alex pass by him so close he could touch him. He spun around. "Alex? Alex Hunter?" he asked.

Alex kept on walking for five steps then stopped. He did not turn around to face Roger. He waited. Roger came up behind him and tapped on his shoulder. Alex turned slowly and faced Roger.

"Alex? How did you?" Roger's face was beet-red.

"Let's not talk here," Alex interrupted.

"The bar?"

"Fine," Alex said and walked toward the revolving doors. Roger tried to keep up.

They sat at a small table in the back of the bar. Many of the tables were occupied. It was nearing seven that evening and Alex knew the bar would pretty much clear out by seven thirty. They didn't say anything until the waitress took their order. When she left, Roger said, "I thought you were dead."

"A lot of people did, I understand."

"What happened? How did you get here?"

"It's a long story and I suspect you know much of it. I walked."

"Walked?"

"From Lanzhou to Kunming."

"Walked? Impossible."

"Okay, so I lied. I had some help. A couple of trucks gave me a lift, and I managed to get a hard seat on a train for a while. I walked in between and ended up at Putao in Burma. I called home and here I am. You probably read about it in the Washington Post. Brady showed the article to me. I looked pretty bad, but boy was I happy."

The waitress returned with their drinks. Alex raised his glass, "Reunion."

"Reunion," Roger said.

"Anyway, enough about me, tell me about Sz An."

"He didn't make it. I'm sure you know that, in fact, I'll bet you know a lot about me."

"I know you lied to everyone about wanting to defect and then told them you were happy you could defect. I know you've been 'cooperative' to an extent, but I doubt you really told them anything important. I also know that your value to Brady and the others is diminishing. After all, we both know things change with time, and it's been what? Two years? They're sure you're out of date."

"They told you that?"

"No. But I know that's the way they think. It's the way all intelligence people think - tomorrow is important - yesterday is nothing - unless yesterday gives you a hint into tomorrow."

"One of Mao's teachings."

Alex nodded. "The man was brilliant. I never knew before my 'reeducation'."

"It didn't take."

The waitress returned with their drinks.

"It did for a while," Alex said. "And, it still guides me sometimes. The problem is I'm not sure when it's going to kick in."

"So why the meeting?"

"I'm not really sure. One minute it's because I want to kill you for killing Crissy, the next is because I want something from you."

"What?"

"I want to know the real story. Why you and she were together in the first place."

Roger sat back and rolled his glass around in both his hands and stared at Alex. He was thoroughly confused. The whole idea of Alex coming back never crossed his mind until the other night when he thought he saw him at the Italian restaurant. Now this sort of cat and mouse conversation. Why? Is he going to try and kill me? Would Brady and his people let that happen? What does he want from me? It sure as hell isn't about his time with Crissy. He decided to play the game a little longer.

"Well, Roger," Alex prodded.

"You want the truth?" Alex nodded. "Okay. The truth is Crissy and I had been making it behind your back almost from the first time you met her. You'd take her to a movie, I'd take her to bed. She liked that. When I told her I wasn't going to marry her, she said she'd marry you. I said 'go ahead'. And she did. On my first R&R to Tokyo, I looked her up, and we started over again where we left off. But she made a big mistake. She thought she'd trap me into marrying her by getting pregnant. When I found out, I told her to get an abortion, and she said no. The day she took a flyer I had come to take her to a doctor and get her an abortion whether she liked it or not. We fought. Things got rough, and I pushed her over the balcony. There. Feel better?"

Alex had been told some of the facts, but when Roger told the whole story with no emotion, he wanted to lash out. He wanted to grab Roger by the throat and never let go. But he couldn't. The truth be told, he had suspected Crissy wasn't faithful even before he left for Korea, but he deluded himself into thinking he was just jealous. Now that the truth was out, it took a lot of the wind out of his sails. He sat forward and grabbed Roger by the shirt, "I hate you." Roger didn't struggle. "But I won't kill you. You know why?"

Roger shook his head.

"Because they knew it. They knew you killed her, and they knew about your past with her and they didn't tell me!" Alex found himself shouting. "I lived with that fucking guilt all those years! They're no better than you!" He released his hold, picked up his glass and threw the remainder of his drink in Roger's face and stomped out.

Roger looked over at the people staring at him, smiled and took a drink.

Alex was shaking violently by the time he got out in the chilly night air. He stopped and rubbed his eyes. The cab pulled up. "I want to walk," Alex said.

"Sorry, Alex." He shrugged and got into the cab.

Three days later, Roger was ushered into Brady's office. "What is going on?"

"What do you mean?"

"I mean I haven't gotten an assignment for two weeks."

"Well, right now we have nothing for you. We did investigate that group in Stanford, but you didn't give us enough to go on and the whole thing fell through. Are you having trouble remembering your agents?"

"No, of course not, but I guess I've been holding back on a couple of names."

"Oh? Why?"

"Pocket aces."

"Poker isn't my strong suit, Roger. I need something to justify having you around."

"I'll have to contact some people."

"I thought we arrested all of them."

"Not quite." He turned and left the room. A few moments later, Alex came in from another door.

"It's working," Brady said. "I saw it in his face. He's getting nervous."

"I like to see him sweat."

"We've got to move on. I just came back from Langley, and they approve of our plan. The President has been informed of the bomb and the Senate and House Intelligence Committees, although they don't really know the details. So, anytime you're ready, Alex."

CHAPTER THIRTY-SEVEN

Washington, D.C., June 30, 1962

The main dinning room of the Mayflower Hotel was bustling with the great and the near great. A cross section of influential lobbyists and Senators and Congressmen and women touting each other's influence and rewards. Scattered among them were international dignitaries and missionaries. Everyone in the room had something to sell.

Nancy was sitting with Lin Bao Sing, a beautiful Chinese woman from the Chinese Embassy. Lin and Nancy had been friends growing up in China. Lin's father was a high-ranking minister and Nancy's father was an ambassador. They grew up and went to school in Peking. Nancy left before either of them went to university. They reunited one day while they both were shopping. They had been good friends, and their affection for one another was immediately rekindled. Nancy told Lin that she was in the Air Force working in the Adjutant General's Office. Lin said she was a secretary for the Assistant Chinese Ambassador. Both lied, and both knew it.

Alex was right on time. He bumped into Nancy and dropped his file. Lin bent over to pick it up, and Alex let her have a glimpse of the contents before he retrieved it. The item she saw was entitled "The Chinese Bomb."

"Oh, I'm very sorry Captain Clarke," Alex said before he bent over to get his file. "I should have looked where I was going."

"That's all right, Mr. Hunter," she said formally.

Alex picked up his folder and made his way through the crowded room to a table where two well-known Senators sat. Lin followed him with her eyes. She saw Alex open the file and hand it to a Senator whom Lin knew to be on the intelligence committee. Nancy watched her friend's eyes and waited. When Lin turned back to look at her, Nancy smiled. "Handsome, isn't he?"

"He is, in an occidental way," Lin said.

Nancy laughed appropriately. "You know, I hear he escaped from China."

"Him? The one the Washington Post said walked to Burma?"

"Yes. I met him when he came to see my boss about some sort of back pay problem."

"Interesting."

"Well, I think he's hiding something."

"Oh?"

"They closed the door when they talked. My boss doesn't do that unless it's really important."

"And you don't know what they talked about?"

"No. Besides, you know I can't talk about work."

"I understand. We all have our secrets."

"Enough. I want to know all about your love life," Nancy said with a smile. "You still crazy about Yao Sung?"

"That was a long time ago. Right now, I'm sans beau."

Alex kept an eye on the two women as they talked. He saw them get up to leave, and as planned, he got up and followed them out of the restaurant. The Chinese Embassy staff car awaited Lin. Alex watched as she got into the limo. Nancy was paying for her car. He walked over to her. "You didn't tell me she was beautiful."

"You didn't ask."

"She got the message?"

"Loud and clear."

Alex smiled and walked over to his waiting cab. Lin's dossier was on the backseat. Alex read her background. She'd been a Chinese intelligence agent in various foreign countries six years before coming to the U.S. Her 'talent' was using men. She had seduced at least six major foreign ministers in four third-world countries over the past six years. She had caused at least two of them to resign. Her rank in the Chinese Army was Captain.

Alex pulled up in front of her apartment house. He and Charlie, his driver got out. Charlie listened to his portable radio. Nothing.

While they waited for a report on her whereabouts, Alex decided they should check out her apartment. A note in the dossier said she had three rooms, one with a camera trained on the bedroom. Using a lock pick, Charlie opened the door. They were about to enter when the radio crackled. "She's on the move. She's stopping at the Belgium Embassy," the voice on the radio said.

"Let's head over that way," Alex said. They ran back down the stairs to the cab.

Ten minutes later, the radio crackled again, "She's on the move again." The cab turned the corner just in time to see the Chinese Embassy limo pass in front of them. "We got her," Charlie said into the mike.

They followed the limo to a small bistro, Le Chamborg, on the edge of Georgetown. She got out and went in. The cab pulled up a half a block away. "What now?" Charlie asked.

"You tell me."

"Shall I ask the boss?"

"Why not?"

Charlie keyed the microphone. "The dame's having dinner. What's the plan?"

"Up to Satan," a familiar voice replied.

Alex sat back. He didn't want to be obvious, but he didn't want to drag this out too long.

"Any idea where the Dodger is?"

"Dodger around?" Charlie asked.

"It's dinner time. Try Le Chambord near Georgetown."

They looked at the marquee - Le Chambord. "Got it," Charlie said. "Now isn't that a coincidence?"

"Or a plan?"

"Or a plan," Charlie said.

"Let's try the money exchange."

"Got it."

A few minutes later, the cab pulled up in front of the restaurant. It sat there for a while, then Charlie got out of the driver's seat and stomped around to the back window. "You son-of-a-bitch! Get out of there." Alex didn't move. A couple came out and watched. Charlie tried to pull the door open, but Alex clung to it.

"Just get me change!" Alex yelled.

Charlie pulled a few more times in vain then turned and walked into the restaurant. He went to the bar and asked for change of a hundred dollar bill. The bartender wasn't too pleased but he didn't want any trouble. While he was getting change, Charlie surveyed the restaurant and saw Lin and Roger in heavy conversation. He got his change and went back to the cab and got in. "They're thick as thieves."

"Drive on, McDuff," Alex said as he waved to the couple standing on the street.

They drove around the block and stopped. "Ten minutes for the first course, then off to work I go."

Alex staggered his way into the restaurant, took a quick glance at Lin & Roger's table, plopped down on a bar stool and ordered a martini. The bartender eyed him carefully, then mixed his drink.

Roger and Lin both saw him come in. "That's him," Roger said. "I think I'll just skip the bill." He got up and went out the back way. Lin waited.

"I need something to eat," Alex confessed. The bartender agreed. Since the place was emptying out, there were several vacant tables. The bartender signaled to the Head Waiter. Within minutes Alex was seated at a table. He'd noticed that Roger was gone. He seated himself with his back to Lin. He ordered another martini and scanned the menu.

Lin took her time. She waited until her food came, ate slowly, paid her bill, got up and walked past Alex. Then she stopped, turned and peered over her shoulder. She cocked her head and said, "Are you that man who walked out of China?"

Alex looked up. He pretended to focus his eyes. Then nodded. "You've got a good eye, lady, to recognize me from that stupid picture in the Post."

"Oh that isn't it. I saw you at the Mayflower this afternoon. You dropped something."

Alex frowned. "I did? Oh, yeah, I did. How did I miss such a beautiful woman like you?"

"Why, thank you."

"Hey, you want a nightcap?"

"I don't think so."

"How about just standing there for a while."

Lin had to laugh.

"I mean it, you make this place look classy."

"Really."

"Sure you won't have a drink."

Lin looked around the room. There were only a few people left. "All right," she said, "Just one."

Alex watched as she snaked her way into a chair across from him. His only thought was - 'hooked'.

They had a drink. Alex feigned getting drunker. She told him her name. He told her his. She asked about his escape. He told her a few details - enough to sink the hook deep. He made a crude pass at her. She deflected it, but only about forty-five degrees. Alex said he had to go home, he wasn't feeling well. She offered him a ride. He declined. He walked her out of the restaurant and said he hoped they'd meet in better circumstances. He said he lived in the neighborhood. He watched her get into a limo. Seconds later, the cab pulled up.

"Home Charlie, and don't lose the tail."

Charlie watched the headlights of the limo come on as they pulled away from the curb.

To make it easier, Alex had lunch at the Mayflower for three straight days before she 'ran into him'. A few charming words by the elevator and he had a date for the next night.

That afternoon, he called Roger. They agreed to meet at Alex's apartment. When Roger arrived, Alex told him he was leaving Washington. He never wanted to see or hear about any of the mess they had made of his life. He told Roger he hoped that he would get what was really coming to him. Roger laughed. He would be all right. As he opened the door, Alex said, " I saw their atomic research center and know they've got the bomb."

Roger stopped in his tracks. He didn't know what to say. He knew they were working on an A-bomb, but he had no idea they had one. "You're lying."

"Little valley near Sining. That jog your memory?"

"Sining?"

"Dr. T.C. Chien? Defector from Los Alamos? Come on, Roger. I know you know."

"Maybe," was all Roger could think to say. Alex knew more than he knew. He was dumbfounded. "Our plant is near Sining?"

"Come on Roger. You know. Our people know you know that you've been holding out on them. I don't think they're very happy."

"But I haven't been."

"Sorry. It's gonna cost you."

"Look, Alex, I didn't know."

"Lin Bao told you the other night."

"How do you know her?"

"You two were very friendly. Bed partners, too?"

"No."

"Get out, Roger. I hope both sides find out what a dirty shit you are."

Roger didn't know what was happening to him. He was confused at Alex's out burst and about the A-bomb and Lin Bao. He stared at Alex for a long time then left. He didn't bother closing the door.

Lin sat at her desk at the embassy and re-read Alex's dossier. The report indicated that Alex came into China as a spy for the C.I.A., got Roger Walters out, and was captured. He escaped by reportedly walking out of China, but about the same time, someone defected in a YAK 6C and was rescued by the American Air Force. Was Alex the man on the plane or did he walk out? The reports by Comrade Su indicated that their 'reeducation' seemed to work well for some time, then something caused his focus to change. Their guess was it had to do with Roger Walters. The question at the end of the report was - how much does Alex Hunter know about Chinese Intelligence, Chinese Military strength, etc. which he may have learned when he walked or rode out. Lin was entrusted to find out. The dinner was to be the first tease, then on the second, he would be invited to her apartment, and on the third she would seduce him and drug him to get the information.

Alex's plan wasn't that elaborate. They met at the San Souci restaurant. She had the pull to get in, and he had the pull to get the right, bugged table. They did the 'mating dance' - cute sayings, lots of compliments on her looks and his charm, and touches under the table. It had been a long time for Alex and he felt very uncomfortable at first, but Lin was easy to look at, and his motivation was very strong. This lasted for nearly forty-five minutes until coffee and dessert came. Alex dropped the first bomb. "So how long have you worked at the Chinese Embassy?"

She wasn't really surprised he knew, but his abruptness caught her off guard.

"Most of my adult life. I find it very interesting."

"I found the Chinese not very hospitable. In fact, downright mean."

"I'm sorry. Shall I leave?"

"No. You know who I am, I'm sure. You know what I went through. I suppose you want to know what I found out as I was getting out. The answer is nothing. I was too busy just trying to stay alive. But, surprise, I found out something the other night that might shock you. I found out one of China's biggest secrets. And you know what. Your own people told me. He told everyone at the C.I.A. and N.S.A. Does the term 'nuclear bomb' mean anything to you?"

Lin swallowed hard. Of all the things she anticipated, this was not one of them.

"In fact, your lover, Roger Walters told me all about it. He bragged a lot. He even told our people where you have your test facilities - near some place called Sining? We talked about it today. You really ought to watch him, he's a lose-cannon when he thinks he's in charge. Too bad he hasn't been since he ran your intelligence operation in China. Or so he says."

Lin kept staring at Alex as he talked. Her mind was whirling. Roger Walters told the U.S. about their atomic bomb? When? Why? He told Alex Hunter about it - even bragged about it? Roger was a traitor. He was just pretending to be on China's side.

"Well, I've got a headache. See you later," Alex said as he pushed back his chair and stood up. I think your embassy can pay for this one." He walked away without looking back.

The phone rang in Roger's apartment. He listened. "Yes, of course," he said and hung up the phone. Twenty minutes later, there was a knock on Roger's door.

Alex, Brady and Nancy sat in the cafeteria at the Pentagon two days later. Brady had a newspaper. He handed it to Alex. On page five, in a small corner column it read, "Roger Walters, a Georgetown resident, was found dead in his apartment by police at 9:50 P.M.. He reportedly committed suicide by hanging himself. No signs of foul play were found on the site. The only inconsistency was a feather in his hand."

Alex looked at the two of them.

"Did you think about our offer?" Brady asked.

"Yes."

"And?"

"I think I'll try real estate again. You guys play too rough."

"I'm sorry," Nancy said. "We could… "

Alex interrupted her. "I thought a lot about 'us'. Nice idea, but I think Ginny is the right one - if she'll have me." He rose. "Whatever you do, don't call me." Alex walked away.

Three months later, on a sunny Saturday morning, Alex Hunter and Virginia Postel March were married in Muncie, Indiana.

EPILOGUE

Page 4, New York Times, October 17, 1964

Reuters announced today that the Chinese Government exploded a nuclear device in the Xinjiang region of the Chinese high desert at 3 P.M. local time on October 16th. It was the first nuclear detonation by the Chinese Government.

Comment

The United States Government wasn't surprised.

Printed in the United States
63096LVS00004B/316

9 781425 971007